STOKER

STOKER

Jenny Brigalow

The Book Guild Ltd

First published in Great Britain in 2022 by
The Book Guild Ltd
Unit E2, Airfield Business Park
Harrison Road
Market Harborough
Leicestershire, LE16 7UL
Freephone: 0800 999 2982
www.bookguild.co.uk
Email: info@bookguild.co.uk
Twitter: @bookguild

Copyright © 2022 Jenny Brigalow

The right of Jenny Brigalow to be identified as the author of this
work has been asserted by her in accordance with the
Copyright, Design and Patents Act 1988.

All rights reserved. No part of this publication may be
reproduced, transmitted, or stored in a retrieval system, in any form or by any means,
without permission in writing from the publisher, nor be otherwise circulated in
any form of binding or cover other than that in which it is published and without
a similar condition being imposed on the subsequent purchaser.

This work is entirely fictitious and bears no resemblance to any persons living or dead.

Typeset in 11pt Minion Pro

Printed on FSC accredited paper
Printed and bound in Great Britain by 4edge Limited

ISBN 978 1914471 513

British Library Cataloguing in Publication Data.
A catalogue record for this book is available from the British Library.

Dedicated to Nixie Patricia, an inspirational Iggy.

1

Frost lay thick upon the ground. Beneath his leather-shod feet, the earth was hard as iron. Cobwebs sparkled in the weak morning sun and the husks of reeds shivered. As a formation of birds flew overhead, Oddie instinctively looked up. His dark eyes narrowed as he peered through the smoke cloud spewing from a brick chimney stack. He scowled and pulled his cap down over his eyes. The geese honked farewell as he trudged down the well-worn path to the mill. A sigh slid through his lips as the coal house loomed, black and ugly and smug.

With one calloused hand, Oddie thrust open the heavy iron door and entered a small, hot room with a stone floor and a bench against one wall. The heat physically stopped him, still as shocking as on his first day; it was like stepping into the mouth of a great, hungry monster. A monster that stank of coal and sweat and grease. And then there was the noise. The monster clamoured to be fed. Not with words but with the roar of the furnace, the hiss of steam, the whirr of cogs and the grinding of the water wheel. Coal dust swirled, lining his nose and mouth.

He removed his cap and hung it on a steel peg. Heat was seeping through to his skin as he rapidly removed his scarf, jacket, vest and shirt. Inside his chest, grief gripped his heart. How had it come to this?

He turned as a door swung silently open and a man stepped through. His blue eyes were the only colour in a soot-stained face. "Oddie," he said. His voice was weary and husky. Taller than Oddie, Huw found the work that much harder, despite the slabs of muscle that bound his torso. Besides, he was old. Must have been near forty. Twice Oddie's age.

Oddie crossed the room. Close up, he could see the lines of fatigue in the man's face. His cheekbones protruded sharply and his flesh clung tight, belly tucked like a racehorse with dehydration. A fine tremor made his hands twitch.

Poor sod. Oddie didn't work the night shift. It was better paid. Huw had a missus and three young to feed. His heart went out to the man. "Long night, Huw?"

Huw shrugged. "Usual." Then he grinned, showing a mouth full of brown stumps. "Could be worse, though. I hear the governor's doing the grand tour today."

Oddie stared at his workmate in horror. "They won't be coming here, will they?" Surely not.

"You never know your luck!"

Oddie scowled. He didn't trust to luck. But he had no time to pursue the issue. He waved goodbye to Huw as he entered the furnace room. Beads of sweat popped up on Oddie's cheeks and chest. He glanced at the coal pile and silently thanked his offsider. The coal was heaped high, ready to meet its fiery fate. He hurried to the nearest of the three furnaces, checked the temperature and moved on to the others. Furnace three was down a bit. He grabbed the huge flat spade that lay at the foot of the coal mountain and set to work.

Soon he had a rhythm. His mind and body bent and scooped and heaved. As he stoked the fires, Oddie felt the mill like a living thing. He felt the engine beating in his heart, the steam streaming from his lungs and the cogs turning in his brain. Dust coated him like a second skin. Flames licked up his bare chest and singed off the stubble of black hair. Sweat ran in rivulets and hissed in the red-hot embers. He tried to shift his mind away, to dwell on something else. But the mill consumed him like the coal.

Then he stopped. He cast down the spade and went to a cubby at the far end of the furnaces. He opened the hatch and lifted out the earthenware jug, full to the brim. Careful not to spill a drop, he drank. The water was warm, but no matter; each swallow was a joy. Untainted. Clear. And clean. The scent transported him to another place. He recalled silver fish swimming in a shallow pool as sunlight danced upon the surface. He captured once more the rich ripeness of the Fens. The grass swaying in the breeze and cowslips gleaming in the hedgerows.

Thirst assuaged, Oddie lifted the jug, tipped back his head and poured the contents in a delicious stream over his face. His eyes closed in ecstasy as the water coursed down his neck and bare chest. And he wondered at the strangeness of a world that forced a man to feed a furnace for his daily bread. He ached for the days before the draining of the Fens. He had been free then. His own man.

Still, there were bonuses. He smiled at the irony of it all. No need to fear the afterlife. Hell was already here.

2

Eliza was entranced. Absorbed, even. Wonders never ceased. She resisted her father's unsubtle attempts to block her view. She planted her two elegantly shod feet, refusing to be diverted, distracted or disrupted. She watched the stoker avidly. She soaked up the determined jut of his jaw, the strong line of his neck and the intriguing muscular matrix of his torso. Tawny streaks of skin were visible in the wake of the water. It made a delicious contrast to the sooty blackness of his shoulders and arms. As her eyes travelled downward she was riveted on a dribble of water that disappeared into the waistband of a pair of filthy, wet, and intriguingly tight breeches.

The scene broke as the stoker's eyes opened. The jug dropped and smashed at his feet. For a second his dark grey eyes made contact. Broody, black-lashed and bloodshot. A damp lock of hair spilled over his forehead in a wet jet spiral. His nostrils quivered as if he were scenting her. A mischievous spirit conjured up a sharp image of her father's black stallion.

Then she was manhandled – yes, actually manhandled – back out of the small room. Humiliation poured over her. She twisted her arm to try and break her father's grip, but he held her like a vice. With prodigious effort she mastered her emotions. After all, she was seventeen now. No longer a child.

The door slammed shut. Her father released her. He smiled. "My dear, I do apologise," he said. "That was not a sight fit for a tender young woman. It was poor judgement on my behalf. I should never have allowed it."

Allow it! Eliza was dumbfounded. She had protested vigorously. Even at a distance, the mill made her uncomfortable. It was ugly. People stared at it and smiled and clapped, as if it were something fine. Eliza felt no such attraction and had tried to push it out of her mind. There were many distractions. Riding, painting, shopping, music and trips to the city. Sometimes she could forget it for days.

Other times she found she could not escape. Even when it was out of sight, she found traces. Black smuts on her herbs. Black dust on her dresser. Black smog in the sky. And the view was ruined. She had entirely given up sketching. It was thoughtless of her pater. He knew full well she loved to paint the Fens.

Only the threat of forfeiting a new wardrobe for the winter season had forced Eliza to submit. Seething at the indignity of being ousted from her bed in the dark and out into arctic conditions, she'd joined her father and the odious Mr Pelham for a tour. It would have served everyone right if she contracted consumption and died.

But death was far from her mind at this precise moment in time. She glared up at her father. "I never asked to come," she hissed, loud as she dared.

In that infuriating way he had, her father seemed not to hear. He patted her shoulder softly. "I'm sure Lord Pelham will be only too happy to escort you home."

Several highly inappropriate words perched on the tip of Eliza's tongue. She pressed her lips together and tried to wither her father with a look instead. Needless to say, she failed. For one blasphemous moment, Eliza wished upon herself the ungodly gifts of Fan o' the

Fens. If she were a witch she'd show them. She'd turn her father into something useful like a fur hat and Pelham into a toad. Although an eel might be more fitting. Then an image of the stoker flashed in her mind. All soot and sweat and shameless nakedness.

Strangely, she felt no desire to change him at all.

3

The hours passed. The clock on the wall seemed possessed by some evil spirit. It stood still for interminable periods of time and then went into overdrive. Oddie couldn't decide which was worse: the long moments trying to foretell the outcome of the morning's mischief or the hours that rushed by like an express train towards the inevitable. Oddie just knew he was going to get laid off. His emotions seesawed from minute to minute. Torn between longing to be released from this purgatory and the fear of losing what was a rare, well-paid position. Other thoughts he held at bay. They boded ill.

So preoccupied was he that he forgot to eat his lunch and to drink until his head began to spin. With a quick look at the gauges he finally paused. He checked the time. It was nearly two. Only one more hour left of his eight-hour stint. Short days by the reckoning of some.

Once he would have agreed, but then his days had ebbed and flowed gently like the tides. His only master had been the rise and set of the sun. He had worked as he willed. Taken his ease when he was weary. Eaten when he was hungry. Slept when he was tired. Filled in his day with small pleasures. But no more. Eight short hours was no compensation for captivity. And besides, it was only short hours because the work did not lend itself to longevity. Men keeled over and fell into furnaces when they were worn out. So, short hours it was, though grudgingly given.

Which reminded him… water and vittles. His lunch was in his jacket pocket. But he was too dry to eat. And the jug was smashed. He'd have to go fill a bucket. Which meant a trip to the well. Damn her! Then he remembered that he'd decided not to think about the girl. Though it was hard. She had made quite an impression. He recalled the moment their eyes had met. And shook his head, forcing his mind back to practical matters. Water. For a minute he wavered; he only had an hour to go. Maybe he'd just push through. But then the ceiling tipped and tilted above him. He had to drink.

Outside, the cold literally took his breath away. Lord, it was perishing. Skin puckering and teeth clattering, he ran around the building to the small yard and privy. With tingling fingers, he let down the bucket into the well, heard a faint splosh and hauled it up. The exercise at least warmed him a little. The water was freezing and splashed down his calves as he hurried back to work. He collapsed onto the bench with the bucket on his lap and stuck his head right in to suck up great draughts of water. It burned down his gullet like whiskey and it took several moments before his head cleared. Oddie completed his meal, wolfing down a slab of crusty bread and two salted mackerel. Rejuvenated, he headed back into the boiler room.

The middle furnace was down. He worked with a will until the needle nudged up to temperature. Not long to go. But the prospect of re-entering the world cranked up his anxiety. Maybe things would work out fine. Maybe no one would blame him for the incident. After all, it wasn't like he'd planned it. A man had to drink! And it wasn't his fault the master's daughter had made a commotion. At least, he thought she was the master's daughter. Must be, for she was legend. A rare beauty, known locally as 'The

Pride of Lincolnshire'. Aye, and she looked proud too. The haughty young minx. Her kind always spelled trouble for the likes of him.

He paused, shovel mid-air, as he recalled the incident. And the more he thought, the less sure he was that she might be to blame. When he really considered it, she hadn't actually *done* anything. Just looked. With those big blue eyes. Forget-me-not blue, they were.

A wave of tenderness rippled through him. He loved those little flowers, so bright and beautiful. And that was another thing. It wasn't just that she was a good-looking lassie; there had been something about her. A quality that he couldn't quite put his finger on.

Coal clinked on his boot; he saved the load and shovelled it into the fire. He recalled the look on her face as she had been removed from the room. He chuckled. She had not looked happy. But his amusement dissolved as he realised that it made no difference. It would be he that bore the brunt of the blame. There was always someone to be blamed. It was the way of the world.

With a grunt he filled the shovel once more. And again. With every motion he began to painfully construct an argument to armour himself with. He had just been drinking water. That was not a crime. He hadn't lost more than a moment of time. This wasn't a fitting place for a young woman of quality to be. She wasn't there at his invitation. No one had warned him.

By the time the big hand teetered on the hour, Oddie felt he'd prepared as good an argument as a man could. All he had to do was say it right. Trouble was, the odds of that happening were stacked against him. Uneasy once more, he counted down the seconds.

4

The journey home was intolerable. Her companion had that unforgivable habit of talking too much. Worse, he was one of those odious men entranced by the sound of their own voice. All in all, Eliza's opinion of Lord Percival Pelham didn't soften. It was as well that she was a refined young lady, or she may have given in to temptation and pushed him out the carriage door.

This last was such an enthralling (and wicked) concept that Eliza spent several moments in silent contemplation. Outwardly, she smiled and nodded at her father's close friend as his words washed over her meaninglessly. Until, that is, a single word broke through her reverie.

"…stoker."

Her chin shot up and she refocused. What was that?

"…the likes of him if we could mechanise the whole process."

Eliza organised her features into her best 'what a clever man you are' expression and waited for Pelham to continue. Not that he needed any encouragement.

Pelham caught her expression and his concave chest puffed up like a courting pigeon. Eliza stifled a giggle. He waved a gloved finger at her. "Yes, I know, it sounds impossible, my dear. But your father agrees that – in principle – it could be done." He then proceeded to bore her rigid with a long sermon on steam engines.

Finally she was forced to accept that the stoker's part in the conversation was over. She tried to find a way to reintroduce him but couldn't think how to do so delicately. After all, she was a well-bred young woman. Well-bred young women did not allow their thoughts to linger on the intoxicating sight of a naked man. Leastways, he was the most naked man she'd ever seen. But that didn't make it proper. And certainly, a young lady would not wish that he'd not been wearing strides too. Not that she did. It just wasn't respectable

Thankfully the drive was relatively brief. Eliza wanted to cheer when her home hove into sight. The Hall sat gracefully before a perfect expanse of frosty lawn. From the bell tower atop to the half-hidden basement windows at the bottom, the massive mansion of yellowstone was perfection. Although she had lived there for as long as she could remember, Eliza was not immune to its majesty. Unlike her father, however, she had no desire to acquire a title to match. Elvidge was a name that she bore with pride.

Mercifully, Pelham was silent, gazing up at the house. Eliza glanced at him under her eyelashes. He was transfixed. His tongue didn't actually hang out, but it may as well have. It was just a shame that his infatuation with her family home did not extend to herself. He may be the third son of the Duke of Lincoln but he was practically penniless. However, that wasn't voiced in polite society.

Gravel crunched as the carriage swept up the driveway. Smoke billowed out of the tall chimneys and Eliza spotted Mary shaking a rug out of an upstairs window. Eliza leant forward and dropped the window, letting in a burst of frigid air as she waved a greeting to her maid. The thought of hot buttered crumpets, tea and gossip before the fire, cheered her enormously. So long as Pelham didn't stay. Then she'd have to sit in the drawing room and make polite conversation instead.

The carriage duly ground to a halt at the bottom of the stairway. Eliza waited in a froth of impatience for Withers, their mealy-mouthed butler, to open her door. Why in the name of god couldn't she get out herself? Did she not have arms and legs! How on earth did society imagine she stayed in the saddle? Really, it was quite ridiculous.

Finally, the door opened, and she hopped lightly down to encounter Pelham striding around to meet her. Pooh. Looked like he was going to invite himself in.

She bobbed a curtsey. "My Lord, would you like to partake in refreshment?"

He managed to peel his eyes away from the grounds that spread away over fallow fields to forest. "My dearest Eliza, forgive me, but I'm afraid I must attend to your father. Our conversation about the stoker was most inspiring. I feel a need to convey these new ideas at once!"

Eliza smiled, genuinely happy. "My Lord, no need for forgiveness. Your dedication to your work is admirable. Perhaps another time?"

He bowed, giving her a brief glimpse of the bald spot on the crown of his head. If he wasn't so obnoxious, Eliza would have felt a little sorry for him. No man under thirty should be balding, especially when already afflicted with bad breath and a body of serpentine proportions. But she hid her contempt and smiled.

As she tripped up the stairs and entered the double doors, Pelham was forgotten. "Mary!" she called. "Mary!" It had occurred to her that Mary knew everyone. Eliza could wheedle out the stoker's name from the maid. What a wonderful day it was.

A small streak of black raced across the marble floor. Eliza scooped up the tiny Italian greyhound and hugged her. The creature wriggled ecstatically and licked her chin.

"Come, Comet," she said. "It's time for tea and crumpets." Eliza hastened up the wide staircase, her mind bent on one thing. The stoker.

5

On the stroke of three precisely the door opened and Billy came in to relieve Oddie of his duties. The lad nodded and plucked the shovel out of Oddie's hand.

"Oddie, you're to see the governor afore you go."

Oddie nodded and took his leave. His heart sank to his boots. He'd expected as much, but still, it didn't make him like it any better. For one, he'd have to wash up. Not a pleasant prospect. But he couldn't go into the office looking like this. Filth put a man at a severe disadvantage.

With the bucket in one hand and his clothes in the other he went to the well. He laboriously hauled up a bucket, braced himself, and poured the water awkwardly over his head and shoulders. He stiffened in shock. By the Imp it was cold! The second bucketful was no more enjoyable, but there was some satisfaction in watching the water run away dark as a bog. Shivering and shaking he put on his clothes, pulled his jacket tight and shook his head to dry his hair. He resisted the urge to put on his cap. Best not.

It took him a short time to make his way around to the front of the mill. At the door he hesitated; he'd only been in here once when he'd come for his job. Whilst he had little love for the furnace room, it was familiar. Heart hammering in his chest, he turned the knob and pushed the door open. Dim and cold, the hallway stretched away grandly with its wooden-panelled walls and thick carpet. Oddie was reluctant to step in and make a mark on the blue, gold and red pattern. It didn't feel right. Maybe he should take off his boots.

To his relief an interior door opened. The governor. Oddie waited. The governor strode down the carpet, his head swathed in smoke from a fat cigar. If he was angry, Oddie couldn't tell. He just hoped he'd get on with it before Oddie froze to death.

The burly man stopped in front of Oddie and removed the cigar from his lips. A draught blew in and chased the smoke away. Whilst he was a handsome man, with a well-formed head and strong, straight nose, he did not resemble his daughter. His eyes were brown and his lips lay buried in a wiry beard like two fleshy shellfish. The governor tapped his cigar and ash flew into the air.

Bits of it caught in Oddie's eyelashes and stuck to his damp cheeks. He resisted the urge to wipe it away. It might be construed as criticism. He was already in deep shite.

The governor gestured with his hand. "Odling, come in."

Oddie looked down at his feet, unsure.

The governor jerked his chin into the gloomy passageway. "No matter! Come! Come!"

Oddie mentally shrugged and without further hesitation followed the mill owner into his office. Heat enveloped him. Oddie moved as close as he could to the fireplace, conscious of his shirt and vest clinging to his wet body. He tried to recall his earlier argument, but it was hard to concentrate under scrutiny.

The governor sat down behind a vast oak desk lined with red leather and stubbed out the cigar in a crystal ashtray. Papers, ink and pens were laid out in ranks like soldiers. A cigar box lay open. The aroma of tobacco dominated the room. Sweet and musky. Oddie wondered what the governor would do if he leant over and helped himself. For a moment an imp perched on his shoulder. "Go on," it cackled. "It's not a hanging offence!" But Oddie wasn't so sure. Seemed to him that pretty much anything was a hanging offence these days. He pushed the temptation away and wished he was home.

"You are a good worker, Odling."

Oddie nodded and looked at his feet. Maybe the governor was just killing him softly.

"I have need of a strong man to help me with a project."

Oddie's head jerked up.

The governor leaned across the desk, selected a cigar, clipped the end and lit it. For a minute or two he puffed away, until the cigar churned out smoke like a chimney. Then he seemed to remember Oddie was still there. "I am building a surgery. Here, on the premises. That way we can deal with any accidents efficiently and better serve the populace." He sucked on the cigar and swallowed the smoke. "Would you give a hand with the fittings?" He released the smoke. It curled in blue banners through the air. "Tomorrow?"

Oddie stared. Not in the shite then. Relief coursed through him but quickly evaporated under the expectant gaze of his employer. A response was necessary. He mentally braced himself, fingers gripping his cap in a deathlock. His left foot began a St Vitus dance on the floor as he concentrated. Then his lips and tongue formed the first sound. Oddie willed it to happen.

"Y…" But it stuck. It always bloody stuck. He ploughed on. What other option was there? "Y-y-y-yes. Of c-c—" His words were cut off.

The governor got to his feet. "We'll start after work tomorrow. Meet me at the front door."

Oddie nodded and turned to leave.

"And, Odling…"

Oddie paused and turned around.

"Not a word about this morning."

Oddie nodded. He rushed out the door, down the corridor and outside. He put his cap on his head and turned his back on the mill. It had been quite a day. One way and another. In the weak winter sunshine, he paused on the riverbank, listening to the water singing its way down towards the sea. A barge lay against the bank, light reflecting off the water to highlight a posy of painted blue flowers.

"Forget-me-not," he whispered. And headed for home.

6

It was not until late afternoon that Eliza orchestrated a moment with Mary. The crumpets were golden brown and swimming in butter. Logs crackled in the fire and the teapot steamed fragrantly into the air. Comet sat at Eliza's feet, her beady eyes fixated on her plate. Eliza tossed her a bit of crumpet, which she caught on the wing. Eliza settled back in the comfortable leather chair and licked her fingers. How to open the conversation?

"Mary, do have a crumpet!"

Her maid paused with an evening gown held aloft. She blushed bright as a boiled shrimp. "Oh, Miss, I couldn't! It wouldn't be decent."

Eliza smothered a smile. They both knew full well that Mary actually could and most certainly would. Both of them, however, enjoyed the game. Eliza shook her head sadly. "It seems unchristian," she said, "to throw good food away when there are children up the hill languishing from lack of bread. Why, Queen Victoria abhors waste!"

"Oh, Miss," said Mary mournfully.

Truth was, neither of them was overly concerned with the welfare of the ragamuffins that ran amuck in Lincoln, begging, stealing and smelling bad. Everyone knew that there was work aplenty for those who had a mind.

"I think, Mary," said Eliza, "that it is your Christian duty to eat these crumpets."

Mary hung the gown carefully back up, as if giving reverent consideration to Eliza's hominy. Finally, she bowed her head in agreement, made her way to the fire and perched on the edge of an ottoman stool. Eliza handed her a plate.

"Ooh, thanks, Miss," said the girl.

For a moment Eliza was silent, pouring tea into the two rose-patterned porcelain cups, and adding milk and six sugars for Mary. Then she settled herself back into her seat and observed her maid eating. This was no hardship, for Mary radiated contentment from the top of her red head to the toes of her black-booted feet. Although not pretty, Eliza decided that her maid was very appealing with her freckled nose and dimpled elbows. They had been childhood companions until Eliza had been coerced into corsets. Mary's graduation to maid had seemed a natural state of affairs.

Mary swallowed the last mouthful and took a slurp of tea from her saucer. She insisted that the Queen drank her tea like that, and what was good for Her Highness was good enough for Mary. Finally, she was done. "Pass me your cup."

Eliza did so and waited.

Mary peered in, twisting the vessel this way and that. Then she put the cup down.

"Well!" said Eliza. "What do you see?"

"Nothing, Miss Eliza."

Eliza didn't believe her. Mary's nose twitched like a rabbit's. A sure sign of guilt. "Tell me!"

Mary crumbled. "I see a cross, Miss."

"A cross? What does that mean?" Eliza picked up the cup and peered at the tea leaves. "Well?"

Mary's sunny expression grew tight and wary. "It don't mean nothing. It's just a bit of fun."

Eliza glared.

Mary sighed. "A cross means trouble. Trouble is coming."

Instantly, Eliza's thought turned to the stoker. Maybe Trouble had already arrived. She secretly hoped so. "I went to the mill this morning." Mary knew this, of course. Mary and all the domestics knew everything.

"Did you now?" said Mary. "And what did you see?"

"Oh, you know – everything. The engine room, the beam, the wheel, the office and the boiler room. Very dull. Very dirty."

Mary frowned. "Is your dress marked, Miss?"

To be honest Eliza hadn't noticed, but it gave her just the opportunity she had hoped for. "I expect so; I had to endure a visit to the furnace room. It was filthy. I don't know how the poor wretch who works there can stand it."

"That'll be Oddie," said Mary. Then she grinned. "Nothing 'poor' about Oddie, I can tell you!"

Eliza was enthralled. She leaned forward eagerly. "Do tell!"

But Mary did not reply. Like Eliza, her attention was drawn to a dreadful din emanating from the fireplace. Detritus cascaded down like hail. Then there was a sound like a giant burping and the chimney blew out a lungful of soot.

With cries of shock and dismay, the pair fled. Eliza slammed the door behind her in a fit of temper. Thwarted by a fireplace. So unfair! 'Oddie' would have to wait.

7

Dusk settled across the flat land. Oddie's breath frosted and fanned out before him. Thin sheets of ice crunched as he stepped in puddles. When he got home he'd build up a fire and boil some water to wash away the day. Then he'd heat up some fish stew. Three days old, it'd be flavoursome. But best finish it up. Four days was pushing the boundaries, even with the cold. His belly growled in anticipation and Oddie pushed on.

Soon he left the river behind. He crossed a ploughed field, hopped over a ditch and followed a drain. A grey shadow flew on silent wings. A heron. Far off, a sheep baaed. Wind blew strong from the sea. When he opened his mouth he could taste it. Salt and seashore. Mussels and crabs and limpets. Maybe he'd go fishing on Sunday. After church. It had been a while. But in the meantime, he'd have to look closer to home. The larder was all but bare.

The drain ended abruptly, flowing sluggishly into a vast expanse of water. Here the marsh began proper. Miles and miles of the wild. To an outsider it seemed a barren, poor place but Oddie knew better. For generations his people had lived and died on the bounty of the land. They had hunted, fished and foraged. They'd kept pigs, chickens and even herded sheep. It had been a hard life, but a good one.

A solitary white ptarmigan broke out of the reed bed that edged the lake. Oddie watched as it was swallowed into the sky and a familiar sadness settled inside him. Once the Fens had seethed with life. Flocks of birds. Shoals of fish. Herds of sheep. But no more. Slowly but surely the land was dying of thirst. It was literally shrinking before his eyes. Every month a new water wheel sprang up, it's steam engine pumping water downriver. The lakes were reduced to mud and bones. The reeds turned to straw that rotted into black mush. It was a slow but sure death. The end of an era, some said. And they'd probably be right.

Guilt stirred. Had he done right? Should he have gone to work at the mill? Some said he was in the right but many argued otherwise. For his part, Oddie didn't know. All he knew was that it hurt. Not in his flesh and bones but in his heart. Many had left in despair. But he couldn't, no more than he could have removed his own limbs. For better or for worse, he was wed to this land. The past and present. The living and the dead.

He stopped abruptly. Slowly he scanned the meadow of hay and thistle heads that stretched away from the water. With a soft plop, a water rat slipped away like a shadow. He shivered and set off once more. He did not believe in goblins or ghouls, but he was wary. These were desperate times. A man could be killed for his coat. Or less.

For the rest of the journey he kept a wary eye out but saw and heard nothing untoward. Until, that is, he saw smoke where it should not be. It rose and blew away in ragged ribbons. As he drew nearer he could smell it. And then he stopped, staring in disbelief. For the smoke was rising from his chimney stack. Someone had let themselves in and made themselves at home! There was no doubt in his mind. The small cottage was huddled in a copse of trees beside a stream. It was the only building in these parts. Whoever it was, they were brazen.

It was crazy, but for one second Oddie thought of the governor's daughter. Her wide-eyed stare. The parted lips. The rapid rise and fall of her bosom beneath the tight bodice. But then he shook his head. He was being foolish. She was a lady. No lady would venture into these parts. In fact, no gentleman either. Whoever it was, it did not bode well. Few knew where he lived. Oddie liked it that way.

At the stream he strode over the stepping stones, barely looking where he was going. He could have found his way blindfolded. Ahead, lamplight spilled out over the water butt and the edge of the vegetable garden. The nerve! He clenched his fists. If he found his supper already eaten there was going to be trouble. There was little enough. Half a loaf of bread and two remaining salted fish in his larder. How was he to work on an empty belly?

He stormed up the track, punched the door open and stopped in his tracks. He stared at the trespasser incredulously. In profile her face was unrepentantly unattractive. Chin like a hatchet and a nose like a hammer. "What in God's name do you think you are playing at?"

The woman stopped stirring the contents of the cauldron and glanced sideways at him. Her dark eyes glinted with mischief. "And a good evening to you too, Master Odling."

She turned around then. Front on, her facial features were transformed. A Madonna with a perfect, oval face, large limpid eyes, a lush mouth and aquiline nose. A true beauty. Oddie never grew accustomed to the transformation. It was queer. Unnatural, almost. Disturbing. Tall, she was, with a cascade of mahogany hair like spun silk. Clothed in a simple woollen gown of homespun, her slender waist was unencumbered. The curves of her breasts and hips needed no corset to accentuate her sex.

Oddie sighed. He should have known. He took a step forward. "Fanny Flowers, explain yourself!"

She lifted a spoon and sucked it. Then she smiled. "I've come to comfort you, Oddie."

Oddie stepped back a fraction. "I've no need of comfort, Fan."

Fan lifted her skirts with one hand to reveal bare feet and slender ankles. "I think you will find that you do," she said.

But Oddie refused to be diverted. "Explain yourself, Fanny."

She sashayed up to him and looked up into his face. She wrapped him smartly on the knuckles with the wooden spoon. "What's the matter? Afraid I might put a love potion in your pease pudding?"

He could not speak, for she had struck at the core of the matter. That was exactly what he feared. But it would not do to say so. Instead, he plucked the spoon from her fingers. "You'd best…" He turned, sure he had heard something. And then – quite distinct this time – a low moan emanated from the room in which he slept. "Fanny, in God's name, who is that?" Although, truth be told, he wasn't eager to know.

8

Undaunted and determined, Eliza bided her time. The whole sooty incident was an irritation, not a catastrophe. Although, the ruination of her blue, silk gown was a burden hard to bear with fortitude. Still, the prospect of a new one comforted her. Meanwhile, Mary was entirely consumed in the removal of all of Eliza's possessions into the green guest room. Thus, Eliza was forced to wait to continue their conversation. Which was most disagreeable.

Dinner was a tiresome affair. The odious Pelham and her parent conversed for endless hours about the mill. Worse, there had not even been a mention of the stoker. Eliza eyed the two men curiously. She never ceased to wonder how it was that the two men had formed such a close association. True, both desired what the other had. His Lordship coveted her father's money and her father coveted the lord's breeding. But it seemed to Eliza that such feeling did not warrant the hours that the two spent together. Of course, it was possible that they just liked each other. A situation she found incredulous.

"Eliza, my dear, would you play for us?"

Eliza stifled a yawn and smiled at her father. "Of course, dear

Papa." After all, the winter season was nearly upon them. She would go into a decline if she did not have a fur to rival Victoria Hughes's. Besides, anything to still their tongues.

Lord Pelham came around and offered a hand. There was no avoiding it. With as good grace as she could muster, she placed her own on his and allowed him to escort her to the music room. Once seated at the piano he lingered to turn the sheaves of music for her. To avoid him, she began to play a gay Irish jig that she had heard at the harvest festival. It had been the eve that Mary had met her match. He was a cooper's apprentice from the city, son of one of the tenants. What a picture they had made, Mary's petticoats swirling as he swept her up above his head. How they had smiled!

Some sixth sense made Eliza glance up. She caught Pelham observing her with a predatory expression that made her neck hair prickle. But what really made her mad was the lord made no attempt to hide his feelings in front of her father. Eliza loved her papa dearly; he was the most generous and kindest of men. But in this moment, she felt a wave of resentment. She wanted him to admonish the Earl's third son. Her father should gently put him in his place. It rankled, to sit meekly like a lamb in the company of a well-bred and very hungry wolf.

Abruptly she switched keys. Her fingers picked up the jaunty tune that Mary had taught her. It was ribald, to put it politely. A song about a milkmaid and a lascivious landlord, it left little to the imagination. The words ran silently through her mind as she played. She looked up at Lord Pelham, to gauge his reaction. To be honest, she doubted he would be familiar with such stuff. It was generally only heard in taverns and two-room shacks.

But her breath caught in her throat as his eyes opened wide and his thin lips parted in shock. The internal struggle was so obvious that the words of the song seemed to write themselves in the air around his head. What a pickle that lordly man was in. He could not admonish Eliza without revealing an unsavoury truth about himself. Eliza played louder and looked over her shoulder at her father, who smiled indulgently at her. Bless him.

Her father's guileless approbation stirred up a filament of guilt in Eliza's soul. She paused, rifled through the music scores and selected a piece that she had come upon by chance. It had no title or composer. But the score was beautifully made, with a tiny face cunningly etched into each note. The movement needed absolute concentration. She bent herself to the task with a rare singularity of purpose. Utterly focused. Absolutely immersed. And, as the notes lifted and fell, her mind seemed oddly clear. It felt… apart. She felt apart. As if she had entered another realm. A secret place. And then she reached the end of the score. And there was silence.

Lord Pelham broke the moment. He clapped loudly. "Bravo, Eliza. A masterful rendition."

Whilst Eliza agreed, she managed to blush modestly and deny the fact artfully. She turned to collect her father's approval even though he was tone deaf. But her expectations were not met. Her father was bent over, his forehead almost touching his knees. Alarmed, Eliza arose, the music stool screeching on the parquetry floor in protest.

She went to him and sank to her knees. "Papa! Papa, what is wrong?"

He did not reply. His chest heaved as he gasped for breath. Eliza looked at Pelham. "Ring for Withers!"

Pelham did as bid and then came to her side, peering down his pointy nose. "Can I help?"

"Help me sit him up!"

Eliza was stricken. Her father's complexion was chalk white, the lips tinged with blue. With shaking hands, she removed his cravat and loosened his collar. She slapped his cheeks, first softly and then with some force. His eyes watered and he took in a sobbing breath of air.

"Get brandy!" said Eliza.

Pelham looked at her blankly. Eliza bit down her irritation. Then the butler entered.

"You rang?" said Withers.

"Father is unwell. Fetch the brandy."

Withers disappeared back out the door.

To Eliza's relief, colour began to return to her father's face. By the time Withers returned he was able to take a glass of spirits.

"Father, we must call for a surgeon," said Eliza.

He shook his head. "No need. I am absolutely recovered. And besides – I am the surgeon."

Which, of course, he was. Eliza said no more but she retired to the green room deeply troubled. Sleep evaded her. The anonymous music seemed to have found a loop in her mind. It played over and over. Memories flooded her consciousness. Some long-forgotten. Some fresh. A picnic by a lake. Her first ride on her pony, Smudge. A white box with a red ribbon. A stoker fuelling a fire. A tea leaf cross. A white nightgown. And something that perched just out of sight. She strained to see it. But it slipped away like a minnow through her mind.

9

There was a boy on Oddie's bed. He twitched and cried and bled. Face white as paper and hair black as ink. Bony wrists grew out of smock sleeves several sizes too small. His feet were horny and bare and had probably never worn shoes. Oddie didn't know him.

Fanny came in behind Oddie. She held a bowl in one hand and a needle in the other. She leaned over the boy and pulled back a rabbit skin throw. Oddie swallowed a wave of nausea as he took in the wound on the boy's thigh. Despite a tight binding, blood oozed ominously.

"The bleeding has slowed, but I have to remove the shot and then sew the wound," said Fanny.

Oddie nodded, but Fanny's dark eyes were fixed on the boy. She glanced up. "You will have to hold him. I have no laudanum."

"Who is he?"

"A ganger."

Pity budded in Oddie's chest. The gangers were itinerant groups of paupers who performed back-breaking employment for a pittance. Controlled by a gang leader, they were little more than slaves. Those more fortunate averted their eyes, lest ill luck rub off. "Poor little sod." Clearly the lad, desperate for food, had gone poaching and fallen foul of a mantrap. A gun rigged with a tripwire that triggered a shot. Illegal, theoretically. "It could have been worse," he said.

"If I don't sew it up, it will be worse," snapped Fanny.

Oddie didn't take offence. He and Fanny went way back. She was sharp when she was upset. "What will I do?"

"Do you have any drink? Gin? Rum? Whiskey? Even beer would help."

Without wasting words he went into the living room. He plucked a bottle off the windowsill. It weighed heavy in his hand. Brandy. He took it to Fanny.

"Sit him up," she said.

Oddie grasped the boy awkwardly about the shoulders and eased him up. The boy's eyes opened wide with shock and he screamed.

For the first time Fanny looked afraid. "Boy! Hush! You will have the patrol on us!"

The scream faded into a low, vibrating whimper. The boy's hands scrabbled at Oddie's wrists as he tried to escape the agony. But it was the feeble fluttering of a moth in a jar.

Fanny lifted the bottle and set it to the lad's lips. "'Tis brandy, boy. You must take some or I cannot help." Without giving him time to react, Fanny tipped the spirit down his throat. The boy swallowed frantically. It was that or drown. The bottle eased off. The lad took in deep, shuddering breaths. Fanny repeated the exercise. Once. Twice. Thrice.

"Lay him down."

As Oddie obliged, he was glad to feel the boy's body relax. "He's got no more meat on his bones than a knitting needle," he said.

"Times are bad," said Fanny. Then she glanced at him. "Ready?"

He was.

"I'm going to cut the cloth off, and then dig out the bullet. You have to hold him hard. If he moves, I risk cutting the big blood vessel. Do you understand?"

He did. How best to do it? His eyes scorched around the room. Then he took a belt off a hook, hastened into the living area and grabbed a bit of fish net. Thus armed, he bound the boy's arms to the bed head. Then he went to the bottom and grasped both ankles in his hands.

Fanny went to work. The bandage split open like a fat caterpillar's chrysalis. The wound gaped and Oddie could see the bullet glint deep in the meat. With a set of fine tongs, Fanny entered the wound. The boy jerked and screamed. Oddie held on ruthlessly and prayed.

As he did, he could dimly catch Fanny's voice. She was singing. He strained to hear, but the song was not familiar to him. Nor were the words. They seemed… foreign. The boy became still and silent. Oddie focused on his task lest his hold falter.

Then Fanny stood up, her expression exultant. "The Goddess be praised. I have it!"

Oddie looked up at the bullet clamped in the metal prongs. He pretended he hadn't heard her words. He released his grip and flexed his fingers.

Fanny dropped the bullet and instrument on the mattress. She picked up the needle and pulled a spool of thread out of a pocket in her dress. Oddie wondered how she would manage to thread it in the poor light. But it presented no problem.

She looked at Oddie. "Ready?"

Oddie anchored the boy's legs once more. Fanny stitched the flesh together. Each stitch was cut and knotted. The knot was as intricate as any sailors. The boy stirred on occasion but made no resistance.

Finally, the last stitch was done. Fanny stood up. "Untie him."

Oddie did so. The boy did not stir. Then something occurred to him. "Fanny, how did he get away from the agents?"

"They lost him in the fog," said Fanny.

Oddie stared, incredulous. "There's no fog. Not so much as a mist!"

Fanny left the room. Oddie followed.

Fanny gathered her things. "I'll be back in the morning."

But Oddie hadn't finished. "How did you get him here?"

The front door opened and shut. "Shit!" Oddie rushed over and flung it open. "Fanny!"

But the marsh was empty. All except for a pair of hare's boxing in the moonlight.

10

Oddie did not sleep well on his makeshift bed of sacking. The boy, surprisingly, did. When the alarm went off, Oddie was already awake, alerted by the distant whistle of the mill. He dressed quickly, groping for his shirt in the dark, grimacing at the grit and dirt ground into his body. Too scared to leave the lad, he'd not washed. Not even his face. He hadn't eaten either and his stomach was tied in knots. He cursed Fanny Flowers softly under his breath. Not for the first time.

As he pulled on his boots he tried to decide what to do if Fanny didn't show. He could hardly leave the boy. But then he could hardly miss work either. There were plenty lined up who'd take his place. He froze as the boy stirred and moaned. He hurried over and peered into his bedroom. Maybe it would be best to wake him and do what he could before he left.

He was still undecided when he heard the front door creak open. No knock. Fanny, for sure. Then his heart missed a beat. The police wouldn't knock. Would they? He glanced at the boy. At his emaciated body, filthy rags and strained, stretched face. Stealthy and silent as a cat, he inched across the room and lifted his rifle off its hooks.

"Mornin', Oddie!"

Weak with relief he sank onto his heels, resting his head on the rifle. That bloody woman would be the death of him. "Fanny," he said.

She poked her face through the door and smiled angelically at him. "How goes the boy?"

Oddie stood up. "How would I know? I'm just a fireman."

Fanny's lips twitched suggestively. "You certainly stoke my coals, Oddie boy."

Oddie ignored her and seethed. Fanny had been hunting him for a long time. This morning it did not amuse him. "He's not moved all night."

Fanny moved swiftly to the boy. In profile, her face was grim. "He lives."

Her words made Oddie feel guilty. His anger with Fanny felt misplaced. If it weren't for her, the boy would be dead in a ditch. Or worse, a pauper's grave. He went closer and waited as she worked over the lad. She was all business as she touched his skin, put her head upon his chest, felt the pulses and gripped both feet in her hands. Then she sniffed the wound. When she stood up her expression relaxed. "His heart is steady; there's no sweats and no smell of corruption. 'Tis early days, but the Goddess be willing, he will survive."

Oddie's empty belly rumbled. Fanny pointed through the door. "There are vittles in the basket. Take some."

Oddie hid a smile. It was as close to thanks as Fanny would come. But no less welcome for all that. "Is there enough?"

"There is plenty. A good pheasant broth and brown bread." She looked at her patient. "I felt he'd earned the pheasant that cost him so dear."

Oddie didn't comment. There was no need. There was not a man, woman or child on the Fens that would not concur. He nodded and went into the living room. There was a hint of light from the embers, but he lit a candle and put it on the table. Soon he had a bowl of broth and a heel of bread still warm from the oven. For sure, one of Fanny's sisters would have baked it. The pheasant was heaven. The broth rich and glistening with globules of fat. They were capable, the Flowers girls.

When his stomach was satisfied, his good humour returned. He had a drink of water and wrapped up a bit more bread, a fish and a withered bunch of crab apples for lunch. Then he fetched the brandy and went back into the room. The wound was unwrapped. It was raw and ragged but there was no bleeding. The stitches held. He lifted the bottle. "Do you need this?"

Fanny took the brandy, popped the lid and took a swig. She smacked her lips. "That's better!"

It wasn't what he had meant but she'd earned it. Then Fanny poured brandy over the wound. The boy twitched. His eyes snapped open and he reached to the source of pain. But Fanny gripped both hands in her own. For a moment he fought but then sank back, obviously exhausted, onto the bed.

"'Tis alright, my boy. You are safe, but you have had a bullet taken out of your leg," said Fanny. "Do you have a name?"

"Bert."

Fanny let go Bert's hands. "Well, Bert. I am Miss Flowers, but everyone calls me Fanny." She looked over her shoulder. "That one, back there, is Oddie. This is his home. You will be safe here, but you must be quiet and not leave unless Oddie or I say so. Do you understand?"

The boy nodded.

Fanny stood up. "I must make a poultice for the wound. Are you hungry?"

Bert nodded once more. He said not a word but his eyes followed Fanny with an almost religious fervour. Oddie grinned to himself. Maybe the boy was older than he looked. He nodded at Bert and followed Fanny. "I must go, Fanny," he said. "Or I'll be late."

"Late!" Fanny spat the word out as if it were poison. "You are enslaved, Oddie. You are chained to that furnace as surely as oxen are chained to plough!"

Oddie sighed. It was an old, cold argument. "I don't have time to disagree."

Fanny snorted. "Tick tock, tick tock, tick tock." She put down a bunch of herbs and lay her hands on her hips. "Tell you what, Oddie. Stay home with me this morning and I'll make you feel like a freeman again."

Oddie shook his head. "N-n-n-no, th-th-th…" Damn it! He grabbed his bait, jacket and hat, and stalked out the door. He wanted to say a whole lot more, but she had tied his tongue up like a turkey with twine.

The door slammed with satisfying conviction behind him. Fanny Flowers was enough to make a saint sin. He didn't believe in witchcraft or any such nonsense. He truly didn't. But she kept on trying to sow seeds of doubt in his head. He always got stuck on words when he was worried or upset. That was all. She had no power over his tongue. Leastways, no more than anyone else.

But deep down he knew that the thing that riled him most, was that Fanny Flowers was right. He was an ox. A dumb beast of burden.

11

At the mill, Huw grumbled at the change of shift that number two furnace was playing up. Smoking like the Puffing Billy. Huw had informed management. It subsequently ran cool, no matter how much coal Oddie shovelled into its starving belly. He looked up and down but could see no cause for the problem. He was no mechanic, but had a good grasp of the system. Outside it had begun to rain heavily. If something wasn't done soon, the wheel wouldn't keep up with the rising water.

Despite his lack of sleep, he was in good form. The fat pheasant sat safe and sound in his belly. It seemed like a small portion of justice. It was wrong that a starving whelp of a boy couldn't take a bird for his supper. Wrong that the men who shot him were aided and abetted by the law. It was no wonder there was uprising verging on rebellion. Not that Oddie agreed with the violence of it. Just the principle. It was no good blaming the gentry. This was not their making. No, it was the machines that were the problem. Everyone knew that. Machines that stole an honest man's work.

The coal heap was getting down. Hopefully the longboat would arrive soon with supplies. He swigged a hasty drink and topped up number one. As he slammed the door shut, a draught of cool air alerted him. A man came in with a hessian bag slung over one shoulder. Without looking up or missing a beat, the haulier made for the coal heap and emptied his load. Then he stood up to reveal a well-made man with shoulders like a bull's. One of the Irish. Wilberforce Riley. Riley was alright. Rough and ready, but honest and a worker.

"Oddie, how goes it?" the man said in his rich Irish brogue.

Oddie nodded. "Can't grumble, Will."

Will grinned showing fine, white teeth in his red beard. "Well, you'd be the only man I've met today who can say that!"

Oddie chuckled. Wilberforce had a wit sharper than a surgeon's blade. "No point grumbling, no sod would listen!"

Another man came in. Young, with hair even redder than Wilberforce's. He nodded at Oddie. 'Twas Will's son, Aiden. The lad emptied his sack, turned on his heel and set off back the way he'd come.

Will watched him go, then turned back to Oddie. "Did you hear the big news? Word is that Lord Pelham's going to make a match with the Elvidge lass."

Judging by the Irish's expression, he was not a fan of His Lordship. But then, he was not alone. The Earl's third son was a bully and a braggart. The locals avoided him at all cost. Particularly the women.

Oddie didn't usually take mind of gossip but Will's words flew into his heart like buckshot. "No!"

Will shook his red head. "Slimy little bastard. The wife says someone should wise up the poor, motherless chit."

Oddie agreed with Will's wife. Trouble was, he doubted anyone would. Wise her up, that was. And besides, maybe Eliza Elvidge didn't mind. A maidenhead for a title was considered fair exchange. The gentry were not like normal folk.

Will made a rude gesture with his hand. "Let's hope he breaks her in kindly."

Oddie felt sick in the guts at the thought. A man that maimed little boys shouldn't be let near a gentle woman. Or any woman, for that matter. He opened his mouth. And shut it smart quick. Close call! Framed in the doorway was the angular, elongated body of Lord Pelham. Some sixth sense told Oddie the man had been listening. Question was, how much had he heard?

Oddie put a polite finger to his forehead. "M-My Lord."

Beneath his sooty face, Will blanched. With a brief bow of his head he snatched up his sack and legged it.

Lord Pelham oozed into the room. "Who was that?"

"N-n-not sure, M-M-M…" But the words stuck.

The lord gave him a narrow-eyed look but was silent as another man came in, emptied his sack and went again. "Stop coaling up number two. There's a blockage."

Oddie nodded. "Y-y-y—"

Pelham cut him off. "I'll expect you later. Doctor Elvidge tells me you are going to assist in the surgery." He gave Oddie a disdainful look and turned on his well-shod heels. Then he paused on his way out and looked over his shoulder. "Go help shift the rest of the coal. It's getting wet."

Oddie simmered with frustrated rage. It was one thing to stammer. There was no shame in that. But to be dismissed like a dumb dog. That stung. It wasn't right. It wasn't fair.

The rain was steady but not torrential. At least, not yet. A draught horse stood patiently in its traces on the canal path, munching on a nosebag of feed. The old longboat was shiny, washed free from coal dust. Oddie joined the other men and waited to get a bag of coal. Will shouldered his way past.

"Sorry, Oddie," he muttered.

Oddie shrugged. What was done could not be undone. He grabbed a sack and marched back still silently seething. It was not long ago he had been his own master. A man who knuckled to no man except when he so chose. Oddie emptied the coal out. A cloud of dust broke into the atmosphere. And suddenly he hated it. It was foul. Like Lord Pelham.

His meeting with the lord did not bode well. Pelham was not the kind of man to let an insult pass. Real or imagined. There would be a reckoning.

Oddie wiped a trickle of black dirt out of his eyes. He was not a man that looked for trouble but neither was he a meek man. He couldn't condone violence. But how much could a man take? He prayed he'd never have to find out.

12

By the time her father had demolished half a game pie, a wedge of Stilton and an apple, Eliza's anxiety retreated. His colour was ruddy and his carriage erect. All in all, he seemed none the worse for the incident in the music room. Eliza decided she was being a goose. Like her, he enjoyed rude good health. Not so much as a head cold.

"Are you well, Papa?" she said.

He flicked the top of his newspaper over and smiled. "Never better, dear Eliza!" He folded the paper and placed it precisely beside his plate. "What do you plan for this afternoon?"

Eliza sipped her tea and considered the question. Her priority was to get Mary aside and finish their last conversation. Sadly there was little prospect of this as Mary was assisting Withers with the chimneys. Eliza looked out the window. It was another cold, clear afternoon. The larch trees danced in the breeze. Bronze and gold leaves swirled around the frostbitten lawn. "I think I will attend the orangery, Papa. The orchids should be blooming."

He smiled indulgently. "Lovely, my dear." And picked up the paper once more.

Once she had formulated the idea, Eliza could not bear a

moment's delay. She pushed her plate aside and went up to change. As she passed her bedroom she slowed to look for Mary. But there was no sign of her. In the guest room, Eliza considered ringing for her maid. But dismissed the idea. She would manage; she wasn't an imbecile after all!

She selected a white linen blouse and a long blue skirt. As she did so, she thought wistfully of the stoker. Of the unhindered, flowing movements of his strong body. Did he know how lucky he was to be blessed with trousers instead of petticoats and skirts that flapped and flopped and grabbed and suffocated? How lucky men were! How well she would work if she had only trousers and boots to deal with.

And then she remembered that she was a lady and pushed such thoughts out of her mind. Getting dressed alone would not be easy, but she was determined to be independent. Several minutes later Eliza paused, red-faced and breathless. No matter how she bent and contorted she could not reach the buttons at the back. "Oh, bother!" she said, and conceded to ring for Mary.

Several interminable moments later, Mary arrived. She was pink and obviously flustered.

"Mary, I am so sorry," said Eliza, "but I wish to go out to the glass house but cannot manage this ridiculous blouse!"

Mary bobbed a curtsey and rushed over to assist. As the maid's nimble fingers made short work of the buttons, Eliza peered over her shoulder. "Mary, is all well? You appear a little agitated."

Mary flushed redder than a radish. "Oh, Miss, there is such a to-do!"

"A to-do? What is the matter?"

"'Tis the chimney sweep's boy, Miss Eliza. He has gone and got himself disappeared."

Eliza frowned. "Disappeared? How so?"

Mary jabbed a finger to the ceiling. "The little ragamuffin has gone up but not yet come down!"

It took a moment for this statement to make sense in Eliza's mind. When she thought she understood, she felt ill. She looked at the fire burning in the grate. "Mary, do you mean to tell me that the wretched creature has gone up a chimney when there are fires still burning? And is still up there?"

Mary nodded. "Yes, Miss, that is clear what I mean."

Eliza was speechless. How had this happened? What idiot had allowed it? She gulped. There was no point speculating. The damage was done. "Which chimney?"

Mary pointed down. "The dining room, Miss."

"How long?"

Mary glanced at the carriage clock on the bedside table. "T'would be nearly half an hour, I'd guess."

Eliza swept out of the room, Mary at her heels. She ran down the staircase, along the hall and into the dining room. Her eyes swept over the glossy length of the mahogany table to the fireplace. A man's bottom and sooty trousers protruded from the space.

"Bates, get down 'ere, you little swine, and stop your malingerin'."

Eliza was dumbfounded. She could not for the life of her imagine that anyone would choose to be lost in a chimney. Then the man removed his torso and head and Eliza stepped back. The man was an evil-looking beast. He would not have been misplaced upon the cathedral wall beside the other grotesques.

On seeing her, the creature bowed his head and shuffled his booted feet. One huge, hairy fist knuckled his forehead, as he muttered some kind of salutation. Two rheumy eyes peered out from beneath the battlement of his brow. His head was shaven to reveal crusts of scabs. A pelt of dark hair grew up his neck to his ears. One shoulder sat high, and one leg twisted like a stunted root. He smelled like boiled cabbage and chamber pots.

Eliza took a step forward. "What is your name?"

"Huggins, Ma'am."

Anything less huggable Eliza had never had the misfortune to meet. "Well, Huggins, I understand you have lost your boy?"

Huggins scowled. "I'll murder the lazy little blighter!"

Eliza ground her teeth. She turned to Mary. "Is my father still in residence?"

He wasn't.

She thought hard and fast. "This room lies beneath the lavender room. Perhaps if we went up, we may be able to find some sign of the boy."

Huggins nodded and knuckled once more. They all trooped up the stairs and into the lavender suite. Being unoccupied, there was no fire. Huggins went dutifully to the grate and peered up. He yelled for his boy but was met with silence.

"What can be done?" said Eliza. She turned and was relieved to see Withers had arrived.

Huggins looked blank for a moment. Then he smiled evilly. "I'll light the fire! That'll shift the little beggar."

"Mary, you will fetch some kindling," said Withers.

Eliza twirled around and glared at the butler. "Mary most certainly will not!"

Then a thin wail floated out of the fireplace. Seconds later, a black figure fell into the grate. The relief that Eliza initially felt at the unorthodox arrival of the child was quickly replaced with horror.

13

For a moment, Eliza's head seemed to float entirely off her neck and up into the air. The chimney sweep lay curled like a baby bird. His mouth opened in a silent scream. His hair was singed away, as were his eyelashes, and the skin on his pate a livid red. When he lifted his hands, they were a mass of blisters. The pitiful remains of his rags smoked. And, even as she watched, the smock top reignited. The sight of those tiny flames licking up the boy's arms bought Eliza back to earth.

Panic-stricken, pulse racing, she grabbed a rug and smothered the flames. It occurred to her then the boy was going to die. Smoke wreathed around her head and choked her. A vision expanded inside her. A vast, cold, clear lake. The soft lapping of water and the tiny plop of fish breaking the surface. And the scent, brackish and salty. Her heart calmed, and her mind followed suit. There was no time to consider. Eliza followed her instincts. "Quick, Withers! Wrap him in the rug and carry him up to my bathing room!"

Withers' thin lips tightened, and he looked at Eliza with an expression that suggested he was not inclined to acquiesce.

"Now!" said Eliza softly. Then she turned to her stricken maid. "Mary, fetch Papa, at once!"

Mary nodded and scampered across the parquetry floor. Then she stopped and turned around. "Miss Eliza, I don't know where he has gone!"

Eliza turned to the butler. "Where is he?"

"The mill, Miss Eliza."

Eliza nodded. "Mary, go to the stables and send one of the grooms with all haste."

Mary lifted her skirts and tore out the room. Eliza silently blessed her. Meanwhile, both Huggins and Withers were still stationary. "Withers – and you, Huggins. Lift the boy. But gently."

Both men edged towards the boy, who made small mewing sounds like a kitten. Eliza's heart contracted with pity. And her patience gave out. She pushed past Withers and crouched down. Carefully as she could, she slid her hands beneath the boy, pulled him close and lifted him. To her surprise he was scarcely a burden at all. The rug probably weighed more than he did. Her nostrils flared at the scent of burned meat and scorched hair.

Withers stirred. "Miss Eliza, I don't think your father would approve."

Eliza shifted the child against her breast and glared at the butler. "I don't believe I asked for your opinion, Withers." She turned to Huggins. "Go wait in the hall." Then she gave Withers the evil eye. "Go and fill the bath with cold water." She set off without waiting for a response.

Halfway down the hall Withers stalked past and swept up the stairs. Every inch of his starched, uniformed body emitted outrage. But Eliza did not care. She glanced down at the boy. His eyes were closed. Was he breathing? Scared, she broke into a jog. Halfway up the stairs she flagged, back aching abominably and her legs like blancmange. Both arms had lost sensation.

"Miss! Miss! Wait for me!"

Eliza could have cried with relief. "Help me, Mary!"

The young maid galloped up the stairs, skirts raised to reveal her booted feet and chubby legs. "The boy's gone with all haste, Miss," she panted as she eased the boy's head and shoulders into her own grip. "But I sent another for Fanny Flowers, just in case."

Eliza nodded and adjusted her hold around the boy's legs. "Hurry, Mary!"

Straining and gasping, Eliza climbed. In her mind she could hear the water gush and gurgle out of the big brass taps and thunder into the deep well of the tub. It called to her.

Fast as they moved, it still seemed too slow. It was an age before they reached their destination. Mary went through the bathroom door backwards and they stumbled to the tub. Over the stench of the boy in her arms, the scent and sound of the water was a balm.

Withers watched on with an expression of deep disgust. If Eliza hadn't had her hands full, she would have probably have slapped him. "Withers, help!"

With infuriating slowness, Withers complied. As he did so, the remains of the boy's clothes disintegrated. The full extent of his injuries were revealed. It was terrible. Eliza looked at Mary. "Hurry! Put him in."

Together, they lowered the boy down into the tub. His eyes flickered beneath the raw, oozing skin of his eyelids. One eye peeled painfully open and he gazed up. Eliza could see his heart beat – like a drum roll – beneath the sunken expanse of his chest. "It's alright, boy," she said gently. "It's only water. It won't hurt you."

He reached out and with raw, puffy fingers touched her cheek. It was a mute but undeniable gesture of trust. And something shifted inside Eliza. Suddenly, he was no longer a starveling boy. He was *her* starveling boy. And she would not fail him.

14

"Hold him, please, Mary," said Eliza. The water was only waist-high.

Mary leaned over and held the boy steady. Eliza raced over to the washstand and picked up the jug. She scurried back, filled it and poured water over the boy's face, head and chest. On and on and on she went until the water was a soupy scum. Inch by excruciating inch, the water rose.

"He's good and wet now, Miss," said Mary.

He was. Thank the lord! There was a pitter-patter of feet. Comet arrived. With a yap of happiness she danced over to Eliza. And then one of the upstairs maids, Ruby, followed the dog in, her white cap askew on her brown fuzzy hair, black eyes wide with excitement.

She bobbed a curtsey to Eliza. "Miss Eliza, Fanny Flowers be down the stairs, demanding to be brought to you!"

Withers gave a hiss of protest.

But all Eliza felt was a huge wave of relief. Thank goodness, someone to help. "Well, bring her up, Ruby! Hurry!"

Ruby, looking deliciously scandalised, hurried away.

Eliza looked anxiously at the boy. For one heart-stopping

moment she thought he was dead. But then the ribs rose, and a shiver ran through his limbs. Eliza breathed again and peered anxiously over her shoulder for the Flowers woman. She felt a tiny twinge of anxiety. What would her father say? He did not have a kind word for Fanny Flowers. He called her a charlatan and a sham. Said she should be locked up in the castle for fraud. Maybe she should tell Withers to send her away.

But then the boy began wailing. It was the most terrible sound. A thin, shrill wail of pure misery. His poor hands slapped the water and his tiny body shuddered like a beached ship. Helpless, Eliza could only hold his head above water. What should she do?

And then there was a bustle of activity. Ruby arrived, her cap hanging by a thread, her hair frizzed out like an unshorn sheep. "She's here, Miss!"

Fanny Flowers had arrived.

Thank God!

Fanny Flowers came over and sank gracefully to her knees beside Eliza. Fanny gestured to the bath with one slender hand. "Who did this?"

Eliza bit her lip. "It was me, I'm so sorry."

Fanny nodded. "You have done well."

Eliza thought she had misheard. "I know it was probably stupid, but I didn't know what else to do…"

Fanny tilted her head and looked at Eliza intently. "It is well done, Miss Eliza. Few would have known the healing properties of water."

The woman's words untied a knot in Eliza's chest. A wave of gratitude rippled through her. It was a fine thing to be told that she was wise. Indeed, she could not recall such a thing before. But to be fair, she had not acted through logic. More panic, really. She opened her mouth to explain but she had lost her audience.

Fanny was bent over the boy, a frown creasing her white forehead. "We must release the water and refill the tub. There are evil humours in scum." Then she stood up. She pointed at Withers. "You, go to the kitchen and bring some apple vinegar."

Withers puffed up like an angry toad. "The kitchen is not my domain!"

Ruby jumped up, her cap tumbling to the floor. "I'll get it, I'll get it!"

Without a word, Fanny knelt again beside Eliza. She smelled nice. Like lavender and… broth. "Give him over to me while you attend the water."

Eliza did as she was bid. Her fingers tingled with pins and needles as she found the plug and pulled it. No one spoke as the water gurgled away, leaving a slick film of slime. Without prompting, Eliza turned the water on and sluiced away the muck from the boy and the bath. Then she put the plug in and let the tub refill. She covered her mouth with her hand as her eyes travelled over the bowed little legs and the sunken chest. There were severe burns all over his body. But the worst was his face, which was dreadful to behold. His eyes were swollen up like golf balls.

Fanny held the boy still and hummed a tune. Eliza relaxed a little. The woman gave off a reassuring aura of calm. Feet thundered and Ruby galloped back through the door, a jug clasped to her flat chest.

"I got it! Apples an' all!" she gasped.

Eliza hastened to the maid and took the jug. She showed Fanny. "All of it?"

"All," said Fanny.

Eliza poured it around the boy as evenly as she could. The water was rising to his knees.

"Get a cloth and bathe his face, then put it over his eyes," said Fanny.

Eliza went to the dresser and picked up a flannel. With trembling hands she wet the cloth and dribbled water over the boy's face. Then she folded the flannel and placed it tentatively over his eyes. She turned to Fanny. "Will he be alright?"

Fanny breathed slowly in and out. "Thanks to you, he has a fighting chance. But it will take time and care. He will need a clean, comfortable bed, as much water as he can drink and then poultices of calendula, lavender and heart of the earth until the skin begins to grain. Then he will need honey applications. His eyes will need close attention, I am also thinking."

Eliza followed all this with intense interest. For the first time since the accident, hope beckoned. "Miss Flowers, how long must he lie there?"

Fanny nodded. "Not much longer, he will become chilled. Where would we lay him?"

Eliza considered the question. "We have rooms aplenty, but perhaps he should be placed close to my quarters, so that I can be on hand." Withers snorted and the two maids twittered like a pair of sparrows. Eliza ignored them. "Should we dress him?"

Fanny nodded. "Just a shift. Light as you can find. Cotton would be best. And I will need something to hold the bed linen away from his body. The weight will be an agony."

Eliza turned to the domestics. "Ruby, prepare the blue room. Mary, fetch one of my summer shifts. And Withers, go to the gardener and bid him make up a wicker frame with much haste."

The two girls galloped off, while Withers stalked out, slamming the door behind him. Silence descended. Eliza went to the bath, leaned over and reached out for the cloth on the boy's eyes. As she did so, Fanny Flowers sucked in an audible hiss of air. Alarmed, Eliza's action was arrested. She looked at the woman. "Is there something wrong?"

"Turn your arm over!"

It was a strange request, but seemingly harmless. Eliza, curious, obliged.

Fanny stared down at the birthmark on Eliza's forearm. "You have the mark!"

Eliza twisted her arm awkwardly and looked. "What mark?"

"'Tis the mark of the cunning folk, Miss Eliza. The fish. Symbol of water."

Eliza was intrigued. "Now you mention it, it does look like a fish." A ripple of unease trickled down her spine. "What do you mean by 'cunning folk'?"

But before Fanny Flowers could reply, the door swung open and Lord Pelham came in like a blast of westerly wind.

15

Eliza stepped into his path. "Sir Pelham, stop!" But he did not stop. He brushed past her as if she were a gnat. The villain! "Sir Pelham, please!"

The beast stormed over to Fanny Flowers. She looked up tranquilly. "Lord Pelham, to what do we owe the pleasure?"

Despite her angst, Eliza was awed by the woman's boldness. Whilst the words were politeness itself, every syllable dripped with disdain.

It was wasted on Pelham, however. He looked over his scrawny shoulder. "Withers, Miss Flowers is leaving."

Withers smirked. "I'll show you out, Miss Flowers."

"You will not!" said Eliza. "Miss Flowers is here by my invitation. She will leave when I say she will leave."

Pelham tutted. "Withers, escort Miss Flowers to the front gates."

Eliza thought she may burst into flames. The nerve! "Where is my father?"

Pelham's face twisted into a victorious smile. "He's busy. He requested I attend this… situation."

Eliza was dumbfounded.

Withers sniffed. "Miss Flowers?"

Fanny looked sideways at Eliza. "Keep him clean and cool. Give him water. Send for me, and I will come."

Eliza's senses revolted. Fanny must not leave. Not yet. But she did not want to make trouble for Fanny. It was clear that Lord Pelham had the upper hand. God smite the lick-spittle. She hurried forward, knelt down and deftly took a hold of the boy. "I thank you, Miss Flowers, for your service."

Fanny Flowers nodded, stood, shook out her skirts and swished out of the room. The door closed and it was just the two of them. Eliza swallowed her pride. It tasted like goat's piss. "My Lord," she said, "the blue room is ready, but I will need help."

Without a word Pelham strutted over. He peered down his bony nose. "Let me," he said.

There was little choice but to comply. Eliza could not lift the child herself. The odious Pelham slid down on his skinny haunches and hunkered at her side. Oh, the horror of it! Her flesh cringed. She turned her face away. A stream of expletives spewed out of Pelham. Leaning over the top of the tub he reefed the boy out of the bath. With one final look of loathing at Eliza, he turned to leave.

The boy screamed. Eliza screamed. "Stop! Stop! For pity's sake, stop!" She ran after him. Her feet skated through a puddle and she crashed to the ground. She struggled up, hampered by her skirts. Pelham was halfway down the staircase. Eliza gripped the stitch in her side and followed. In her haste her foot caught, she slammed onto her back and went bumping down the stairs. She lay winded at the bottom, scarcely able to breathe. She struggled to her knees. "Lord Pelham, I beg you!"

Pelham paused at the front door, water dripping from the limp form in his arms.

Eliza raised her eyes to his. "Please, My Lord, don't take him. I beg you. Don't punish him for my transgressions." She felt sick. Shamed. "Lord Pelham, don't take him. Please."

He sneered. "You don't know what punishment is. Yet."

How she hated him! He was monstrous. Rage swelled inside her. It consumed all other emotion. If only she were a man. A big strong man. A stoker! Then she would make him sorry. She'd rip his ugly head off. She'd fill him full of lead shot. She'd—

Her eyes darted to her arm. The fish. It leapt and dove, water rippling across her skin. In a dark corner of Eliza's mind, something shifted. She stood and closed her eyes. Written on the insides of her eyelids were words. Words that she had never seen nor heard. They rolled effortlessly off her tongue. Outside, thunder clapped. Wind roared. The doors burst open, hail and rain lashing the floor.

Her eyes opened. Pelham was struggling towards the door, the climbing boy in his arms. "NO!" Eliza stamped her foot. Lightning cracked. The house trembled. Mary scurried into view. She was shouting, but Eliza couldn't hear. The maid ran towards her, pointing. Eliza turned. Her head exploded. She went down and was shrouded in darkness.

16

At the end of his eight-hour stint, Oddie was all but done in. He longed to head home and see what was happening. Longed for a bite of bread and a mug of beer. Longed for a deep breath of cold, clean air. But instead he made a sketchy wash at the well and headed round to the front entry. Best get it done. With luck, the governor wouldn't keep him late.

To his irritation, it was not the governor waiting on the front step, but Lord Pelham. Glumly, Oddie took off his cap. "M'Lord."

"Follow me," said Pelham with a jerk of his chin.

Oddie followed and fumed. Not so much as a please or thank you! Rude. Good manners cost nothing. That's what his mother had always told Oddie. And she was right. Give the governor his due, the man was courteous enough. More of a gent than this pumped-up little popinjay.

From the rear, the Duke's third son was an unattractive specimen. His stockinged legs were bowed, and his waist would have been the envy of many a young maid. Oddie tried to envisage Pelham with Miss Eliza Elvidge. It wasn't easy, yet there had been odder couplings made. Still, he felt for the girl. She might have silk dresses and satin bonnets, but it amounted to little if she were to be harnessed to the likes of this one. Why, Fanny Flowers might be a baggage, but she was as free as a bird. No man mastered Fan.

Absorbed, Oddie almost walked into Pelham when he stopped abruptly beside a stout oak door. There was heavy cloud cover and it was almost dark, but Oddie could hear the river running and the creak of the water wheel.

Pelham took out a key and unlocked the door. Light spilled out as it opened, making long, skinny shadows dance on the muddy ground. Then he stepped inside and seemed to vanish.

Oddie hurried after him and nearly went headfirst down a steep flight of steps. The air was close and hot. Not as bad as the furnace room, but unpleasant all the same. Oddie wrinkled his nose. There was a cloying, sickly smell. It occurred to him then that this narrow, steep entry was not sensible. It was an obstacle for anyone sick or injured.

The stairs ended, and he followed Pelham through another door. Oddie stopped and looked around. It was a huge room. Centre was an empty space dwarfed by three tiers of balconies. The fourth wall was given over to row upon row of shiny metal shelves. There were books. More books than Oddie had ever imagined existed. Glass bottles gleamed and displayed all kinds of weirdness. Oddie stared in fascinated horror at a row of pickled remains. A heart, a kidney and an eye were easily identifiable. The rest he really didn't want to know. At least it explained the smell.

"Ah, Odling!"

At the sound of the governor's voice Oddie turned away from the display, eyes grazing over an array of gleaming instruments. He recognised a row of saws and another of clamps. It was a scene more fit for the horrors of a butcher's yard than that of a respectable physician. A prickle of fear ran through him. Surgery was the last roll of the dice for the desperate. And a loaded dice it was too. He made a brief bow to the governor. "Sir."

The physician put down a slender knife and came to him. He

pointed to a pile of steel stacked neatly in front of a glass cabinet. "Odling, that is to be our surgical table. It will screw together but is heavy. Between us, no doubt we can erect it easily enough."

Tongue-tied, Oddie nodded. He felt uneasy in close confines with two immaculately turned-out men. While he knew he'd never compare even in his Sunday best, it would have been good to be clean. Still, there was naught that could be done. Best get the job done and get out.

It turned out the governor was right, it wasn't difficult. Although Pelham was as much use as a chocolate teapot. Mind you, he was good at giving out the orders. Oddie was tickled pink to find the governor rushing to obey alongside himself. Wait 'til he told Fanny! He forgot he was mad with her long enough to wonder what was for supper. He was starved.

Then the last screw was turned and the last bolt hammered home. They all stood back to inspect the result. The structure was very impressive, shimmering beneath the gas lamps.

The governor slapped Pelham on the back. "Excellent!"

Oddie smothered a grin as the engineer's legs buckled.

Pelham gave Oddie a sour look. "You can go, Odling."

Oddie's spirits lifted at Pelham's discomfort and the prospect of a brisk walk home, followed by an evening on the Fens. He had a mind for some more fowl. Maybe a duck or a late goose if he were lucky. There were some mealy potatoes and carrots stored that'd make a fine mess. Maybe he'd find some wild oats still clinging to their stalks in the meadows. The Flowers girls weren't the only ones that could make a meal. Besides, that starveling boy could do with a bit of meat on his bones.

His sense of wellbeing waxed as he recalled that tomorrow was Saturday. Followed by the Sabbath. Day of rest. But his good humour vanished like ale at a wake as he caught the tail end of a hushed conversation.

"Have you decided what to do about the boy?" said Pelham, softly.

"That scoundrel Huggins has disappeared. So, it'll be the workhouse," said the governor.

Conscious of the governor's eyes on him, Oddie had no choice but to head out of the door. The only other word he caught was 'Fanny'. Whilst Fanny was not an uncommon name, Oddie knew exactly to which Fanny the governor was referring. And he knew which boy too. The one sleeping in his bed. His heart clenched like a giant fist in his chest. Someone had blabbed. He had to get home.

He took the stairs two at a time and crashed out the door. He ran down the towpath, beside the long drains and across the marsh. Birds took flight and a fox stopped dead in his tracks as Oddie whisked by. He came to the creek, keen eyes probing the darkness ahead. But there was no welcoming light where he knew home to be.

Up the slope he charged. "Fanny!" But there was no answer. Nerves humming, he pushed open the door. "Fanny!" But inside it was as quiet as a crypt. "Fanny," he said, but softly this time as his senses quested. The only sound was the air roaring in and out of his windpipe.

He went to the table, fumbled in the dark and found a flint. After a few futile attempts he lit the lantern, picked it up and headed for the back room. The door was ajar. He lifted the light. A white face and a pair of stricken eyes stared up at him from the bed. The boy was still there.

"Where's Fanny?" said Oddie.

The boy shook his head. "I don't know."

"When did you last see her?"

"Long hours since."

Oddie was deeply disturbed. The fear that he had held at bay all the way home now swelled up inside him. If Fanny wasn't here, then something was very wrong. They both startled at a knock at the door.

"Shit!" said Oddie. He put a cautionary finger to his lips and left.

Someone rapped again sharply. Oddie hesitated, raced over, grabbed his rifle and went to the door. He whipped it open, rifle at the ready.

Fanny Flowers placed a finger delicately on the end of the barrel. "Well, Mr Odling, I'm pleased to see you too," she said.

17

When she awoke, Eliza winced and gingerly touched a lump on the crown of her head. Had she fallen? It was all hazy. She remembered chasing Pelham. Remembered begging him not to take the boy. And a storm. A bad storm. But then – nothing. Just waking up in her bed with a dreadful headache and a sense of foreboding.

She sat up. Where was he? What had they done to him? She felt physically ill. As if wildcats were clawing at her innards. The screams of the boy would haunt her until her dying day. And she scarcely knew how to contain her loathing for Lord Pelham. Her father would have to drug and hogtie her before she would agree to become his wife.

For one brief instance, Eliza wished for the mama that she had lost so long ago. But just as quickly, she pushed the emotion aside. It was a locked box that she was too afraid to try and open. She stood and went to the window, pressing her hot forehead against the cool pane of glass. Eliza peered out into the darkness, hoping to see a sign of her father's return. In her papa lay salvation. When he heard what Pelham had done, Papa would go and bring the climbing boy back.

There was a knock. Eliza tensed. The bedroom door opened and Mary came in. Eliza searched the maid's face for news. "Mary, tell me quick, what have you heard?"

Mary looked over her shoulder and then shut the door. "Miss Eliza, the house is abuzz with speculation, but…" She flushed and shuffled her feet.

"It's alright, Mary, you may be frank," said Eliza, sensing the maid's discomfort.

"Well, Miss, Cook says the boy will go to the poor house and Lord Pelham will go to hell!"

Eliza was aghast. "The poor house!" Every Sunday she passed the bleak building with its high walls. She had never given much thought to what went on inside. But now she understood it could not be anything good. Then a tiny spark of hope flared. "What about his master, Huggins?" she cried. "Surely he must hold some responsibility for the child?"

Mary shook her head. "He is not to be found, Miss Eliza."

Hope was pinched out. "What are we to do, Mary?" Although she did not really expect the girl to know.

"We should go see Fanny Flowers, Miss Eliza."

Eliza stared at the maid. "Fanny Flowers? What can she do?" Once more Eliza sensed Mary's reluctance to speak. "Please, Mary, speak, I beg you!"

Mary glanced once more over her shoulder, even though the door was shut. Then she walked over and put her lips almost to Eliza's ear. "Do you not recall?" she whispered.

Eliza was at a loss. "Recall what?"

Mary stepped back and put a trembling hand over her mouth.

Eliza was alarmed. Mary was the most steadfast of girls. Not one easily upset. "Mary, I remember Pelham took the boy. And I tried to stop him. But I couldn't. And then he left in that storm." Eliza frowned and put a hand to the egg on her head. "And then – I must have fallen…"

Mary shook her head. "'Twas no accident, Miss. 'Twas Withers. He whacked you on the noggin from behind!"

Eliza was stunned. It was impossible. Withers wouldn't dare! But the truth shone from Mary's eyes. She had no cause to lie. But – Withers! That verminous villain. When she told him, her father would dismiss him on the spot. "Mary, don't fret, my father will send Withers packing. There is no need to trouble Miss Flowers."

Mary shook her head. "Miss, it is not Withers that you need to consult Fanny about. It is the… other business."

Eliza almost laughed; the young maid looked so tragic. "Mary, what 'other business'?"

Mary was silent for a moment. "Miss, the storm. It was no ordinary storm." She stopped, clearly unwilling to continue.

Eliza stamped her foot. "For the love of god, Mary, spit it out!"

Mary flushed. "Miss Eliza, truth be told, the storm came on your command. That is why you must seek out Fanny. You and her are kin of a kind."

Eliza wondered if she were running mad. Nothing Mary said made a speck of sense. "Speak plain, Mary. What do you mean?"

Mary wrung her hands. "Miss, I do not want to say it out loud!"

"Mary, whisper it!"

Mary did.

Eliza assumed she had misheard. "A… witch?"

Mary gasped. "Hush, hush, you must not speak it out loud."

Eliza understood that Mary was right. To think such a thing was questionable. To speak it was insanity. Poor Mary. The shock of it must have been too much for her. "Oh, Mary, that's silly. There's no such thing as… what you said. It's just superstitious stories to make naughty children behave."

Mary just stared back.

"Really, Mary," said Eliza, "Fanny Flowers is just knowledgeable in herbs and healing, is all. And she and her sisters are all unwed and live alone. You know how people will gossip."

Mary sniffed. "Well, Miss Eliza, if you say so."

It was transparently clear that Mary was not willing to disagree. And Eliza did not want to create bad feeling between them. She was very fond of Mary, and Comet adored her. "Perhaps we would both benefit from a pot of tea?"

Mary bobbed a curtsey and rushed from the room.

Eliza went back to the window. To her joy, her father's carriage was rolling down the drive, lanterns just visible in the misty rain. Thank goodness! She rushed to her wardrobe and dragged out a cloak. She could not wait another second. As she swirled it around her shoulders, the sleeve of her gown rode up. On her forearm, the fish-shaped birthmark swam fluidly across her skin.

With a cry of alarm Eliza dropped the cape and staggered back. A pulse hammered in her forehead. "No, no, no," she said. She leant against the mantelpiece and willed herself to be better.

When she was composed, she turned her arm over. She fixed her eyes sternly on the mark and watched and waited. But nothing happened. It was as still as a Lincoln lake. A nervous laugh escaped her lips. Goodness but her nerves were pulled tighter than her corset strings. Must be the blow to her head. That damnable butler! Wait until her father found out!

She retrieved the cloak, put it on and set off. As she raced down the stairs she regained her equanimity. The birthmark was not a fish. And, even if it did resemble one, it certainly could not swim.

18

Whilst Fanny checked the boy's wound and reapplied a compress, Oddie told her of the strange happenings down at the mill.

Fanny – being Fanny – appeared unperturbed. She pulled the blankets carefully over the boy's lap and gave Oddie her full attention. "Don't fret. The boy is safe here. No one will breathe a word of his whereabouts."

Oddie shook his head. "You don't know that, Fanny."

She raised an eyebrow. "Do I not?"

Oddie glanced at the boy. He dropped his voice to a hiss. "Fanny, for goodness' sake, he was poaching on Lord Pelham's ground. The people may be loyal but his pockets are deep. Times are hard!"

Fanny turned to the boy, giving Oddie the full benefit of her chisel-like chin. "I'll get you some soup. Would you manage some cornbread?"

The boy nodded. "Aye, Miss, I would that." Then he ran a hand through his tangled hair. "You wouldn't have a nip of gin, would you, Miss?"

Fanny laughed. "No, but how about a bit of beer?"

The boy grinned. "That'll do."

Oddie was pleased to see the boy in such fine spirits. Gin was poisonous stuff, though.

"Oddie, come and set the table. We'll all sup."

Oddie smiled at the lad and followed Fanny into the living quarters. He put three bowls and spoons out whilst Fanny served up. His mouth watered. He was ravenous.

Minutes later he was engrossed in meat, carrot and potato broth, relishing the fragrant herbs. For a moment he almost wanted to give in to Fanny and marry her. Then he realised that she had managed to distract him entirely from the topic. She was a cunning one, that was for sure.

His appetite sated, Oddie put down his spoon. "Fanny, I heard what I heard. Pelham is on to the boy and yourself. My ears were not mistaken."

Fanny sipped her tea. "No, your ears heard the right of it. But this is not the boy in question."

Oddie was amazed. How many boys could there be? "Who then?"

Fanny leaned forward and unfolded a tale so strange that he was hard pushed to believe it. He sat back in his chair for a moment to allow the facts to sink in. He picked up his tea but simply stared into it. Then, putting it down, he leaned forward across the table towards Fanny. "So, you are telling me that a climbing boy was grievously wounded, that Eliza Elvidge tended to him but then Lord Pelham intervened and the boy was taken away."

Fanny tutted and shook a finger at him. "Don't be so perverse, Oddie. You are deliberately sifting out the facts that don't suit you!"

Oddie glared at her. "What, you expect me to believe in your hocus pocus, Fan? It is ungodly, I tell you. For sure, you are a good woman with a gift for kindness and knowledge of herbs and healing, but I do not hold with your talk of… devilish things."

Fanny laughed. Long and loud. "Oh, hark at you! Say it and be done, Oddie. It is magic! A craft that has passed in the blood from generation to generation for time so long it is forgotten."

Oddie glanced anxiously towards the bedroom. "Hush! The boy will die of fright with your devil's talk!"

Fanny sobered up and nodded. "Yes, mayhap. I should hate to undo all that has been done." She leaned towards him. "You can deny it all you like, Oddie, but the day will come when the craft will have its way with you. This I know." Then she leaned back, stretching voluptuously and smiling angelically. "Mayhap, it already has."

Shards of ice spread through Oddie's veins. For all his denial, some primitive part of his soul shivered. He tried to rally a response, but the seed had been sown. He sensed trickery but was not able to put his finger on it.

Outside an owl screeched and Oddie's senses stirred. "I'm going out."

Fanny nodded. "Where?"

"Where the fancy takes me." He stood up abruptly and began to gather his belongings.

"Don't be going to Pelham's, Oddie."

"Don't be telling me where to go."

Fanny got up and began to tidy. She poured ale for the boy. "Please, Oddie. Keep away from the estate. You are already in his sights. Don't push your luck. There is no charity in him. He is a cold, cruel man."

"What happened to the climbing boy?"

She shook her head, her brow creasing into a frown. "I don't know." Then she picked up the ale. "But I will find out."

Oddie didn't doubt it. Little escaped the Flowers girls when they cast their net. Part of him wanted to know what she would do when she found out, but the more prudent side of him shied away from the prospect. He was a peaceable man. Not given to looking for trouble. And these days there was trouble aplenty.

He put on his cap and shouldered his rifle. "Will you stay?"

Fanny shook her head. "Only until the boy is sleeping. I will give him a draught of Saint John's wort before I go. The wound is clean and healing. Tomorrow I will get him out of bed. He is young and will mend quickly. We must think where he will go when he is able."

Oddie's head snapped up sharply, and he stared her dead in the eye. "'We'? There is no 'we'. I'll not turn him out, but he is your responsibility."

Fanny ignored him. "Best thing would be to take him to Lincoln. He can lie low for a few weeks 'til he is walking. Then we will have to find him some sort of work." She was silent. "Maybe, you could find a job at the mill?"

"No."

"Yes," said Fanny, obviously warming to the idea. "Yes, you can take him to Lincoln on Sunday on the pretext of attending church. I'll organise a ride for you both."

Oddie sighed. A man must know when to accept defeat. "Well, alright. But that's it. No more, Fanny – do you hear me?"

Miraculously she did. She came to him and, holding the ale carefully aloft, pressed her body to his and kissed him. Hopelessly aroused, his hands passed around her waist.

Then she stepped away. "You are a good man, Mr Odling. You should make an honest woman of me."

He grinned. "That'd take a better man than me, Fanny Flowers."

She smiled and carried the ale into the back room.

Oddie stepped outside at last. He breathed in the moist, cold air. The stream muttered and mumbled over its stony bed and the wind moaned across the moor. As his eyes adjusted to the darkness, the hay meadow swayed and bent its heavy head as if in prayer. The misty rain settled into the grooves of his face and upon the work-hardened skin of his hands. He felt his spirit unfurl like wings ready for flight.

It was strange, but out here, everything seemed so much simpler. The Fens had nurtured his family for generations. It had given fish, fowl, plants and feathers and fur. And it still did. But each year that passed there was less. Each year the waters receded and the black soil was taken and ploughed and planted. Inch by inch his beloved Fen was being stolen from him. And he was helpless to stop it.

He cut across a ridge of marsh and stopped beside a pool. It was black as pitch. But he knew that below, fish and eels abounded. He unwound a net from his waist and deftly cast it. As it sank without a trace, Oddie found himself thinking about a birthmark shaped like a fish. About a burned boy and another filled with bullets. About the slow starving of the Fens. And, about Lord Pelham.

Oddie listened to the night. It told him that it was time he paid Lord Pelham a visit.

19

It was the strangest thing, but once Eliza was in her father's presence she found that she struggled to speak. At least, to speak about those things that lay heavily upon her mind. Sat beside him in his study, with warm milk, sweetened and sprinkled with cinnamon, the details of the day melted like snowflakes. As she sat, listening to him read a verse from an ancient book in a foreign tongue, Eliza felt soothed.

But then reality returned with a rude awakening. The insidious Withers knocked and entered to inform them that Lord Pelham had arrived. With that, the whole horrible day came tumbling down.

"Papa!" she said. "I must speak to you! About Lord Pelham – and Withers."

Her father put down the book and smiled at her. "Eliza, it is alright. I know all."

Of course he did. How could he not? A surge of resentment shot through Eliza. That sneaky, slimy little bully had already told his side of the story. And she could just imagine how that must have sounded.

She jumped up, desperate to have a say. "Papa, please listen to me. Lord Pelham was exceedingly cruel. And worse, he disrespected me in my own home. He took away that poor boy against my express wishes. If you had been here he would not have dared!" Breathless, she paused, her passion so high that she could barely breathe. For the second time in her life she railed against the whalebone and steel corset that constricted her. She felt that everything conspired against her.

Her father looked at her gravely and stroked his thick, curly beard, a gesture that usually indicated some inner conundrum. "Eliza, calm yourself. You raise your voice like a common fish wife. As I understand the situation, Lord Pelham was only acting as he believed appropriate as my business partner and friend. And I believe that he did so with the best of intentions."

"Best of intentions! You believe that dragging a grievously injured child away from a sick bed was well intentioned?" exclaimed Eliza with outrage.

Her father frowned. "Eliza, you do not seem to understand the depths of your impropriety. It will be common knowledge by now that you invited a… common trollop into our house. It is only Lord Pelham's intervention that saved you from utter social ruin." He stood up. "Indeed, you owe him a humble apology."

Eliza was confounded. The conversation was not proceeding as she had envisaged. Everything was topsy-turvy. Her papa was not taking her side. He was not being agreeable at all. This was such a novel turn of events that she hardly knew how to proceed. The only thing that she was utterly sure of, was that she would never, ever apologise. Fanny Flowers may be all that her father insinuated, but she had come in an hour of need. In return, she had been abused. Reassured that she was on the side of the angels, Eliza pressed on. "Papa, perhaps my behaviour was out of character. But you were not here. You did not see. Fanny Flowers helped. You must see that. Why, you would have done the same, I am sure."

Her father shook his head. "I am a physician, Eliza. Not a hedge healer. That woman is a renowned baggage. And as for her 'healing', it is little more than native cunning and a quick tongue. Believe me, Eliza, you are quite out of your depth. But then, you have lived a sheltered and refined life, as befits a young lady. Therefore, I do not hold you accountable for your behaviour."

Eliza took a moment to digest this last statement and found it bitter. To be judged to be in the wrong was bad enough. To be judged as if she were of no consequence was far worse. She breathed in as deep as she was able and drew herself up to her full five foot and two inches. "Not accountable? Am I a scarecrow stuffed with straw?"

"You are a young lady. It is not your natural state to understand the more complex matters of this world."

Eliza opened her mouth to speak but her father held up a restraining hand and she was silent.

"Be that as it may," her father continued, "you will apologise to Lord Pelham."

"I will not!"

He smiled. "You will, if you wish to acquire a new winter wardrobe."

These last words hurt her. Not because they were insulting, but because they conjured in her mind a startling and unpleasant view of herself. She felt a little sick in her stomach. Was she truly that shallow? Did her father honestly believe that dresses and shoes and fur tippets were more important to her than a poor, burned boy? More important than her – self respect?

And then an even worse thought struck her. Was that how other people saw her? Did they look at her and see a spoiled, selfish and indulged young woman? Reluctantly she came to the conclusion that was exactly what people saw. And why wouldn't they? Tears of shame and humiliation welled in her eyes. She refused to blink lest they fall. She found she could not meet her father's eyes. "Where is the boy?"

"He is in good hands."

"But where is he?"

Her father stood up. For the first time in her life, Eliza was aware of how big he was. Not just tall, but wide and solid. She felt like a sapling in the shadow of a great elm tree.

"Where he is, is none of your concern, Eliza."

She knew she should not pursue the matter, but she could not help herself. The images of the boy's terrible suffering were etched into her mind like a charcoal rubbing. "Please, Papa. I just want to see him. I feel it is my fault that he has been so hurt."

"It is nobody's fault!" her father said. "Such accidents are commonplace. Chimneys must be swept and boys must do the sweeping!"

"But Papa, the fires were lit. How did it come—"

"Enough, Eliza!"

Eliza shrank back from her father as if he had dealt her a bodily blow. Never, in all her seventeen years, had her beloved papa raised his voice in anger. She was entirely undone.

Then Withers cleared his throat. Eliza had entirely forgotten he was still there.

Her father turned away from her. "Bring Lord Pelham to us, Withers."

Withers gave Eliza a triumphant look and went. Eliza watched him go silently. Her father went to his desk and took a cigar from a box. He lifted it to his nose and sniffed it. Then, apparently satisfied, snipped it and put it to his lips. He struck a match. Smoke billowed and twined around his face. He did not so much as look at Eliza.

He turned at the sound of footsteps. Seconds later Withers reappeared with Lord Pelham in tow.

"Lord Pelham," said Withers.

Her father beckoned Pelham in. "That will be all, Withers."

The butler shut the door softly.

Eliza's father picked up the cigar box. "Lord Pelham?"

Lord Pelham obliged. He lit up and turned to Eliza. "Miss Eliza, I do hope you are recovered."

Her father nodded and smiled. "I think Eliza has something she wishes to say to you, My Lord." He looked expectantly at his daughter.

Eliza dropped a curtsey, sinking almost to the ground, her gown spreading like a flower over the carpet. When gracefully she arose, she looked at Lord Percival Pelham. She smiled. "My Lord, I would just like to say that you are – truly – the most repulsive person I have ever met." With that, she turned on her heel and fled.

20

Saturday. Oddie loved a Saturday. Mainly because the next day was Sunday. And this Sunday promised to be a good one. The main reason for this was – naturally – the weather. He woke that morning shivering and shaking in his makeshift bed. Later, as he made his way briskly to work, the rising sun revealed a sparkling landscape of ice. Trees like iced confection, spider webs sparkling like jewels and frozen heads of thistles shimmering like a million stars. And such a freeze meant just one thing – skating.

At work Oddie shovelled with a will as he contemplated the whereabouts for this activity. On reflection, it turned out that Fanny's plans were fortuitous. Not that he'd tell her so; she'd just give him a look that suggested that she had already seen it in her teacup. Or some such nonsense. But the truth was that the best skating lay at the foot of Lincoln. So, he'd drop the boy off, go to the cathedral for service and head on down for a race or two.

Oddie's feelings of wellbeing were muted at the unexpected and unwelcome arrival of Lord Pelham. Rather reluctantly he downtooled and nodded politely. "M'Lord." He hoped he wasn't required to go back down to the surgery. The place gave him the willies.

Pelham observed him as if he were something nasty stuck on the bottom of his shoe. "Odling, the blockage in number two has been cleared. Now the furnace has cooled it can be cleaned out."

Before Oddie could muster a response, the engineer abruptly turned and left.

"You shite," said Oddie softly.

The furnaces were traditionally only cleaned when the fields were dry and the wheel at rest. And that was a rare occurrence. It was unheard of this time of year when it could rain for weeks without ceasing. He had the sneaky suspicion that Pelham was just finding an opportunity to get at him.

Glumly, he went to the furnace and opened the door. It was not an inviting sight. Big enough to fit a man but too small to stand or turn around. And filthy, of course. Before he could even begin to scrape off the build-up of soot, he'd have to shift the thick layer of ash on the bottom. Oddie hated ash worse than coal dust. It made him sneeze something fierce.

With resentment burning in his heart, Oddie set to his task. Once he started, he decided to get as much done as he could on his shift. Huw had gotten a cold on his chest and he wasn't as young as used to be. So Oddie put his rage to good use and attacked the furnace like a man possessed. He filled bag after bag with ashes and dragged it out to dump near the canal. It was so cold that the perspiration on his bare skin froze. It popped and crackled as he moved. And then melted in a black river in the heat of the furnace house.

Winded, he paused for a while. He drank deep from the jug. As he put it back, whole and unbroken, he recalled the governor's daughter. Eliza. It seemed a long time ago since she had been here with her forget-me-not blue eyes. How exotic she had seemed in this place, like a breath of fresh air. But, if Fanny were to be believed, she was somewhat more substantial than air. In his experience, there were few who extended the hand of charity in the sanctity of their own homes. And fewer still who would put their hands voluntarily on a pauper. The closest most came was to toss a coin from the confines of their carriages. It warmed him to know that there was good inside that girl. Not that it helped the boy in the end, he reflected bitterly.

He stoked the furnaces once more before returning to his toil. He picked up his shovel where it had fallen at the rear of the furnace. With a yelp he dropped it and put his finger in his mouth. When he took it out a big blister blossomed on the calloused pad. Something was still very hot in the ashes. Odd.

With an iron poker in hand he went back to investigate. A couple of prods detected a foreign object buried right in the corner. Curious now, Oddie began ferreting around. He grunted with satisfaction as he caught sight of a dark object. He worried it out of its sooty bed, peering down to get a look. It took a moment for his eyes and brain to reach a mutual conclusion. It was a watch. Unwilling to touch it, Oddie swapped tools once more and scooped it up carefully with his spade.

He deposited it gently on the furnace-room floor. Then, impatient, he grabbed the jug of water and poured the remains over the watch. It steamed and hissed softly. Oddie filled in time checking the furnaces, topped up number one and came back to his find. Tentatively he touched it. It was barely warm, so he picked it up. The face was all but destroyed, the glass and both hands lost. A few Roman numerals were barely visible beneath the black, burned surface of the face. A long, charcoaled bit of a chain still clung tenaciously to top of the timepiece. It was light, though, as if hollow. Oddie turned it over to inspect the back. When he did, he let out a cry of shock and dropped the watch

For a moment he stared stupidly at it lying smashed at his feet. He tried to make sense of it all, but his brain felt stuffed with cotton wool. Then he shook his head. He must be suffering from heat stroke. That's what it was. It had been an exhausting and stressful couple of days.

"Get a grip, Oddie, you idiot!" he growled to himself. He picked the watch up and peered minutely at the inscription at the back. And all doubt ebbed away. This was, without a shred of doubt, his father's watch. True, the name was barely decipherable, but the pair of skates etched below was clear. His father had won the watch in an ice-skating race several years before he died. The watch had been his most prized possession.

Trouble was, the watch in Oddie's hand was all that remained of his father, whose body had never been found. The authorities had said he had been swallowed by a bog. There had been no search. Truth was, no one had really cared about the fate of a Fen slodger. The police hadn't even hidden their disdain, making jokes about webbed feet and other offensive innuendos. And Oddie had been too heartsore to protest.

Not that it would have made a difference. Outsiders only saw what they wanted to see. It made them feel superior to look down their noses at an old Fen man. They were too ignorant to either comprehend or value the cornucopia of knowledge inside his father's head.

Memories swamped him. Oddie recalled how his father could almost magically make a meal out of thin air. How he could shoot a hare on the foot, catch a fish with his bare hands and whistle a pheasant out of its hide. How he could shear a sheep as easy as he could mend a boat. And put him over a pair of skates, he was swifter than a roe deer. But outsiders only saw a wattle and daub hut in a swamp and decided that they understood all there was to understand about a man.

Tongue-tied with misery, Oddie had said nothing, but he had searched for his father night after night. After a year he had finally accepted that he may never find him. And now, years later, there was this. His father's watch. Sorrow, loss, anger and love engulfed him. For, while his father had been gruff, impatient and quick to temper, he had also been honest, hardworking and fair.

Not only that, he had passed on to Oddie a deep, abiding love of the land.

Oddie's hand closed around the watch as he waited for his grief to pass. When it began to ease he opened his fist and looked once more. As the shock wore off, his brain ticked back to life. He looked over at the furnace and wondered how it was, that his father's prized possession had come to be buried in the ashes. Who had put it there? And what was their motivation? Ultimately, he was led right back to the place he'd been when his father disappeared, left wondering what had happened. A chill ran through him as he filled once more with the conviction that his father's disappearance was suspicious.

With the watch snug in his trouser pocket, Oddie returned to work. He methodically raked the soot and ash with the poker and his eyes. But by the time his shift ended, he had found nothing more. He wasn't sure to be glad or sad.

When he bid Huw a farewell, he made no mention of the watch. He couldn't really say why. In part, it was a natural reticence to discuss his private life. But there was more to it than that. Fanny would have said it was a portent of some sort, and while Oddie didn't hold with all that superstitious twaddle, he was deeply disturbed. Truth was, he suspected that Percival Pelham was involved. Maybe he was paranoid, but Oddie couldn't let go of the suspicion that the lord had deliberately set him up to clean out that furnace.

The bottom line was Oddie couldn't let that rest. Not now.

21

The atmosphere in the house was tense. Or, at least, Eliza thought it was. But she was in such a dither it was possible it was just her. After her outburst at Lord Pelham she had expected her father's wrath to descend upon her head. But there had been nothing. Indeed, she had not seen him since. It was unnerving, although Eliza didn't know exactly why. It raised a host of unanswered questions.

Dressed and ready to attend the cathedral for morning service, Eliza peered anxiously out of her bedroom window. For a moment she forgot her woes as she looked out over a winter wonderland. The garden glittered and sparkled in the pale morning light. Not snow, but a splendid mantle of ice. Movement broke into her reverie and she turned her head to watch the carriage coming around to the front door. Both horses wore blankets over their glossy quarters and the driver jumped down from the box and stamped his feet.

Eliza went to her wardrobe and pulled out her fur cape and fox muff. But once she had put on her outdoor clothes, she hesitated. She was apprehensive about going but she was equally afraid to stay. With no other rudder with which to steer by, thus far she had stayed in the familiar groove of routine. Up until this moment she had believed her father would send for her and that there would be some sort of resolution. Horrible though that was to contemplate, she felt that it would be better than this drawn-out state of affairs. But he hadn't come or summoned her to him. And she did not know what this meant.

Then a horrible thought crossed her mind. Was it possible it was only herself that was upset? The more she examined the idea the more likely it became. Yes, it was quite within the realms of possibility that her father had banded together with the odious Pelham and dismissed her outburst entirely. Her imagination went into overdrive. Most likely they had lit a cigar, poured a whiskey and sat down to discuss the deficiencies of the feminine sex in general, and of Eliza in particular. Yes, she mused. Then it would have led to a lengthy discourse of hysterical women. And finally they would have decided that all 'poor Eliza' needed was the steadying hand of a good husband and a dozen brats. Then the pair of them would pat each other on the back at the prospect of bringing her to heel.

Her anxiety crystallised into ice-cold anger as she contemplated her insights. It seemed that her life was all mapped out for her whether she liked it or not! She was a golden pheasant raised up, pampered, and groomed only to be released into a hostile environment. And Pelham was a slavering hound, just waiting to find her in the open air, defenceless and exposed. Nausea roiled in her stomach and her head felt fuzzy.

There was a tap at the door and Mary entered. She bobbed a curtsey. "Carriage is waiting. Ready, Miss?"

Eliza stared at her maid. Ready? Was she ready? No. She was not ready at all. Maybe it would be best if she made her excuses and stayed at home. It was an attractive prospect. She could take her Welsh cob, Windsor, for a ride. It was a lovely day, sunny and dry. But then she pouted. One of the grooms would insist on accompanying her, even though she rode like a centaur. Why, even the hunt Whip said so! She had been the toast of the season.

Windsor was as calm as he was capable and Eliza was in no danger. Maybe she could just sneak out. But then she sighed. There was no hope of that. The men and boys in the stables were too scared for their places to neglect their duty. It was so frustrating.

"Miss?"

Eliza looked at Mary still undecided. "Is Papa waiting?" To her surprise her voice was remarkably steady.

Mary shook her head. "No, Miss. He rode out with Lord Pelham earlier."

Upon hearing this, she made up her mind to go. If she didn't, her father and the perfidious Pelham would assume they had won. They would give each other a knowing look and assume she was cowering in her boudoir, too ashamed to show her face. And that, she could not allow. She smiled at Mary. "Yes, I'm ready."

As she swept out of the room, Eliza glanced in the full-length mirror near her bed. She did look fetching. The sleepless night had left beguiling smudges of fatigue beneath her eyes. And the dark mink cloak and hood emphasised the blue of her eyes and the clear, porcelain complexion. Invisible beneath the fur, Eliza was brutally laced into her favourite Sunday gown of palest blue silk. Her waist was no bigger than a man's hand span. It would be a shame to waste all of Mary's hard work. To say nothing of her own.

As she swept down the main stairs and across the hall, Eliza had a thought that lifted her spirits considerably. There would be just herself and Mary in the carriage. Very private. It was a goodly drive and presented the ideal opportunity to finally finish the conversation they had started before the accident. It would be a welcome diversion from her worries.

Outside, her breath fanned out in a white spume of air and her nose tingled. Impatient to be away, she could barely bring herself to wait for the footman to assist her into the carriage. Once inside she settled onto the broad, cushioned seat as the coach began to move, her fingers drumming restlessly against the timber door. She knew it was unladylike but this morning, she frankly couldn't have cared less. It seemed to her that being a lady was thoroughly overrated.

Finally, confident they were going at a speed that would prevent the driver and footman from overhearing, Eliza clapped her hands together. "Mary, do tell me all about the stoker!"

Mary grinned. "What does Miss want to know?"

22

It was a slow journey in the back of the milk cart. Oddie felt that he could have carried the boy faster on his back. Sitting still for hours froze him to the marrow. The boy's lips were blue and his teeth chattered like warring conkers. But he made no word of complaint; he stared adoringly at the back of Fanny's bonneted head.

The cart began to vibrate. The milk churns rattled and danced as if possessed. The boy jerked his eyes away from Fanny and looked fearfully at Oddie. Oddie patted his arm gently. "Not to worry. It's just the cobblestones shaking us like milk into butter. Means we are nearly there."

The boy visibly relaxed and closed his eyes. His skin was pale as whey but his cheeks had filled out and his mop of black hair was shiny and clean. Oddie doubted his own mother would have recognised him.

A carriage came up the steep hill behind them. Oddie recognised it at once. There were few so fine. It was the governor's. He admired the high-stepping black horses between the shafts and the blood-red coat of the driver. His admiration turned to concern as the carriage gave no sign of slowing as it approached. "Fanny!" he yelled. "Fanny, look out!"

Fanny turned. Her lips twitched dangerously and Oddie stifled a groan. It wasn't the time to be playing silly devils. A horn blasted. The boy's eyes shot open and he sat up. Oddie pushed him firmly back down and shook his head. He was going to murder Fanny.

The driver was bearing down on them, whip aloft, his lips forming profanities that they could not hear for the combined cacophony of milk cart, horn and shod hooves. It was going to get ugly. The governor would be onto them and then they'd all be in for it.

But then, Fanny's draught horse turned and meandered to the side of the road. With a blast of the horn and crack of the whip the carriage pulled out to pass them. Oddie knew it was unwise, but he couldn't help himself. As the windows drew level he looked inside. His heart swooped and soared as he glimpsed a pair of forget-me-not blue eyes. And she smiled. And was gone.

Oddie sagged back against the side of the cart, dazed. He'd almost forgotten how beautiful she was. She was as delicate and refined as a lace doily. A creature so far removed from his world as an angel from heaven. And she had smiled at him!

The cart turned into a side street and half a dozen milk churns tumbled into Oddie's lap. After a violent struggle, he set them to rights and turned to Fanny to vent his displeasure.

But Fanny caught his eye. "Put your tongue back in, Oddie," she said waspishly. "She was smiling at me."

Oddie snapped his mouth shut. Damn the woman. She was too sharp for her own good.

The boy plucked at Oddie's sleeve. "She was looking at you, Oddie," he whispered. "I swear!"

"I'm not deaf!" Fanny snapped. As if to reinforce the fact, she pulled the carthorse to a sudden stop. "We're here," she said.

Oddie swore softly as he set the urns to rights once more.

The boy grinned but said nothing.

Fanny jumped down from her box and came around. She didn't say anything but her lush mouth was set in a straight line. Oddie watched her for a moment. Fanny was clearly miffed. He nearly laughed out loud when the penny dropped. Fanny Flowers was having an attack of jealousy! Who'd have thought? Fanny had never made a secret about her designs upon him but neither had she seemed even remotely concerned when he walked out with other women. Indeed, she mocked him. Well. Well. Well.

But he let it go. Not the time. He made his way to the edge of the cart, careful of the boy and the churns, and dropped to the ground. They were outside an inn. Three storeys high, it was tidy as a pin. A fresh-painted sign of a black dog swung back and forth in the breeze. Oddie had had a few bevies there. It was a pleasant inn, with fine ale and plain, well-cooked fare. The landlord, William Calcraft, was the hangman. His wife was Fanny's aunt.

Fanny glanced up and down the street. "Can you carry him round the back?" she said.

He could. Minutes later they nipped down the alley into a yard stacked with casks and pallets of empty bottles. Fanny's aunt was waiting. Oddie could see a strong family resemblance in the stout woman's dark hair and eyes, but she did not have Fanny's profile. Nor her full-frontal facial charm.

"Bring him in, Fan," she said, and smiled at Oddie.

Oddie smiled back. "Hello, Molly."

Oddie went into a narrow passage and followed Molly up a flight of stairs. It was a tight squeeze and Oddie was hard pressed not to knock the boy's bony elbows on the walls. They reached a landing, but Molly led them to another staircase. At the top was a garret. Small but snug enough. The boy was soon settled into the narrow cot in a corner.

Fanny turned to her aunt. "I cannot thank you enough, Aunt Moll!"

The landlord's wife smiled. "It's what families are for, Fanny."

Fanny squeezed her hands and then turned to Oddie. She smiled sweetly. Oddie was instantly on his guard.

"Come, Mr Odling," said Fanny breezily. "We must hurry, or we will be late for the service." Fanny swept out the room.

Shocked into silence, Oddie had no option than to follow.

23

Eliza's brain was abuzz. Truth be told she had not recognised the stoker at first glance. She had been riveted by the sight of Fanny driving the milk cart. The sight of her had been a slap in the face. All the horror of the climbing boy's accident had reared up inside her and she had been filled with a desire to speak with the Flowers woman again. Eliza guessed that if anyone would know the fate of the boy, it would be this woman who some called 'witch'.

It was only as the carriage overtook the slower vehicle that Eliza spotted the man in the rear, almost hidden by milk urns. She had been struck by his good looks. It was only as his intense, charcoal eyes met hers that she twigged. Her initial response had been one of pure, unadulterated delight, expressed in a spontaneous smile.

This unladylike behaviour was subsequently followed by an attack of intense embarrassment. Her emotions were sparked for twofold reasons. Firstly, Eliza remembered that on their first encounter he had been practically naked. Secondly, Mary had disclosed several fascinating but curiously disturbing facts about the stoker. Primarily, Mary had assured Eliza that he was the most lusted-after man in Lincolnshire.

As the carriage reached the crest of the hill, Eliza was silent, lost in contemplation. Once her galloping heart settled she tried to sort out the conflicting and confusing thoughts that assailed her. She wondered what the stoker was doing in the company of Fanny Flowers. What was their affiliation?

She harboured a secret desire that they be cousins. And not of the kissing kind. She glanced at Mary who was watching her with undisguised curiosity. Eliza hesitated, but then plunged in. "Tell me, Mary, how does the stoker come to be in the company of Fanny Flowers?"

Mary's eyes glittered. She leaned forward a little. "Well, Miss Eliza, I would not like to say, it's just idle gossip."

It was clear that Mary was actually dying to say. Eliza knew it and Mary knew it. But there was a way of doing things. "Yes, of course, Mary," said Eliza. "Gossip is an ungodly act."

Mary nodded. "Indeed it is, Miss."

The carriage was sweeping up to the cathedral and time was running out. "Of course," said Eliza, "some say that where there is smoke, there must be fire."

Mary grinned and conceded. "Well, they say that Leon Odling and Fan o' the Fens are – you know – an item."

Eliza didn't really know but she could imagine. And what she imagined made her feel decidedly ill-tempered. She knew it was wrong, but she didn't want Leon Odling being an item with anyone. Not even Fanny Flowers, whom she liked very much.

It was in this state of discontent that Eliza stepped out of the carriage and swept into the cathedral. The soft hum of conversation swelled as heads swivelled to watch her walk up the long isle. Usually the avid attention of the congregation leant to Eliza a sense of wellbeing. Usually, she would take great delight in the pretty picture that she presented. She loved being the centre of attention. But today, she found she didn't care. Truth was, she was far more concerned with whether her father was sitting in their family seat.

She spotted the back of his iron-grey head. Beside him was the oily, dark hair of Pelham. Her heart sank like a stone. What a presumptuous prig! Sitting there, in the Elvidge seats as if he were already one of the family. It was too much to bear.

"Over my dead body!" she hissed softly.

Both men nodded in unison as she stalked past them and settled herself in the row. She sat as far away from Pelham as she could without making a public spectacle, ignoring them with steely determination. The injustice of it all built inside her like a great head of steam. Tears of frustration prickled in her eyes, and she blinked them back furiously.

A rainbow of colour on the flagstone floor distracted her. Her gaze travelled up to the stained-glass windows. Lit up by the morning sunshine they made a dazzling display. Eliza gazed up to the ornate arched ceiling. Her eyes alighted on one of the many grotesques that decorated the cathedral. He was an ugly little fellow, perched on one leg and leering down at her with a horned head. Eliza rather warmed to him. He was considerably better-looking than the pernicious Pelham.

And then she let out a small scream of shock, which she quickly smothered in her gloved hand.

"Eliza, are you ailing?"

Eliza turned haughtily towards Pelham. "I am in excellent health, thank you, My Lord." But it was a lie. She wasn't well at all. The stress of the last days was getting to her. For, without a doubt, what she had witnessed was impossible. Yet, she would have sworn on a Bible what she had seen. That naughty little man had stuck out his tongue at her.

A giggle bubbled up in her chest. She clasped her hands to her bosom as if she could compress her hilarity. Despite her efforts, the giggle wiggled up her throat and perched on the back of her tongue. Eliza shifted her hands to her mouth and her eyes shifted sneakily upward. This time, the impish fellow winked. The giggle escaped and became a most unladylike guffaw.

Behind her, several rows went still and silent. Eliza could feel her father and Pelham looking at her. She did not dare turn around. Her self-control was stretched to snapping point. She rolled her lips between her teeth and stared steadfastly ahead. Frantic to regain her composure, Eliza sought a distraction. In desperation she picked up her hymn book and opened it at random. She began to read the Christmas carol under her breath. By the time she reached the third verse, the vein in her head had stopped throbbing and she relaxed a little. Finally, as the congregation picked up conversation once more, Eliza convinced herself that the moment had passed. She did not, however, dare look upward.

When the entire congregation took a collective breath, Eliza gripped the edge of her seat in consternation. For a horrible moment she thought she had had another... episode. But then a silence settled through the cathedral so profound that she could not resist. Eyes cast down, she slowly turned, peeking under her eyelashes. What she saw wiped away her fears.

Her mouth opened, and she stared, transfixed. Sashaying down the centre aisle was no less than Fanny Flowers. Then Eliza's attention shifted to the man at her side. It was him! The stoker. Leon Odling. Eliza looked around. To her vast amusement the congregation was agog.

If Fanny Flowers was perturbed, she made no outward sign. She looked neither left nor right until she reached the top of the aisle. Then she paused and stared pointedly at an elderly couple sitting in the row. They both glared and grumbled but shuffled over. Fanny moved gracefully into place and sat down. The stoker, hat in hand, sat beside her.

Eliza was delighted, for she had a clear view. Squashed into the tiny pew, the stoker was forced to let one long, muscular leg extend out into the aisle. His broad shoulders were beautifully emphasised, encased tightly in a worn leather coat. His hair was glossy and clean, swept back from the high forehead, revealing a hawk-like nose and a stubborn thrust of clean-shaven chin.

It was only as the bishop bustled into his lectern that Eliza dragged her attention away. As she did so it did not escape her notice that she was not alone. There was not a woman or girl in the vast cavernous cathedral who was not enthralled. Eliza was not amused by the attention lavished on the stoker. It had become clear to her in those few moments that Leon Odling was clearly destined to be entirely hers. The only question was how.

She looked up at the bishop and then above his head at the crucifix. Poor Jesus looked back down and Eliza knew exactly what was needed. It was time to make a deal with God. She had struck quite a number of very satisfactory deals over the years. Not that she abused the system. She never asked for anything that she felt she was not entitled to. And she was never greedy. It seemed to her that, in the big picture, securing the undying love of a humble stoker was a minor request. She had no doubt that God would surely see that. The tricky part was what she should offer in return for God's kind intervention.

The bishop began his sermon. Eliza wished he'd be quiet. It was very difficult to concentrate with him hammering on about someone and 'Gomorrah'. She clasped her hands together, shut her eyes tight, and mentally plugged her ears. Then she began to pray. With every iota of her being she begged the good Lord to grant her very modest request. If he did, she swore that she would forgo her winter wardrobe for the season. It was a great sacrifice, but she felt it was only fair. She conveniently forgot the pending apology to Lord Pelham upon which her winter wardrobe depended.

Satisfied that she had presented an equitable case, she said a hearty 'Amen' and opened her eyes. Her nerves quivered as a voice whispered in her ear.

"Oh ho! Have a care for what you wish for, Eliza!"

Eliza stared fearfully up at the imp. But he did not wink. This time, he smiled.

24

It was the longest service Oddie had ever endured. It was bad enough to be the centre of a seething, infuriated and outraged community. But it was ten times worse to be exposed to the unhappy gaze of the governor. What was Fanny thinking? Long as he'd known her, she'd never put foot in church. He'd believed her to be a heathen. And he was not alone. Mind you, he did not think as many did that she was in league with the devil. That was just ignorance and spite. Fact was, he was utterly bemused.

For her part, Fanny seemed utterly unfazed by the furore she had created. She behaved with utmost propriety even when the bishop sprayed spit over her in his passionate attempts to publicly shame her. Indeed, Oddie was amazed as she joined in prayer word perfect and stood, sat and kneeled right on cue. And she sang all the hymns in a clear, pure soprano. Not to mention, on top of that, he was acutely aware of the proximity of Miss Eliza Elvidge.

If he turned his head a fraction to the right he had a clear view. It was hard not to stare, for she was as perfect in profile as she was from any other angle. Golden strands of hair curled from under her bonnet like delicate fronds of flowers. As he sank awkwardly down to his knees to pray he bashed his head on the Bible rack. It made a sharp crack like a cannon.

Oddie subdued a curse and couldn't help looking over. He was just in time to catch a blast of blue eyes as the governor's daughter sunk gracefully down. Maybe it was his imagination but she looked a bit put out. Not surprising really, he thought darkly. She probably didn't appreciate the attention of a common, working man. After all, she was most likely engaged to Lord Pelham. He'd best keep his eyes to himself. Likely he was in enough trouble already, thanks to Fanny.

As the congregation murmured responses to the bishop's incantations, Oddie took a moment to wonder why Fanny had come. Had he misjudged her? Maybe her avoidance of church wasn't lack of faith at all. Perhaps she just didn't want to suffer the undisguised hostility of the bishop and the congregation. It would be understandable. You'd have to be deaf, dumb and blind to miss the whispering, pointing and pained expressions. And yet, when their wives screamed in agony in the birthing bed, it was to Fanny that they begrudgingly turned. That was the thing that stuck in his throat. Not their hostility, but their hypocrisy.

He was roused from his reverie when Fanny kicked him – none too gently – in the shins. To his chagrin he found everyone else already seated. He tried to get up in a dignified manner, but it was damn near impossible when you were jammed in tighter than cork in a bottle. Behind him someone giggled and was hushed. The back of his neck grew hot as he extracted one leg and then another and slid onto the wooden pew. Fanny glanced at him and grinned evilly. Curse her!

The rest of the service ground on. Oddie kept himself sane by focusing on the pair of blades waiting for him in the milk cart. Outside, the wind cut like knives but it was more sheltered down the bottom of the steep hill. The ice would be perfect. He couldn't wait to cut loose and see how far and how fast his skates would take him. Maybe he'd win a race or two. Put another treasure on the mantelpiece beside his alarm clock. No one else he knew had such a thing. It was a source of great pride for Oddie. Sometimes he'd just sit and look at the second hand skate around and listen to the deep, steady tick and tock. It was a magical thing, that clock.

Which brought him back to the fob watch that had belonged to his father. It was in his pocket. Somehow, now he had found it, he couldn't bear to be parted from it. He hadn't said anything to Fanny about it but decided he would. She was sharp, was Fanny Flowers. Maybe she'd be able to shed some light on the mystery. Indeed, maybe she'd show that there was no mystery at all. Then he could stop obsessing over Pelham and settle down to the quiet life that he loved.

Finally it ended. Oddie leapt up, eager to be away. In the aisle he waited impatiently for Fanny. But Fanny was faffing about with her button boots. "Fanny!" he hissed. "Hurry up!" Fanny gave him an insolent look, tapped her foot and slowly stood up. Then she opened her purse and began to dig around in its depths.

Just as Oddie decided to leave without her, she clipped her purse shut and sauntered out of the pew. There was something in her expression that caused Oddie a twinge of concern. Instinctively he looked around and his heart plummeted. Clearly Fanny had been delaying.

He stood aside as Lord Pelham advanced at the head of his small entourage. Oddie held his breath as they walked slowly towards him. Oddie prayed they would pass by peaceably. Apparently, God wasn't listening. Fanny stepped out into the middle of the aisle.

"Excuse me, Lord Pelham," she said politely.

Pelham stared determinedly over her head and kept on coming. It was only when he was a whisker away from Fanny's face that he ground to a halt. "Begone, woman!" he snapped.

Fanny's chin jerked up and Oddie felt all hope wither and die. He knew that gesture of old. Oh dear.

"Don't 'woman' me, Sire," she said softly. "I have come to give you fair warning."

Pelham's nostrils flared with ire. "You'd be wise to keep your counsel, Fanny Flowers," he said.

Fanny snorted. "No. You would be wise to listen. There is talk in town and none of it to the good. Feelings run hot and high when men cannot put a crust of bread in the mouths of their babes. Feelings run over when children are mutilated by mantraps. Try another tack. A little bit of Christian kindness goes a long way. Turn a blind eye until the cold, dark times are behind us."

Lord Pelham looked like he was going to burst into flames. His face was livid red and a pulse the size of a hosepipe throbbed in his forehead. "Beware, Fanny Flowers. I have your mark!"

Fanny's lips twitched and she lifted her arm to peel back the edge of her sleeve. She turned her hand over to reveal the smooth, creamy underside of her wrist. "This mark, Lord Pelham?"

Pelham stared at the birthmark as if he'd like to bite it out of its fleshy bed. Oddie daren't look at the governor. But a sharp intake of breath caught him unawares, and before he could think, his eyes followed the sound. Miss Eliza Elvidge looked white as paper. She was all eyes, staring down at the purple mark on Fanny's skin.

It was funny, but Oddie had never thought about it before, but the wine-red birthmark strongly resembled a rabbit. Or maybe… a hare. No sooner had he thought it than his intestines shrivelled inside him. Fanny may as well have thrown down a glove at the man's feet. He glanced around and was not surprised to find they had an audience. Many whispered and pointed. Some were dragging curious children away, as if they were in danger. Oddie felt a wave of contempt. So much for their books and learning. They were as superstitious as a shoeshine boy.

Pelham dragged his eyes off the birthmark and opened his mouth. But he did not have a chance to speak. The governor laid a heavy hand on the man's narrow shoulder and propelled him forcefully forward. The three of them passed in a grim procession. The young miss followed, eyes cast down, lips tight. She looked deeply unhappy.

As Oddie turned to watch them go, he noticed the governor had hold of his daughter's delicate wrist. Red marks flared from the pressure of his grip. Outrage ignited in Oddie's chest. And shock. He could scarcely believe that the governor would lay a hand upon his daughter. Everyone knew how devoted he was to his only child. Unsure and upset, he took a step forward, not even sure of his own intent.

"No!" said Fanny, grabbing him by the elbow.

Oddie pulled away for a moment and then stopped. What was he going to do? Call out the governor for a duel? No. Fanny was right. There was naught to be done. A father had the right to chastise his child. But he could not still the unease that writhed like a barrel of eels in his belly. There was something amiss. Something just beyond his ken. As if he were in a fog where he could sense things but couldn't see them.

The congregation all drifted away until the cathedral was empty for all but a cat. It popped out of the clock and scampered silently across the flagstones. Fanny bent down and picked it up. It purred and rubbed its black face on hers. Oddie put out his hand to stroke the glossy coat and was rewarded with a hiss and paw full of claws. Fanny laughed.

Oddie stifled a curse. He looked up at the great, arcing ceiling and felt an urgent need to escape. He looked at Fanny. "What's going on, Fanny?"

She shrugged. "I came to warn Pelham. There is trouble brewing."

But Oddie didn't entirely believe her. Without a word he walked away. As he strode briskly back to the cart to collect his blades, the scene whirled around and around in his head like a carousel. The men's behaviour he thought he could fathom. But what of the young miss? Why had she looked so shaken? Strange.

When he reached the cart, it came to him. Fanny was crafty. The whole thing had been a charade. It hadn't been about Pelham at all. It had all been about the governor's daughter. Eliza Elvidge.

Trouble was, Oddie couldn't work out why. But he intended to find out. He was tired of being kept in the dark.

25

Eliza felt funny. The world around seemed peculiarly distant. As if she was peering down the wrong end of a pair of binoculars. And sound was muffled as if she had put her head underwater. Her father was walking so fast across the cobble stoned square that she could barely catch her breath.

When they reached the carriage he did not wait for the footman, but flung the door open and pulled her around. Eliza stared up at him, too shaken to speak. She felt like a ragdoll whose stuffing had spilled out. She twisted, snatching her arm away. Her wrist throbbed and black spots danced before her eyes. It occurred to her then that she may faint. The idea was abhorrent. She despised weaklings. With a deliberate effort she straightened her spine and leant against the carriage. With something solid behind her she felt better. She closed her eyes, trying to breathe as deeply as she could.

"Get in!"

Her eyes snapped open and she looked carefully at her father. Had he gone mad? "Why, Papa? What have I done to warrant such unkindness?"

His eyes glittered. "Get in!"

She stiffened as Lord Pelham slid around the corner of the carriage. At the sight of Eliza and her father, his face twisted into a triumphant leer. Eliza gripped the door and willed herself to stay upright. She'd die rather than give them the satisfaction of witnessing her complete collapse. Pelham crowded into the space between her father and the carriage. She felt claustrophobic. "Get away, Sir!" she hissed.

To her vast relief, her father nodded, and Pelham backed off. With the tatters of her dignity drawn around her like a cloak, Eliza turned and stepped up into the carriage. Mary stared bug-eyed from the far corner. As the door slammed shut, Eliza sat mutely, too shocked to think. She looked down in disbelief at her wrist. At the purple bruises flowering around the bone. But in truth it paled in comparison to the pain of her public humiliation.

A tear trickled down her cheek and melted into her fur cape. And another. With a murmur of sympathy, Mary came and sat beside her. Abandoning all pretence, Eliza leaned against her maid's shoulder and wept. Grief poured from her like a river, until finally she ran dry and sat up. She hiccupped, stared out the window, and pulled out her kerchief. As she blew her nose she was distracted by the picturesque scene unfolding before her eyes. Wistfully she watched the skaters dart and glide across a great expanse of silver ice. Sounds drifted on the breeze. Laughter, squeals of mock terror and yells of excitement.

And then she stiffened and pressed her nose to the glass. Her mouth opened wide in surprise, fogging the window. By the time she'd rubbed a peep hole in the glass, the carriage had passed by. But she peered back, trying to catch one more glimpse of the skater that she was sure had been the stoker.

She blew her nose once more. "Mary, does the stoker, Mr Odling, skate?"

Mary nodded. "Oh yes, Miss. Why, he is famed for it! He is a champion in these parts. He's won trophies and prizes and everything!"

Eliza leaned back into the plush upholstery and mulled this fascinating snippet over in her mind. She felt a flicker of excitement. It seemed that God was already on her side. Surely it could not be pure coincidence that the stoker happened to skate right past her carriage at that precise point in time? Clearly there was a message here. All she had to do was make a plan. After all, didn't the clergy sincerely preach that God helped those that helped themselves? Yes. Eliza must take charge of the project. And it quickly became apparent what should be done.

She leapt out of her seat, nearly sending poor Mary into an apoplexy. She opened the window, stuck her head out and yelled out to the footmen to stop. Her cries went unheeded and she withdrew with a curse of frustration and banged furiously on the roof. The message must have got through, for the coach slowed and came to a stop.

Seconds later the footman peered anxiously through the window. His thin, acne-scarred face was furrowed in a frown. "Everything alright, Miss Eliza?"

Eliza nodded. "Ted, please instruct Oswald to turn around. I wish to go back to the ice field."

Ted stared at her with a startled expression. "But, Miss, the Master said you was to go straight home."

Was she indeed! Her grief hardened to be replaced by a simmering resentment. On careful consideration, Eliza found that she no longer held her father's authority in such high esteem. "You will turn the carriage around this instance, or I will get out and walk!" she said.

Poor Ted looked as if he was going to cry but withdrew smartly instead. Eliza waited in a lather of anxiety. She did not want to walk. But she would if she had to. She let out a long sigh of relief as the carriage began to move, circle and retrace its passage.

Terrified but determined, Eliza trembled with suppressed emotion. The unconditional love that she had always felt for her father now seemed misplaced. She felt lost and afraid. As if she had died and been reborn into a foreign place full of strangers. Indeed, it felt as if strangers were more familiar to her now. She had a growing conviction that Fanny Flowers had been at the cathedral for the explicit intention of seeing herself. There could be no doubt that Fanny had wanted to show off her own birthmark despite her baiting of Lord Pelham.

It was with rigid self-control that Eliza resisted looking at the fish-shaped mark on her arm. If it so much as shed a scale, it would push her over the edge. She shied away from the thought. For right at the nub of Eliza's distress was the shadow of insanity. No one spoke of it, but everyone knew of it. There were few secrets on the Fens.

The carriage slowed, manoeuvring onto the frozen footpath that led to the lake. The sights and sounds buoyed up her spirits. Here was a golden opportunity not just to strike up an acquaintance with the stoker but with Fanny Flowers too. As she hopped down onto the frozen field, Eliza gathered her courage. She wouldn't fail. After all, God was on her side.

26

Oddie saw her straight away. He was not alone in that, of course. There were few present who would have missed the carriage's progress. She made a striking figure in dark fur, silhouetted against the sparkling ice field. He could not recall the governor's girl attending a skate before. Other members of society appeared regularly. Like the hunt, a good hard freeze drew rich and poor alike to the common land. But never Miss Elvidge.

Afraid to be caught gawping, Oddie skated upstream but she remained forefront in his mind's eye. He absentmindedly acknowledged the cheerful greetings sent his way and forced himself to keep going. Soon he left the crowd behind and joined the ranks of the stronger skaters. The Fens spread out, flat and frozen as far as his eyes could see. The rhythmic swish of his bone blades soothed his ruffled spirit. He breathed in deep breaths of frigid fresh air. As he emptied his lungs he could almost feel the coal dust blowing away. It was good to be alive. But his movements gradually slowed, and he found himself fighting a growing urge to return. Finally, he gave in and circled back.

"Oddie!"

He looked over his shoulder at a furiously fast figure coming up behind him. The figure came into focus. It was Bennet Forsythe, local blacksmith and avid skater. Known as 'The Bull', Forsythe was built like the proverbial and skated like a bovine pumped on cracked barley.

The blacksmith's baby face cracked into a smile. "Bet you a pint of best bitter I get back afore you!" he yelled.

A vision of Forsythe sweeping into the arena, victorious under the approving eyes of Eliza Elvidge, filled Oddie's mind. For the first time, Oddie was acutely aware that Forsythe's fine physique and halo of blond curls cut quite a dashing figure. It was not an insight that made him happy. Not happy at all.

With a flurry of activity, Forsythe swished past, grinning from ear to ear. And a kind of madness possessed Oddie. A savage hunger erupted inside him. A hunger to win. All he knew was that Eliza Elvidge's forget-me-not blue eyes must witness his triumph. How he wanted to shine! He wanted her to clap her little gloved hands and cheer for him. To look up at him with approval and admiration. Nothing else would do.

With a "Hah!" he set off in pursuit of his rival. Forsythe had already forged a gap and was rapidly pulling away. Adrenaline burst through Oddie's blood like a firework. He leaned forward, clasping his hands behind his back, and began to work in earnest. The months of hard labour had conditioned him like a racehorse. His legs felt like pistons and his lungs felt like a vast steam engine. As he accelerated, the wind blew his cap off and his hair streamed back. When he passed Forsythe, he gave the blacksmith a victory sign before pushing on.

Forsythe swore and sped up. But Oddie was not concerned, he just pumped up the ante and kept the lead. Teasing his quarry. As they approached the road the dense mob of skaters parted. With the wind whistling in his ears he couldn't hear but could see the mouths of the mob yelling and cheering. Ahead, a couple of youngsters dashed in and set two barrels across the centre of the ice. Oddie glanced over his shoulder. The blacksmith's grimly determined face scowled back. With effortless ease, Oddie stormed down the last length and shot through the finishing gates. He slid gracefully to a standstill in a shower of ice as the crowd erupted. The bets must have been laid thick and fast. Men and women groaned and grinned in a frenzy of exchange.

For a few moments Oddie was besieged by an enthusiastic cluster of admirers. They only fell back as Forsythe shouldered his way through. The big man shook his head and held out a gloved hand. "You're in good form, Oddie," he said. "Well run!"

Oddie shook briefly. "Maybe next time, hey, Ben!"

Forsythe smiled ruefully. "See you in The Dog then?"

Oddie nodded. "Sure," he said. But the conversation barely registered. His eyes kept slipping away to check out the crowd. She was still there, he knew. He could see the driver of the carriage sitting shivering on his box. And then the crowd melted in his mind, as he glimpsed a sight of her. She was standing on the frozen dark earth, a skate blade grasped in one hand. She was staring right at him. He could not see her expression clearly but her slender form was utterly still. Like a mouse frozen beneath the shadow of a hawk. Or like a cat about to pounce. It could have been either.

The world folded in upon itself. Time stopped ticking. And then he was moving although he had no conscious recollection of deciding to do so. Like metal to a magnet he was pulled forward. Closer and closer until he could have put out his hand to touch. But he didn't. Instead, he stopped. Up close she was as bright and beautiful as he remembered. Delicate and dainty as a flower, she was. Her creamy cheeks flushed with cold and her lips rosy red. But it was her eyes that undid him. Big and blue, wide apart, and warm, they could have been the ocean. Or the sky. It did not matter. Oddie was happy to sink inside them.

Then she smiled. Her teeth, white and perfect as the inside of a shell. "It is Mr Odling, I believe?" she said.

He nodded, afraid to speak in case the words stammered and stuttered into the air like hammer on anvil. She was silent for a moment, head cocked slightly to one side, revealing a plump pearl of an earlobe nestled in a curl of gold. Then she bit her lip as if pensive. As if she were as unsure as he.

Like a revelation he realised that Fanny Flowers had got it wrong. The smile had been intended for him after all. Without a doubt, the governor's girl, Eliza Elvidge, had come to the frozen fields with him in mind. Oddie was awed. Oddie was exhilarated. But most of all, Oddie was hopelessly, helplessly in love.

27

To her irritation, all the clever quips and gay comebacks that Eliza had hoped to ploy seemed to dribble out of her brain via her ears. Instead of being scintillating she just stood there, staring up into his deep grey eyes like the scarecrow she sincerely did not want to be. But it was hard to form any lucid thoughts at all.

Close up and squeaky clean he was devastatingly handsome. How she longed to peel off her glove and run the tips of her fingers along the hard line of his jaw. And her eyes kept flickering back to his. Deep grey, like slate and framed in lush black lashes. And his lips, full but firm, drew her gaze next. And then there was his aroma. Without thought she breathed him in. It was a heady concoction of leather, carbolic, peat smoke and… healthy, virile man.

It occurred to her then that such thoughts were not proper. She dropped her eyes as a flush of heat crept up her neck and into her face. What must he think? Before she could dwell on this she was distracted by a figure shooting into her vision and coming to an artful halt. It was a young girl. Buxom and brunette.

"Oddie," said the girl, insinuating herself between Eliza and the stoker. "Come take a turn with me!"

Eliza was furious. How rude! But her anger turned rapidly to acute anxiety. Her confidence took another blow as it occurred to her that the man before her was somehow different here. It was, she decided, the difference between admiring a tiger held in captivity and meeting said tiger in the wilds. In the bowels of the furnace room, Eliza had witnessed the stoker. But here, amidst this dashing crowd, he was practically a king. It was she who seemed less. It was not a very palatable thought.

The dark girl moved back a little and Eliza willed her to keep going. But she didn't. Instead she slowed a fraction and then began to circle; round and round she went until she was no more than a mad spinning top. With a flourish, and a smile, the girl came to a standstill. "Come on, Oddie!" she gasped.

Eliza curbed a burning desire to go out onto the ice and give the trollop a good shove. How lovely it would be to have her flat on her back with her legs and bloomers waving in the wind. She took a deep breath and looked square at the stoker.

For a paralysing pulse of time he looked down at his boots as if they were some fascinating form of fauna he'd just discovered. Eliza had just decided that she would not stand around to be humiliated one fraction of a second longer, when he glanced up at her and smiled. And as he did, he was transformed. His dark eyes glinted, his teeth flashed and a dimple danced on his cheekbones. Her heart skipped several beats. Why, there was something positively devilish about him. Then he looked at the hopeful face of the young woman. And shook his head.

Eliza knew it was vulgar but she couldn't suppress a burst of triumph. The twirling trollop gave Eliza a look that would have stripped the rind off of bacon. Eliza merely raised an ironic eyebrow. After all, she had been raised as a lady. And ladies were always as gracious in winning as they were in defeat. The trollop turned tail and pummelled her way through the skating crowd. She was instantly forgotten. Eliza decided that God really did work in mysterious ways.

They faced each other silently and Eliza searched frantically for something intelligent to say. Then she remembered the heavy timber blade dangling in her hand. With a small smile, she lifted it up by its long leather thong. "I have a confession to make," she said.

He moved a fraction closer. Eliza waited apprehensively for his reply. Really, he was the most self-contained human being she had ever encountered. She longed to hear his voice. She sensed it would be deep and resonate. Or maybe a bit musical. She thought he looked upset. Had she said something amiss?

But to her relief his lips parted and Eliza leaned in, eager not to miss a word.

"W-w-w-what is it?" he said.

She was right the first time. Deep and resonate. And he stuttered. Her heart melted. There was something utterly adorable about such a flaw in this man. It made him a little… vulnerable. A bit like Achilles and his heel. Or Samson and his hair. Eliza wanted to reach up and kiss away the worry lines that crinkled at the corners of his eyes. But she wouldn't. That would hardly be ladylike, would it?

Instead, she bent down and picked up the other blade that she had exchanged for her fur muff. "I have to confess that I cannot skate!"

And then he tipped back his head and laughed. It was a good sound. Full and uninhibited. There was no holding back like with his words. Then he sobered, reached out, plucking the blades from her hands. "Here, l-l-let me," he said.

To her delight, he knelt on the frost-hard ground and put out a hand. Deliciously self-conscious, Eliza lifted the hem of her gown and exposed the minimum amount of foot and ankle. In a few seconds he had cradled her boot in his hand and deftly strapped on one blade. She put her foot back to the ground to test it. To her relief, she balanced quite easily. But when he lifted the other foot, her leg wobbled dangerously. Panicked, she put a hand onto the nape of his neck to balance herself.

He froze. Then continued as if nothing had happened.

Beneath her gloved fingers, Eliza could feel the strong muscles in his neck contracting. Despite the frigid atmosphere, she felt an alarming flush of warmth. Perspiration dampening the small of her back. Her heart racing. And she felt a disturbing but pleasant tingle in her private parts. She wished could strip the silly gloves away and feel the texture of his tawny skin and dark hair. Just as she decided that it might be wiser to risk a fall rather than to continue this alarming but curiously pleasurable activity, her other foot was released.

In a fluid, graceful motion, Leon Odling was up on his feet, watching her anxiously.

Whilst Eliza found she could stand up on two blades with considerably more ease than one, she was filled with apprehension. Never in her short life had Eliza wanted to shine more. It would be unbearable to be a duffer. Everyone else looked as if they had been born to skate. She must be the only lady in Lincoln who'd never skimmed like a swan over the ice. She would die of shame if she fell. Worse still, the twirling trollop would die laughing. The county would gossip about it from dawn till dusk. Her friends would whisper from Epiphany to Easter.

There was only one answer. But it wasn't very ladylike. Not ladylike at all. She took a deep breath. "Will you hold my hand?"

He nodded and smiled. A smaller, softer smile. Gentler. More... intimate. It was as unexpected as it was welcome. He made her feel special. A jealous little voice in her head reminded her that he probably used the self-same smile with Fanny Flowers. But she shoved the thought away. No one was going to spoil this day. Especially not herself. Besides, she was here. Fanny Flowers was not.

Her stomach fluttered like a kaleidoscope of butterflies as she put out her hand. It hovered there, airborne, a white, bright, lonely thing. And then it was enveloped. His hand on hers. It was a perfect fit. And Eliza was lost. Forever.

28

With her hand in his, Oddie felt an enormous sense of responsibility. To his eyes she seemed as fragile as a forget-me-not. The ice field was an unforgiving place. Ankles turned and arms and legs snapped like twigs. Here the elements ruled. It humbled the strongest of men. The cold could kill. And it did. If anything happened to the governor's girl, Oddie didn't think he could bear it.

Truth was, he didn't want to lead Eliza out onto the ice. He wanted to sit her back in the carriage, safe, snug and swaddled in furs. For a minute he considered doing just that. But she gazed up at him with expectant, trusting eyes. Her small hand trembled in his. And he could not deny her.

He took a single step back and waited for her to follow. She bit her bottom lip and stepped after him. Despite having his back to the crowd, Oddie sensed a hundred pairs of eyes watching. With a jolt, he realised that there would be many out there who might think a common stoker was stepping outside the social order. But then again, he wasn't at work now. He was on the ice. And here there were few that were his equal. His status here was that of an experienced skater. A prize-winning skater, at that. All in all, it would be best to carry on. Put on a show of professionalism. To pull out now might make things worse.

Confident he had a handle on the situation; Oddie turned his mind to the job. Over the years he'd aided many rookies to find their feet. This was at least something he could do well. And really, there was no need to actually teach. Preservation was the order of the day. All he had to do was to lead her about carefully and then deliver her back to the carriage unharmed. With a plan readied, he moved back onto the ice proper. For a second, she wavered, their hands pulling almost apart, until he barely held the tips of her fingers. Maybe she had changed her mind, after all.

Oddie was conflicted. The situation was fraught with peril. But he baulked at the prospect of letting her go. The conflict was quashed as she moved carefully forward, one tiny footstep at a time. A frown of concentration etched in her smooth brow. And two teeth nipped at her full lower lip. Perhaps she was scared?

She stepped tentatively onto the ice. It wasn't as smooth as Oddie would have liked. All the blades had sliced it up. Still, she was safe enough. With a glance over his shoulder, he rolled easily back. As she jerked forward she gave a little cry and gripped his hands compulsively. Worried, he checked she was alright. But he need not have worried; she was travelling steadily. Better still, the frown had flown and her bottom lip curved into a smile. Her eyes shone with health and happiness. Golden curls escaped from beneath the blue bonnet, corkscrewing onto her shoulders. Oddie felt as if his heart had been clamped into a vice. She was so beautiful it hurt to look at her.

For a few magical moments all was well in his world. He towed her carefully across the ice. She was as light as thistledown. If he hadn't felt the grip of her hands, he would have not known she was there.

Then she frowned. "Stop!"

Oddie did as she bid. Unfortunately, the governor's girl did not.

With her mouth open in an O of surprise she kept on coming. They came together with more force than her slight form suggested. Her body closed in to his and with a small huff of fear, she grabbed his jacket front. Instinctively he clasped his hands around her waist, fearful she would fall. Briefly she relaxed into him and he could feel the swell of her breasts and the beat of her heart. His response was spontaneous. And rampant.

Oddie wished the ice would crack and swallow him. Mortified, he pushed her away. Dear God! What must she think? She'd think he was a brute. And she'd probably be right. He didn't know what to do. Or what to say.

Luckily, the governor's girl was not so afflicted. Stood alone, unaided on the ice, her face was as red as a sunset. "I'm sorry," she said. "My fault. I forgot I didn't know how to stop." Then she was silent. But not for long. "I don't want to seem ungrateful, but the thing is – I want to be like them." She made a graceful arc of her arm, indicating to the flying figures around them.

Oddie's embarrassment was forgotten. She must be joking? But Miss Eliza Elvidge seemed quite serious. What to do? Best thing would be to explain that it wouldn't be wise. His anxiety was exacerbated by the people swirling past, eyes and ears on stalks. Best to explain just how dangerous it was. On so many levels.

But she stared up, wordlessly pleading. And he caved. "Alright." He thought for a moment. "Most important thing is to stay relaxed. Open your arms. Bend your knees a little and lean forward a bit. And walk."

She blinked. "What, on my own?"

He suppressed a grin. This was not what she had anticipated. Truth was, there was no other way. It was do or die. Suddenly he was very curious to see just what the governor's daughter was made of. Maybe she was just a canary in a cage. Or a chicken?

She gazed around the ice once more. "What if I… fall?"

"You get up."

"Oh." And with that, she spread her hands, sank a fraction and took a step.

Oddie watched. And prayed.

One step followed another as she inched her way over the ice. As Oddie followed her progress he felt a bubble of respect expanding inside him. In no time she had found a rhythm and was skating proper. And then she really got into the swing of it, flitting across the frozen water. She accelerated away from him and looked triumphantly over her shoulder. "Look at me!" she cried joyously. And fell flat on her back.

Oddie died a thousand deaths as he streaked to her side. The magnitude of his actions crashed over him as he crouched down beside her. His eyes searched her face frantically, and then ran over her body, searching for signs of injury. "Miss Elvidge!" he shouted. "Miss Elvidge, are you hurt?" His soul shrivelled inside him as she lay limp and mute.

Then her eyes opened, bursting with mischief. "My pride is severely dented, Mr Odling, but my person is quite intact." And then she burst out laughing.

Oddie couldn't decide if he wanted to kiss her or strangle her.

29

Even looking straight up his nostrils, Leon Odling was delectable. From this angle she noted that he had a tiny, sickle-shaped scar on his forehead. It shone white in the morning sun. Eliza wondered what else there was to know about him. For a fleeting moment she was forcefully reminded of their collision. Of the hardness of his body. Of her own response. Of her deep-seated curiosity to understand the odd workings of his maleness.

Heat sprang in her cheeks. These were not the musings of a well-bred young woman. But she still lay, grazing her eyes over him. Despite the cold seeping through her clothes and the numbness of her fingers and toes, she felt quite content. She laughed again. Not at him or even herself, but at the wonderfulness of the world. She laughed at the sheer brilliance of the sunshine, the exuberance of the dancing skaters, the brittleness of the air and the tantalising possibilities of life.

Her laughter skipped away and Eliza became uncomfortably aware that the stoker did not seem amused. She sobered up and reluctantly raised herself up onto her elbows. A rather challenging feat, as it turned out. Her elbows slipped and she was once more relegated to the ground. "I may need a helping hand," she confessed.

Without a sound, the stoker leaned over and grasped both her hands. In a trice she was up on her feet. She had barely time to find her balance when he set her free. His features looked set and angry, his lovely eyes narrowing as he observed her. Her heightened sense of wellbeing melted.

Then, for the first time, Eliza became aware that she was the object of some interest. People skated to and fro, surreptitiously watching. Perhaps this was why her stoker looked so sombre. "I'm sorry, but have I done something to upset you, Mr Odling?"

He shook his head. "No. You just gave me a scare is all."

It did not escape her notice that his stammer had gone. She wondered what this meant. Eliza let out a huge sigh of relief. "Oh, I am sorry!" But then she heard someone calling her name. With a mutter of irritation, she turned to look. A flash of bright-red hair caught her eye. It was Mary, standing on the bank of a dyke, waving at her. Eliza's heart sank. Pooh. She didn't want to go home.

"Miss Eliza! Miss Eliza!" Mary waved frantically again.

Something in the girl's demeanour tweaked Eliza's consciousness. A premonition of impending doom swept over her. She glanced at the stoker and the premonition hardened into fear. His face was set like stone, as he stared towards the road behind her. Then she heard the clip-clop of shod hooves. Her stomach dropped as she caught sight of two horses trotting rapidly towards the parked coach.

It was undoubtedly her father and the poisonous Pelham. Had they come upon her by chance or had someone sneaked? Not that it mattered. Here they were, spoiling her fun. She cheered up when she remembered that they knew nothing of her recent pact with God. Let them chastise all they liked; it was too late. Already her plan was well on the road to completion. The stoker was as good as hers. There was nothing they could do to stop her now.

With an imperious toss of her hatted head, she looked at the stoker. "Escort me back to my carriage!" For a horrible moment she thought he might refuse. Flustered, she remembered her manners. "Please, Mr Odling." Then he came to her side and she thanked him.

As she progressed over the ice, Eliza's confidence shrank under the full force of her father's furious stare. Her chat with God seemed less of a done deal. In just minutes, she would have to say goodbye. It occurred to her that time was of the essence. If she were to have any hope of seeing him again she must act at once. But in her panic, nothing coherent came to mind. When and where? Anguished, a snippet of conversation popped conveniently into her head. "I'll meet you tomorrow night, ten of the clock, at The Dog," she whispered, staring resolutely ahead.

His progress stalled a fraction but then he moved on. It nearly killed her, keeping her eyes off him. There was no way of knowing his reaction. No way of assessing the impact of her words. Was he pleased? Or was he surprised? Of course, he might be offended. Might think she was a foolish little girl. Perhaps he didn't want to see her. Or – worse – maybe he was disinterested. Maybe he was madly in love with Fanny Flowers. It was all just too horrid.

Further speculation was abandoned as the frozen road drew inexorably closer. All her earlier distress reignited in her breast. Her confusion, hurt and humiliation bubbling up in her brain at the sight of Pelham's censorious pasty face. Even mounted on a fine Irish hunter, he managed to look unattractive. She didn't dare look at her papa. Not yet. She couldn't bear another public scene. And it occurred to her to wonder what possible hold Lord Pelham could have over her father. Could her father be so desperate for a title? It seemed unlikely.

And then she was at the edge of the ice. The horses snorted, dancing in the cold. Her father sat well in his saddle. Still and relaxed. Pelham gripped his horse's reins so tight that its bit was in danger of sawing its head off. Eliza looked up at him and gave him a frosty nod of her head. Then she steeled herself, turning to look at her father.

But he wasn't paying her any attention. His eagle eyes were on Leon Odling but his expression was unreadable. "Odling." He spoke the single word in a way that could have been either a greeting, a question or a warning.

Horror-struck, Eliza realised that the consequences of her actions may overflow onto the stoker. What if her father punished him in some way? What if he sacked him from his work? Or accused him of behaving in an improper manner? Or had him horsewhipped. Or any number of unkindnesses. And if that happened, how would Leon Odling then feel about Eliza Elvidge? It did not bode well.

Sick in the stomach she rushed forward and scrambled onto dry land. "Papa," she said. "Mr Odling has been performing a service. He has been instructing me on how to skate. Unfortunately, I have no coin. Would you make good for me?"

Beside her, the stoker stirred but before he could speak, Pelham jabbed his horse in the ribs with his spurred heels and came down the slope. At the edge he halted, put a hand in his coat pocket, drew out a coin and tossed it. It glinted as it arced through the air. There was no discernible sound as it went skimming lightly across the ice to land at Leon Odling's feet.

It was too horrid for words. The insult was so unsubtle it took her breath away. No one moved or spoke. Over the swish of skates, a soft murmur arose. The incident had been noted. Eliza waited in anguish, entirely unsure what she should do. Leon Odling stared down at the coin as if transfixed.

She looked up at her father. His face was expressionless. And then she moved her attention to Pelham. His Lordship made no attempt to disguise his pleasure. He positively gloated. Eliza snapped. Back onto the ice she went. With her heart in her throat she managed to keep her balance. It took little time to reach her goal. Slowly, carefully, she crouched down at the stoker's feet. Without looking at him she pulled off one glove, grasping the coin in her fingers. Then she arose, holding out the coin to him.

"Please, take it. For my sake," she said softly.

He looked at her, his mouth set in a grim line. Then his lips twitched, and he reached out and took the coin. He tossed it high and caught it effortlessly. Then he bowed slightly towards Eliza's father. And – ignoring Pelham – tipped his cap to Eliza and sailed away.

30

The incident with Lord Pelham served to remind Oddie that a visit to his estate was long overdue. The cloudless day delivered a suitably bright night, the moon soaring like a silver sickle in the sky. Perfect for a spot of poaching. Should it be fish or fowl? There were pheasants galore, but he hadn't had a bite of trout in a longish while. Tricky. In the end he settled for a bit of both if the opportunity arose.

The coin lay on the table beside his bowl. A silver half-crown. Oddie couldn't decide how he felt about it. He was torn between a violent desire to throw it into a lake and an urge to put it in his vest pocket close to his heart. His loathing of Pelham was met in equal measure by his growing desire for Eliza Elvidge. What to do?

He polished off his supper whilst he considered the matter. As he chewed his bread, he picked up the coin. The only answer was to keep it and spend it on something that Pelham would heartily disapprove of. Oddie smiled. The answer was obvious. He'd spend it on Eliza Elvidge. Supper at The Dog.

Relieved to have sorted out this knotty problem, Oddie jumped up and set to. He whistled tunefully as he gathered up his gear. No need for a gun; all he needed was his net. Pheasants weren't renowned for their powers of deduction. The gentry would never catch 'em if they could think. And trout could be tickled. Either way, Oddie would be as silent as a crypt.

The night was bitterly cold. Wind sighed across the Fens from the sea. The scents of salt and soil mixed in his nose as he strode towards the mill. The Pelham estate lay about five miles north and west of the mill and, since the draining of great swathes of Fen marsh, was easily approached cross-country. Now the wetlands were just a memory. The rich, dark peaty soil was turned, ploughed and planted in an unending cycle of orderliness. He never got used to the emptiness of it. The land had no soul.

The world was peaceful when Oddie met the canal. Even the mill slumbered, her wheel idle until morning. He walked silently along the towpath. A lone longboat lay moored across the frozen water. But no lights shone within. Pleased, Oddie relaxed, picking up the pace. At the lock he crossed the metal bridge, passed the lock keeper's neat cottage, and came out onto the road. Half a mile along he made out the graceful lines of The Hall, silhouetted against the moonlit sky. He could nip through the governor's fields to meet the back end of the Pelham estate. Handy.

A scream sliced through the silence. It was an incongruent sound. Not the shriek of an owl or the squeal of a vixen. No. It was something else. It could almost have been human. Maybe a very young child. Troubled, Oddie paused in the shelter of the hedgerow and gazed across the water at the mill. He was almost certain the sound came from that direction. Senses aquiver, he waited. And waited. But time pressed and he reluctantly moved on once more. And, just as he vaulted a gate into a paddock, he heard it again. An elongated scream of agony. A shiver rippled through his body.

And then he spotted a light shining up at The Hall. It was high, on one of the upper storeys. An irresistible urge came over him and he set off towards the mansion. It was mad, but Oddie couldn't shake the idea that it was the governor's daughter. Like him, she had heard the blood-curdling shriek and was awake. He didn't know what he hoped to achieve but it made little difference. The Pelham estate could be accessed just as easily from the woodlands as it could through the fields.

At the foot of a pair of great iron gates Oddie paused. They stood open, two dragons eyeing him from lofty perches. Their wings were set in stone, forever flexed in flight. A smooth, pale gravel road swept away to a circular driveway bounding a manicured garden. Of the light there was no sign. The window must be set on the eastern side of the mansion. Undeterred, Oddie slipped through the entry and made his way along the clipped hedgerow. In a short time he found himself on the outside of a walled garden. Yellow light spilled out of the window halfway down the building.

He knew he should move on. But the closer he got, the greater was his belief that the light belonged to Eliza Elvidge. Quite simply, against all reason, he could not tear himself away. His fingers touched the wall inquisitively. It was well made, the mortar well bedded and the bricks even. It was too high for a running leap. But there could be a door around the other side. Jogging now, he travelled around the wall. His spirits lifted as he spotted a dark patch in the brickwork. It seemed too good to be true when it proved to be a stout timber door. Doubtless it would be locked.

He lifted the latch and pushed. He nearly fell through when it swung open with a bang. Oddie swore and stepped back into the shadow, half anticipating a pack of dogs descending on him. He paused, ready for flight. His eyes watched for more lights to appear in the facade of the house. But all was still. It seemed that Lady Luck was with him. When his heart rate resettled he moved into the garden. Midwinter it was sparsely vegetated, but he could pick up the fresh scent of mint and the sweet smell of rotting pears. Garden beds were neatly laid in squares with paved paths running in a criss-cross pattern.

In the centre, light flooded over a bird table laden with seeds and crusts of bread. Glass frames glinted, and weeds spilled out of a flat reed basket beside a bed of parsley. Oddie looked up and let out a yelp of surprise. Eliza Elvidge was standing framed in the window. Her hands were pressed flat to the glass and her nose almost touched. Her head was bare, hair flowing and curling over a pale blue gown to her waist. She stared down at him as if transfixed.

Indeed, Oddie began to think that she could not see him. Or perhaps did not recognise him. But then she lifted a hand and waved. Without thinking, he waved back. She moved away from the window and he watched as she reached up to open the latch. The lower half of the window rolled smoothly up and her head popped out. Her hair fell over the sill and unfurled like a golden river.

It belatedly occurred to Oddie that his impromptu visit might not be viewed in a positive light. Maybe Miss Elvidge might think he was not there by chance. Keen to explain himself, Oddie moved forward until he was directly below her. He craned his head back to see.

She leaned further out, until her shoulders were freed. The lace neck of her gown gaped a fraction and revealed a disturbing glimpse of what lay below. Oddie's mouth went dry. He had habitually thought of her as a girl. But of course she was not. Young she might be, but Eliza Elvidge was every inch a woman.

Then she smiled down at him. "Mr Odling!"

Oddie smiled back, delighted by her warm reception.

She glanced briefly over his head at the garden. "What brings you here?"

Oddie felt it was one of those occasions when honesty wouldn't do at all. He decided to sidestep the question rather than outright lie. "Did you suffer from your fall?"

She tossed her head. "Just a bruise on my buttocks, is all."

The mention of buttocks effectively killed the conversation.

Oddie became excruciatingly aware of the foolishness of his actions. His discomfort was enhanced by a longing to examine the said bruise for himself. It would not do at all. Silence descended over them like a fog. Both enfolded in horrible self-awareness.

It was broken by a shrill scream. Oddie heard Eliza gasp. "I heard it earlier," he said.

She nodded. "Me too. What can it be?"

He did not wish to alarm her. "Probably weasels hunting."

She lifted her head and stared out, revealing the tender underside of her throat. "I hope so," she said. Then she looked back down at him again. "It's just that…"

But the sentence was never finished. With a fearful glance at him, she slammed the window shut. Seconds later the drapes swept closed and the garden plunged into darkness. In the distance he heard the metallic click clicking of a pheasant. Time to go.

31

Eliza was frantic. She had hardly slept a wink. Where, oh where was Comet? As the sun tinged the horizon with a pale yellow ribbon she got up. Mary snored softly on the bed, one toe poking through a hole in her much-darned stockings. Despite the scare she had given Eliza that night, she was glad of the girl's company. A little guiltily, Eliza shook the girl's shoulder.

Mary sat bolt upright and yawned. "S'morning, Miss?"

"Yes. Mary, I need to dress and go look for Comet."

Mary scrambled off the bed and scurried over to join Eliza. "What'll you be wearing, Miss?"

"My riding habit." Eliza did not plan to ride, but the outfit was designed to allow for the maximum waist expansion fashion prescribed. She could at least breathe in it. Wide-awake now, Mary deftly drew in the strings of Eliza's corset. Hanging on to the post of her bed, Eliza peered over her shoulder. "Tell me again, Mary," she begged.

Mary tied off the strings and picked up the habit. "Well, Miss Eliza, word has it that the chimney sweep's climbing boy is not in the workhouse."

Not in the workhouse. How exasperating. "Where else could he be?" said Eliza, more to herself than the company.

Mary dropped the habit over Eliza's head. "No one could be sure but…"

Eliza resurfaced and waited expectantly but her maid dried up on the subject. She tutted. "But what?"

"Well, some say that Lord Pelham did for him, Miss."

Eliza was mystified. "Lord Pelham 'did' for the boy. What do you mean?"

Mary looked over her shoulder as if she suspected Eliza's wardrobe of eavesdropping. "They says that he murdered the poor creature and threw him in the bog," she whispered.

This was so ridiculous that Eliza burst out laughing.

Mary planted her hands on her hips. "It is no laughing matter, Miss Eliza! There are some that swears they has seen the climbing boy's ghost wandering on the Fens!"

Eliza didn't want to hurt the maid's feelings, so she composed herself. She turned to look on the bed for Comet. But of course, she was not there. "Come, Mary. Let us go search the grounds. Comet may be locked in the stables or the greenhouse." Or caught in a snare or a trap. But she could not bring herself to word such dreadful thoughts.

The two of them put on boots and cloaks and sped out the door. As they progressed through the house, they passed only Withers on his way up the stairs. Eliza pretended he didn't exist. If she wasn't a lady she'd shove him violently back the way he had come. How lovely it would be to see the nasty creature cartwheel down the stairs to land in a crunch of bones. Eliza would jump over his broken, beaten, bloody body without a second glance. And serve him right. Lucky for Withers, she was better bred.

As they hurried across the hall the clicking of leather boots echoed from the direction of the study. Eager to avoid a confrontation with her father, Eliza grabbed Mary's hand and they ran out the door, down the steps, hastening down the path. They did not rest until they had turned the corner of the walled garden. In the shelter of the wall, Eliza stopped to catch her breath. Soon as she was able, she set off for the stables. Her eyes lingered on the garden gate as she passed it, recalling the strange nocturnal sighting of the stoker. What had he been doing there? Was he looking for her? It was an intriguing thought. Perhaps she would ask him that night. At The Dog.

But her anxiety for her pet overrode all as she came to the back gate of the horse yard. Unlike the house, the place was seething with activity. Grooms were pushing wheelbarrows full of manure, throwing hay into mangers and filling buckets with fresh water. The horses peered over their half doors munching corn, breath streaming out their nostrils like smoke.

Eliza automatically headed over to her horse's stall. The black cob whickered, dropping chaff and corn onto the cobblestones as Eliza slid the bolt and opened the door. "Comet!" she called. There was no answering yip or whine. Unwilling to accept failure, Eliza went in, patting the cob reassuringly. She looked in every corner, but clearly Comet wasn't there. Panic fluttered at the periphery of her mind.

Back in the yard, one of the grooms went past, carrying a saddle. "Jake," said Eliza.

The boy paused and looked at Eliza, blinking like an owl beneath a shaggy dark fringe. "Yes, Miss Eliza?"

"Have you seen Comet?"

The boy shook his head. "Can't say I have, Miss. Sorry, Miss."

Eliza nodded but was afraid to speak lest she blubber like a baby. She set off again, asking each stablehand the same question. But all answered the same. No one had seen hide nor hair of Comet.

"Where now, Miss?" said Mary anxiously as they left the yard.

Where indeed? Poor Comet could be anywhere. But it wasn't like her to go astray. She wouldn't go far. Not unless she was chased or afraid. These thoughts did not reassure Eliza. She shivered. Part from cold, part from a growing trepidation. "We'll check the greenhouse," she said.

Several minutes later they made their way across the back lawn. The frostbitten grass swept down to the lake and beyond to the edge of Pelham's forest. The glass house was situated between the house and the lake. It was a huge, elegant building, with a domed roof and a glistening expanse of glass and scrolled iron frames. The glass was opaque with condensation and the heat swamped Eliza as she opened the door.

"Comet! Comet, here girl!" she called.

Mary came in, shedding her cloak. "Any sign, Miss?"

Eliza looked around, eyes raking through the palm trees and orchids and down to the orange trees. "I can't see her," she said. She hurried down the white shell path, calling as she went. After two full circuits she had to concede that Comet was not there. She looked out the windows down to the lake and woods. With fear flowering in her heart she knew she must continue on.

The two of them parted on the edge of the lake, travelling in opposite directions, to meet on the other side. Eliza could hear Mary calling for Comet. The world was waking, and ducks quaked on the frozen water, ruffling their feathers and waiting for a thaw. A large tabby cat took flight into the shrubbery and crows carved Vs into the pale sky. But of Comet there was not a sign.

Eliza stared helplessly at Mary. Dark thoughts shadowed her mind, all kinds of terrible ideas taking root. Comet drowned. Comet caught in a trap. Comet taken by a fox. Comet shot by a poacher. Comet down a well, swimming frantically. Tears sprang and teetered on her eyelashes. "Oh, Mary, what shall I do?"

Mary looked around the splendid grounds. Finally she perused the encroaching trees. "We must go look in the woods, Miss Eliza. You will not rest otherwise."

A burst of warmth ignited in Eliza's heart. She stepped forward and gave the maid a fierce hug. "You are very wise, Mary," she said, letting the surprised girl go.

Mary's face grew red but she did not look displeased. "Let's be getting on then," she said.

It was hard to know where to begin. In the dim light the trees seemed endless. In the end they followed the main path, calling. But they had no joy. Thrushes pecked noisily in brambles and squirrels whisked their red tails up tall trunks of trees. Eliza's heart soared and then sank as a crackle of undergrowth startled a herd of roe deer.

Finally they reached the fence that divided the properties. Eliza sighed and went to the stile, looking listlessly over at the Pelham woods. And then she felt as if a stick of dynamite had exploded inside her. Sick with dread, she climbed up and over.

She tore through the brambles, fell to her knees, staring down, aghast. She had found Comet. But how she wished she had not. The little hound's slender limbs were splayed akimbo tied to four points of a cross. Her mouth was open, teeth bared as if in terror. Glazed dead eyes stared up at the stark, bare canopy. Her belly was a cavity. Empty. Blood was smeared and coagulated over the once satin-smooth coat.

Someone started screaming. Terrible it was to hear. Like a man being flayed alive. It took time before Eliza realised that it was her.

32

The day seemed endless. The last hour an eternity. Oddie had got the news from Huw first up. Huw had got it from his daughter who had heard it from her third cousin Mary, who worked up at The Hall. And Oddie had now listened to the tale thrice more through the day. Indeed, it seemed no one talked of anything else. And could you be blaming them?

Truth be told, it was all Oddie had thought of as he toiled in the furnace room. Huw had it that the governor's girl had lost her reason entirely. Prostrate she was, with shock. Mind you, such a thing would undo the strongest of men. The poor little dog gutted and crucified on a cross. 'Twas unnatural. Oddie shivered. Who would do such a thing?

He took the problem with him at knock-off time. It did not escape his attention that the corpse had been found on Pelham land. For sure there was no proof, but it seemed suspicious to Oddie. But perhaps he was just looking to lay blame to assuage his own sense of guilt. Had he not heard the poor beast? Why hadn't he gone and investigated?

But he knew why. He had been hell-bent on exacting a revenge on Pelham. He had eyes and ears only for fish and fowl. The brace of pheasants and two fat trout in his home were testament to that. He had let Eliza Elvidge down. He would never forgive himself.

So absorbed was he that he barely acknowledged the landscape as he strode furiously across the Fens. His lack of attention was rewarded by an impromptu baptism in a stream. Judas but it was freezing! That'd teach him to look where he was going. He got to his feet and made his way up to the croft with more care. The wind rippled through his wet clothes, numbing his toes in sodden boots.

Inside Oddie stripped down and redressed in double-quick time. He stoked the embers and fed the flames. Once his fingers had feeling again he poured a cup of water and contemplated the trout. The pheasants hung in the pantry. He planned to take them that night to The Dog. Bit of payment for the boy's keep. The trout would salt but he decided he'd do best to eat the evidence.

Once the fat fish were sizzling in the pan, Oddie contemplated the night ahead. It seemed unlikely that the governor's girl would show up, what with all the goings-on. The more he thought about it, the less likely it seemed. Not just because of talk of her affliction. In all likelihood she would have thought better of her promise. The governor's girl wasn't titled stock but she was gentry all the same. Her sort and his didn't mix. It was a fact unpalatable as it was true.

Still, he'd go anyway. The Dog would be full of people. People were full of talk. They might even have something to say that Oddie wanted to hear. And it was already arranged with Fanny. She'd be waiting for him out on the Mill Road with her pony. Too late to change the plan now and of course it was best not to upset Fanny.

With his thoughts in order, Oddie transferred the fish to a platter. The poached trout was delicious straight up on a slab of well-buttered rye bread. Washed down with an ice-cold cup of water and a nip of good brandy, Oddie doubted a king would fare better. A glance out the window at the darkening sky reminded Oddie to get a shove on. He threw the dishes in a bucket and donned his jacket and cap. His father's watch sat hard and cold against his chest. Though why he took to carrying the thing around was beyond him; he must be going soft.

As he turned to the door, he nearly died of fright as Fanny came bursting in.

"Fanny, please, come in!" he said furiously.

Fanny threw her bonnet on the table. "Have you heard?"

Oddie nodded. "Strange happenings, they say."

"Yes, but more – it is dark magic. This I know."

Oddie did not like such talk. Not of magic – dark or otherwise. "Fanny, give it a rest. It is no more magic than I am."

Fanny smiled lasciviously. "Oh, Mr Odling, you have your own brand of magic, I'll be bound."

Oddie scowled but refused to be bated.

Fanny sobered up. "If you choose to walk the world with both eyes crossed I cannot help you," she said. "But you should be aware that Eliza Elvidge is in great danger."

"Danger! How so! 'Twas just a wee dog. It was most likely the work of some passing lunatic."

Fanny snorted. "Tosh! Passing lunatic? You do not believe that any more than I."

Against his will, Oddie was forced to silently agree but kept stum. "Fanny, why are you here?"

"I am on my way to the Ternings. Tess is birthing. I must go. I'll meet you at The Dog later."

Oddie nodded. "No matter, I'll make my own way."

"I must go." She turned but then looked over her shoulder. "Do you know there is still no sight nor sign of the climbing boy so badly burned at The Hall?"

Of course he knew. He shrugged. "So?"

Fanny rolled her eyes. "So – where is he? And what about the hauntings?"

"Hauntings! Don't be nesh, Fanny. You'll be telling me there's boggarts next. People do love to imagine ghosts and ghouls and such like. Too much white poppy and gin." But despite his protest, Oddie was not so sure. Not that he believed in ghosts and such like but more that he suspected dark dealings of Lord Percival Pelham.

Fanny turned the full force of her beautiful face on him. "So, Leon Odling, what would you say if I was to tell you that in the chest cavity of the dog was found not a cold heart, but the smoking remains of a silver watch?"

Her words stung like a hornet. "NO!" His hand went up to the hard nub over his heart. He pressed the burned remains of his father's fob against the wild beating of his heart.

Fanny's expression softened and she leaned towards him. "Oddie, what's wrong?"

But Oddie didn't know what to say. He unbuttoned his jacket and fumbled until he located the watch. He withdrew it and opened his hand.

Fanny looked down at the watch for a long time. She looked back at Oddie. "Why, Oddie, isn't that your father's watch?" she said.

To hear the words spoken out loud was a vast relief. The secret had been festering quietly inside him. "Fanny, I found the watch in the ashes of a furnace at work but a few days ago. It was on the order of Percival Pelham. And…" Oddie paused, unwilling to voice that which was unfounded.

"And… what?" Fanny prodded him, not unkindly.

Oddie decided that Fanny could be trusted. She was wise in her way. "And I had this feeling that he already knew the watch was there and he wanted me to find it." Oddie closed his hand tight around the watch. "Fanny, don't say anything, I beg you. There could be any number of innocent explanations as to how the watch ended up there."

Fanny shook her head. "Young Eliza insisted the poor beast be buried. Word is that she laid out the remains herself. When she came to wrap the dog, the watch fell free. At first no one could tell what it was, so charred and ruined was it. It was a small watch. A ladies' watch. The governor's girl claimed it had belonged to her mother."

"God save us!" said Oddie. It was so much to take in. His heart bled for Eliza Elvidge. What a cruel way to be reunited with her mother's possession. Far worse than his own experience. He frowned. "These are strange goings-on, Fanny. What do they mean?"

But Fanny did not reply. Oddie looked at her and was shocked to his core. In the many years he had been acquainted with Fan o' the Fens he had never seen her afraid. Until now.

33

As soon as the door closed Eliza slipped out of bed, opened the window and spat out the foul poppy tea. She would have no more of it. It fuddled her mind. Worse, made her hear and see things that were not there. As she pulled the window back down, her eyes spotted a curious thing. Laid in a neat row along the window ledge were several buttons.

She picked one up and examined it. It looked familiar, but then buttons were not an item that she paid attention to unless they were missing. Or particularly pretty. Which this one was not. How odd. As she reached out to collect the others the door opened. Eliza turned fearfully and then sagged with relief as Mary slipped through the door.

"Mary! You gave me a start!"

Mary shut the door softly. "Sorry, Miss. I was afeared of awakening you." The maid's freckles stood out in stark contrast to her white face.

Eliza managed a wan smile. "No need to be sorry. As you can see, I am quite awake."

Mary hurried forward, looking anxiously at Eliza. "Miss, are you yourself? I have been worried to the death."

Eliza took the maid's cold hands in her own. "I am utterly myself, Mary!" To her consternation the maid collapsed onto a chest at the foot of the bed and began to weep. Eliza hurried over.

"Mary, what is wrong?" But Mary just wailed louder and buried her head in her lap. There was nothing to do but wait until the girl had recovered herself.

Mary's sobs turned to hiccups. She lifted a woebegone face. Her eyes were swollen and bloodshot. But she pulled out a kerchief and blew her nose heartily. "Miss Eliza, do you not remember?"

Eliza considered the question for a while. "Not clearly, Mary. I remember that the poppy tea made me have terrible visions." She stopped and shut her eyes tight to try and stem her tears. "I remember burying poor little Comet. And I remember that there was a watch. And then after the tea I saw terrible things. I saw Comet." Grief gripped her and she could say no more.

Mary looked up. "Miss Eliza. It is true that you saw the spectre of poor Comet. Not surprising when you think of the terrible violence done to her!"

It was not what Eliza had expected to hear. "Mary, it was not a ghost! It was just my mind mazed by the poppy. That is all. It can do that, you know it can."

Mary bobbed her head but her mouth set in a stubborn mould. Clearly Mary did not really agree. Exasperated, Eliza tried again. "Really, truly, Mary. The poppy has worn off and I am myself. I see nothing in this room but you and I."

"Yes, I see, Miss," said Mary in a voice that clearly stated that she did not see at all.

Eliza let it go. She turned and pointed to the buttons. "Mary, do you know how these buttons came to be here?"

"Yes, Miss. I did place them there for your protection."

"My protection?"

"Yes. 'Tis a charm to protect you from the devil, Miss Eliza."

Eliza opened her mouth but, on seeing Mary's expression, shut it again. There was no harm in it after all and she didn't want to argue. Not when no one else seemed to be on her side. She looked at the carriage clock over the fireplace. It was seven o'clock. What to do? She paced up and down, trying to think.

She knew, despite all the denials, that the watch had been her mother's. But it was impossible to prove. True, she had taken the poppy tea willingly enough when Pelham had bought it. She had been overwhelmed with grief and close to collapse. Now she wondered why it had not been her father who had come in her moment of need.

Once more she struggled to make the connections. Why did her father allow Lord Pelham so many liberties? What power had he over them? She now acknowledged that her loathing of the man had hardened into fear. Fear of what it would mean if she were wed. It seemed more and more likely that her father desired this match above and beyond all things. Worse, it seemed that her father would not take no for an answer.

And her mind was made up. "Mary, do you have a dress that I could borrow?"

Mary gawped at her. "A dress, Miss?"

"Yes. A gown. Any gown."

Mary nodded. "Well, I do only have two other than the one which I wear now. One other for work and my Sunday best. I do have some old ones at home, but they are much patched and worn."

"Bring both that you have close at hand."

Mary stared at her, her eyes narrowing in suspicion. "What would you be needing them for, Miss?"

Eliza weighed up the pros and cons of telling her and decided that it would be impossible to keep it a secret. "I am going to Lincoln and I need a disguise."

Mary put her hands on her hips. "And what business would you be having in Lincoln after dark?"

"I am going to meet the stoker. Mr Leon Odling. At The Dog, at ten."

Mary's indignation vanished. "Well, we'd best hurry it up then."

"You are not going!" said Eliza but she spoke to thin air. The maid had already whisked out the door.

It felt like Mary was gone for an age although the clock showed just five minutes had passed when she returned. The maid laid the dresses out on the bed. The work dress was plain cut and dark grey. Respectable, starched and pressed to perfection. The other was clean but threadbare. A homespun, a hideous shade of pumpkin.

Eliza stared longingly at the grey. It'd bring out the blue in her eyes. But it was rather too smart. Too eye-catching. Not the dress of a dairy maid or a weaver's daughter. She sighed. The pumpkin it would have to be.

The pumpkin was too big in the waist, even when Mary let out Eliza's stays to scandalous proportions. The dress was so tight around her chest that both her bosoms were thrust together in a most unladylike fashion. Mary, in a fit of giggles, tied a muslin scarf artfully around Eliza's shoulders, disguising the fact most effectively.

Eliza perused herself in the mirror. It could have been worse. The length was fine, only revealing the toes of her button boots. But it was cold out. She'd need some warmer clothes too. After a frantic search in her wardrobe, Eliza donned a black woollen cape she only wore in the garden and a black bonnet. Once the ribbon had been ruthlessly removed and the peak bent about, the bonnet did not look out of place. At the last moment, Eliza took her good gloves. She needed them and could be easily hidden.

"Will I do?" she asked Mary.

Mary nodded. "You will not attract attention, so long as you take care to speak little."

The maid was right. Eliza's voice would be a giveaway. She must remember. "Mary, you must put on my nightgown and cap and get into the bed. I will put out the lights and if anyone comes it will appear as if I am still asleep."

"I must come with you," said Mary.

"I wish you could, really I do," said Eliza untruthfully. "But I must venture out on horseback."

Mary's expression dropped. They both knew that the maid would not be able to ride, even pillion. "I will do as you bid, Miss Eliza. But you must let me do your hair before you leave."

Eliza tutted in exasperation. "Mary, I do not have time for such trifles…" Mary's jaw set stubbornly. Perhaps it would be quicker to agree. Eliza sat down before the mirror and passed the brush to the obviously relieved maid.

In minutes Mary carefully divided Eliza's long hair into three sections, braided it, and pinned it close to her skull. Mary nodded. "Do not take it out for any reason. The power of three will protect you."

Eliza nodded uncertainly but made no objection. Indeed, foolish though it may be, the peculiar dress of her hair gave her comfort. She arose from the stool and put on her bonnet, cloak and gloves. She hugged Mary. "Put out the lights and huddle beneath the quilt," she warned.

With her heart beating like a military band, Eliza slipped away into the night.

34

The quickest way to travel was on water. Oddie's skates skimmed silently up the frozen waterways towards the city. In a velvet sky the moon shone like a slice of lemon. His breath fogged, forming ice crystals on the edge of his scarf. Elongated shadows spread thin upon the ground. A vixen screamed, and an owl skimmed over hedgerows. The dark shape of the mill grew until Oddie came to the end of the canal. Here he paused, looking anxiously at the three longboats tethered to their moorings. Light spilled out and voices murmured softly. He deftly removed his blades and slipped into the shadows.

At a steady jog, he passed the towpath and made it unseen across the lock bridge. From here he would follow the road until he found the shallow frozen stretches that would take him to the foot of Castle Hill. He couldn't help but cast a lingering look towards The Hall. His heart lifted as he spotted a yellow light. Was Eliza getting herself ready to meet him? He couldn't help but hope. Truth was, he ached to see her again. Longed to hear the lovely, lyrical notes of her voice. Wanted to hold her small, warm hand in his own. Dreamed of having her close to breathe in her sweet scent. Even an imaginary Eliza awoke his senses. Desire flooded through him and he groaned softly to himself.

And then he froze as an unearthly sound cut through the still of the night. All his senses on alert, he held his breath, straining to hear the sound again. Every fibre of his body warned him that something was amiss. There was someone – or something – out there. A ripple of dread shivered through him. But all he could hear was the rustling of wind through the brittle leaves of the hedge and the lapping of water against the canal walls. His pulse steadied, and he turned, ready to fight or flee. But the road was empty.

Feeling foolish, Oddie let out his breath and set off once more. Still anxious, he blamed Fanny. Any wonder he had the jitters with her talk of dark magic. It'd be enough to scare a saint. He tried not to think about the charred watch pressed against his chest. There would be an explanation. But then, there was the other watch. The one that Eliza had found in the grisly remains of her dog. Could it be coincidence? He cursed Fanny. Of course it was!

Oddie forged on, his boots clinking on the stony ground and crunching through icy puddles. He swore long and loud as a marmalade cat shot out of a hole in the hedge. It propped and turned to face him, lips bared and hair on end. With a snarl and spit, the feline darted off, squeezing through the brambles on the other side of the road. Oddie stared in surprise at the empty space where the cat had been. Known affectionately at the mill as 'Hungry', the cat was something of a personality. Hungry was a good-natured animal who kept down the rodents and begged food in his spare time. Tonight, however, Hungry was unrecognisable. And Oddie wondered why.

And then he heard it again. But louder. Clearer. It was a piteous sound. A sound of suffering that chilled him to the marrow of his bones. It was weird. Oddie was familiar with every creature, great and small, that dwelled in these parts. This one was not familiar. And guilt prickled. Last time he'd ignored his instincts the consequences had been dire. Because of his ill judgment, Eliza's little dog was dead. And a terrible death it had been. Despite the hard lump of dread in his chest, Oddie flexed his fingers and made up his mind. This time he would get it right.

Once more the sound carried on the breeze. Oddie concentrated, trying to identify it. His mind churned through the possibilities. Bird, perhaps. It wasn't a fox, or an otter, or even a dog. It was a thin, raspy tone. High-pitched. And then he knew. Oh my god! It was speech. Actual words. He concentrated for a moment, then nodded. It was human. A babbling, indecipherable cacophony, but it was words. Even as the thought coalesced in his mind, he burst into action.

He raced down the road, heading for the next gate. It wasn't far. He skidded to halt, grabbed the top bar and vaulted over. The fallow field spread away into darkness. If there was anyone there, they were not visible. "Hello!" The word boomed across the landscape, echoed, and faded. Oddie waited, but there was no reply. Just silence.

Unsure, he travelled on, over the hard earth, hopefully heading in the right direction. The black silhouette of the mill dominated the skyline. And then he froze, scarcely believing his ears.

"Ma-ma-ma-ma-ma…" came the cry.

It was a bleating, staccato sound but not made by any sheep Oddie had ever heard. And then his heart contracted with pity. Dear God. It was a child. The high-pitched, desolate wailing of a child. "I'm coming!" he yelled and broke into a run.

At the far boundary of the field ran a wide drain. It was frozen solid. Oddie slipped and slid, barely cognisant of what he was doing. His eyes scanned the Fens beyond, searching desperately for signs of life. His imagination ran riot with visions of an infant trapped in an icy bog, or worse, clinging desperately to the sides of a drain. Or maybe wandering, lost and alone, injured and afraid, suffering a lingering death from cold and hunger.

"Hello!" he shouted once more. Then again and again. Silence reigned supreme. The land seemed empty. Even the wind stilled.

Oddie had just decided to raise the alarm and organise a search party when he heard it once more. This time he was sure that the noise came from the mill, or very close to it. His heart leapt. "I'm coming!"

He set off like a jackrabbit. His hat blew off as his blades did a St Vitus dance over his shoulder. With uncanny accuracy he travelled over the perilous landscape. Finally, his feet found solid ground on the track to the mill. He stopped and caught his breath. His eyes probed the darkness. His ears strained, but he could hear nothing more than the rush of the river. Oddie reconsidered. Maybe it would be best to get help. The Fens were still a formidable place. He half turned, and then whipped back around. And he stilled as he spied a small figure moving left of the mill.

"Hey! You! Wait!"

But there was no reply. Oddie swore and set off, aided by the flat, even ground beneath his feet. He sped past the front of the mill and caught a glimpse of a tiny, tatty figure slipping around the corner. Oddie felt his heart lodge in his throat. That way lay the river, raging towards the sea. Unfrozen and treacherous.

Fear put wings on his feet. His breath came in ragged gasps. He wanted to call out a warning but didn't dare risk losing momentum. Finally, he rounded the corner of the building, frantic for a glimpse of his quarry. And found it!

Stood in the shadow of the mill was a boy. At least, Oddie thought it was a boy, for his hair was shorn and he wore a pair of ragged pants above booted feet.

Oddie slowed, afraid to scare the child. "Hello," he said softly. "It's alright, I just want to help."

But the boy was mute.

Oddie walked tentatively forward, hands held up. "Are you hurt?" The boy turned his head left and right as if assessing an escape route. As he did so, light reflected from his face. Strange.

Perhaps he was wearing spectacles. Although this seemed unlikely given his unkempt appearance.

Step by step, Oddie inched closer. He kept up a steady stream of placatory nonsense to try and reassure. Despite expecting the boy to bolt any minute, he made it to the edge of the long shadows that encased the child. With a smile he edged closer. "Hello. My name's Oddie," he said. "What's yours?"

The boy hung his head and fidgeted with his feet.

Oddie was encouraged. "Are you hungry?"

To his horror the child began to cry. Great heaving sobs of misery.

Oddie reached out a hand to comfort him. His fingers touched the boy's shoulder. The child looked up. Oddie staggered back, his heart thumping like a piston. "No!" he said. "Oh God, no!"

In that moment, Oddie's life changed forever.

35

Eliza had never ridden astride before but she decided she liked it. Worried that her own pony would be recognised she had taken one of the draught horses instead. The only saddle broad enough for Polly's pied back was her father's. Eliza found riding astride easy-peasy. It was wonderful to feel her weight evenly distributed on either side of the saddle. Infinitely better than perching sideways. Honestly, men had it every which way.

The only downside was that Polly wasn't built for speed and no amount of urging on Eliza's behalf encouraged the mare to engage in more than a sedate trot. And Polly's shod, plate-sized hooves sounded louder than church bells on Sunday. But there was nothing to be done; she was committed now. It was The Dog or die!

She put the reins into one hand and pressed the other hand against her breast. The cold, hard surface of her mother's watch nestled against her skin. It was the only thing she had that linked to her mother. Everyone else could deny it up hill and down dale, but Eliza knew absolutely that her mother had worn the watch. The image was clear in her mind. The small, silver surface pinned on to a grey dress. And, even though she could not conjure up her mother's face, she could recall a soft voice singing nursery rhymes and the scent of bluebells. All she needed was some proof. Someone who would be honest. Eliza was pinning her hopes on Mr Odling and Fanny to help her. The Fen folk were a close-knit community. Someone must know something.

As the landscape slipped by, Eliza thought about her mother and the little that she knew. Most of it had been learned when she was young when maids and tradespeople did not give a child the benefit of wit. Mad. That's what they'd whispered. Her mother was a madwoman who'd lived her last days in an asylum. Eliza had never doubted her scantily harvested crop of knowledge. Until now.

Now, the more her father denied the watch had ever been in the house, never mind upon her mother's person, the less Eliza believed him. And – almost against her will – Eliza had begun to ponder upon another possibility. What if – and it was a huge what if – her mother had not been mad at all? What if her mother had been like Fanny? A witch or wise woman? And what if her father had locked her away for it? And – last but not least – what if Eliza was just like her?

After all, it wasn't just what Fanny had said to her about the fish-shaped birthmark. There was more. The strange happenings in the cathedral. Her own instinctive ability to care for the poor little chimney sweep. The storm. And Mary's insistence that Eliza protect herself against the devil. It was clear that the Fen folk believed in witchcraft. Were they truly the vicious, lowlife, ignorant people that her father despised? Eliza could not believe it. Not now.

But there was a pool of reserve too. For if these thoughts were true, what did it mean for herself? Panic erupted inside her. Her father had incarcerated her mother. If he could do that to the mother, what about the child? It would certainly explain in part her father's determination to marry her to Pelham. Maybe he thought that if he didn't marry her soon, no one would take her. And as for Pelham – there would be no understanding there. It was all the more reason to stick to her plan to never marry the dreadful man.

Eliza, absorbed in her thoughts, gave lazy Polly her head. When Polly propped Eliza was undone. She shot out of the saddle, nosediving past Polly's shoulder. She landed forcefully onto the frozen ground. Her spine felt like it was exploding out of the top of her head, but she clung to the reins, gritting her teeth. It would be a disaster of unmitigated proportions if Polly escaped.

Consequently, the spooked mare proceeded to drag Eliza down the road. A most distressing situation. The friction pulled Eliza's garments upward until her skirt rode up to her thighs. Grit and stones shredded her stockings and grazed her legs. The strain on her shoulders was horrible. And, just as it seemed life could get no worse, a sudden jerk on the reins flipped Eliza over like a fish on a griddle. Face down, neck straining to keep her chin off the ground, Eliza had to let go.

And then Polly stopped. Thanks goodness! Eliza gathered herself together and prepared to get up. But before she could do so, she heard the scrunch of heavy boots approaching. Panic-stricken, she rolled over, her hands slipping and sliding on the treacherous ground.

A large, dark figure appeared from behind Polly's apple-shaped bottom and stopped, gazing down at her. "Are you alright?"

Eliza met the stoker's eyes with mixed emotions. The instinctive delight she felt at the sight of him did battle with the knowledge that she was not looking her best. This, followed by acute embarrassment at the exposed length of legs. It was not the reunion she had envisioned.

She sat up, tugging frantically at her skirt, which had wound tighter than ivy. "I'm fine," she snapped. And immediately flushed with shame at her rudeness. After all, she was a lady, born and bred.

The stoker stared at her silently, his expression unreadable. Eliza gave up all pretence and put out her hand. "Help me, please." Leon Odling stepped forward, grasped her hand firmly and pulled her to her feet. She stumbled forward a few steps as her skirts finally unravelled. When she stopped, she was a mere hand's breadth from him.

He was bigger than she remembered. Both taller and broader in the chest. And he smelled good enough to eat. Like leather and wood smoke. And – even though she knew she shouldn't – her senses tingled with the knowledge of what lay beneath the clothes that he wore. She dared a peep under her eyelashes and was relieved to find his expression softening beneath her gaze.

With her modesty restored, Eliza's confidence flowed back. "Mr Odling, it would seem that I owe you thanks."

He nodded. "G-g-g-glad to be of s-s-service, Miss Eliza."

Happiness swelled in her bosom like fresh baked bread. He was even more adorable than she remembered. "Mr Odling, I was on my way to The Dog to meet you!"

He plucked at a pair of skating blades slung over one shoulder. "Likewise."

Eliza was silent as she contemplated the wisdom of her next words. In the end she decided it would not be proper to speak. Not proper at all. But the words just gushed out. "Mr Odling, Polly is a strong mare. Perhaps we could travel together?" Her hand rushed to her mouth as if she could push the words back inside. But what is said cannot be unsaid. Oh, what must he think?

He did not answer. He turned, looking up and down the road. Eliza felt a quiver of apprehension, for there was something in his expression that was disquieting. Finally, he gave her his full attention.

"I think it would be wise to travel together," he said softly.

Eliza nodded nonchalantly but on the inside her heart was fluttering and flittering. "If I mount, you can sit behind. It will be a bit snug…" Heat raced up her neck. 'Snug' didn't really do it justice. Desire fizzed through her, her body aching and throbbing in a most disturbing fashion. Eliza wondered if such sensations were at all ladylike. Yet, she was helpless to help herself. Tongue-tied, she fell silent.

Luckily, the stoker seemed oblivious of her internal turmoil. He stepped back and eyed Polly critically. Then he nodded. "Let me help you." So saying, he tossed the reins over Polly's head, hunkered down and cupped his hands to give her a leg up.

Breathless with anticipation, Eliza placed a hand onto his shoulder. As her weight transferred she could feel the strength of him, muscles like steel, beneath the leather. She lingered for one lovely moment, unwilling to break contact, and then placed a foot delicately in the palms of his hands and sprang up in a flounce of petticoats.

Settled in the saddle she gathered the reins and looked at him expectantly. She did not have to wait long. He placed a hand on the pommel of the saddle, bounced once on his feet and vaulted aboard. Polly sighed resignedly but made no protest. As the mare walked down the winding lane, Eliza froze, as two arms passed around her waist to hold her lightly. Her back felt on fire, as his torso moulded to hers. Like Polly, she made not a murmur of protest. Rather, she wished that the slow ride to Lincoln could last forever.

36

As the fat, piebald mare clopped down the frozen road, Oddie felt as if he had fallen into a dream. The world as he had known it had faded to be replaced with a landscape that was both intoxicating and terrifying. If anyone had told him an hour ago that he would both doubt his faith and ride pillion on a pony with Miss Eliza Elvidge, he would have doubted their sanity. Now, it was his own that seemed questionable.

Oddie's discomfiture was further compounded by his proximity to Eliza's person. He was inflamed by the feel of her, pressed hard against him. Her wisp of a waist gently expanded and contracted with each breath of air. He was acutely aware of the cage of whalebone beneath his hands. He recalled the glimpse of the lush valley of her breasts as she lay prone. And then his mind's eye conjured up the slender, coltish lines of her legs. The expanse of thigh above her stockings gleaming like ivory.

Oddie groaned to himself as his body reflected his emotions. Eliza would not be able to miss the iron rod that swelled in his trousers. Lord have mercy! Best think of something else.

He switched back to the other major event of the evening. To the terrible spectre he had witnessed at the mill. His blood still turned to ice. Stunned, he had watched as the ghostly apparition moved away, still sobbing, to be swallowed into the night. Such a sight had led him to wonder if he had seen the ghost of the climbing boy. What else could it have been? No angel, for sure. But some hellish demon with lamps where eyes should be. Great glass globes that reflected his own terrified visage.

The pony's gait suddenly increased, lurching into a spanking trot. Oddie slid sideways. Hells bells! There was no other option than to reach around to grasp the front of the saddle. In doing so, he enfolded Eliza Elvidge in an embrace. Thankfully, his recent recollections meant he was in no immediate danger of offending Eliza with his manhood. Although, as he inadvertently caught an eyeful of her pert breasts, that could very well change.

With his balance regained, he wiggled back a bit and glanced over the hedge to gauge their progress. He could just make out the lights of Lincoln flickering and the glistening expanse of the frozen Fens at the foot of the hill. They were making good time. With luck, Fan would not be too far away. The thought was comforting. For Fan was the one person Oddie could count on to listen to his story without ridicule. Mind you, there was bound to be a certain amount of smug, unspoken 'I told you so' hanging in the air.

Still, Oddie could live with that so long as he could unburden himself. Maybe, with the telling, some rational explanation would present itself. Somewhat reassured by this prospect, Oddie allowed himself the luxury of contemplating the evening ahead. What would Fan o' the Fens want with Miss Eliza Elvidge? Did she really think that Eliza was a witch? It was laughable, even if he believed in such tosh. Anyone less like a witch he'd yet to meet. Fan, on the other hand, could pass for a crone when looked at in profile. Not that Oddie was game enough to say so.

And then there was the watches. Watches that were found where watches shouldn't be. It was something that he had in common with Eliza Elvidge. And Oddie wasn't sure how he felt about that.

On the one hand, he was entranced with the idea of a common bond. For they were socially as far removed as it was possible to be. But, on the other hand, Oddie was deeply disturbed by the business of the watches. Fan was right about that. There was something very wrong about the brutal slaying of the wee dog. No wonder the girl had been deranged. He felt a bit edgy himself.

And there was another matter. He had never believed any of the talk about Eliza losing her mind. At least not in any permanent fashion. And now he had seen strange sights himself, he was even more disinclined. The Fen folk were a superstitious bunch. God-fearing too. But inclined to embroider on a tale until its origins were hidden within the tapestry of repeated telling. He too had heard the talk about Eliza's mother. About how she had believed in faery folk, although it didn't mean her daughter was so afflicted. Did it? In his experience, nothing in her demeanour leant itself to such a conclusion.

And – when all was said and done – would people say he was mazed in the mind when his own story was retold? That being the case, Oddie could only conclude that if Eliza Elvidge was demented, then he was too. Without thinking about what he was doing, Oddie drew her body protectively towards him. He bent his head and briefly brushed her cheek with his. Cold but smooth as silk, he revelled in the feel of her flesh and bones. Eliza responded with a tiny return of pressure. With a surge of happiness, Oddie reluctantly relaxed back. His cheek tingled with the memory of the moment. It was such a small thing. The tentative touch of two people. But it spoke louder than any number of words.

Of course, the truth was, Oddie didn't really care whether she was crazy or not. All he knew was that he adored her. And that he was – and always would be – her humble servant.

As they crossed the bridge and began the steep climb up the hill, the pony slowed back to a plodding walk. The city was quiet, few venturing out in the frigid night air. Both Oddie and Eliza started as Polly let out a trumpet of noise. And then Fan materialised over the hump of the bridge. How in God's name had she gotten there? Oddie waved and Fan returned the gesture. She hurried towards them.

Oddie stared. Puzzled. "Why have you got that broom, Fan? And what about the baby?"

Fan gave him an insolent stare. "What broom?"

"That broom." Oddie blinked. Fan's hands were empty.

"Baby was birthed when I got there. I got a lift with a tinker on the road," Fan said smoothly.

Oddie glared, sure he was being hoodwinked. Fan smiled slyly and set off.

No one spoke as they trailed up the steep hill but Oddie could feel the tension building in Eliza's slight frame. Occasionally Fan glanced over at them, her expression troubled.

Eliza's patience must have snapped as they turned off towards The Dog. She clicked Polly on and then laid the whip on the pony's shoulder, slicing the silence. Polly's ears went back and she snorted, but her speed did not increase. Indeed, the pace slackened somewhat. Oddie grinned to himself as he heard Eliza mutter a few choice words under her breath. Her ladylike demeanour was under threat, it would seem.

Finally, they arrived. An old ostler shuffled out of the stables and held the horse. Oddie slid down and turned to offer Eliza help. But she was already dismounting, with a flash of ankles and button boots.

She landed lightly and looked up at him. "I have a thirst, Mr Odling," she said. "How about you?"

Oddie ignored Fan's rude snort. He smiled at Eliza. He was thirsty alright. But not for spirits. "Let's get a drink, shall we?"

Eliza turned towards Fan. "Miss Flowers, we must talk!"

Fan nodded. "Yes, but mayhaps the time for talk is nearly done, Miss Eliza. Time has come for action."

Oddie felt a twinge of disquiet. He liked not this kind of talk. But he had to acknowledge there was merit in Fan's words. Certainly, Eliza seemed to be of a like mind. She stepped towards Fan, grasping her hand.

"Miss Flowers, I fear you are right." She turned to Oddie. "Come, let us find a discrete spot inside. Time is not on our side."

Fan led the way, followed by Eliza with Oddie at the rear. They filed down the narrow corridor, through the taproom and into the bar. It was busy. The atmosphere thick with smoke and the sour scent of spilled ale. In unspoken agreement they threaded their way through the press of bodies and squeezed into an empty nook beyond the fireplace. Eliza perched on a half barrel, her back to the bar. But no one cast more than a cursory glance in their direction.

Oddie patted his pocket where the silver half-crown nestled. One in the eye for Lord Pelham. "What would you like to drink?" he said.

But Eliza's focus had shifted. She was leaning over and patting the air. She glanced up at him, a smile dimpling her cheeks. "He's lovely!" she said. "What's his name?"

Oddie did not reply. What was she talking about? He glanced left and right, thinking that he had missed something. Then thankfully, Fanny intervened.

"What do you see, Miss Eliza?"

Eliza's hand froze mid-air. "I'm just wondering what this dog's name is," she said in a little voice.

Oddie shifted his feet awkwardly. So far as he could tell, there was no dog.

Something like triumph flared in Fan's eyes as she leaned in towards Eliza. "His name is Drifter. And he has been dead for seven years."

Oddie decided he'd better make his drink a double.

37

Eliza assumed that she had misheard. She shook her head and laughed. "I'm so sorry, Miss Flowers, but I thought for a moment that you said that this dog was dead!"

As the words fluted into the cramped room a silence fell, louder than a drum roll. She could feel eyes boring into her back. Confused and upset, she rested her hand on the dog's head. His short, black coat felt smooth and warm. Almond-shaped brown eyes peered at her, slightly crinkled against the smoke. A ridiculous tail curled over his back like a pencil shaving. He was roughly the size and shape of a collie. His tongue poked out and he panted softly.

Eliza dragged her eyes away and looked at Fan o' the Fens. "I don't understand…"

But Fan turned on the staring crowd, legs akimbo and hands planted on hips. She cast a long, hard look across the throng. "What?" she said.

There were a few mutterings and grumbles, but the mob subsided, picked up their pipes and glasses and made a show of minding their own business. Fan sniffed disdainfully and settled on a stool. She looked at Oddie. "What do you see, Oddie?"

Eliza turned eagerly to the stoker.

He met her gaze steadily, but tiny pricks of perspiration popped up on his forehead. "W-w-w-well now," he said.

Fanny Flowers snapped her fingers in his face. "Oddie can see nothing," she said softly.

Eliza was silent, digesting this with reluctance. Then the dog moved away, winding between the tangle of legs until he vanished through the door. His passage was not acknowledged by anyone. There was not so much as a flicker of interest. She looked at the stoker. "Is it true? Can you not see him?"

The stoker ran a hand through his thick, dark hair. "'Tis true enough. I cannot see anything in this place with more than two legs."

"And nor will he," said Fanny, with a touch of impatience in her tone. "I can see him and so can you because we have the gift – or curse – of seeing." She pulled a pipe from her skirt and began to tamp down the bowl. "That dog belonged to a thief that the landlord executed seven years ago. Since then the dog has haunted him. And so, to try and appease his spirit, the landlord changed the name of his house. Sadly, the beast is still here, as you see."

"So the landlord can see him too!" This made Eliza feel better.

Fanny shook her head. "Not see him exactly. But hear him bark and howl, and the tick tack of his claws when the place is quiet. And he feels the dog's grief and loneliness too. For whilst not a seer, the landlord is well acquainted with death and has some affinity for the afterlife."

A wave of unease rippled through Eliza. A vision shimmered in her mind of her own dear Comet. But then she relaxed a little. "It is the poppy tea!" she said. "Just a side effect, is all! It is the poppy."

Fanny raised an eyebrow. "In a way." She leaned forward, fixing her gaze upon Eliza. "The poppy can act to open the inner eye." She was silent, watching Eliza carefully. Then she continued. "Eliza, poppy can do this, but it is an unnatural and uncontrolled experience."

The witch's words sifted through Eliza's brain. And where they fell they found fertile ground. Eliza knew that it was the truth. It was an uplifting revelation. It had not been hallucinations. She was not crazy. She had seen Comet's spirit or ghost. Dear little Comet had come back. Tears pricked her eyes as she recalled her pet's terrible end. But she clamped down on the emotions. It was a luxury in which she could not indulge. If Fanny was correct, something was happening that she had no control over. She wiped her eyes. "What must I do?"

Fanny let out a deep breath of air. "You must learn to tap into your power. It is there but buried. But it has awoken, and it is spilling out unbidden. You must train your mind to control it, otherwise it could become dangerous to you and those around you."

The Fen woman's words were reassuring. It finally made sense of everything that had been happening. But more importantly, it offered a way to put her life back into order. "How?" Beside her, the stoker stirred. Eliza looked at him, hoping he might speak. But he did not, although he looked deeply troubled. Which was not surprising, really. What must he think? Fanny was his friend, maybe more than that, but what did he make of all of this? Was he repulsed?

As if he had read her mind, he reached out and took her hand in his. In the calloused warmth of his grip she felt the strength of his kindness. She gripped on, grateful.

Fanny cleared her throat and Eliza looked at the older woman, half expecting to find her angry. But instead she caught a flicker of amusement.

The woman leaned in, until her lips were almost on Eliza's ear. Her breath was hot and scented with rosemary. "To control your power, you must master your mind. You must learn to wipe your mind as a rag removes chalk from a board. Only then will you be able to channel your gift at will."

Eliza wobbled inwardly. It sounded impossible. "But how?"

Fanny sat back and shrugged. "Everyone is different. Some concentrate the mind through incantations, others use cotton and thread, some can create tranquillity from the making of intricate knots." She was silent once more, possibly to give Eliza a chance to take it all in. "And," she continued, "some make use of words written on parchment." These last words were spoken with an emphasis that may or may not have been deliberate.

Eliza felt a little lightheaded. Whilst it was wonderful to know that there were many ways to manage her… condition, Eliza was no closer to the key. "Miss Flowers, how will I know which to choose?" But her brain was already leaping ahead like a hound on the scent of a fox. She thought hard. "The first time I felt something like this, I was playing piano. I was truly lost in the moment. Perhaps that is the key."

Fanny nodded. "Perhaps."

Encouraged, Eliza explored further. She visualised herself hauling the grand piano around on her back wherever she went. Her spirits drooped. It was hardly practical. Then she had another idea. "I can embroider. And read and write a fair hand!"

"Then you are blessed, Eliza," said Fan. "Few have so many choices. But you must decide soon. I sense that forces gather against you. You must arm yourself."

Her words chilled Eliza to the core. Fan o' the Fens forced Eliza to frame all her fears. There had been many strange and disconcerting events but she had not connected them before. Indeed, logically one wouldn't. There was little that seemingly bound Oddie (what a lovely name), the pernicious Lord Pelham and poor little Comet. To say nothing of the climbing boy and strange storms. But logic now seemed somehow inadequate.

Aware that both Oddie and Fanny were watching her anxiously she tried to collect her thoughts. "Tell me, Miss Flowers, when you speak of bookish things, what do you mean exactly?"

But Fan had jerked upright with a hiss of warning. Oddie looked over Eliza's head and his expression set into grim lines.

Eliza instinctively started to turn, but Oddie gripped her forearm and held her fast. He dropped his head low and whispered urgently. "He's here!"

Eliza did not have to ask. She knew only too well who it was. Dear God! If Lord Pelham found her here it would not end well. Not for any of them. Especially Oddie. And she could not bear to damage him further.

Panic-stricken, her mind scurried about like a rat in a run. What on earth was she to do? While it was fine for Oddie and Miss Flowers to be here, her own situation was as inflammable as tinderwood. The resultant fire would burn them all. She must get out and get away. If she were caught, they were all undone.

38

The situation could not have been more volatile. Eliza was pale as a sheet of paper. It could have been pure coincidence that Pelham had popped in for a pint. Or not. Frankly, it hardly mattered. What did matter was the immediate danger his arrival posed. Oddie decided there and then that desperate measures were called for. Pelham must be headed off before he got wind of Eliza's presence.

He looked at Fan, who – in that way she had – gave a reassuring nod of her head. Fan understood as well as he that the lord must not get an inch closer. Whilst Pelham was a monstrous human being, he was not a stupid one. Oddie glanced surreptitiously around, hoping for inspiration. But nothing came to mind. Pelham was heading for the bar, intent on a drink, his back to Oddie and his friends. The rowdy crowd fell away to allow him through, although some did so with poor grace. Lord Pelham was loved by few.

The barmaid rushed to serve him and Oddie knew the chances of discovery escalated with every passing minute. He had to intercede. But he could think of no justifiable reason to approach Pelham without creating suspicion. Unless… he put his hand on his chest and pressed his father's watch. He knew what he must do.

He glanced at the two women. "Stay here. Soon as I have his attention, be off, quick smart. I'll meet you under the bridge."

Both Eliza and Fanny looked as if they were going to protest, so Oddie didn't hang about. He slapped his cap on his head and set off. Hurrying forward as best he could, Oddie elbowed his way through the crowd. When he finally reached the bar, he heard the barmaid flirting with his quarry. Oddie blessed her for holding Pelham's attention even whilst he wondered at her wit. The lord took his pleasure where he would. But he took no responsibility for the string of sprogs he seeded. The maid would end up on the streets with a big belly like the others if she wasn't careful.

The lord flipped a coin at the girl, picked up his glass, and turned. His eyes darted around the packed room like a pair of minnows. Oddie surged forward. Pelham's eyes slid over him, and then slid back. And moved on. Clearly, he either didn't recognise Oddie or deemed him too insignificant to acknowledge.

The slight was not unexpected. But still, it rankled to be dismissed like a dog. Oddie was so close now that he could count the black heads that pitted Pelham's long, pointed nose. What he would have liked to do was blacken both eyes. Instead, he doffed his cap and dropped his eyes to the ground, in as servile a manner as he could stomach. "M-M-M-My Lord," he said.

Pelham shifted his gaze with obvious reluctance to Oddie. A sneer spread over his face. "Ah. The s-s-stammering stoker," he replied loudly.

The atmosphere in the bar thickened like cold porridge. Heat raced up Oddie's neck as humiliation and rage fought for pole position. His hands curled into fists. It took every ounce of self-control not to hit the arrogant little prick. Oddie focused on Eliza. And kept his temper.

He gripped his cap and nodded. "L-L-Leon Odling, L-Lord Pelham."

Pelham took a sip of ale. "So, what do you want?"

Everyone stared. Oddie knew he was done for. Under pressure his stammer worsened. Whatever conversation ensued would be painstaking, to say the least. But there seemed to be no other option but to try. And – on the plus side – he had achieved his goal. He had the lord's undivided attention. All he had to do was hold it.

Aware Pelham would soon grow bored of his company, Oddie moved to plan B. He groped inside his leather coat and extracted the watch. For a moment, he gripped it in his hand. The burned and battered relic was the last link to his family. All that remained of his father. It may be a humble inheritance, but Oddie did not relish exposing it to Pelham.

However, there seemed to be little choice. As the lord sipped his beer, his eyes began to wander. Oddie panicked, held out his hand, uncurling his fingers. "S-S-S-Sir…" he said.

Pelham rolled his eyes and sighed but finally cast his gaze towards Oddie's hand. His expression froze. Time stretched painfully like limbs on a rack. Then Pelham reached out.

Oddie submerged an instinct to snatch the watch away. Not least because he glimpsed the edge of Eliza's bonnet to his right. Relief ran through him. They were on the move. Almost safe! He forced himself to keep his eyes focused on Pelham as his bony fingers grasped the watch. Oddie felt a pang of grief as the timepiece was lifted free.

The lord looked in turn at the watch, and then at Oddie. "What is this?"

Oddie eyeballed the man. "That," he said softly, "is a watch."

Pelham tutted impatiently but his deep-set eyes narrowed. "Well, what of it?"

Oddie realised then that the truth would not do. If Pelham was involved, it would be unwise to reveal his suspicions. The whole thing had Fan spooked. Best be careful. But what to say without looking either idiotic or suspicious? His mind was blank. "I f-f-found it," he managed.

Pelham jiggled the watch in his palm. Breath whistled through his teeth. He smiled dangerously. "And where did you find it, Mr Odling?"

Oddie knew then that it made no matter how he responded. Without a doubt, Pelham was on to him. It was time for damage control. "I c—"

But he lost his audience. A frigid gust of air billowed into the stifling, packed room as a man burst in. He stopped and looked around, mouth flapping like the broken sole of a shoe. His lips were pale in his dirty face and his eyes bulging. Oddie recognised him. An old slodger, Albie, who eked a meagre living trapping eel. Not a bad old cove.

Albie caught sight of Oddie and staggered across the floor. The reek of gin preceded him. "Oddie!" he gasped. "I done seen the devil!"

Silence fell. Mugs of ale paused halfway to waiting lips. Darts missed their mark. Dominoes fell. The barmaid stood staring, ale spilling over the rim of a mug.

Poor Albie seemed insensible to his audience as he gripped Oddie's sleeve. "Oddie, I seen him! The ghost of the climbin' boy! He was cryin' and wailin' in the Fen. And then he sees me. And comes after me with eyes burning bright like the gates of 'ell!"

Oddie was rocked. He didn't know what to say. He flashed a look at Lord Pelham, only to find the man was on the move. Despite the excitement, the crowd parted in an almost biblical fashion as he strode out the door.

Oddie watched him go, patted Albie on the shoulder and took off, praying Eliza and Fanny were clean out of sight. As he stepped out into the freezing night, he remembered that Pelham had taken his watch. He cursed but pushed it aside. If Pelham happened on Eliza, the watch would be of small consequence.

He hurried out into the courtyard, pausing to let his eyes adjust to the dark. He heard the lord's boots tapping rapidly away, and then made out his tall, thin silhouette against the stable wall. At a safe distance, Oddie followed. His motivation was twofold. The first to be sure that Eliza and Fanny were safe. The second to see where Pelham was going in such a hurry.

As Oddie slipped into the shadows, he could not shake off a superstitious dread. What if Fanny was right? What if there really was some dark magic at work in the world? What if Eliza really were a witch? Was it possible?

He didn't want to believe it. But there was one thing he was sure of. If there really was a devil, then Lord Percival Pelham was a strong contender.

39

Underneath the bridge, Eliza shivered. Her breath blew white, spuming into the night air. Her nose, toes and fingers were numb. She leaned into Polly's neck for warmth and comfort. Beside her, Fanny was silent, peeping around the mossy, dripping edge of the bridge.

"Is he coming?" said Eliza.

By way of reply Fanny shot back beneath the bridge. Under Eliza's demanding gaze, she shook her head in warning and put a finger to her lips. Shod hooves trotted down towards them in great haste. Someone was coming.

"Pelham?" Eliza silently worded.

Fanny nodded. Then she let out a gasp of horror as Polly whinnied a welcome.

In panic, Eliza took a hold of the mare's bridle, pulling her muzzle into the crook of her arm. Polly snorted and huffed, straining to lift her head. Perspiration popped out on Eliza's forehead as she tried to contain the struggling horse. Her anxiety quadrupled as the rapid trotting slowed to a walk. Then silence. Evidently the poisonous Lord Pelham had paused in his journey. Damn his eyes. And his ears for that matter!

Eliza stared at Fanny as the hoofbeats proceeded once more. However, the pace was much slower than before. Eliza could picture Pelham in her mind's eye, his pointy nose sniffing her out like a ferret. How she loathed him! If he found her he'd be the sorry one. Eliza Elvidge was a force to be reckoned with. She was no simpering milksop. Not anymore. There was magic in her soul. And power. All she had to do was tap into it. She tensed as the hoofbeats ceased once more. Her heart hammered. What to do?

Fan turned to her then. "Give me the mare," she breathed gently.

Eliza didn't want to hand over Polly. Without the mare, she would be severely restricted. It was a very long walk home and it didn't bear thinking about what would happen if she weren't back by daylight. But she also saw the logic in Fanny's request. Pelham wouldn't recognise Polly. She was a carthorse. Not for carriage or saddle. It would be natural for Fanny to be in possession of such a horse. Reluctantly, she handed over the reins.

Fanny lifted a hand and motioned for Eliza to stay put. Eliza nodded.

Minutes later Polly's wide rump turned out of sight and her large feet could be heard on the stony, hard ground.

"Well, well, what have we here?"

Pelham's insolent voice was loud. Eliza felt lightheaded. He must be very close. She held her breath, praying he couldn't hear the wild palpitations of her heart.

"My Lord," said Fanny, in an uncharacteristically sweet tone.

Despite her misgivings, Eliza felt a twinge of amusement. Fanny hid her venom well.

"What are you doing, lurking in dark places, Fan o' the Fens? What mischief are you making?"

Fanny chuckled. A fluting, flowery sound. "My Lord, what kind of mischief would you like me to make?"

Eliza clapped her hands over her mouth to mask an explosion of mirth. How she wished she could see the look on Pelham's face. She waited, ears on stalks, for his response.

Eliza heard him clearing his throat. It was a phlegmy gurgle that made her want to gag.

"Miss Flowers," he said, "I am flattered."

Flattered? Really? The man was a dolt. Eliza edged forward, unable to resist. She slid along the wet wall, fingers feeling the way. As her fingers curled around the end of the brickwork, she peeped around. What she saw was both disturbing and wildly amusing.

Pelham was halted on his bay hunter, looking down at Fanny like a starving hound. Eliza expected him to start drooling any moment. What, she wondered, would her father make of this byplay? What a raving hypocrite the wretch was. Still, Fanny clearly had the upper hand. Which was most gratifying.

Fanny pulled off her bonnet, her dark skein of hair unravelling in a black waterfall. The dairy maid tossed her head. Pelham's eyes were riveted on the flowing, sleek hair. Then Fanny smiled up at him. "'Tis I that is flattered, Milord. I came here in the hope you would pass this way. You have been on my mind."

Eliza inched forward. Her foot kicked a stone. It shot away and clinked against the footings of the bridge. It sounded like gunshot to Eliza's ears. She froze as Pelham's narrow face turned. His eyes, black as ink, glittering in the moonlight.

"What was that?" he snapped, suspicion dripping from every syllable.

If Fanny were concerned she showed no sign. She looked around innocently. "What was what, My Lord?" She stepped forward, tugging Polly in her wake, to lay a pale hand on Pelham's skinny shank.

Eliza felt a shaft of pity for Fanny. Fancy having to touch him. Yuck! She'd rather stroke a slug. But, at the same time, she was impressed by the woman's nerve.

Unfortunately, Pelham was not so easily distracted. His head twisted right and left, as he leaned forward in the saddle.

Eliza shrank back and closed her eyes tight. It seemed a prudent moment to remind God of their recent pact. The only thing that came to mind was the Lord's Prayer. "Our Father, who art in heaven…" she intoned silently and fervently. "Forgive us our trespassers…" If he found her she would die!

Then the conversation resumed. Her eyes snapped open and she sighed with relief. Pelham was once more distracted. Eliza could only pick up the odd word, but it was clear that Fanny had his undivided attention. Eliza slipped back behind the bridge.

On tenterhooks, she waited. What was going on? What should she do? She jumped as horse's hooves clattered overhead and away across the bridge. The sound echoed and boomed like thunder. For the life of her, Eliza couldn't decide if it were one horse or two.

And then, after an eternity of agonising indecision, Polly and Fanny came back into sight.

Eliza rushed forward. "Are you alright! Thank goodness he's gone!" Then she let out an involuntary yelp as a dark figure strode under the bridge.

The figure hesitated and then moved forward. "Miss Eliza, it's me. Oddie!"

A rush of gratitude filled Eliza. The stoker must have been there all the time, watching and waiting. She should have known. She wondered what would have happened if Lord Pelham hadn't been so cooperative. Several scenarios popped into her fertile imagination. But she squashed them down. It wasn't ladylike.

Fanny sniffed, gathered up her hair and rammed it back beneath her bonnet. "That was a treat," she said sourly. Then she glowered at Oddie. "What in seven hells do you think you were playing at?"

To Eliza's surprise and secret delight, Oddie grinned broadly, white teeth glistening. "You're welcome, Miss Flowers." Then he slipped a set of blades off one broad shoulder and bent down.

Fanny pointed a finger at Oddie. "Oddie, what are you doing?"

He glanced up. "No time. Gotta go."

Cold fingers of dread fanned Eliza's frazzled nerves. "Where are you going?"

The stoker tied on the second blade and stood up. "His Lordship is off to the mill, if I'm not mistaken. If I go cross-country, I'll get there before him."

Eliza was horrified. "Don't! Please."

"I forbid it!" hissed Fanny.

Oddie looked at Eliza and smiled. "Wait at the window," he said. He stepped onto the frozen water and struck off, blades sighing over the iron-hard surface. In minutes, he was no more than a memory.

Fanny uttered a few choice words.

A terrible premonition settled about Eliza. She took Polly by the bridle, led her out from beneath the bridge and scrambled up into the saddle.

Fanny turned and stared. "What are you doing?"

But Eliza didn't reply. She dug her heels into Polly's fat sides and they lurched up the bank onto the road.

Fanny raced after her. "Eliza, no!"

But Eliza was committed. Maybe it was madness, but she had to go. Oddie needed her. He just didn't know it yet.

40

Without any headwind, Oddie had made good time. He hunkered down into a drain, gazing at the mill and the canal. He should be able to see Pelham above the hedge on his big blood horse. Then he heard the distinct sound of a horse fast approaching.

Oddie twitched violently as a high-pitched scream rang out. Then he berated himself for a fool. Just a vixen on the Fens. He looked out over the marsh, his eyes burrowing into the waterways and reedy beds. Albie, though not a bad man, was prone to too much gin and tall tales. In the ordinary way of things, Oddie would have laughed and shouted him a pint. But now he knew better. Plus, Pelham's covert interest and subsequent speedy defection strongly suggested that he had believed the old slodger, even if no one else had.

Metal struck a spark on a stone as Pelham's steed came at speed around the corner, parallel to the canal. To cross the water, the lord would have to go down to the bridge, which gave Oddie plenty of time to reach the mill first. He slipped out of his hide and made his way across the boggy ground. His feet instinctively found a safe passage, avoiding bog and sand sinks. He skirted around the driveway, taking cover behind the tangle of stunted trees and brambles that grew in the shallow soil. In the shadow of the chimney, he paused, senses stretching like spun silk.

It was a still night and the sound of the rider carried clearly. The pounding of hooves grew louder until Oddie caught a glimpse of them charging up the drive. Soon he could hear the horse's stressed breathing as it flew towards the mill. Lord Pelham was in a hurry, spurring the poor beast along like a man possessed. Not surprising, if Pelham had seen what Oddie had seen.

Except, of course, Oddie wasn't sure what he had seen. A boy? Probably. A ghost? Possibly. But a demon? Surely not. And then he recalled the weird incident at The Dog. Unless his ears deceived him – which they never did – Fanny had told Eliza there was a dog. A dog that Eliza could see but Oddie couldn't. A dog that was dead. A ghost dog. So, logically speaking, if the boy was a ghost, Oddie shouldn't be able to see him. This revelation was not a comfort. Indeed, under the circumstances, a ghost seemed a sane solution. Anyway, in Oddie's experience, it was the living that one had to look out for. Not the dead.

He lay flat to the ground, barely breathing as Pelham hove into sight. At a walk now, the man approached the mill, his head turning left and right. What was he doing? With fierce determination, Oddie held his place. Whatever Pelham was up to, Oddie needed to know. For himself and for the two women in his life. And perhaps for the poor, lost soul that wept and wailed in the darkness.

And then he heard it. That terrible, anguished cry. It rose into the sky in a ragged ululation. Inside Oddie's chest, pity warred with dread. He wanted to creep away and vanish into the wetland. But he held fast as compassion for the creature with lamps for eyes won out. In the end, it was a boy. Perhaps even the climbing boy that Eliza had so heroically tried to help. How could he walk away? How could he live with himself if he did?

He breathed in slowly and then let it out. His breath silvered in the air. In control once more, he shifted his attention to Pelham. Despite it all, he was wildly curious. The man had headed out here with purpose. If Fanny was to be believed, that purpose was dark. Dark and deadly… and magical.

Magical. The word shimmered in his mind like a distant, mysterious planet. Even now, after all that had happened, Oddie struggled to comprehend what this really meant. To him magic had been the realm of childhood imaginings. Of the bogey man lurking beneath his bed. Of Tiddy Mun dancing in the moonlight. Of the Imp encased forever in stone by an angel. But Oddie had cast these aside in adulthood. Now he found magic in the tender, green shoots of spring and the push and pull of the moon on the tides. So, what was this other magic?

Oddie tensed at the soft scrunch of booted feet approaching. Somewhere in the darkness, the horse whickered anxiously. Pelham was on the move and heading his way. Then the lord came into view. He walked briskly past the furnace room and down to the corner of the mill, heading towards the eerie, desolate wails that carried in the still night air.

As Pelham vanished from sight, Oddie bounded to his feet, sprinting along the rough tussocks of grass and weeds. His passage was barely perceptible. None but a fox or water rat would know he was there. Reaching the path, he forced himself to pad gently over the gravel. By good luck he crossed without so much as a clink. At the corner he paused, listening for signs of activity. But there was only the pounding of his heart and the keening of a lost soul.

Finally, scared he would lose Pelham, he dared a peek. His eyes opened wide with shock at the scene that greeted him. Pelham stood face to face with the spectre that Oddie had seen. Oddie could only see his back. A skull stripped bare of hair. A body ragged and starveling-thin. Twisted like a tree that grows in poor soil. Oddie's mouth set into grim lines. He watched, willing Pelham to offer solace to the child.

An uncanny calm had settled. The only sound was the rush of the stream down to the water wheel. The boy rocked back and forth like a pendulum. Even mute, he exuded an air of anguish. Oddie watched Pelham, trying to grasp the man's motivation. It seemed impossible that the lord and the starveling were strangers. When Oddie had first encountered the boy, he had been shocked. So shocked that he had lost all ability to function. And Albie had been distraught, even considering his inebriated state. Pelham, on the other hand, exhibited no such emotion. He seemed collected. Both parties appeared to be at a standoff. As if one was weighing up the other.

And then Pelham reached a hand into his overcoat and withdrew something. Something black and shiny. Long and lean. A revolver. The lord lifted it, and pointed straight at the boy's face.

Like a stone from a catapult, Oddie launched himself out of hiding. He tore across the moonlit, silvered expanse of the riverbank. "Nooooo!" he yelled. "Stop!"

Pelham jerked, his angular, spindly body an uncoordinated collection of limbs. And the boy turned too. He emitted a drawn-out, piercing whistle of protest. As he did so, a great gust of steam erupted from his mouth. Oddie skidded to a halt as the heat enveloped him. He shook his head in disbelief. Incredulity turned to horror as the steam shrivelled rapidly in the freezing air, revealing the tortured face of the climbing boy. His eyes burned bright with yellow light. Spot-lit, Oddie, half blinded, backed away.

A shot rang out. Oddie looked down at his chest. But he was whole. A soft whimper of sound slipped through the boy's lips and the lights faded away. Oddie surged forward as the boy crumpled to the ground. Oddie dropped to his knees, swallowing down his shock. For, where the boy's heart should have been, there was a gaping, meaty, hole. Slivers of metal and glass glimmered in a river of blood. The remainder of a watch twitched and shivered in its fleshy bed. Oddie gathered up the tiny body and pressed it to his chest. He wept as he felt the last vestiges of the boy's life ebbing away.

He lifted his head and his eyes swept the scene until they found Lord Pelham. "What have you done?" said Oddie.

Pelham sneered. "It's not what I've done that should concern you, Odling. It's what I'm g-g-g-going to do that you need to pay mind too."

Oddie eased the boy gently to the ground and stood up. He felt at sea. Lying at his feet was the hideous proof that Fanny was right. There was something unnatural going on. There was no other explanation. It was a fearsome, dark magic that turned a boy into… well – what? A monster? A machine? Neither seemed appropriate.

He appraised Pelham acutely. "I'm leaving," he said firmly. "Let's not have any more bloodshed."

Pelham lifted the revolver, jabbing it towards Oddie. "You're not going anywhere."

Oddie sighed. "I'm not going to hang around long enough for you to reload."

A smug, satisfied smile lifted Pelham's mouth. "I don't need to reload."

Wary now, Oddie looked down at the dead boy. "I beg to differ," he said. "I just saw you shoot him."

Pelham giggled. "No, I didn't."

"He didn't," said a familiar voice. "I did."

Oddie turned around. His mouth went dry. He stared in disbelief. "No. Not you!"

Primal fear sent adrenaline surging through Oddie's body and he ran. He got no more than a few yards when the gun fired. His leg exploded. And the world went dark.

41

The journey seemed interminable. Every agonising mile had felt like a furlong. Eliza could not shake the dreadful certainty that something bad was going to happen. As she finally turned a reluctant Polly over the stone bridge towards the mill, her head felt hollow with anxiety. A pulse beat a rapid tattoo at her collarbone and her mouth was dry as coal dust.

It was impossible to hide her approach. So, making no attempt, she urged Polly on to their destination. She stared up in trepidation as the mill loomed ever larger until, reaching the end of the gravel drive, it dominated her line of vision. She halted the puffing mare and looked around. The place was empty of life other than the rush of water and the sigh of wind through the reed beds. But Eliza wasn't deterred. There was a distinct atmosphere. Like the imprint of emotion left behind in a room where violence has occurred.

Eliza nudged Polly forward. Without a doubt, something had happened. These insights had haunted her all her life. Although, Eliza had never thought too much about it. But she did now. She didn't worry if it was magic or not. This time it was different. This time she must take responsibility. Leon Odling's life may depend upon it.

With her stomach clenching like a fist, Eliza pushed on. She travelled down the front of the mill and around the corner towards the water wheel. With a snort of protest Polly stopped. Eliza almost spilled over her shoulder. Impatient, she urged the mare on. But Polly snatched at the bit and backed up.

Finally, realising that the mare was set on having her way, Eliza dismounted. She looked around to find a place to tether the mare but there was nothing. In the end, she hooked the reins through a stirrup leather and left her. The mare snorted, and walked away, snatching nervously at mouthfuls of brittle grass.

Spooked by the horse's behaviour, Eliza looked carefully around. There was no movement whatsoever. Not a living soul. But perhaps it wasn't living souls that she should be wary of? Quietly as she could, she walked down the gravel path. Her eyes darted around the moonlit riverbank in nervous anticipation. She stopped, her nostrils flaring as a metallic scent flooded them. Dreadful images flickered through her mind. Comet dissected and spread-eagled on a crude cross. Her tiny teeth bared in anguish. Eliza strangled down a sob and forced her legs to keep walking.

A dark, shiny puddle spread out over the cropped turf. The smell was strong. Her right foot slid beneath her. Slick with blood. So much blood. A bucketful? A barrel? Nausea rolled up her throat and she backed away. Sweat glissaded down her brow, dripping off her nose. She willed herself to be calm. There could be any number of reasons for the sticky, dark pool. It was probably poachers. They'd killed a sheep and slaughtered it there. Most probably she'd caught them unawares.

Eliza stared around. What if they were still there? What if they were watching her? What might they do to keep her silent? Men were hanged for less than a dead sheep. What would one more death matter? Desperate men would care little that she was the governor's daughter. Indeed, it probably made things worse. They could only hang them once. Couldn't they? Faint at the thought,

Eliza backed away. An overwhelming longing to get back to the safe harbour of home engulfed her.

All atremble, she turned back towards Polly. She grabbed at her skirts with both hands, hoisting them above her knees. By the time she took the corner, her breath came in great, heaving gasps. She blessed Mary for the freedom her borrowed clothes gave, and kept going.

Her fingers were like bunches of bananas as she gathered up the reins. She grabbed a stirrup iron, hopping around feebly as Polly reefed at the reins to carry on grazing. Eliza fought for supremacy and failed. She was too weak. How she hated being a woman!

It was then that she saw it. It must have been there all the time. Indeed, she would have ridden straight over it. It was filthy and torn. She bent down and picked it up. Her eyes filled with tears. There was no doubt in her mind. The cap, though tattered and torn, was Oddie's. He'd been wearing it when she had seen him last. Every detail of their encounter was etched into her mind.

Shame flooded through her. How utterly cowardly and self-absorbed she was. The pool of blood wasn't from a silly sheep. There were no poachers. Her stoker had been here. His hat told her that. And that meant that something bad had happened to him. Eliza quailed at the thought but gritted her teeth. She had nearly failed him! Nearly run away like a silly, selfish little girl.

With the hat gripped in her hand, Eliza forced herself to face the facts. There were two probabilities. The first – and most abhorrent – was that Oddie was dead. But lots of blood didn't mean death. Death took time and it hadn't been long since she'd last seen him. No. The second option was much more likely. He was hurt. Panic receded to be replaced with crystal-clear clarity. If he was hurt, then he needed her. She must find him.

"Oddie!" she called. "Oddie!" The only answer was the wind moaning through the tall stone building. She walked up and down and called and yelled. But there was nothing. It was hopeless. Even if Leon Odling had been there, he wasn't now. She didn't know what to do. Best go home and wait. The stoker's disappearance would not go unacknowledged. Mary and Fanny would have an ear to the ground. And besides, Oddie's last words had been to wait for him at her window. And so she would. Perhaps he would come.

But she did not really believe it. She believed that Lord Pelham had done him harm. This was no accident. Somebody had spilled his blood. Her stoker. The man that she loved. And Lord Pelham would pay. She was Eliza Elvidge. A cunning woman. There would be an accounting.

42

Oddie awoke with a jerk from the most dreadful dream. One of those dreams that was so vivid, so real, that it travelled with you into waking hours. Still, no time to linger on such fancies; the mill's siren screamed, and he must answer. There was coal to be shovelled. Best not be late. The governor didn't tolerate poor timekeeping.

He opened his eyes reluctantly. And blinked. Puzzled, he looked left and right. Maybe he was still asleep after all. This was the room he'd dreamt about. Small and dim and damp. Deep, it was. Like a cellar or cave. A stub of candle burned half-heartedly on a raw pine plank. The sharp resin mingled with other less savoury aromas. In the candle's flickering light, Oddie could see stone walls and a patch of dark floor. Beyond that he could see an old door, its green-painted surface mottled with rust and mildew.

As he continued to lie there, he realised just how cold it was. He shivered. Better wake up and stoke the fire. Must be another frosty morning.

The siren blasted. Oddie put his hands to his ears to block it out. He sat up and smacked his head. He cursed emphatically. Then fell silent as a warm trickle of blood rolled between his eyes. He reached up and encountered a cold, hard metal beam. That wasn't right. What the hell was going on?

Then the truth hit him. He was neither sleeping nor dreaming. Thoroughly disturbed, he lifted his fingers and ran them tentatively over the beam. To discover that it wasn't a beam after all. It was round. A pipe. Where the hell was he? And – more to the point – why?

On the verge of panic, Oddie wiggled awkwardly towards the open space on his left. He pulled his torso to the edge and then shifted his left leg. For some reason his right leg refused to follow. Fragments of his dream played in his mind and Oddie felt a stab of fear. A fear fuelled by exhaustion. His eyes closed as he braced himself. Really, more than anything, he wanted to go back to sleep. Instead, Oddie scrunched himself up and reached down to grab a hold of his trouser leg. But his fingers wiggled into empty space.

He lay still, too confused for thought or action. Then, straining every sinew, he inched his hand down a little more. But there was nothing. Just air. He crept his hand sideways and encountered the coarse cloth of his trousers. His hand swept back to the right. Nothing. Which was queer. How was that possible? His breath came in shallow pants. He groped around until his fingertips encountered something alien. A thick wad of cloth. He prodded the lump. Big mistake. Pain engulfed him. It wasn't agony. There was no word to describe it. It felt like someone was sawing his leg off.

Then the dream died and coalesced into reality. And Oddie screamed.

43

She stood at the window, the curtain opened a fraction. The walled garden was clearly illuminated beneath a moon bright and round as a new penny. Despite the coals burning red in the fireplace and her warmest, quilted dressing gown, Eliza shivered. She did not even attempt to sleep. Fear and hope mingled in her breast like water and oil. With her nose pressed against the freezing pane of glass, Eliza willed Oddie to appear.

She prayed to God for him to be alright. This time there was no talk of tit for tat. This time it was the desperate, fervent plea of a terrified woman. A grieving woman. She could not bear to think of his hurt. Oddie was good. Surely God couldn't be so cruel as to let harm come to him? It wasn't fair!

Her shoulders stiffened and she sucked in an involuntary gulp of air. Something was moving in the garden. She was sure of it! Then she slumped, wiping tears from her eyes with angry fists. It was a cat slinking atop the wall. Her eyes were playing tricks on her. But she couldn't push away the possibility that something might have scared it. She concentrated on the shadow that was the garden gate. Oddie might emerge any minute. Once more she leaned into the window, watching intently. Please. Please. Please. She prayed silently.

On the mantelpiece the carriage clock ticked and tocked. Time hung heavily upon her. She longed for the night to be over. Still abed, Mary snored softly, a long strand of red hair floating up and down with each breath. The sound was strangely soothing. It gave Eliza a sense of belonging. Of normality. Of being connected to the world. It was why she had not woken the maid. While she slept, Mary still belonged to yesterday, where life had been set in the old pattern. A life that – despite its frustrations and irritations – was familiar and predictable. There was no doubt in Eliza's mind that the old life had gone. When morning came, her new life would begin. And she was afraid.

When tomorrow came, there were two possibilities. The first was that she would be reunited with Oddie. If so, Eliza had made up her mind that she would persuade him to leave and go with him. The prospect made her lightheaded with happiness. She would take her jewels and her bag of coins and her most serviceable clothes, and they would leave. Where they would go, she did not know or care. All she knew was that they must go far away. Start a new life. And never look back.

The second possibility was that Oddie would not come. Her lips trembled but she held herself together. She had to be strong. She drew strength from the knowledge that if their roles were reversed, Oddie would do anything for her. It was only right that she did all that was in her power for him. When the thin winter sun rose over the Fens, Eliza may have to go to war. She would have to fight for Oddie. For his freedom. Perhaps even his life.

She shuddered to think of the price Pelham would demand for Oddie's survival. But she was determined that she would do whatever she must. Once Oddie was free, then she would work things out.

If there was anything she had learned over the weeks, it was that there were no rules anymore. Or at least, no rules that she recognised. If Fanny Flowers and Mary were right, then Eliza had created a storm of frightening ferocity. And then she had seen the spectre of Comet, followed by a dog dead seven years. This was an alien world. Yet, somehow, she must learn to live in it.

There was a certain sense of relief, in facing the facts, ugly though they were. But the waiting was a torment. When a dark figure emerged into the space below Eliza cried out. He had come! How foolish she was to doubt it! She fumbled at the window casings, unwilling to take her eyes off him. "Oddie!" she called, even though sense told her that he could not hear. Finally, her fingers flipped the brass fastening of the frame and she pushed the sash window up.

Eliza stuck her head and shoulders out, bracing her upper body with her elbows. Her hair swung down across her face, blocking her view. She tossed her head in frustration, catching a glimpse of Oddie, now almost directly below. "Are you alright? I've been beside myself!" she said, in a half whisper. But he did not answer. A shadow slipped over her heart. Something was wrong.

Clutching the ledge with one hand, she thrust her hair aside; and nearly fell headfirst out of the window. Oh God! It wasn't her stoker. It was Pelham. She staggered back into her bedroom as his laughter mocked her. She slammed the window shut.

"Miss Eliza! What ails you?"

Eliza turned to her maid, who was now wide-awake and scrambling out of bed. For several fraught moments, she could not speak. Her thoughts darted around her skull like mice beneath the thrasher's blade. What to do? Then it came to her. "Mary," she said, "I must go find my father! Papa will bring that scabious cur to heel. He has done something bad to Mr Odling and must be made to answer!"

Once she had spoken the words, Eliza felt her confidence returning. This disclosure would surely bring her father around. If necessary, Fanny would speak out too. Then Papa would be forced to see the truth about Lord Pelham. And when Oddie was free, the evidence would be overwhelming. Papa would have to acknowledge the Earl's third son as a scoundrel and scallywag – and an entirely unsuitable match for a lady such as herself.

Determined now, she tightened her sash and headed for the bedroom door. She grasped the handle and began running her words through her mind. It was important that she present her case with care. There must be no hint of hysteria or she would be undone. And her stoker too. With a mental deep breath, Eliza pushed the heavy door aside and stepped over the threshold.

And stopped. She goggled at her father. "Papa," she said, reaching out a hand. "Papa, how strange, I was just coming to find you. There is something that I must disclose, though I know it will be unpalatable." Aware that her hand hovered in the air in expectation, she fell silent. Her fingers extended a fraction towards him, in silent supplication. A cold dread slithered down her spine like a serpent. Slowly, her arm fell back to her side.

"Papa…" she said. Then her words dried out at the sound of approaching footsteps. Eliza looked down the carpeted corridor and stared in disbelief. Pelham approached. He positively swaggered. As if he were already resident in her home. The arrogant wretch! She would swing for him. How she would delight in the sound of hemp creaking as he danced to the hangman's tune.

She turned to her father. "Papa, you must listen to me! Your fine lord is up to his skinny neck in dark deeds. He has done something dastardly to my poor climbing boy and your own stoker. You must make him tell you what he has done, before it is too late!" She paused to collect herself, aware that the pitch of her voice was rising at an alarming rate. Her body was atremble with passion.

She pressed on, forcing herself to be calm. "Papa, I have been out tonight, to the mill, and there is blood spilled upon the riverbank. Great quantities of blood. I know that something terrible has happened. He has—"

Her words were cut like an umbilical cord as Pelham closed in. To her dismay Eliza saw the two men were observing each other with expressions of resigned agreement. Something unspoken in the air made Eliza take a step back.

Pelham's hand snaked out, grasping her wrist.

Eliza looked to her father expectantly. "See!" She reefed her arm violently, to reinforce her words. Rage flooded through her as her parent failed to respond. The feel of Pelham's cold, clammy hand on her person was sickening. With a snarl, she snatched her hand up, fastening her teeth into his bony hand.

She felt a wave of triumph as he squealed and let her go. She glared at her father. But he seemed unmoved.

Then his eyes flickered over Eliza's head. "The maid," he said coldly, "she will have to be silenced."

All the fight went out of Eliza. "No, please, Papa, don't hurt Mary. I beg of you! I'll go. Just leave her be."

Pelham sniggered, and her father said nothing but his head nodded a fraction.

As she followed Pelham to the stairs, Eliza wondered how she could have gotten things so wrong. Had her love for her father blinded her? Or her loathing of Pelham? But it hardly mattered. At this point conjecture was pointless. Her beloved father was a monster. A man in league with Lord Pelham, that dreadful man! Oh God!

And then she knew. He had hurt Oddie. And he was going to hurt her too.

44

Oddie watched the flame flicker, gutter and die. The darkness was complete and as effective as a blindfold. The only sound was his laboured breath and the gurgle of water in the pipe overhead. His mouth was parched and his head was aching abominably. The stump of what had once been his leg throbbed. Fear, pain and anxiety made it increasingly difficult to think.

Time passed, as oppressive as the silence. Unbidden, terror washed over him. Oddie clenched his lips; he didn't want to start screaming again. It was exhausting. Some primitive instinct warned him to keep his mouth shut. What strength remained must be preserved. But another part of his mind whispered that it was too late. How could a one-legged man help himself? A one-legged man who was weakened by blood loss. Panic welled up. How could he live with one leg?

He tried to force his focus away from such dark thoughts. Eliza's image shimmered to the forefront of his mind. For a few precious moments, Oddie sank into a reverie as he recalled her exquisite form. The perfection of her tiny waist. The clear, soft complexion. The brilliance of her blue eyes. The golden head of hair cascading through a window casement. The mischievous twist of her lips when she laughed.

Then reality crashed in. What would Eliza think when she saw him next? Would she turn away in disgust? Or would her lovely face fold into an expression of pity? With luck he wouldn't live long enough to find out. Yet, this last thought snagged on his consciousness. He was forgetting something. Something important.

He worried over it like a dog with a particularly meaty bone. Something to do with Eliza. He shut his eyes tight until a memory flickered. Oh God! He had been shot by Eliza's father. The governor had shot him in cold blood! All the time they'd been obsessing over Pelham, it had been the governor all along. Eliza's own flesh and blood.

Eliza needed to know. Oddie had to survive. Survive and make good his escape so that he could warn her. Everything else was secondary. Fanny had been right all along. Dark times were upon them. There was evil at work. And – though he grudgingly acknowledged it – magic too. He'd known it when he'd encountered the climbing boy. Known it, but still refused to believe.

This whole thing was beyond him. But perhaps that didn't matter. What mattered was that Eliza was in mortal danger. And not just Eliza. Everyone.

This last cleared his mind. The governor had killed the climbing boy. He had shot Oddie. It didn't take much of a stretch to link him with the brutal vivisection of Eliza's little dog. And then there was his father's watch. It wasn't coincidence that Oddie had found it in the furnace. It too was connected. Whatever the hell was going on had been going on for a long time. His father had been missing for ten years. Oddie was now certain that his father was dead. He shied away from the thought. He couldn't deal with it now.

He shifted restlessly. His legs cramped. Sweat poured from his body, pain stabbing through him like red-hot pokers. Oddie cursed to keep from crying out. If he started screaming he couldn't hear. And – at this point – that was all he had. His ears. With that being the case, Oddie resolved to listen for all he was worth.

It occurred to him then, that if the governor wanted him dead, he'd have finished the job already. Once Oddie was wounded, it would have been only too easy to follow through with murder, then find him an unholy grave out in the mudflats or the bog. So, it seemed unlikely that Eliza's father would leave him here to rot. What was the gain in that? No. The governor had plans for Oddie. The thought of this filled him with both hope and horror. Would he end up like the climbing boy? Or could it be something worse? Worse was hard to imagine. But then, if he lived, he could find a way to warn Eliza.

For the first time since his return to consciousness, Oddie felt anchored to reality. He had a plan. Vague though it was, he had a purpose. He must live and find his way back to Eliza. With time, he would recover. He was young and strong. After all, the poor twisted and starving climbing boy had survived whatever tortures were inflicted upon him. Logically, therefore, Oddie could too. There was, he reassured himself, no point in trying to think too far ahead. That road would lead to madness.

The pipes gurgled. It was a comforting sound. Almost human. Like blood pumping through an artery. A sound that he connected with people. The water in the metal pipe was travelling somewhere. To a tap, perhaps. Maybe even to the boiler room. And near to the boiler room a stoker was fuelling the fires. Life went on without him.

So consumed was he by these thoughts that a subtle new sound didn't fully register. It just nibbled on the periphery of his mind. It was only as the pipe silenced that Oddie stiffened, senses buzzing. He held his breath to better hear. But there was nothing. Perhaps he was hallucinating.

Then he heard it again. A muffled murmur. The air rushed out of Oddie's parched lips. He gripped the pipe above him, craning his neck. Was someone out there? Then he heard it. This time it was louder. Not a noise anymore. Voices. People having a conversation. Oddie knew it was men by the deep tones, although the words were too muffled to distinguish.

Whilst the prospect of facing the governor was daunting, Oddie felt a sense of relief. What could be worse than lying here locked away in the darkness? It was twisted, but Oddie understood the governor was both tormentor and deliverer. Oddie was still alive. Therefore, he must be of value. A bargain could be struck. He tried not to think about the price to be paid. He'd already paid with his liberty and a limb. It didn't take a genius to guess that may not be the end.

A rumble of laughter echoed around the darkness. Oddie stiffened, instinctively knowing they were close. Sure enough, the laughter ceased. There was a soft click of a lock. The door whined open.

Light flooded in and Oddie let out a cry of shock. His eyes closed tight, and he turned his head away. Silence. But they were there. Oddie could feel eyes upon him and smell their aggression in the air. He hated them. Hated himself for cowering like a cur. He forced his eyes open and turned his head.

It took a few minutes to focus, two blobs slowly evolving into men. Well-dressed men with two legs apiece. The governor and Pelham. Who else? They stared down at him. The governor's expression was as inscrutable as ever. Indeed, he almost looked benign. Pelham, however, seemed thoroughly overexcited. His pale face was unusually flushed as he rubbed his spidery fingers up and down his thighs. Oddie couldn't get rid of the notion that the lord was in the throes of some sexually charged moment. Which was altogether disgusting.

Oddie refused to look at Pelham lest he be sick. A humiliation he'd rather be spared. Instead he fixed his eyes on the governor, deciding that he wasn't inclined to polite conversation. Indeed, he wasn't inclined to converse at all. Silence was his only weapon. Therefore, he'd wield it for all it was worth.

Unfortunately, the governor did not seem perturbed by Oddie's tactics. He too was silent. Then he lifted his hand with a magician's flourish and something glinted. It was a clock. Oddie's guts turned to water and his heart to stone. It was no ordinary clock. It was Oddie's clock. His own precious alarm clock.

Pelham grinned widely. "Tick-tock, tick-tock," he said, one finger describing each second in the air.

Oddie tried to summon a response. Some act of defiance. A short, snappy retort. But he had nothing. He'd never considered himself to be a fanciful man. But now all he could do was stare and imagine. And all that he imagined was not nice. Not nice at all.

45

Her father's office was snug and warm. The fire popped and hissed softly. The drapes were closed but a gas lamp lit the room up like day. It smelled of boot polish, cigars and leather. Scents that had always been a source of comfort for Eliza. But not today.

Today, everything had changed. It was a topsy-turvy world where nothing could be taken for granted or trusted. She felt as if she were living in a maze, with no idea of where she had come from or where it was that she was trying to go. Life had warped into something dark and scary. How had she gotten things so wrong? How had she made such a mess of things? She felt foolish. Humiliated. Angry. Heartbroken.

Eliza's anguish was two-pronged. First was the fear that she harboured for Oddie. Every instinct warned her that her stoker was in trouble deep. But that grief was matched by the loss of her father. She felt that the man she had known and loved all her life was lost to her. As good as dead. Her father had been the centre of her universe. She had lived her life confident that she was loved and cherished. She felt abandoned.

Eliza shivered. She looked at the door and wondered if it

was locked. She contemplated getting up and testing it out. But she didn't. Her limbs seemed disconnected. Shock, probably, she reflected. But that wasn't quite true. Part of her was unwilling. If it weren't locked, Eliza had no idea what she would do. She had lost all confidence in her own ability. In the face of her father's power she felt inadequate. Even if she possessed some kind of magic, what good had it done for her or those about her? What of Fanny and Mary? Had they too met some terrible fate?

And there was something else. What about her mother? Had she really been mad? Was she really dead? If so, had her father killed her? And if so, why? Would he kill her too? A tear ran hot down her cheek. She strangled back a sob. If she started to cry, she'd never stop. And besides, she couldn't bear Lord Pelham to see her abject misery. That would crush her altogether. He was a despicable human being.

Dwelling on Pelham's defects was oddly satisfying. What a weak, dishonest, cowardly man he was. And pig ugly too! So ugly in fact, that such a comparison was an insult to pigs. Pigs were smart and cute. Pelham was a weasel. He wasn't fit to wipe his hands on Oddie's working boots. How she loathed him. He was as disgusting as a slimy slug. The thing one expected to find when one lifted a rock.

Such contemplation had the effect of stiffening Eliza's spine. She lifted her skirt hem and wiped her eyes and blew her nose. She must pull herself together. She must think. There must be a way out of this mess. After all, she was alive and kicking. Well, not so much kicking, more flopping about a bit. But still, her father and his odious offsider had bought her here for a purpose. Whatever that was, she must find a way to turn it to her advantage. Blubbing and snivelling was not the way to go about it. She must remain outwardly calm. She must think! If there was one thing she had learned in the last few hours, it was the depth of her own ignorance. What she needed to do was to wait and watch. She must convince her father that she was utterly conquered. Her spirit entirely quenched.

Her cheeks flushed in shame. The last shouldn't be too difficult. She had not set the pole very high, thus far. Mostly she had hissed like a feral cat and indulged in a few undignified episodes of slapping. Whilst the slapping had been very satisfactory at the time it had been wretchedly futile. Violence really wasn't the answer. And besides, she didn't really trust Pelham not to slap her back. Worse, she believed that if he did, her father would abet him.

No. It was time to take a different tack. She took a deep breath and stood up. Her legs felt like junket, but she made it to the door. With a burst of resolve, Eliza reached out and grasped the brass knob, giving it a turn. When there was no more give, she pushed. The door stayed sullenly shut. Locked. But at least she knew.

She turned and leant against the door, gazing around the familiar room. Her eyes brushed over the huge, leather-lined desk. It was so tidy. Everything laid out like soldiers in a battalion. Even the bookshelves were regimented. Sets of matching books perfectly aligned on the oak shelves. Her curiosity was piqued. What kind of books interested her father? It was hard to imagine. She moved across the carpet, pausing before the long library.

Most of the books were dull, dry tomes. Law, medicine, history and a large collection of books about steam machines. Listlessly, Eliza plucked one off a shelf and flicked through it. Chapters sped by, revealing an indecipherable conglomeration of engineering texts and diagrams. She put it back and moved on. At the end of the row she found a collection of books that stood out by way of being uncharacteristically shabby. The spines were peeling and faded. Some sagged like old flour bags. One book had a mottled appearance suggestive of mould.

Eliza bent down and examined the texts more closely. As her eyes grazed over the titles she felt an odd tightening in her chest. The advanced age and dilapidated appearance of the books was not the only thing they had in common. They were all written in a foreign language. The alphabet was entirely unorthodox. Curious, she pinched a leather spine in her fingers and levered it out.

Eliza moved nearer to the lamp. She gazed down at the title page, at the peeling gilt print. And, the longer she looked, the less unorthodox the language appeared. A sense of vertigo gripped her. What had initially presented as rows of haphazard dots and dashes became increasingly legible.

"*Aspinall's Superior Anthology of Spells and Incantations*," she said.

She repeated the title. Louder this time. The second time around the title seemed less intimidating. A frisson of excitement coursed through her. Here, in her hands, was a book of… magic. A book of spells! The very thing that Fanny had said was the key to mastering the wild, tempestuous power inside her.

Then the gas lamp shivered, throwing her shadow into a frenetic dance. A cool draught of air made her skirt rustle. The door swung abruptly open.

"Aspinall was a better anthologist than he was a practitioner," her father said.

Eliza did not reply. She hardly knew what to think, never mind say. She peered over her father's shoulder, into the dim corridor, to see if Pelham was there. To her relief, he was not.

Her father advanced across his study and took the book from her unresisting hand. He tapped the cracked, burgundy leather cover. "Of course, many of these spells are not superior. Some are more cheap tricks for children's parties."

Eliza waited, her emotions seesawing as she wondered where this disturbing and most unconventional conversation would lead. It was strange, her father looked the same. Tall, stern, handsome and strong. He emanated an aura of benevolent patience. Only now she knew that this persona had no more substance than smoke. An insight that she decided it would be wise to keep to herself.

She stepped forward and repossessed the book. Without a

word, she moved back into the light and flipped the pages open at random. She perused a spell that could turn a tide. As the words infused her mind, she felt an awakening. She tingled from her nose to her toes. She felt a frisson of energy at her core.

"Eliza, I have the stoker."

The book dropped. Eliza stared at her father in horror, his words conjuring up all her worst fears. "Why?" she said.

He bent down and picked up the book. "The stoker is to be part of a scientific experiment. Part of a new movement that will revolutionise our world." He lay the book softly on the desk. "And you are going to assist me."

Eliza stared at him. Comet's desecrated body filled her mind. He was mad! He couldn't possibly believe she'd be party to his abhorrent practices. She shook her head. "No! Never!"

Her father seemed unperturbed by her resistance. "You will help me, Eliza."

She gripped the edge of the desk and leaned towards him. "I'll be damned if I do!"

He smiled. "Oh, you'll be damned alright." He turned lightly on his heels. "Come!"

Filled with trepidation, Eliza watched him sweep back out the door. Her heart felt fit to burst.

Seconds later, she followed.

46

Her father led her briskly down a confusion of stairs and corridors. He walked so fast that Eliza could scarcely find breath. When they finally came to a stop, she found she was in a surgery.

Despite herself, Eliza was impressed. It was a large surgery, with several tiers of seats and a shiny display of new instruments. This seemed entirely appropriate given her father's chosen profession. Surgeons were increasingly inclined to invite prominent members of society to witness their skill first-hand. Obviously, her father was set to do the same. Ordinarily, Eliza would have been proud. At this point, she was just scared stiff.

She watched her father walk around a shiny steel operating table. He ran a finger down its smooth surface. "Comet looked very small on the slab," he said.

Despite all that she knew, and much that she suspected, Eliza was shocked. She hadn't expected this callous cruelty. She reined in her emotions with supreme effort. A hysterical outburst was probably what he wanted. And she wouldn't give him the satisfaction. "Comet is small," she said softly. "Was small."

Her father turned to look at her. "The stoker will leave little space to spare."

Eliza gave him a disdainful glance. "If you say so."

Her father's facade cracked a little. "I do say so!" he hissed. Then he drew in a deep breath and circled the table once more. When he stopped, his mask was back in place.

"Eliza," he said, "I apologise. My passion for my science sometimes overcomes my sense of propriety."

Eliza snorted, and gave him the evil eye.

He pretended not to notice. His arms opened in a gesture of pleading. "Eliza, what I am doing here will revolutionise our world. Imagine, a world where mankind is no longer limited by the weaknesses of their own flesh. Where a man is transformed by the power of steam and steel. Where he is immune to the ravages of time and disease. A perfect, precision-made man that can work without fatigue. Whose strength would rival that of Samson himself. A man who could live forever. Imagine that if you can, Eliza!"

She couldn't. It beggared belief. Mankind was imperfect, it was true. But was this necessarily a bad thing? Eliza didn't think so. After all, these very imperfections were sometimes more lovable than qualities that were judged to be superior.

Her thoughts flew to Oddie, but she pushed them away. She dared not go there. Instead she chose Mary. Mary, who was hardworking, honest and god-fearing. All qualities that Eliza valued. But it was Mary's quirky faults that were truly endearing. Like the buttons on the windowsill. Her silly superstitions. Her snoring. And then there was Rosie, whom she valued for her physical strength and loyalty. But it was her misplaced enthusiasm and unkempt appearance that Eliza enjoyed. She didn't want them to be better. Or perfect. She loved them just as they were. Human. Warts and all.

Then the full force of her father's words punched like a pugilist. He was not talking about mankind at all. He was talking about just one man. Leon Odling. Her stoker. Her love. Her mad father planned to turn Oddie into a monstrosity. A man of steel and steam. A man doomed to live an eternity.

The revelation almost undid her. Blood drained from her head and she thought she would black out. How she wished that she were a man. Then she could pick up a scalpel from its velvet bed and thrust it through her father's heart. How she ached to feel flesh and sinew tear asunder beneath the force of her fury. How she longed to see his blood burst out in a fountain of red until he lay cold upon the floor.

Aware of his eyes upon her, Eliza tried to focus. Violence would not serve her. She must fight some other way. But how? How could she, a weak woman, possibly hope to win? If violence was not the key that only left cunning. *Cunning.* The word reverberated inside her. Was that not what she was, after all? A cunning woman?

With her heart in her mouth, she walked to the metal slab and looked down at her father's reflection. "Comet didn't live forever," she said softly.

Her father bowed his head, as if both honouring her pet's memory and acknowledging the truth of her words. "Alas, Eliza, it is true. I failed. But her sacrifice was not in vain. I learned much from the experiment. And the climbing boy lived, did he not?"

His casual attitude towards the destruction of life was mortifying. He who should be dedicated to the preservation of life evinced no signs of remorse for his actions. Did he truly believe that the end justified the means? True, the boy had lived, but by all accounts, it was a terrible, cursed existence. If that was the price to be paid for immortality, Eliza was almost glad that little Comet had not survived.

She swallowed her revulsion and forced herself to look at her father. "I am somewhat overwhelmed by it all," she said. "It is all so... new. So very alarming. I hardly know what to think! And yet, I must confess that I find myself intrigued. The idea of creating a man with such powers is astonishing!" She hoped the tremor in her voice would be interpreted as womanly temerity, rather than suppressed rage.

She waited, on tenterhooks, praying that the fish would take the bait. To her profound relief, her father's lips lifted into a smug, self-satisfied smile.

"Eliza, it is true that you are handicapped by all the weaknesses of your sex. Yet, you show uncommon insight into the situation. I think that you may even begin to understand that I am giving the stoker a great gift! It is a gift that men will soon be begging for. Imagine, once the stoker has exhibited his unnatural qualities, how much men will pay to become his equal."

Most of what her father said was such lunacy that Eliza struggled to follow. A few choice pieces of prose did resonate, however. His vision of Oddie as an 'exhibit' for one and 'a great gift' was another. Clearly her father was a megalomaniac. He obviously believed that he was doing his stoker some vast favour. Equally clear was, if he succeeded, Oddie was going to be no more than a caged tiger in a menagerie.

Aware that her father was expecting a response, Eliza cast around for something to say. It wasn't easy. "Father, I am speechless," she whispered.

He rubbed his hands together, nodding vigorously. "Indeed, I did not intend to overtax your mental capacity."

Eliza marvelled that she did not spontaneously burst into flames. It was on the tip of her tongue to query how she could assist her father in his scientific endeavours when she possessed the intellect of an ant. But she bit her tongue. She must keep her passions subdued or she would undo everything. Instead, she looked meekly at her toes and kept her counsel.

Her father came, taking her arm. "Come, Eliza, I think it's time to start your education."

A door opened behind them and her father looked over his shoulder. "Excellent timing, Lord Pelham. You must accompany

Eliza and myself to visit the patient. It is time to begin preparations."

Eliza forced her features to remain impassive. Inside she was anything but. The thought of being in Oddie's presence filled her with both delight and desolation. Delight to be near him. To speak with him. To look upon his beloved face. To have proof that he breathed. Desolation as to the circumstances of their reunion. She desperately wanted to know how he fared. How had they taken him? She could not imagine it was without a fight. Had they hurt him? Tears pricked at her eyelids and she blinked them furiously away.

"Come, Eliza!" said her father.

Eliza linked her arm through his and walked away with him.

Pelham watched on sullenly. Eliza avoided his gaze. Clearly, Lord Pelham was not altogether pleased with the situation. Eliza could not hazard a guess as to the root of his disquiet. But one thing was sure: she must be wary. Pelham was a weasel. She must beguile him if she were to succeed.

It was a nauseating prospect.

47

Time ticked by silently. But the image of the clock lingered. There was no doubt in Oddie's mind what his fate would be. The governor was going to take out his heart and replace it with a clock. Perhaps he would replace his lost limb with a pitchfork. Maybe he too would wake with lamps for eyes.

If he were lucky, he'd die under the knife like poor little Comet. If he were unlucky and lived, then he would become some ghastly spectre. Like the climbing boy. Not a man. But not a spirit either. Would he wander the Fenlands wailing his fate for an eternity? Or did the governor have something else planned? It was impossible to guess. There were no longer any landmarks by which he could navigate his life. Life as he'd known it had been extinguished. Now there was just darkness and pain and fear. And waiting. It was the waiting that was the worst.

This time, when he picked up the sound of approaching footsteps, Oddie felt a surge of gratitude. Followed by confusion. What was wrong with him? Perhaps it was just that he was so thirsty. At this stage, he would have supped a pint of ale with Satan himself. It would be easy to lose his sense of self in his present predicament. He must try and hold on to the man he had always been. The man that Eliza loved. In the end, no matter what, he must hold on to that. Eliza would be his compass in the darkness.

No voices this time. Just the march of feet. Louder, he thought. A clink and click. A gust of cold, fresh air. Light.

It took longer for his eyes to adjust this time. His eyelids were dry, sticking together and sore. The governor came into focus first, being closest. Pelham stood behind in shadow. Oddie stared at them both hopefully, but his hopes were dashed when he failed to find either in possession of so much as a thimble of water.

A small gasp of sound alerted him to a third party, stood half in and half out the door, partially obscured by both men. He craned his head as far as the cramped space would allow and glimpsed a length of gown. Pale. Blue. It was a woman. Oddie couldn't imagine what a woman would be doing here. At the best of times, the mill was a male domain. And now, at the worst of times, it felt all wrong. No woman should be exposed to such deeds. And besides – he was ashamed. Ashamed that a woman was privy to his wretchedness.

A rustle of material signalled that the woman was on the move. For a moment she was hidden and then she pushed a passage between the two men. His initial reaction was acute embarrassment as he realised that the woman was in a state of undress. Why, she was in her night attire! And even as the thought formed, a familiar scent stole over him. His eyes moved up the pale gown and followed a golden curtain of hair to a pair of brilliant blue eyes. His heart expanded like a hot-air balloon. Eliza!

His lips formed her name but his parched throat could not utter a single sound. For an eternity, they simply stared at each other. He prayed that Eliza would read all the unspoken words. How could she not feel the emotion that raged inside him? How could she not feel the power of his love?

To his relief, she looked well. True, there were purple bruises under her eyes, but no other harm seemed to have befallen her. How beautiful she was. Her skin was as white as fine china. Loose, her golden hair curled to her tiny waist, accentuating the pointed chin and wide-spaced eyes. Her neck rose from the white lace collar like the stalk of a snowdrop. She was perfect. If he could have drawn his last breath there and then, he would have slipped from the world without regret.

He watched in dismay as a tear welled, trembled and fell down her cheek. He stretched out his hand towards her. She lifted a dainty foot and then stopped. Her lips set in a hard line and she clasped her hands together at her breast. Then, almost imperceptibly, she shook her head. The movement would have been missed by the watching men.

Oddie was panic-stricken. Heartbroken. Oh God! She was disgusted! Who could blame her? Gone was the slodger. The stoker. The skater. Instead, there was a cripple. Any woman would turn away from such a pathetic, ugly sight. Why, even Pelham was more of a man. He turned his head away lest she see the desolation in his face.

"What happened to his leg?"

Oddie barely recognised her voice. Gone was the vivacious, teasing tones he had adored. Now, Eliza sounded as cool and calm as a Fenland lake.

"An eight bore," said her father, without a hint of apology.

Pelham laughed. "Not so pretty now, is he?"

"No," said Eliza. "Young Mary will be so disappointed."

"Mary?" said the governor sharply.

"Oh yes, she is absolutely sweet on the stoker. It was most amusing. Indeed, I was arranging a tryst when Lord Pelham put in an appearance."

There was a silence.

Then Eliza giggled. "Was that terribly naughty of me?"

It was the giggle that did it. It just wasn't Eliza. Eliza didn't twitter. Not the Eliza that Oddie knew. It struck him then that the tiny shake of her head was not rejection at all. It had been a warning. Clearly, she had started towards his outstretched hand and bought herself up short. There were things that he did not understand. But that didn't matter. All that mattered was that Eliza was on his side. That was everything.

If anyone had told him an hour ago that he could feel happy, he'd have called them crazy. But that was exactly how he felt. Despite it all, he felt more like himself than he had since he'd woken in the cellar. Hope rekindled. His Eliza was here. She was good and brave and strong. Her mere presence gave him strength.

Slowly he turned his face to observe his audience once more. His joy was clouded by a new and particularly fearsome thought. Her guarded behaviour told him that she was in mortal danger. He must be careful not to do her injury or to compromise her position. He thanked God for his parched throat. What might have escaped his lips had he been able to speak? He remade his vow of silence. It seemed the only safe option.

Eliza turned to her father. "I see," she said. "Is he strong enough for the… procedure? There was a loss of blood."

The governor stepped forward, peering down at Oddie. His eyes ran up and down. His gaze lingered on the bloody stump of leg. Then he turned his back. "He is strong. He will survive."

Oddie was not reassured. What did 'survive' mean? Perhaps it was better that he did not know. It was clear that Eliza must now be acquainted with the facts. It was also clear that her father had not bought her here purely for sport. Or punishment. There was a tension between father and daughter, drawing them together like an invisible thread. It had never occurred to him before that the two were alike. But they were. Especially in this moment. And Oddie wondered if the governor had any inkling of just how smart and strong his daughter was. He hoped not, for therein lay Eliza's salvation.

And what purpose did the governor have for his child? Oddie was almost too scared to think about it. Fan had long suspected dark magic. And now Oddie had no doubts on the matter. It was just that he couldn't equate Eliza with such evil. By what means was her father manipulating his daughter? It was impossible to guess.

The governor retraced his steps across the floor and out the door without a backward glance. Pelham moved to block Eliza's exit. She stopped abruptly before him before backing away. But, swift as an adder, Pelham had her pinned against the wall. He slid a hand down the front of her nightwear. Oddie felt blood rushing to his head and he screamed silently as he watched the beast fondle Eliza's breast.

Pelham looked over his shoulder and smiled evilly at Oddie. "Her father may be a fool but I'm not," he said sibilantly. "You'll never have her. I'm going to tup this ewe."

Then the lordling let out a shrill squeal and dropped to his knees, gurgling and gulping like a landed fish. Oddie watched in delight as water gushed out of Pelham's mouth.

Eliza smiled angelically at Oddie. "Oops," she whispered.

Pelham began to recover. Coughing and retching he staggered to his feet and scurried out as the governor strode back in.

"Eliza!" he said curtly.

"Coming, Papa," she replied meekly.

Oddie's eyes embraced her until the door shut and darkness engulfed him once more. He lay still and closed his eyes. The future still seemed bleak. But there was hope. He must fight to survive. For any life on Earth with Eliza was better than eternity in heaven without her.

48

Back in the study, Eliza's father requested she sit at his desk. She complied, waiting anxiously as he browsed his library, selecting books. When his arms were laden, he came, dropping them on the desk with a crash.

Her eyes skittered over them, trying to register their titles. But she couldn't take anything in. She was too shaken by her encounter with Oddie. Her heart felt as if it had been ripped from her chest and thrown on a red-hot brazier. The agony of seeing him mutilated, imprisoned and shamed was almost beyond endurance. Yet, at the same time, she knew she must hold on to her sanity. Everything depended upon it.

Her father picked up a small, burgundy book. "We will start here. Thus far, my scientific endeavours have been extraordinarily enlightening. I now have a firm foundation of knowledge and an absolute understanding of not just how I have succeeded, but also where I have failed."

Eliza was astonished. Clearly her father was not only proud of himself but also expected a standing ovation. She dutifully nodded her head. "Indeed, Papa, it is an awe-inspiring achievement."

He made a show of humility, but it was obviously a mockery. "I have succeeded in melding man and machine. But the end result has been… disappointing. I am, however, confident that I can still achieve my goal." He paused and appraised Eliza. "There are four elements that harness the Earth's power. Fire, water, air and earth."

Eliza was spellbound. Whilst she abhorred her father's methods, the subject matter was an entirely different thing. She knew in this moment that she would never be the same again. Incredible though it was, she was about to be initiated into an undreamt of world. A place ruled by magic. Her father could call it science or whatever he liked, but magic it was. And she was part of it. It was a heady moment.

Her father continued. "An individual can tap into one of the elements. And one only. It is not a matter of choice. This is nature's way. But individuals can join. This fusion of power creates a whole new potential." He put the book down carefully on the desk. "And that is the reason you are here today."

Eliza drew in a deep breath and held it in her lungs. The most astonishing thing was it all made absolute sense. As if none of it were new, more like a lesson learned long ago that she recalled. A wave of excitement enveloped her. "Water!"

Her father nodded. "Indeed."

For a few minutes, Eliza pondered. Quickly she reached a conclusion. Fanny was earth. Fanny with her love of herblore and gift of healing. Which left fire and air. Her father's element must be one of them. But then she frowned. Not so. His could be any but her own. She looked at him. "Which is your element?"

"Guess," he said.

The invitation indicated that there was an obvious answer. It was a test then. Eliza hid her dismay and nodded calmly. What did her father need? And why? He was melding man and machine. She knew which man. For a moment, she faltered. Oddie's mutilated body burst into her head and threatened to overwhelm her. Ruthlessly she thrust the thoughts away. It did no good. Not now.

Eliza refocused. Where was she? She knew the man. So, on to the machine. But what kind of machine? A watch? Perhaps. But that seemed too simple. And then it came to her like a lightning strike. It was obvious. Steam.

"Steam!" she said. Her father nodded curtly. Emboldened, Eliza dared to press on. "To make steam you need water and… heat." Therefore, there was only one possibility. "Fire," she said. "You are fire." It made sense. Fire and water were opposites. Were they not? Whilst she knew little of science, her every instinct told her this was the correct combination.

"Well done, Eliza," he said. "My element is indeed fire. Fire, the most powerful element of all. Nothing, not even stone, can stand up to fire. Fire is the destroyer of all."

Eliza was silent. Her father sounded absolute. Yet, a little worm of doubt wiggled in her brain. Fire was powerful, there was no denying it. Fire did destroy. It was deadly. But did water not extinguish fire? Did that not make water the most powerful? Then she relaxed as the answer came to her. The elements must be equal. Otherwise the world would have been a living hell. Wind could fan a flame. The earth could disgorge lava. Water flooded land. And so on and so forth.

Clearly, though, her father did not wish it to be so. It would be wise to keep her thoughts to herself. "Fire is a mighty force," she said.

His whole demeanour changed. He leaned in towards her, his eyes burning with a fanatical flame. "Eliza, together we can be mightier still!"

Eliza was struck by an observation. "Papa, if the fusion of two elements can magnify power, what about more? Would not the fusion of all four be the optimal outcome?" The look on her father's face warned her she had said the wrong thing. But not even magic could unsay words, so she waited on tenterhooks.

He turned from her, pacing up and down. "There is some truth in what you say," he said finally. "But in the same way that fire is the superior element, it is still limited – or advanced – by the wielder's power."

This was true. Fanny had said as much. Eliza wavered. Clearly her father's confidence in his own abilities was absolute. What if her own ability turned out to be inferior? What would that mean? Would it mean that her hopes of aiding Oddie would be diminished?

Her father stopped at the fireplace, his fingers tapping angrily on the mantel. "Take the hedgewitch," he snapped. "Any potential she may have is strangulated by ignorance. She is well suited to her role, treating the rabble in the sinks and bogs."

That he spoke of Fanny, Eliza had no doubts. His tone discouraged any further discussion. But Eliza wasn't convinced. Even her father had inadvertently acknowledged that Fanny had 'potential'. To divert her father from the subject, Eliza turned to a point on which she was curious. "Father, is there anyone that you know of who wields the power of air?"

Her father was duly distracted. He turned and chuckled. "Indeed, I do." He went back to his desk and spent an infuriating amount of time lighting a cigar. Shrouded in smoke, he looked at Eliza. "As a matter of fact, you too are well acquainted with this individual," he said silkily.

For one heart-stopping moment, Eliza thought that he was referring to Lord Pelham. It would be too dreadful to be born! She felt physically ill.

Perhaps her father guessed her thoughts, for he smirked. "Let me give you a hint. You have met him in the cathedral."

Relief suffused her. Thank God! Not him. But who had she met in the cathedral and nowhere else? She racked her brains. Could it be one of the clergy? No. She'd encountered all of them elsewhere. The same went for the congregation. Unless her father meant one of the many poor parishioners. It seemed unlikely. Her father's disdain of the lowlier members of the community seemed to negate the idea. But, for the life of her, she could think of no one else. Except… no… it was ludicrous.

She shrugged. "I'm sorry, Papa. I cannot think of any noteworthy person that I have encountered only within the confines of the cathedral."

He lifted a sardonic eyebrow. "He would be disappointed. The pair of you seemed to be on quite intimate terms only the other day. I recall that he amused you immensely."

She could recall the incident very clearly. Yet, still she was loath to put it into words. "Papa, I think I know to whom you refer. But I fear to speak lest I be labelled an hysterical woman."

Her father removed his cigar from his lips, puffing out three beautiful smoke rings. "Then let me set your mind to rest. It is the Lincoln Imp."

The words set her heart racing. She wasn't mad at all! It had been real. That impudent imp had really spoken. "How is this possible?"

"Oh, he always was an impudent fellow. A wilful, arrogant fool. And a dangerous one. He meddled in magic that should not be meddled with. Three combined to seal him in stone, to put an end to his meddling."

To Eliza it seemed a cruel fate. "But, will he never be free?"

"I doubt it."

Doubt. Not a negative then. Interesting. "So he could be freed?"

Her father tapped ash into a marble pestle. "No," he said. He didn't wait for a reply. Instead he reached across the desk and picked up an ancient tomb, setting it before Eliza.

He had lied. Eliza just knew it. But she let it go. For now. Best play dumb. "Poor Imp," she said sadly.

Her father rolled his eyes. As if to say, "Women!" Then he opened the book. "Read this."

Eliza looked down, eager to see what sorcery it held. She blanched. Not magic. Biology. Diagrams of a human heart. Oh God!

Her father eyed her, clearly amused. "Heart surgery. Better get busy." He stacked four more texts, pages open, before her. "Mug up on these incantations and spells. I'll be back in a couple of hours to check on your progress." And, without waiting for a response, he left.

Black spots dancing before her eyes, Eliza gripped the edge of the desk. She forced herself to be calm, taking deep breaths. Oddie was depending on her. When the room stopped spinning she pulled the book close. Best be detached. The heart. Four chambers. Four valves. Blood in. Blood out. It actually made sense.

She pulled her hair into a knot and took a deep breath. She was scared. She was furious. But most of all, she was determined. Oddie was not going to die.

49

When they came for him, Oddie didn't want to go. Maybe it was the thirst. Maybe it was the cold. Maybe it was the pain. Or maybe he'd succumbed to madness. Whatever the reason, he resisted with all the fury of a baited bull.

The governor watched from the doorway as Pelham tried to drag his resisting body from its rude bed. Pelham's hands on his person disgusted Oddie. Those same hands that had ravished Eliza! Oddie was in no mood for niceties. When the lord's fingers came into range he whipped his head forward and sunk in his teeth. God, it felt good! Flesh exploding, blood spurting and bones breaking. Shame it wasn't the pervert's heart.

And how that servile serpent screamed. Worse than a vixen in heat. Oddie could have listened forever. Oddie clamped down, shaking his head violently. Pelham's screams reached a satisfying crescendo. The governor stared down, apparently unmoved. Disappointing.

The governor shook his head, pulled a stick from his pocket and began to sing. Or maybe chant would have been a better word. It made no sense to Oddie. It was some foreign gibberish. But then he watched in disbelief as a jet of sparks spewed out of the end of the cane, spiralling towards him. Fire flew at his face, burning his lips and scorching his tongue. He released Pelham.

Shocked, he stared up at his tormentor. Even if he could have spoken he would not have known what to say. Somehow, he'd known that this moment was approaching. Fan had warned him. And here it was. This man that he had once respected, was finally revealed. The governor was in league with the devil. He could wield the fires of hell.

Then the burning stopped. The sparks floated away like fire fairies. And died. Unfortunately, Oddie observed, Pelham hadn't. He was still howling like a scalded cat, holding his injured hand against his puny chest.

The governor snapped his head around. "Shut up, you imbecile!"

Oddie was grimly amused.

Pelham's eyes goggled. His petulant mouth opened but then shut again. Apparently he wasn't idiot enough to take his master to task.

The governor reapplied himself to Oddie. "Mr Odling," he said, in a smooth tone, "there are two ways we can proceed. There is the easy way. And then there is the hard way. It makes no odds to myself. The end result will be the same."

Oddie took a while to digest this indigestible nugget of wisdom. The governor's words were undeniably, depressingly believable. Was there really any point in further resistance? Antagonising his torturers wasn't going to endear him to them. Perhaps he should play along for a while. Save his strength. Accept his fate.

But his spirit rebelled at the thought. Did a fish stop fighting on the end of a line? Did a deer lay down for an arrow? No. It wasn't nature's way. The governor was a demon and Oddie was damned if he was going to aid and abet in his own destruction.

He looked up at the governor, shaking his head.

The governor's cool façade cracked. He leaned over until his breath broke on Oddie's brow. "I can always find another stoker," he whispered. "Fen scum are two a penny."

Oddie didn't dare blink.

"But," continued the governor, "that would be a waste of my time. So, have it your own way." He stood up and snapped his fingers at Pelham. "Bring her here." He chuckled. "She may have no interest in the stoker, but he has plenty in her. Let's see just how much, shall we?"

Pelham snivelled, but looked mollified as he shuffled across the cell.

Oddie was distraught. It seemed the governor's potential for cruelty was limitless. He would happily hurt his own child to get his way. Oddie opened his mouth but no words came out. He lifted a hand, rapping loudly on the pipe. The governor glanced over. Oddie nodded.

"Lord Pelham," said the governor, "cancel that last. It seems we have the stoker's full cooperation after all."

Oddie sagged back. He was exhausted. The effort had cost him dear. A fact that did not fill him with confidence for the future. It was true, he was expendable. A horrible thought flitted across his mind. Was Eliza expendable too? Surely not. He didn't think he could bear to witness her suffering. But of course he must. What other choice did he have?

Pelham came back and jerked Oddie out of his rough cot. The pain was indescribable. It consumed him. As he slid over the stone lip of the ledge he blacked out.

When he awoke he wished he hadn't. He stared up at tiers of seats and knew where he was. The surgery. Beneath him the metal bed was as cold and unforgiving as the steel from which it was wrought. His body was anchored to it by bonds that were welded to the table. Despite his determination, he was scared nearly witless. This was beyond any fate he had ever imagined. Even the prospect of seeing Eliza again could not subdue the tide of primeval terror rising inside him.

Reason flew out the distant window. He had to get away. He tensed, straining with all his might, chest swelling and biceps contracting. Sweat burst out of his skin. His mouth opened in a silent scream. A phantom heel on a phantom leg levered against the slippery surface. But it was in vain. There was not an ounce of give. Not so much as a turn of a screw or a stretch of a link. Not a hint of weakness. Except within himself.

When his strength gave, he lay on the slab like a dumb beast. A gasping, pathetic, bleeding piece of meat. And suddenly he thought of the climbing boy. What must that child have suffered? A stunted, twisted and weak child at that. Alone and unloved. Now Oddie understood why he had wailed. If he'd had a voice he'd wail too. But the thought bought him comfort. Gave him strength. That pitiful child had survived. If that pathetic scrap of humanity had clung to life, so then could he. He owed it to the lad.

Footsteps clicked over the hardwood floor. They were coming. Oddie began shaking. He didn't want to, but he couldn't help it. Maybe it was because he was so dry. If he could just have a drink. Just a cupful, he'd do better. Be braver. Stronger. He wondered then what he was wanting to be stronger for. The governor hadn't been very clear on the subject. It was all very vague. Eliza had called it a 'procedure'. Which wasn't terribly helpful either. All he had to go on was the monstrous abuse of the little dog and the boy. And of course, there was his father's watch.

For the first time, it occurred to Oddie that his father may have suffered a similar fate. But he pushed that away. He couldn't bear to think of it. Not now. When it was all over, then he'd think about it. And then… well… he didn't know. Best not to think too much. The footsteps clacked closer. Best just pray. He closed his eyes and began the Lord's Prayer. It was all he could remember in this dark hour.

Then a soft, cool hand closed around his arm. Even before he painfully opened his eyes, he knew it was her. Her scent washed over him. Her hair was pulled up into a severe bun, and her face was pinched and pale. But her eyes were as blue as the Fen sky. She did not speak for a long moment. Then she removed her hand as her father stood beside her.

"He is as dry as a date!" she snapped.

The governor looked unimpressed. "It hardly matters."

Eliza's bosom swelled beneath her blue nightgown. "I disagree!"

Oddie was stunned. There was something different about Eliza. She'd always been sassy, but now there was another element. It was a kind of... confidence. She reminded him of someone, but he couldn't think who.

"Eliza, you must trust in my superior knowledge."

Eliza turned to her father with an imperious air. "Your knowledge is centred around the element of fire, is it not?"

The governor eyed her curiously for an instant and then nodded curtly.

Eliza flicked a hand at him dismissively. "My element is water. Therefore, I am the expert in this case, and I say he is too dry to work with."

The governor looked like he wanted to protest. Indeed, Oddie thought he was going to. But he tutted, turned on his heel and clicked away.

Immediately, Eliza grasped his hand. "Oddie, it's going to be alright. I promise, my love," she whispered. Then she snatched back her hand as her father stalked back.

The governor held a jug in one hand and a glass in the other. It smelled like heaven. Oddie craned his head up anxiously. Eliza reached for the glass, but the governor, ignoring her, moved to Oddie's head. Seconds later he placed the glass to Oddie's lips. Oddie swallowed frantically. When the last drop was gone, the governor moved away.

"That's not enough," said Eliza. "He must have more."

Oddie had always loved her but now he worshipped her. He looked up, hoping that she could read it in his eyes. In the curve of his mouth. In the pores of his skin. Just having her close made him feel like a person again, his sense of isolation easing. Eliza was with him. Eliza was on his side.

Eliza loved him.

50

At the fifth cup of water her father lost patience. "Enough!" Eliza did not argue. Best not push her luck. The jug was nearly empty. It would help. At least the worst ravages of Oddie's thirst would be assuaged.

"Eliza, come!"

She jumped at her father's command, even though she knew what was expected of her. Her nerves felt exposed to the elements. But perhaps that was how it should be. After all, she was water. It was liberating in its way. Terrifying. But liberating. Within her dwelt a power undreamt. She did not doubt it. But, despite her father's reassurances, she doubted her ability to wield it. If only her initiation were anything other than this. The consequences of failure were too dreadful to contemplate. It took every ounce of willpower not to break down and beg her father to spare Oddie. But the risk was too great.

Like a puppet, she carried out her instructions. She moved slowly, afraid of error and afraid of revealing her inner angst. It was ghastly to handle the shiny array of surgeon's tools. The knowledge that the rows of blades, forceps and saws would slice unmercifully through her beloved's flesh shrivelled her soul. It was a living nightmare. How she would live with the knowledge of her actions, she could not imagine. Yet, if she didn't proceed, then Oddie's hope of survival was dramatically reduced. Ultimately, it was the best choice of a bad bunch.

There had been one positive. She couldn't bear to see Oddie so distressed. Even without her sixth sense, his condition was abysmal. She had been scared witless when she'd confronted her father. The outcome had been unexpected. And welcome. Clearly, her father was not the font of all knowledge that he professed to be. This, she decided, was a two-edged sword. On the one hand, she had discovered a weakness. On the other, Oddie might pay the price.

Her father placed a roll of silk thread beside a row of needles. "It is time," he said. "Are you prepared?"

Of course not, she wanted to shriek. Instead, she nodded. "Yes, Papa."

Footsteps alerted her. She turned, glaring contemptuously at Pelham. He too had his part. But clearly he was not happy. Eliza rejoiced in his discomfort. She turned her back on him and marched to the surgical table. Oddie's eyes followed her every move. The only sign of his fear was a tremor in his remaining leg. It broke her heart.

Aware that her father and Pelham were engrossed in whispered conversation, she smiled at Oddie and blew him a kiss. He grinned up at her, and he was transformed. Once more he was the most lusted-after lad in Lincolnshire.

Then her father moved around to the opposite side of the table. Oddie's gaze didn't falter. He held her in his sights as a lighthouse drew a ship safely to the shore. It steadied her. Anchored her. His trust gave her strength.

Even when Pelham stood beside her with the clock in his hands, she did not waver. She understood its significance perfectly. Indeed, there was a logic to the usage of the timepiece. Her father was convinced that part of the problem lay with the pocket-sized watches he had thus far utilised. Bigger was infinitely better. This was a large clock and of superior quality. All to the good. With luck.

Then it began. Her father's voice lifted, incanting an ancient spell. Eliza felt the atmosphere shift subtly. It was as if the very air had awoken. The room grew warmer. It was harder to breathe. The incantation insinuated itself into her mind. And Eliza welcomed it, for it resonated inside her like a familiar tune. She concentrated with all her might. She must not miss the moment.

Strapped and defenceless upon the steel table, Leon Odling gazed up into her face. His breathing accelerated and his hands clenched. Then his eyes flickered. And the lids drooped. A minute later they were closed. Relief infused her. It was as her father had foretold. He slept. Pray to God that he did not wake.

Still chanting, her father held out a hand to Pelham. The lord passed him a fine scalpel. Eliza didn't want to watch, but she could not draw her gaze away. The blade sliced cleanly through skin and flesh. In a blink of an eye, her father held a serrated saw. He brutally severed the sternum. Pelham leaned in and forced the bone apart with a pair of ratcheted forceps. And the heart was exposed.

Eliza felt faint. Not at the sight but at the full magnitude of what was happening. She gripped the steel table, fighting down nausea. It was not just the butchery that distressed her; it was the unimaginable effect it would have on the man she loved. Perspiration burst out over her body, her gown clinging to her breasts and back. The room was now hot as hell. Which seemed somehow appropriate.

Her knees turned to jelly as her father inserted a silver knife, slicing around the beating muscle. Blood fountained, soaking them all. Eliza parted her lips and tasted the metallic fluid in the air. This was her love! This was his life! She did not know that she could bear much more.

And then the heart was gone, leaving a livid space. Oddie stopped breathing. His life spent. A carcass. Eliza prayed for his soul. She prayed that his suffering be at an end. She prayed that he'd come back to her. She prayed for the strength to make it happen.

Her father's voice expanded, filling the surgery. And, with sleight of hand, it was done. The clock lay snug in the warm cavity of Oddie's broad chest. Needle and catgut flew. Flesh met flesh in a rude, jagged line. She looked expectantly at her father, but he was oblivious. She turned to Pelham, to find his hands full. He held a long, slender metal rod, intricately riven with springs and levers. One end was clawed. What was it? And then it became clear. It was a limb. A leg. Of course. For what good was a one-legged slave?

The object was rudely inserted by means of a screw. Sickened, Eliza turned away. It did no good to distress herself further. She must stay calm for what must be done. Eliza felt a growing sense of urgency. But could not say why. What was it? Perhaps it was exhaustion. Or stress? No. That wasn't it. Something swam on the peripheries of her mind. She forced herself to focus. And found the answer. Time. Time was running out.

She turned and picked up a willow wand that lay beside the surgical tools. It had no magical property; her father had assured her. It was purely a prop to help her channel the force. She had practised feverishly and proficiently performed simple spells. Her father had told her she was ready. And she believed him.

Still, her hand trembled. "Papa, we must begin!" she said. Both men paused in their grizzly work and looked at her. Almost, she thought, as if they had forgotten her.

Her father pushed Pelham out of the way and drew his hazel wand from his pocket. He pointed it at Oddie's mutilated body. His voice was hoarse as he cast his spell. Perhaps her father was not as confident as he professed. Then a red spark emitted from the wand. It was the signal Eliza had been waiting for. It was time. She spiralled down into the dark side of her mind and found the source.

With every ounce of strength that she possessed she summoned her element. And water answered.

In a great geyser, her wand spilled water into the air. It met the sparks and sizzled. The sparks ignited into flame. Fire and water coalesced in a hissing, roaring explosion. And there was steam. Oddie's corpse was enveloped in a boiling, roiling silver haze. Her father's voice fell silent. Eliza's wand slipped from her hand. She staggered but gripped the edge of the table. The mist swirled, shifted and evaporated. Anguished, Eliza waited.

Finally, Oddie's body emerged. The fearful wound no more than a livid scar. His battered body lay still. But his chest slowly rose and fell. Eliza held herself silent but inside she exulted.

Leon Odling lived!

51

Oddie was awoken by the persistent, rhythmic tick-tock of a clock. He listened, waiting for the alarm's strident voice to summon him from his warm bed. He tried to recall whether or not the mill's siren had blared. But he couldn't be sure. Not that it mattered, it was time to rise and shine.

He stretched and wished he hadn't as an exquisite pain seared through his chest. Without thinking he put his hands to the source of his discomfort. He breathed, nostrils flaring at the scent of burnt meat. Fanny must have burned the sausages. Beneath his fingertips he encountered a ridge of proud flesh. His eyes opened wide and reality reasserted itself. Christ alive! What had they done?

Air whistled through his dry lips. His fear accelerated apace with the loud tick-tock of the clock. His hand trembled as he pressed it to his chest. The pain was almost welcome. Proved he was alive. Tick. Tock. Tick. Tock.

It was impossible. But he knew it to be true. Fantastical and frightening. Weird but oddly wonderful. Inhuman. Unholy. Unimaginable. There weren't really the words. How could there be? He didn't know what to feel. Perhaps he couldn't. Perhaps he had no feeling left. Now he had no heart.

A whisper of silk caught his ear. Soft footsteps. A cool, gentle touch. A pair of bonny blue eyes.

"Eliza!" But the words were in his head. His tongue was swollen, sticking to the roof of his mouth.

Eliza bent over him, her mouth trembling. "Hush, my love. Save your strength. All is well. You will soon be yourself again."

For a moment, her lips alighted like a butterfly upon his brow. Soft and sweet. But then flew away. Oddie watched in mute dismay as Eliza abruptly retreated. Understanding swiftly followed as footsteps rang out. Someone had come. Oddie tried to see but the movement made him lightheaded. He closed his eyes. He was so weak.

A malapert finger inserted itself under his eyelid, prising his eye open. The governor swam into sight. Then hands prodded and poked his person. It wasn't the pain so much as the indignity of it. Angry and humiliated, Oddie could do nothing but seethe silently. He vowed that when he was back on his feet the governor was going to be sorry.

And that reminded him. Feet. Plural. When he had last been awake he'd had only one foot. One leg. One limb. The wound had been bleeding. A raw stump. Had they cauterised it? Was that what he could smell? He reached down, fumbling around his thigh. Nothing made sense. His hands pressed around something hard and cold. His fingers followed, sliding down and then up a shaft of metal. Oddie tried to make sense of it. His hand was reefed away.

"The artificial limb seems to have taken," said the governor.

"Yes, Papa."

Oddie was stunned. Artificial limb? What in God's name was that? Artificial? Was that possible? Could a leg be formed from metal? But he knew the answer almost before the question had formed. Naturally it was possible. Or maybe unnaturally was more the case. After all, he had a clock for a heart! The poor climbing boy had lamps for eyes. A limb of steel was probably child's play.

Question was, would it work? Of course, there was only one way to find out. With a silent prayer on his lips, Oddie tensed and wiggled his toes. The left toes obliged. The right did not. But he didn't panic. Not yet. After all, he might not have anything toe-like. He gathered his wits and tried to visualise the lost leg. He imagined bending his knee. This time his effort was rewarded. This time he had a sensation of movement. Without being able to see, he couldn't gauge what he'd achieved. But the metal contraption was a reality.

Oddie felt a twinge of hope. The loss of his leg had devastated him. Now it seemed that he had grown a new one. Well, not grown exactly. More… magicked one. Which was insane. But there was no other explanation. He tried to imagine what it looked like. What he looked like. The image that he conjured was ludicrous. Laughable.

A great bubble of hilarity collected in his chest. It blossomed, bursting out in a muted guffaw of laughter. Paroxysms of uncontrollable mirth cracked into the surgery. The governor stared down at Oddie with a look of disbelief. Which only served to fuel Oddie's amusement.

Eliza stepped closer. "Oddie, stop!"

But he couldn't. It was all just too ridiculous for words. He was a mechanical man. Who'd have thought? Not him. Not ever. Only Fan would listen and nod her wise head. Fan had tried to tell him, but he hadn't listened. But he'd bet his peg leg that Fan wouldn't have seen this coming. No one could. Not in their wildest dreams.

A hand gripped his. Hard. He was surprised. Who'd have thought there was such strength in Eliza?

"Oddie, stop. Please!"

Something in her tone set Oddie aback. She sounded concerned. Frightened, almost. He tried to rein in his emotions. He didn't want to upset Eliza any more than she was upset already. To his dismay, he found he couldn't. More than that, he felt like he was being swept up by an uncontrollable force.

Alarmed, he closed his mouth and tried to swallow his mirth. For an instance he succeeded. Then he felt a pool of heat gathering deep in his belly. It pulsated and writhed, warmth radiating, as if a furnace had been lit. Then, it began to rise.

Oddie felt it travelling through his flesh and bones. Up, up, up it came. Into his chest. Into his throat. Then into his mouth. The heat was unbearable. His mouth opened. A great gust of steam billowed out. Hot. Hot. Hot. It met cold air and fogged around him.

Oddie stared. Too shocked to speak. What the hell? How did that happen? It was scalding-hot. His shock turned to horror. Where was Eliza? Was she alright? Please, please God, let her be alright.

Then the mist melted away. He tried to sit up but found he couldn't move a muscle. His body ached as if he'd been stoking a hundred fires for a hundred years. Then Eliza bent over him. Oddie's eyes raked over her, afraid of what he might see. But her complexion seemed unblemished. Pale, and a little dirty, perhaps, but untouched.

He closed his eyes. Utterly wrung out. A terrible thirst gripped him. And, almost as if she had read his mind, Eliza proffered a cup. He lifted his head. With Eliza's support, Oddie managed to drink. The effects were immediate. And dramatic. With each swallow, his body revived. By the time the cup was empty, Oddie felt almost human.

He looked up at Eliza. "Please, more."

Without a word, she turned away. Tap, tap over the flagstone floor. Then quiet. Then back once more. Eliza, cup in hand, smiled down at him. This time, Oddie was able to appreciate the experience. The delicious sensation of Eliza's fingers nestling in his hair. Her delicate scent. The tender expression on her face.

But the cup was empty all too soon. Eliza lowered his head gently to the table and moved away. He closed his eyes as waves of exhaustion swept through him.

He didn't want to sleep. He didn't want to lose sight of Eliza. He was scared that if he slept, on awakening, she would be gone. Gone, never to return. And that was unbearable. But in the end, fight though he did, it was not a choice. Sleep took him anyway.

52

It was almost a relief to see Oddie slip into unconsciousness. Eliza was shocked by his appearance. Despite the 'success' of the procedure, he looked desperately ill. He had shed so much weight his ribs looked like a washboard. And his eyes were sunken and dull. But more than that, was an instinctive knowledge of unbalance within. As with the burned climbing boy, Eliza was filled with a desperate need to succour. But this time she had no idea what to do.

She turned to her father, trying to decide how to best word her thoughts. Whilst he seemed blind to her passion for his stoker, Eliza knew Pelham was not. Everything she did and said must be carefully weighed. It would be unbearable to betray herself.

To gain a moment, she took the cup back to the bench and made a show of tidying up. Then she smoothed down the front of her gown and re-tied her hair.

"Eliza."

She turned and looked at her father. "Yes, Papa?"

"You have done well."

She was cross with herself for the flush of pleasure his words created. The reasons for this were many and contradictory. First, she had never expected to gain her father's respect. Nor his approval. Something, that in retrospect, she realised she had sought all her life. And now it had arrived, it was bittersweet. For those words had been hard won. Not so much by herself as by the man she loved.

She managed a prim smile. "Thank you, Papa. I believe that I have been tutored by the best."

Her father smiled back. "You are too kind."

Eliza smothered a snort of derision. Her father was patronising her. How infuriating. She bowed her head to hide her anger, in a mock show of humility. After all, two could play at that game.

"My dear, you must be exhausted. Lord Pelham awaits in the study to escort you home."

Eliza was horrified. She couldn't leave Oddie. Not like this. Could her father not see that his life hung by the finest of threads? Leon Odling was a young, strong man but he had endured more than any man had ever had to endure. Shock may still cause him to fail. She must convey this to her father, but not in a way to arouse suspicion.

She laughed, a tiny tinkle of ladylike titillation. "Oh, Papa, I am not the least bit tired! Please, I beg you, let me stay a while longer, for I am loath to miss even a moment of this grand adventure!"

He tutted, shaking a forefinger at her, as he often had when she was a child. "Now, Eliza, whilst I am delighted by your enthusiasm, I fear that you overestimate yourself. You will overtax your delicate constitution."

Delicate constitution be damned! But what could she do? If she were to protest too loudly it may only serve to undermine her own position. It was critical that her father did not suspect that his daughter was anything other than the dizzy little lady that he desired her to be. But she still had to say something.

She bobbed a demure curtsey. "Papa, you are quite right. But, I am concerned for you. The stoker will need careful observation and care. How will you ever rest?"

Her father turned to stare at Oddie. "Don't worry your pretty little head on my account," he said. "It is all in hand. When you go to the study, please tell Lord Pelham to bring our guest down before he leaves."

Eliza waited, expecting her father to enlarge upon his last statement. But nothing more followed. Realising that there was nothing more she could do, Eliza reluctantly took her leave. It took every ounce of strength she possessed not to look back.

She shut the door of the surgery, sagging back against it. Her body shook as if she had an ague. It was delayed shock, she knew. Hardly surprising but unwelcome all the same. She couldn't allow Pelham to see any signs of weakness. Once she was home and safe in her room, then she could let herself go. Eliza metaphorically steeled her spine. The sooner she faced the pernicious Pelham, the sooner she could leave. And the sooner she could return.

And if she were honest, she was more than a little curious as to the identity of the 'guest'. Who else could be privy to her father's insane necromancy? Rack her brains as she might, no one came to mind.

Eliza set off through the passages, hurried up the stairs and into the hallway. All was quiet. Gas lamps flared bright, lighting up the space like day. She squared her shoulders, smoothed her nightgown and moved to the closed door of the study. Without pause, she flung the heavy door open and marched inside.

To her delight, she caught Pelham with his sticky little hands in her father's desk. His pasty face flushed to the unbecoming scarlet of a boiled lobster. The drawer slammed shut and he gave her a dirty look.

Eliza pretended not to notice. A quick glance around the room revealed that the lord was alone. Perhaps the person in question was waiting on the front steps, cap in hand. "Father requests that you take his guest down to the surgery. Now."

A sly smile slid over Pelham's face. "Indeed. But I think an introduction might be in order, before I go."

Eliza shrugged. "If you insist."

"Oh, I do."

Eliza waited for him to take his leave, but he reached down behind the desk instead. When he stood up he held a heavy wicker basket in his hand. The kind usually associated with picnics. "I'm not hungry," she said.

He ignored her and placed the hamper on the desk. He flicked open the buckles. Then, with a flourish, he whipped the lid open, dove his hand in and pulled out a rabbit. Held unkindly by its long ears, the poor creature kicked and jerked frantically.

Eliza stared in astonishment. What was this? Was he trying to impress her with conjuring tricks? Did he really think that his cruel handling of the poor creature would warm her to him?

"Put it back!" she cried. "At once. For pity's sake, let it go or put it out of its misery. It may only be a rabbit, but it is one of God's creatures."

Pelham giggled. "A rabbit? I think not. Look again, Eliza."

And of course, on closer inspection, he was right. It wasn't a rabbit. It was a hare. "Rabbit. Hare. What difference?" she snapped.

Pelham swung the hare like a pendulum. The poor creature gave a high-pitched squeal of distress.

Despite her determination to reign in her emotions, Eliza's eyes welled up and tears fell. "Please, put it down."

He lifted the hare and bought it around until its tiny nose was almost touching his own. "What say you, Fanny?" he said. "Shall we put you down?"

Eliza felt her grip on reality slip. What was this new mischief? Was he insane? Perhaps he often held conversation with hares in private. It was not entirely out of the question. Lord Pelham was a seriously creepy man. "You're mad!"

As if to underscore her words, he laughed, drawing the animal closer. Eliza watched in disgust as his tongue slid out of his mouth and insinuated itself into the hare's furry neck. The hare exploded.

Legs raking at his chest. Teeth snapping. Body bucking. Actions that Eliza fully understood and respected. Pelham's tongue on her neck would have elicited the self-same response.

Disgusted, she ran forward, leapt on the desk and plucked the hare from Pelham's hands. He swore profoundly and snatched back. He missed, swiping at the air. Then he came for her around the desk. Eliza backed away towards the door, determined to get outside and free the animal.

But she had misjudged the man. Contorted with rage, Pelham grabbed an armchair and flung it full at her. She scurried back, tripped on her hem and fell. With a cry of dismay, the hare slipped from her grasp.

Eliza lay, eyes wide, as she watched the hare huddle on the rug. Then, before she could say 'abracadabra' it was gone. In its place stood a woman. But it was not just any woman. Naked, and defiant, it was Fan o' the Fens.

53

Eliza stared. Pelham stared. Fanny Flowers seemed the only one present unperturbed. She smiled at Eliza.

"Miss Elvidge, how do you do?"

Eliza scrambled to her feet and curtsied. "The better for seeing you, Miss Flowers." It was true. Fanny Flowers was like a marigold in a midden. Then, aware that Pelham was ogling Fanny in a most ungentlemanly manner, Eliza slipped off her dressing gown and held it out to Fanny. Left in her chemise, Eliza felt almost as naked. She crossed her arms over her breasts, even though they were not the least visible. Pelham just had that effect.

With a swirl of silk, Fanny enveloped her shapely form in the wrap. She tied the waist ribbon firmly, flicking her luscious dark hair free. "I thank you, Miss Elvidge."

Taller than Eliza, the gown fell to only mid-calf on Fanny. Her ankles were exposed. Eliza stared in dismay at the woman's right ankle. "Why, Fanny, you are hurt!"

Fanny glanced down. "Ah, yes. Lord Pelham has mastered the manly art of hare snares."

Eliza wished she'd had a gun. She'd have shot him there and then. "Fanny, this is a surprise meet," she said lightly. She tried to keep her expression bland. "Did you know that the stoker is here too?"

Fanny's lips set in a thin line. Her face turned white as chalk. She turned to Pelham. "Is this true?"

Pelham did not disguise his delight in Fanny's distress. "Oh dear, are we upset? What a shame. If I'd have realised that you were lusting like a bitch in heat for the stoker, I'd have saved myself all the trouble of snaring you."

Fanny laughed. "No, you wouldn't, you weasel. You are a twisted man. Others' pain gives you pleasure. It is a well-known fact on the Fens." She turned to Eliza. "Keep far from this one, Eliza. He will use you ill."

The wise woman's words came as no surprise. Bluntly put though they were, they served to underscore Eliza's own suspicions. But having her fears made a reality did not help. Oddie was in mortal peril. And instinctively she knew that if anyone could help, it was Fanny.

As she faced Fanny, Eliza wondered how she could communicate all that had happened without compounding the complexities of the situation. She did not wish for Pelham to be privy to her friendship with Fanny. If only out of sheer perversity. Also, there may be still some advantage to be gained from his ignorance. On the other hand, Eliza had to reveal her own part. But how?

"Miss Flowers, I have done something terrible," she said.

Fanny's face softened. "Tell me and let me be the judge."

"Miss Flowers, I have aided my father in the darkest of arts." Behind her, Lord Pelham drew in a sharp breath. Eliza rushed on, afraid he may object or intervene. "Below lies the stoker, grievously ill. I fear for his… life." Eliza did not say that which she wanted to say. That she also feared for Leon Odling's soul.

Fanny was silent for a long time, her dark eyes searching Eliza's, as if she could read in them some profound truth. Finally, she sighed and turned to Pelham. "You must take me to the stoker."

She turned to Eliza. "Go and rest. Sleep and eat. When you are recovered, you must return. Bring with you water from the well beneath the church wall."

Eliza felt giddy with relief. Fanny was a healer of great renown. Only now did Eliza understand the depths of her knowledge. And the depths of her love for Oddie. Without a doubt, Fanny would stop at nothing to heal him. Strangely, Eliza felt not a jot of jealousy. It mattered not who Oddie loved. Or who loved him. At this stage, Eliza would have welcomed a coven of smitten witches if they could have helped.

"Thank you, Miss Flowers," said Eliza. "I will do as you bid."

Fanny reached out, taking Eliza's hand. "Do not be too hard on yourself, Miss Eliza. The future is not written. Things may still be well." Fanny turned back to the lord. "You will take me to the patient and then go to my home and collect my herb box and suitable attire."

Pelham looked peeved. "You are my prisoner, Flowers. I'll be the one giving out the orders!"

Fanny sniffed. "Lord Pelham, I do believe you are fearfully pale. Are you unwell? Perhaps your stomach ails you?"

Pelham looked as if he would have liked to slap Fanny. Alarmed, Eliza stepped forward but halted as Pelham groaned and clutched his belly. He doubled over, dry retching. Filled with awe and not a little satisfaction, Eliza watched as the cowardly man's mouth opened to expel a bundle of fluff. Although, on closer observation, Eliza realised it wasn't fluff. It was fur. Hair of a hare.

He choked, coughing and heaving with such violence that Eliza almost had reason to believe he may expire. Sadly, her hopes were extinguished when the lord spat out another clump and took a deep breath.

"Better?" said Fanny solicitously.

Pelham gave her a look to kill, but wisely remained mute. He jerked his head towards the door and stalked out. With a tiny smile on her lips, Fanny sailed after him. The door shut, leaving Eliza alone. She shivered and looked around the room for something to put on. It would be bitterly cold outside, and she loathed the idea of being near Pelham in a state of undress.

Thankfully, one of her father's shooting jackets hung over the back of the chair behind the desk. Gratefully she plucked it free and put it on. The arms hung to her knees and the hem to her ankles but she cared not. It was deliciously warm. The wool coat emitted the familiar scents of her father. And Eliza felt a wave of grief as she realised that the smoky smell no longer elicited feelings of comfort and love. All affection and respect had been replaced with repugnance and fear. Her father was lost to her as surely as if he lay in the graveyard.

The door swung violently open and Pelham swept back in. A tiny ball of fur clung to his chin and Eliza decided it was best left alone. Indeed, it made her feel closer to Fanny. She felt braver for it.

"Eliza," he said in that pompous tone that so irritated, "I will escort you home. On no account are you to leave the premises. I will return when your father commands. You will remain in the company of your maid and the butler will instruct any visitors that you are indisposed."

His words did not dismay her. Quite the contrary, the mention of Mary reassured her that the maid was well. Her heart lifted at the thought of being reunited. And as for receiving guests, she had no desire for company. Indeed, she felt as if she were unfit for society. The idea of sitting and making inane conversation about bonnets and balls seemed ridiculous. That world was gone.

Without a word she crossed the room, making a wide path around Pelham. He hurried after her, almost treading on her heels. She snapped the door open and hurried down the corridor. Outside, it was dark. Clouds hung low, spitting rain. Wind buffeted the brick façade of the mill, chafing across the canal. The carriage was waiting in the lee of the mill. At sight of them the driver clicked the horses on.

When it paused, horses chomping at their bits, manes flying in the wind, the postillion jumped down. He bowed and opened the door. Ignoring Pelham's proffered hand, she leapt up the steps. Inside, she planted herself in the centre of the seat, hoping it would prompt her unsavoury escort to sit opposite.

It did. But it was a small consolation. Once the door shut and the carriage rolled away, Pelham licked his lips and leant towards her. "When we are wed, I will have to teach you some manners."

Eliza borrowed Fanny's snort. "I will never be wed to you. You have no power over me."

His lip curled as he reached inside his coat pocket and pulled out a key. "Do you know what this is?"

She did not deign to answer.

Pelham pretended not to notice her defiance and swung the silver key back and forth. "This, my dear, is a key, which is wed to your stoker's new heart."

Eliza started and sat up. He had her full attention.

He giggled and put the key away. "I mean that in a most literal fashion. If he survives, his life will be forever enslaved to said key."

Eliza felt sick. She sensed what was coming but was helpless to stop it.

Pelham reached out, placed his hand on her calf and slid it up beneath the hem of the coat.

With a gasp of horror Eliza reached down, grasping his wrist. Repulsed, she gathered herself to finish what Fanny had started.

But he tutted and wiggled a finger in her face. His hand stilled but did not retreat. "If you do not agree to be my wife, I suspect that I may inadvertently lose that key. It is so very small."

And Eliza knew that she was bested. She did not doubt his words. She must submit to his will. For now. And, as his fingers slid up the tender skin of her thigh, Eliza closed her eyes. Hell was here.

54

Oddie was restless. He wasn't used to idleness. His body was twitching with tension. What he wanted was to walk. Or at least to try. Sleep had restored him to a degree. On waking he found himself, if not reconciled, then at least less terrified by the changes wrought upon him. The steel bed beneath him was unforgiving and cold. And he was heartily sick of staring up at the empty tiers of benches.

Once he stood up, he would be able to cast his eye over his body. Would reality be better or worse than anything imagined? Curiosity began to displace his anxiety. Methodically he worked through his muscles, flexing and relaxing each in turn from ears to toes. Everything seemed to work. Even the 'artificial' leg had become progressively more in tune with his thought process. Yet, he hesitated. Fear of falling strapped him to the bed as effectively as a chain.

He was parched. He tried to ignore it and think about Eliza. But he couldn't. He felt dry as bleached bone. His stomach made a noise like thunder. He was hungry too. Not as hungry as he was thirsty but famished all the same. He looked around the surgery as best he could from his prone position. Food seemed out of the question, but he was sure he could just see the lip of a stone jug.

He breathed in. It was water. It was tantalising. "Come on, Oddie, you idle swine," he muttered. With grim determination, he slid his elbows back and levered himself up. His head swam with the effort and he closed his eyes. Once his head floated back onto his shoulders he peered down.

"Oh, shit!" he said. Shock set his timepiece off. It tick-tocked frenetically inside him. He took several deep breaths and forced himself to continue. The steel leg was every bit as weird as he'd imagined. Strangely, as the first shockwaves settled, Oddie was filled with awe. The steel structure was almost a work of art. Shimmering and shiny, it was an intricate design of rods, cunning pulleys and springs. So delicate was the false limb that Oddie wondered if it would have enough strength to hold him.

But he consoled himself by recalling that many things that appeared fragile often possessed great strength. Like spider's webs and bees. And Eliza. Who would have ever suspected the power that lay within her? She who seemed as substantial as thistledown.

Oddie peeled his eyes away from the steel limb to inspect his other body parts. Thankfully he could detect no other interference. Mind you, he was skinnier than a stray cur. No wonder he was hungry. If he bent his neck to a painful angle, he could just see the top half of the scar mid his chest. His breath caught in his throat. What had they done with his heart? Was it buried or burned or pickled in a giant jar? To be honest, he wasn't sure he was ready to know. Not yet.

He licked his cracked lips and considered his next move. Slowly he looked around the room. It was exactly as he remembered it. It seemed like a lifetime since he'd been here last. How ironic that he lay on a steel bed of his own making.

Someone cleared their throat right behind him, nearly sending him into orbit. So quiet had it been, that Oddie had assumed he was alone. Although, in hindsight, this was probably foolish. Feet tapped around to the side of the steel slab. It was the governor. Oddie eyed him suspiciously but said nothing. Indeed, it was hard to know what to say. Seemed to him that words were superfluous at this stage.

"How are you?" said the governor.

"Thirsty."

"Mmm." The governor swept away to return immediately with a jug and cup. Water splashed and the cup was proffered.

Oddie gritted his teeth and pushed himself into a sitting position. Scared the governor may change his mind, he grabbed the cup and drank. Without a word, he held out the empty vessel. It was refilled. Rejuvenated, Oddie decided to push his luck. "I'm hungry."

But he was diverted as the door opened. Oddie watched, heart (or clock in his case) in mouth to see who would appear. Let it be Eliza! Let it be Eliza! Let it be Eliza! But it wasn't. Instead (almost), dressed in Eliza's pretty gown, was Fanny. Although he knew it was selfish, Oddie couldn't suppress a rush of joy. In the chaos that was his life, Fan was a link to his old self. Indeed, he'd known Fan… well… forever.

This last made Oddie pause for thought. As Fanny walked towards him, giving him the full benefit of her beautiful face, Oddie tried to recall how old Fanny was. He'd met her when he was a lad of eight. Yet, now he thought on it, Fanny had been a grown woman. Yet, to his eyes, she looked not a day older. How could that be?

Fanny stopped at the foot of the table. Silently she raked him up and down as if he were a horse at the market. When her dark, mocking eyes lingered on the bulge of his crotch he felt heat rise to his face. It had been a long time since someone had made him blush. Damn the woman. Yet, despite his discomfort, Oddie felt oddly reassured. Fanny appeared unperturbed by his predicament.

Finally, she moved around to his side. "Well, well, Mr Odling. I hear you have been letting off a bit of steam. So's to speak."

To his surprise, Oddie grinned. But then a wave of nausea rolled over him and he lay back. He felt like shit. Fanny's fingers moved stealthily over him. She probed and pressed his body until he felt that no orifice was sacred. Then she laid her ear against his chest. Her hair was fragrant and smelled of fern. Oddie felt a deep yearning stir inside him. For with Fanny came the call of the wild. How he longed for the Fens. For the mizzle and the mires. For the fish and the fowl. For the rustle of the reeds and the swish of skates. For home.

It hit him then with the force of a runaway steam engine that he may never go home again. For this dread thing had been done unto him not for his own sake. Rather, for some dark purpose. Some purpose that pleased his master. What that purpose could be Oddie could not begin to fathom.

He felt it then. That gathering of heat inside. Once more the clock began to tick and tock fit to bust. Fanny's breath expelled harshly against his skin. She stood up and for the first time Oddie sensed an underlying tension. He searched her face, trying to meet her eyes. But she seemed oblivious. She turned away, her hag's profile harsh and strained.

"We must work swiftly," she said to the governor. "The force within him threatens to overwhelm the flesh. The elements are unbalanced. He must be kept watered until your daughter returns. Or I fear…"

Oddie knew what Fanny feared. As heat surged and swelled inside him like a pupa bursting its cocoon, he feared it too. This time, it was worse. He felt aflame. All atremble, his limbs contorting. This time it hurt. He opened his mouth in agony, emitting a silent scream. Instead, it was all steam. On and on it went until his body was wracked and his mechanical heart beat so fast it must surely falter and fail. Death would have been a welcome release.

But he did not die. Fanny gathered his ravaged body in her arms and pushed a cup to his lips. He drank and drank and drank.

Inch by inch he was dragged back from the abyss. Yet he knew that this time he was less restored. He felt… diminished. He knew that he would not survive many more such happenings.

When his thirst was finally sated, he could not hold off sleep. He tried, for he knew now that Eliza was coming back. He didn't want to miss her. Not by so much as a tick or a tock. It may be the last time. In this world, that was. "Fanny," he whispered.

Fanny leaned close, her hair a curtain about his face. "Yes, Oddie?"

"Wake me, when…" He stopped, aware of the folly of speaking Eliza's name. But he need not have feared for Fanny nodded.

"I will," she said.

Oddie would have kissed her but he didn't have the strength. He observed her smooth skin and lush, youthful figure. His curiosity was rekindled. "How old are you, Fanny?"

Fanny's lips twitched. Then she brought her mouth to his ear. "Mr Odling, I am as old as my tongue and a little older than my teeth."

Her answer, slippery as an eel, only served to exacerbate Oddie's curiosity. "Fanny, don't tease, not now," he begged. "Tell me."

But it was no good. His eyes shut and he fell into darkness once more.

55

Rain fell in sheets through the churchyard. Low cloud enveloped the spire and thunder rumbled in a bruised sky. The yew trees groaned as wind whipped their green, gnarled branches and rivulets of water rushed down the flagstone path. Despite her hat, water dripped down her face and trickled under Eliza's collar. But it barely registered; she was insensible to all but her mission.

She hurried past the church door and down past the ostentatious Pelham crypt to the far wall. The spring bubbled up over the lip of a low trough and ran merrily across at an angle to duck once more beneath the dry stone wall. Mary had once told her the spring had healing powers and had been the site of worship long before the church had been built. To be honest, Eliza had taken little note. Indeed, she was ashamed to recall that she'd dismissed her maid's words as superstitious twaddle.

As she crouched down beside the water, Eliza wondered how she could have been such a silly little fool. She removed her sodden gloves and tentatively dabbled her fingers in the small pool. "Oh!" she cried. "Oh my God!"

But her words were meaningless. For Eliza understood now

that there was no god. God was a creation of men. A sham. There was only the mighty force of nature. This world in which she lived was the Mother. And she, Eliza Elvidge, was no more or less than the Mother's handmaiden. She was blessed (or cursed) to be able to commune with Her. It was both humbling and awe inspiring.

She cupped her hands and bought a mouthful to her lips. She drank, eyes closing in ecstasy. It tasted like… life. She felt the whole of Earth in that single swallow. And she knew that she was changed.

With that change came clarity. She now grasped how wise Fanny Flowers was. A fact that escaped her father entirely. Eliza was grimly amused. It seemed her father was in the habit of underestimating others. His daughter included. She bent, filling a silver flask with the life-giving water, hands absolutely steady. She screwed the lid shut and pushed it deep into the pocket of her sable cloak.

With a last heartfelt thanks to the water spirit, Eliza retraced her footsteps. The carriage waited, the poor horses sodden and miserable. The carriage driver looked little better. At sight of her he made a move to scramble down.

"Don't," she cried. "I can manage." Without waiting, she tugged the door open, fought for control as the wind wrestled with her, and then scrambled inside. She slammed the door shut and sank down upon the seat with a sigh of relief. At least she was rid of Pelham, if only for a while. He'd reluctantly gone to Fanny's before returning to the mill. Which was a mercy.

The carriage rumbled away and they set off at a spanking pace towards the mill. Eliza stared blindly out the window at the sodden landscape, fingers tapping an impatient rhythm on the door. The journey seemed interminable.

At long last the mill emerged from the curtain of rain. Eliza's heart leapt at the prospect of being reunited with Oddie. But she must be careful. She must be in control. She must project a demure but obedient demeanour. The tiniest slip would seal both Oddie's and her own fate.

Even before the carriage came to a halt, Eliza was half out the door. She hit the gravel drive hard but didn't stop. Skidding and sliding in the mud, she hastened to the entry. Her hand had not even touched the door when it opened. Lord Pelham leered down at her.

"Let me by!" said Eliza.

He smirked and inched back.

Eliza glared at him, willing him to move. But he stood firm. She wrapped her fur tight to her body and sidled through the narrow gap. Just as she felt that she had won free, his arms caught her around the waist. Nauseated, she fought her instincts, submitting as he drew her close and bent to kiss her.

His tongue forced its way into her mouth, slithering around like a snake. He tasted like fish. For a moment, she contemplated biting it off. But she didn't. His threat still stood at the forefront of her mind. She didn't dare doubt him. There was too much at risk. Sickened, she tried to turn her mind elsewhere. But it was impossible. She felt violated. His hands roved over her body with sickening confidence. She feared that his restraint would crumble altogether and she would be dragged into a distant room and assaulted.

When he released her, she staggered into the hall, watching him warily. He ran a hand down the front of his tailored trousers. With horrified fascination, she watched his hand caressing a huge bulge before adjusting himself. Eliza refused to look at him. She may be a maid, but she was no fool. Servant girls whispered and giggled their secrets to her. And she'd watched her father's stallion serve a mare. It was clear that the lord's ardour would not be contained for long.

Pelham smirked down at her. "You show promise but you have much to learn. I look forward to your instruction."

Eliza struggled for control as the power inside her stirred and strained to be released. It was tempting. Why not finish him now?

Then his pathetic threats would die with him. How she longed to unleash upon him the terrible end that she had in her mind. But she dare not. There was no knowing what the repercussions may be. This wasn't the time. Oddie and Fanny were counting on her. She must not fail them.

With revenge burning her heart like a brand, she curtsied meekly. "May I go now, M'Lord?"

The idiot puffed up like a pouter pigeon. He gave a mocking bow. "After you."

Eliza didn't waste time. She turned and made her way quick as she could to the stairs and along the passage below. Her skin crawled with every step, anticipating another assault. But she made it unscathed to the door of the surgery. As her hand reached to the handle, her eagerness to see Oddie was tempered by a surge of anxiety. There was no knowing what waited for her.

Dread settled over her as she pushed the door open. Her imagination went into overdrive as she stepped into the room. She feared finding Oddie's corpse shrouded beneath a sheet. All her faith in Fanny disintegrated beneath the weight of her fear. When she found him wide-awake, eyes fever-bright, she struggled to contain her emotions. She dragged her eyes away and found her father's gaze upon her.

"Papa," she said brightly, "how are you?"

He smiled. "The better for seeing you, my dear."

Movement caused Eliza to turn around. It was Fanny, now more appropriately attired in a day dress and linen apron.

Fanny dropped a small curtsey. "Miss Eliza," she said.

Eliza plunged her hand into her pocket and pulled out the flask. She held it out. "Here."

Fanny stepped forward and took it. She looked at the silver flask and then her gaze turned to Oddie. "Mr Odling, in this flask is water from the sacred well that sits within the churchyard. Its origins are known to few."

The silence was absolute. As if the very walls of the building were listening. Fanny lifted the silver flask. "Long ago the world was birthed from this water." Fanny looked around at her rapt audience. "Once its healing properties were celebrated. Today, that power resides there still for those that know how to harvest it."

Fanny came to Eliza and pushed the flask back into her unresisting hands. "Miss Elvidge, that knowledge resides within you. Only you can free the water spirit."

It was true. Eliza knew so, in the same way that she knew that fish swam and birds flew. Yet, she also sensed that there was risk. As her father had already proved. Risk for her stoker. Risk for herself. Risk for her mother, Earth.

"At what cost?" she asked. Her question was for both her contemporaries.

Her father answered first. "If you do not do this, the stoker will die, you will have failed in your duty to science and to your father. Science may be set back for years. "

Eliza strangled down her anguish. She dared not look at Oddie. How must he feel? How dare her father relegate a fellow human being to an experimental specimen! But still, callous though his words were, she knew that he spoke true. Oddie would die.

She turned to Fanny, hoping against hope, for words of comfort.

Fanny shook her head. Then she turned to Oddie, who lay, as if hypnotised, upon his steel slab. "Mr Odling," said Fanny. "You have expressed an ungentlemanly interest in my own age." She paused. "I think the time has come to satisfy your curiosity. Truth be told, I am seventy-three years old, almost to the day."

Eliza laughed. It was ridiculous. But then she realised her amusement was purely her own. She sobered quickly, a prickle of unease teasing down her spine.

Then Oddie spoke for the first time. Eliza turned to see him sitting up, his dark eyes beseeching. "Eliza," he said hoarsely. "Don't… do it!"

Fanny turned her back on him and took Eliza's hand. "The greater the power that you wield, the longer your lifespan. This is the price you pay."

Eliza took a deep breath and let it out. It mattered not. She would live an eternity if she must.

56

There was no doubt that Fanny Flowers was the worst kind of woman. Wilful, wanton and wicked. Oddie wanted to strangle her. She had no right to decide his fate. Or Eliza's. Whilst the grand puppeteer did not understand what drove his daughter, Oddie had no doubt. Eliza would sacrifice herself to save him. And he could not allow it.

Yet, as he watched the three witches preparing for what was to come, he was at a loss to know how to stop them. He scrambled around in his mind, like a rat in a trap, trying to find a solution. Now, he wished he had not survived. Now, he bitterly regretted the colossal constitution that pinioned him to the world. Eliza wasn't thinking straight. Hardly a surprise. To some, the promise of eternal youth, an unnatural lifespan, may seem more like a gift than a price to pay. But Oddie wasn't so sure.

He thought about the grief of losing his parents. About Eliza's grief at the loss of her pet. In each life, there must be loss. But how would it feel to watch as all your loved ones left you behind, without hope of ever being reunited? How would it feel to watch your beloved dwindle into winter with frost in their hair whilst your own face remained fresh and fair? It would be a lingering, sorrowful life. He could not bear that fate for Eliza.

Behind him he could hear the rustling of paper. Books being opened and closed. Murmured words that were incomprehensible to his ears. He may not be magical, but Oddie could feel a change in the air. In the same way he felt the subtle change of seasons, so now he felt a gathering. A gathering of what, he did not know. All he knew was that it was amounting to some great and ghastly end.

Unless… unless… he ended it on his own terms. After all, there was general agreement that he was mortally ill. It was clear that with each episode of overheating, his power of recuperation was severely compromised. Would it, therefore, be possible to bring about his own demise? He decided that it was. All he had to do was build up a degree of rage sufficient to cause a literal meltdown. And quickly. Before the coven started sprinkling their holy water about.

With the decision made, Oddie was confident that he could put thought into deed. After all, he had a whole host of grievances to draw upon. Many suppressed by the more immediate challenge of survival. He barely knew where to begin. The tick tock in his torso reminded him of the moment he found his father's watch in the furnace. He still did not know how it came to be there. But he had no doubt it was by foul means.

He turned his head, observing the four of them. Eliza, Fanny, the governor and Pelham. All four of them had revealed aspects of their character that shocked him. But it was the governor's treacherous nature that had hit him hardest. Oddie had always respected him. Thought of him as an ally in a world gone mad. Now he knew better. In reality, the man was the biggest cog in the wheel. It was he who had orchestrated this whole nightmare. His lips hardened and his hands curled into fists as a wave of fury gripped him. Then, he felt a rush of heat gathering inside him.

Oddie looked at Eliza. At the tender, pale stem of her neck as she bowed her head to whatever work she was at. She looked fragile as gossamer. Her hair bound up beneath a net, golden tendrils escaping from their bonds, gleaming in the gas light. She wore a lemon gown that emphasised her tiny waist and slender arms. Oddie ached for the touch of her even as his heart broke for her.

The loss of his own father had been a blow. But at least he had the comfort of remembering him as a hard but fair man. How must Eliza feel, understanding the terrible truth about her own parent? She must be reeling. How would it feel to know that your own father was the devil? What kind of man used his own child thus?

The heat swelled and burst into flames. But this time Oddie embraced the scorching, searing agony. All he needed now was to fan the flames and he would burn up. Pelham sidled into sight. Oddie watched in outrage as the fiend proceeded to place a hand upon Eliza's right buttock. Eliza's head jerked up, her body visibly stiffening. Oddie waited for her to admonish the lord. But she didn't. Stiff as a marionette, she continued to work as the hand massaged through the silky material. Oddie snapped. With a snarl, he pushed himself upright. He leapt to the ground. Fixating on Pelham, he lunged forward.

And fell, screaming with frustration. On his hands and one good leg he crabbed across the floor. It wasn't so far. Pelham was so close he could smell his fear.

But then he was accosted. Hands grasped him, dragging him back the way he had come. He lashed out. Bullseye! Pelham's eyes watered as he collapsed to the floor, clutching his balls. Oddie's body was a furnace. He felt a flush of triumph. He was close to his end!

Then Eliza crouched down before him. She was crying. Her lips moved but he couldn't catch the words. He was forced to quiet himself, from fear of doing her damage.

"Leon, stop. Stop! Please stop!"

Then Fanny moved in. "Oddie, enough! You'll kill yourself!" Then a knowing look came over Fanny's face. "Oh no you don't!" she snarled.

Oddie stared her down. But he'd lost his audience.

Fanny turned to Eliza. "Now, Eliza! It must be now. Or it will be too late!"

Eliza stared at Fanny for a moment. Then she turned to Oddie. And nodded. In one hand she held a wooden wand and a silver flask in the other. But Oddie didn't mind. Pain wracked his body. His time was near. He let go of his anger, wanting nothing more than to leave the world with Eliza's image burning in his mind.

Eliza's eyes narrowed, a butterfly of concern etching between her eyebrows. She lifted the wand, circling it above him, speaking words that he did not understand. But there was poetry in the tone and rhythm. As the words fell Oddie strained to hear. He was entranced. Absorbed. And utterly helpless.

As Eliza's voice gathered in power and cadence, Oddie felt his life force dwindling. Thank God! He was going to win.

When the first drops of frigid water sprinkled across his face, Oddie took no note. They scarcely touched him as they sizzled and steamed. He closed his eyes and lay back, content. Utterly spent. Ready to meet his maker. But his eyes snapped open as the delicate spray became a downpour, drenching him from head to toe.

"No!" he cried. "No!"

But there was no mercy. Eliza sang her secret songs. The water poured. His body sizzled like a sausage in a pan. He fought with all his might. He dredged up every wrong, every injustice and every humiliation that he could wring from his memory. Eliza's expression tightened, and her shoulders squared. Her blue eyes bored into his, like cut diamonds. For a time, he held his own and hope blossomed.

It withered as a second voice joined the strange song. It was deep and strong. The governor. Even in his fraught state, Oddie could feel the atmosphere thickening. He strived and struggled but there was no escape. Father and daughter delivered a deadly duet from which there was no escape. Inch by painful inch they stole his will away. Slowly, but surely, he felt the fire fade. Flicker. And die.

Cold now, he lay in a pool of water and stared up at Eliza. Despair resonated through him. He had failed. He would live. And so would Eliza. Forever. As they hauled him onto the steel table top, Oddie wondered what would happen. Strangely, he felt almost at peace. Things could not be any worse. What more could they do to him?

He did not have to wait long to find out.

57

The silence was serenaded by the steady ticking of Oddie's heart. Eliza closed her eyes to hear the better. She could scarcely believe he was still alive. And – though she loathed to acknowledge it – that was largely thanks to her father. Without his help, Oddie would have had his way. Why he had chosen to self-destruct she could not guess. Clearly Fanny had some grasp, but Eliza dare not ask. Not then. It would have to wait.

Leon Odling lived. For now, that had to be enough. She looked at her stoker and ached to hold him. But forced herself to maintain a cool persona. As she glanced surreptitiously at her companions she became aware of the side effects of her efforts. Everything and everyone around her was wet. Soaked. Saturated. Except for herself. Eliza alone remained dry as a ship's biscuit.

This observation was satisfactory on two levels. Firstly, it presented an opportunity to orchestrate a few moments alone with Oddie. Secondly, the pernicious Pelham was blue with cold. It was gratifying to see him suffer. If only a little.

She fixed a smile on her lips. "Papa, you are wet through." Then she pretended to note Pelham and Fanny's predicament for the first time. "Why, you are all soaked! Go at once and repair the damage. I will stay and tend to matters here."

Her father's eyes narrowed and he looked at Leon. Eliza

sensed his reluctance to leave. But then, shivering involuntarily, he nodded. He glanced at the lord. "Come, Pelham, let us hasten, for there is still much to be done." Then he turned to Fanny. "Miss Flowers, you must leave. If I have need of your services I will send word." Then he fixed her with a hard look. "You will speak to none of all that has passed. On pain of death."

Her father's words seemed to amuse Fanny. She dropped a mocking curtsey. "I can keep a secret, as you well know," she said.

Eliza refrained from comment, but her curiosity was piqued. Clearly it was some private joke. And yet, there was something peculiar in her father's expression. It was a… wary look. Uneasy, perhaps. Eliza made a mental note to chase it up. But meanwhile, there were more important matters.

She could barely control her impatience as the three finally dripped their way towards the door. Lord Pelham fussed and stalled like a reluctant racehorse at the barrier. Eliza ignored him, busying her trembling hands at the worktop. At last the door snicked shut. Eliza hastened over to Oddie.

But, she found she could not look at him. A flush of shame heated her cheeks. She had done what she had to do. Yet now she feared that his love may have perished amidst the magic. And she could not bear the thought. Life without his love stretched away like a vast, dry desert.

She gasped as his hand found hers. He held her as if she were made of china. The hard pad of his thumb caressed her palm and her insides melted.

"Eliza."

In that one small word, he communicated the depth of his feelings. Eliza took courage, lifting her eyes to his. What she found swept away her fears and her sorrows. For his love for her was written as clear as stars in the night sky. Overwhelmed, exhausted, her emotions finally flowed over. She lay her head upon his scarred chest and wept.

Oddie said no more. But his arms cradled her until she was

spent. When she lifted her head, she found he was smiling. And – on impulse – she leaned close and pressed her lips to his.

And then he kissed her.

She felt no shock nor shame. Only rapture. Bliss. It was an all-consuming blaze of desire that she had no intention of denying.

Her hands explored the hard planes of his body and her fingers twined through the wet tangle of his hair. With her cheek, she swept the unshaven length of his jaw. And, as his hand encased her waist, she slid onto the steel surface, cleaving to him.

"Eliza," he said.

But she took no note. She was utterly absorbed in the extraordinary effect his proximity had upon her person. She sensed she may not be entirely within the bounds of etiquette but frankly she couldn't have cared less. Being ladylike had ceased to hold any attraction.

"Eliza!"

The urgent tone of his voice broke through her ardour. Reluctantly she lifted her head from the rippling muscles of his torso. "What is it, my love?"

"Someone is coming!"

His words were as effective as a bucket of ice-cold water. Eliza slipped hastily to the ground, hurried to the bench and began frantically clattering instruments around. The serpent Pelham slithered into the room.

Eliza sniggered. He looked like a badly bred stork with his pale, skinny legs exposed beneath her father's coat. But the snide smile he sent her way sobered her as he shut the door.

"You will be laughing on the other side of your face, Eliza Elvidge, come the morning," he said.

Eliza felt her soul curl up. "Your threats don't scare me," she bluffed.

He giggled, rubbing his spidery fingers over his crotch. "Well, my dear, they ought to."

Eliza sensed rather than saw Oddie rise from his bed. She held her breath, suddenly scared. His last brave attempt to walk had ended disastrously. "No, Oddie!" There was no need for pretence. She hastened to his side. But there was no cause for concern. Her stoker was standing tall and proud. He stretched, and Eliza was distracted by the delicious play of his musculature beneath his tawny skin. Oh, he was so lovely!

Pelham, however, did not share her sentiments. To Eliza's delight, he looked close to piddling his pants (had he been wearing any). With a great sense of satisfaction, Eliza stepped aside as Oddie crossed the surgery floor. He moved slowly but surely. His gait was even, creating a distinct sound. The soft fall of his foot followed by the clink of the other. It was a strange and wondrous sight.

Pelham slid backward, his bare feet slipping in puddles of water. He pointed at Oddie, hand shaking. "Don't touch me, you… you…"

Eliza could only assume that Pelham couldn't think of a word bad enough to sum up his assailant. She waited for Oddie to tear him apart.

Oddie walked steadily, his expression calm but determined.

"Fee… Fie… Foe… Fum," he intoned softly, "I smell the blood of an Englishman."

Pelham turned tail and legged it. Eliza gasped as Oddie went surging across the flagstone floor. He moved with all his old grace but more swiftly, unimpeded by his steel limb. One hand whipped out, snagging his quarry by the scruff of his scrawny neck.

Pelham squealed like a little girl.

Eliza clapped.

Oddie lifted him, shaking him like the rat he was. Pelham's terrified face turned red, then blue and then an interesting shade of purple. His eyes bulged, his tongue protruding like a swollen slug.

Eliza jumped as the door banged open, slamming against the bookcase. Glass jars shivered and shattered. Books bounced onto the floor with a bang. All of Eliza's bonhomie evaporated at the sight of her father.

His face was dark with fury. "Enough!" he cried. He pulled his wand free from his pocket and lifted it, pointing it at Oddie. Eliza felt power resonating from within him. Frantic to protect Leon, she flung herself forward, trying to create a barrier. She braced herself for the onslaught. Fearful but ferociously determined.

But then, to her amazement, her father lowered his wand. Instinctively, she turned. Her heart leapt up into her throat. Oddie dropped Pelham. A look of bewilderment flitted across his face. Confusion turned to dismay, and dismay to fear as his whole body twitched and shuddered. Then, like a puppet without strings, he crumpled to the floor.

The room was silent. Eliza gasped, shocked and dumbfounded. It was then that she realised she couldn't hear a single thing. Not even the sound of a clock ticking where a heart ought to be.

58

Oddie awoke with a start. He sat up and stared around. He was half relieved to find himself in familiar surroundings. Even if it was the boiler room. Trouble was, he couldn't recall getting here.

Behind him someone cleared their throat. He rolled off his back and onto his side. His eyes climbed up a brand-new oak door riveted with heavy iron studs. There was no handle on the inside. At head height, there was a small opening through which a pair of eyes peered. The governor.

He stared up blankly. The last thing he could recall was bearing down on Pelham with violent intent. Eliza had been clapping. An involuntary smile lifted his lips for a second. But receded as he struggled to follow the thread of thought. His hand went to his bare chest, pressing down to feel the clock tick inside. This gave him cause for concern. But why?

He sat up as the answer swam into his mind. His clock had stopped. He recalled it quite clearly. How the ticking had slowed, grown irregular and then… ceased. Yet, it was working now. Making good time. Regular and rapid.

"Curious, is it not?"

Oddie stared at the governor, alerted by his sinister tone. He did not answer, as it was clear the governor did not really expect or desire one.

"Run your hand down the scar."

Filled with trepidation, he did as he was bid. At first he came up a blank, his fingers finding nothing but the ridge of scarring. Then he found a circle of calloused skin. His finger probed, dipping into a hole.

Even while he could not see the governor's face, Oddie knew that he was smiling. This was reinforced by the governor's next words.

"Ah, I see you have found it. Excellent!"

Oddie pulled his finger away as if it had been burned. "What is this?"

By way of an answer, the eyes vanished to be replaced by a hand in which a key was swinging rhythmically.

Oddie blinked. "That's my key."

The governor sounded delighted. "Indeed it is! Help yourself."

Oddie stood up, uneasy and suspicious. He advanced slowly, expecting some trickery. But the governor stayed fast until Oddie took the key. The hand disappeared, and the governor's eyes peered in once more.

Oddie examined the key. He looked at the governor. A kind of dread began seeping through his bones. The ticking inside him accelerated. He could not speak.

The governor blinked slowly. "That, Mr Odling, is the key to your heart." He chuckled. "Quite literally."

Oddie dropped the key, eyeing it as if it were a serpent. His hand reached to the hole in his sternum. What kind of a freak was he? A cold, hard anger settled in his soul. He stood up tall and stalked over to the door. He brought his mouth to the aperture. "I'm going to tear you into pieces and feed you to the furnace."

The governor's bedside manner disappeared. He retreated a few steps. "You are no more than my creation, Odling. A mechanical marvel, it's true. But like all machines you are dependent upon your maker for your existence." He paused for a long moment as if inviting conversation.

Oddie did not oblige.

"If you work hard and show your gratitude, I will let you wind yourself as regular as… clockwork." He paused, tilting his head as if to calculate the impact of his words. "If you are troublesome… you will forfeit. And you will cease to exist."

Oddie wondered if he desired an existence. There seemed little incentive. All was lost. His love. His soul. His humanity. Would it not be easier to throw the key into the flames? And end on his own terms?

The governor cleared his throat. "I thought you might like to know, Lord Pelham and Eliza are to be wed on Tuesday. Still, if it's any consolation, it's you that she loves. Her cooperation will ensure your survival. And your cooperation her own."

He knew! Oddie's desire for oblivion died. There would be no easy path out. That was clear. He must live. He picked up the key and took it to his master. But when he got to the door, the key vanished. Perplexed, Oddie stopped, casting his eyes around, thinking he must have dropped it.

The governor's hand slipped through the slot and, with a magician's flourish, he extracted the key from behind Oddie's ear. He peeped in once more. "Best get to work. It would be a good idea to not disappoint, Mr Odling."

The mocking eyes vanished. The metal flap banged shut. Footsteps receded.

Oddie exploded, flinging himself at the door, pounding it with his shoulder and then his fists. It did not budge. Desolate, Oddie slumped to the ground.

As he lay there, a few revelations came bubbling up to the surface of his mind. The first was that he seemed to be finding his feet. *Literally*. To quote the governor's demonic words. Indeed, he felt well. More than well. Fighting fit, in fact. Thirsty and hungry. But damned fine.

Oddie gazed around the grim, grimy space and made up his mind. He would escape. He would find Eliza. He would be avenged.

Trouble was, he didn't know what day it was.

How much time did he have until Tuesday, exactly?

59

Eliza paced up and down her room like a caged tiger. No matter how hard she tried there seemed no way out of her predicament. On her mantelpiece, the carriage clock cheerfully chimed the time. It was six o'clock. Sunday morning.

She went to the window and drew back the curtain. It was dark. She gazed towards the east, to where she knew her love lay. A vision of him, alone in the dark, wounded and helpless filled her. She wept, although she despised herself for her weakness. What good were tears? What good was she? Why was she so weak? How she longed to be a man. Big and strong with a pistol in each hand.

Utterly spent, she slid to the floor and sobbed until she felt wrung dry. The shedding of tears seemed to help. Eliza felt better. She found her capacity to think improved. And she felt her inborn optimism reassert itself. After all, she wasn't Lady Pelham yet! There was still time. And that time would be better spent actively searching for solutions.

She went to the fireplace and picked up her wand. It felt weightless in her hand. The horrible happenings of the previous day circled chaotically in her brain. She knew that without her, the dark deeds could not have been done. But how great had her contribution been? It had felt great. Indeed, it had been the greatest feat of her short life. Not just in physical endurance but in mental application. Yet, how could she gauge the significance of effort? She had no stick by which to measure. Was her father's power far superior to her own?

There seemed no way to an answer other than to put it to a test. And, the truth was, Eliza was afraid to try her father out. If she failed, the consequences would be dire. Not just for herself but for Oddie. She had been foolish to believe she could deceive him. He had known her feelings for Oddie all along and had played her like a piano. She returned to the window, pressing her forehead on the cold pane of glass. What to do?

Ultimately, it was the key that presented as the biggest problem. Whoever held it, held Oddie in the palm of their hand. Eliza's temper simmered. As a girl she had always lived under her father's 'protection'. Now facing enslavement as the wife of a man she loathed, she would again be caged. But she had at least been trained for the part. But not Oddie. For him, such subjugation would be nigh on intolerable.

Outside, in the distance, a light flickered. Her eyes followed listlessly as she wrestled with her problems. Another flame flared. And another. And another. Alert now, Eliza tried to work out where the little lights were coming from. She couldn't be sure, but she thought they were beyond the mill, out on the wetlands of the Fens. It was curious. Who would be wandering across the treacherous marsh at such a time? And why?

For a long while she peered out, watching the lights bobbing and weaving around. They moved at speed but not unnaturally so. Then the lights were stationary. And went out. Eliza waited and waited but they did not return. She finally shut the curtains and put it out of mind. There were more pressing issues at hand.

The key. What to do? The obvious solution was to steal it from her father. This seemed possible. It seemed likely that such an important artifact would be kept on his person or close by. Therefore, he would bring it home. Eliza didn't doubt she could find it given enough time.

Trouble was, under the circumstances, the key's disappearance would be soon noted. It wouldn't take a genius to work out who'd taken it. She jumped at a soft knock on the door. She felt a surge of panic, sure it would be Pelham or her father. "Who is it?"

"Ma'am, it's me, Mary, Ma'am."

Mary! Dear, sweet and loyal Mary. Eliza was mortified. She had scarcely given the poor girl a thought. She rushed to the door and swung it open, pulled the shocked maid inside and enveloped her in a hug. When she let her go, Mary laughed, her cheeks colouring with embarrassment.

"Miss, be you mazed?" she gasped.

Eliza smiled. "I do believe I am." She took Mary's hand and led her to the fire. "Are you alright, Mary?"

Mary bobbed a curtsey. "I am well in body, Miss Eliza, but somewhat ruffled in spirit."

"How so?"

Mary leaned close and whispered. "There is much unrest in the shire. Lord Pelham has enclosed the common lands and fenced the woods. He has put his henchmen to capture any who trespass. And there has been a disaster in the cotton mill. A man dead and a boy without an arm. No compensation has been made. There is talk of uprising. Of violence."

Eliza knew then what the lights signified. There was a gathering on the Fens of desperate and angry folk. And who could blame them? Desperate times made for desperate measures.

Mary took Eliza's hand, holding it in her work-rough ones. "I have bought a warning from Fanny Flowers. She said to tell you to have a care. There are many who resent your father's new made fortune. Empty bellies make for empty heads."

Eliza was more saddened than surprised. A week ago, she

would have been undone by such news. Today, however, she had other things on her mind. "Mary, do you know anything about keys?"

Mary shrugged. "Never had a key. They lock things up. Doors and treasure chests." She wrinkled her freckled nose and gave Eliza a curious look. "Why do you ask?"

Eliza sighed. "My father has a key and I need it. But I cannot ask him for it. And to take it sly would be too much of a risk." Exasperated she stamped her foot. "If only I knew a locksmith!"

Mary chewed her bottom lip.

Eliza knew that look. Mary was thinking. "What?"

"Well, Miss, I know one who is a… kind of locksmith."

Eliza was delighted. "Why, Mary, that is marvellous! Would he help, do you think?" Then she fell silent, aware that Mary did not share her enthusiasm. Indeed, the maid looked positively awkward. "What ails you, Mary? Do you have piles?"

Mary shook her head. "Well, Miss Eliza, it's like I say, she's not a locksmith exactly."

"Well, what is she… exactly?"

Mary blushed scarlet. "She be a house breaker, Miss. She is a dab hand at the making of new keys from old, or so it is said."

A duplicate key! "Mary, you are brilliant!"

Mary turned magenta, shook her head but smiled.

Eliza hardly dared believe it. Could it really be so simple? "Mary, what must I do?"

"Well, you must make an imprint of the key in question in wax or a cake of soap and Sarah will do the rest."

Eliza's mind raced over this new prospect. It was simple in theory yet dangerous in practice. Without a doubt her father would return with the key upon his person. He would secrete it in his room or library for sure. What she would need was an opportunity to sneak in and make the impression. Once she located the key it would be quick enough.

She went to the window, tapping her fingers on the glass. Trouble was, her father would be watching her every move. He was acutely aware of her feelings for his stoker and was fixated on her forthcoming nuptials. How could she create a safe window of opportunity?

Think, Eliza! Think! Then she had it. She turned to her maid. "Mary, will you hasten to Fanny Flowers and ask her for a sleeping draught? Tell her it must be subtle but strong."

Mary nodded vigorously. "'Tis only a step away, Miss. I'll be back within the hour."

Eliza looked out the window. "Have a care, Mary. The Fens are fractious this night. Do not take any risks. I could not bear for harm to befall you."

Mary laughed. "None will harm me, Miss! They would fall foul of Fan o' the Fens if they did. They knows better than that. Rest easy."

Only a little reassured, Eliza gave Mary a quick peck on her cheek. "Keep off Pelham land, the man is a menace."

Mary's eyes twinkled. "Mayhaps not for long, Miss!" And with that, she twirled her worn cloak around her shoulders and slipped out the door.

Eliza stared after her, Mary's words resonating in her mind. What did Mary know that she did not? Would there be an uprising against her intended? It was a heady prospect.

With an effort, she pushed the thought away. She must focus. Oddie's life depended upon it. She must find a way to feed her father the draught without awakening his suspicions. But how? Then her eyes rested on her wand. She felt a wave of embarrassment. Was she a witch or wasn't she?

With a candle in one hand and her wand in the other, she set off for the library. Fanny had said knowledge was key to the most powerful magic. Surely there must be something in one of the ancient tomes that could aid her.

All she needed was a little time.

60

The furnaces were at full speed. Oddie paused for a second to inspect the gauges. All of them were perfect. Full steam indeed! How long he'd been working he did not know. There was no way to gauge time. No clock. No window. No sense of routine. All he could do was make a guess by the size of the coal pile. By his reckoning he'd used about a quarter. So that would be roughly half a day's work.

Except that now he was working at a ferocious speed. There was no correlating fatigue. He felt fit as a flea. As if he could stoke for bloody Britain. But he was thirsty. This presented no immediate problem. Several buckets, filled to the brim, were arrayed along the back wall. They were all a bit scummy with dust and dirt, but in all honesty, Oddie didn't mind. In fact, he was growing increasingly fond of the slightly singed flavour.

He was, however, absolutely starving. There was not so much as a crumb to be found. He knew the governor would feed him. After all, he was an 'experiment' that must be kept alive. Trouble was, it felt way past teatime.

Fed up, he went to the door and gave it a good battering. "Hello! Pelham, you piece of piss, I want some bloody dinner!"

When the flap flopped open, Oddie took a step back. He'd not really expected a response. When he recovered his equilibrium, he bent down to look outside. At first, he thought there was no one there. But the delicious scent of bread drew his gaze down.

A boy stared up with a look of abject terror on his thin face. A pair of sunken hazel eyes leaked tears that trickled in a muddy stream down his face. In one hand, he held a tray. He held nothing in the other, mainly because it was missing. As was his arm. A threadbare sleeve hung empty at his side.

Oddie's heart sank into his boots. It wasn't difficult to deduct the fate of the child. Another of the governor's 'experiments'. He smiled. "Hello. I'm Oddie. Who are you?"

The boy did not answer but hoisted the tray awkwardly upward. Oddie reached out and grasped the loaf of bread and chunk of cheese that lay on it. The tray retracted.

"I'm... boy."

Oddie was nonplussed. Boy? Was the lad simple? Or just scared out of his senses? "Where do you hail from? Who is your father?"

It was the lad's turn to be puzzled. "No father. No mother. No nothing." He looked at his sleeve. "Machine ate me arm. In t'mill."

Dear lord. Another lost boy. He wasn't mazed. He just had no name. Probably been chained to a machine since he could walk. If he'd had a name, he'd forgotten it. Oddie forced a smile. "Well, Boy, I'm pleased to meet you."

The boy nodded. Looked over his shoulder. And slammed the flap shut.

Alone once more, Oddie settled down on an upturned bucket and applied himself to his food. The loaf was soft inside and golden crusty on the outside. Wheat and oats. Bloody lovely. The cheese was pale and crumbly with a sharp bite. Just how he liked it. He'd half expected week-old rye bread and rancid bacon. All in all, he was pleasantly surprised. Mind you, a swig of tea would have been welcome.

He devoured the whole lot in minutes, his mind chewing over the appearance of Boy. He wondered how long it would be before the governor got going with his diabolical dark arts. Was there already a clock waiting? Sat ticking merrily away in the surgery. Would Eliza be forced once more to assist?

His jaw stopped chewing as his mind dwelt on his love. Where was she now? Was she alright? There was nothing that he wouldn't have given for one more moment with her. He drew the memories of their last meeting forward and lingered over them tenderly. He recalled the sweet taste of her mouth. The curve of her lips as she smiled. The forget-me-not blue of her eyes. The magical mystery of her.

And then the ugly image of Pelham possessing her surged through his brain. A groan arose deep from his psyche. It was unbearable. He leapt up, padding around his prison. He must get out! He must! He must! He must! If only Fanny were here. Fanny would know what to do. Fanny was a clever one. What would Fanny do?

Up and down the space he strode. Up and down. Up and down. The bread was gone. Thirsty once more he drank. Then resumed his pacing, his clock heart ticking away the seconds as if to mock him. A horrible thought stopped him dead in his tracks. Could it be Tuesday already? Why in God's name hadn't he asked Boy? What an imbecile he had become!

Overwhelmed, he opened his mouth and screamed. "Help! Help me! I'm in here!" Even though he knew it was futile. The sound would not carry through the walls. But hearing a voice, even if it was only his own, made him feel better. It relieved the pressure inside, like a leaky valve.

He sat down on the bucket once more. No good behaving like a hysterical woman. What he needed was a plan. Think, Oddie, bloody think! The key was the thing. That damn key. He had to get it from the governor. But no matter how he strained and strived, he could find no answer. The governor possessed demonic powers the likes of which Oddie had never even dreamed of.

Even if he could get out, how would he wrestle the key free? Brute force? Well, he was strong. Unnaturally strong. But that was no protection from spells and enchantments. And, if he tried and failed, what would happen to Eliza? The prospect of her being wed to Pelham was dreadful, but he did not doubt her father would find worse ways to punish her if necessary.

Pelham. His hands curled into fists and he slammed them into the wall in an outburst of impotent rage. Maybe the governor was untouchable. But Pelham wasn't. If Pelham was to die, then Eliza would be free. A widow. A titled widow. Not an ideal outcome, but better than a poke in the eye with a big stick.

Oddie checked the furnaces, mostly out of habit and ruminated on this last. And, the more he tossed it around, the more he liked it. He may not be able to save Eliza from her fate, but he could try and limit her suffering. Pelham must be eliminated.

With a plan in place, Oddie unwound a fraction. He inspected his hands. The knuckles were bloody. But no real damage. He stared blankly around. His belly felt full, but he wasn't satisfied. He craved… something. But he couldn't quite put his finger on it. Tea? Strong contender but, on reflection, no. Not the thing.

He went over to the corner and picked up the broom to sweep back the stray bits of coal. As the lumps skittered obligingly back to their rightful place, dust drifted up his nostrils. It smelled unfamiliar. Which was peculiar because he'd been breathing the stuff in for weeks. He picked a piece up and examined it. And what he found amazed him.

Perched between his fingers, the black nugget of fuel was an object of beauty. Its surface twinkled and glinted like a rare jewel. How had he never seen this before? And then, there was the texture. He rolled the coal gently between his palms. It was cool and sugary. Then, lifting it to his nose, Oddie breathed it in. How sweet it smelled! His senses expanded, a new awareness awaking inside him.

The hard lump of black in his hand wasn't coal. Not now. It was something else entirely. He looked at the great pile of fuel. Fuel! The word now possessed new meaning. Coal wasn't just the fuel of furnaces.

With a flick of his fingers, Oddie tossed the nugget into the air. It rose and fell. Oddie snapped his head back and caught it neatly between his teeth. He drew the coal into his mouth. Chewed slowly. Swallowed and smiled.

Well, well, well, who would have thought it? Damned stuff was good. More than good, in fact. Seriously satisfying. He felt fantastic, like a fire was igniting in his belly. His whole body began twitching and jittering. He rocked back and forward on his feet and looked around the confines of his prison, seeking an outlet for this excess of energy. But found none.

Finally, he bounced over to the door, slamming it with his fists. It shuddered and shivered beneath his assault. But held. He banged again, then paused to listen. But silence mocked him.

He backed up, tensed and shot forward, hitting the door with all his strength. The door stood firm. Shit! Lifting his metal leg, he kicked out. Again and again and again. Splinters of wood flew but the door remained obdurately shut. Almost screaming in frustration, Oddie was forced to accept defeat.

For a while he just stood, contemplating his failure. Whilst the door looked worse for wear, it'd take a month of bloody Sundays to chip his way through. It occurred to him then that, unlike the door, his body showed no signs of wear and tear. Not so much as a scratch. Interesting.

Unable to settle, Oddie checked the furnaces and set to some serious stoking. It was soothing to feel his body flexing and flowing effortlessly. His mind steadied and he thought about this weird new discovery. Somehow, the magic or the ingestion of coal – or a combination of the two – gave him unnatural strength. Not just that, though. His body seemed resistant to injury. Or, could repair itself super speedily. Very interesting.

Smiling grimly, he put down his shovel, reflecting that this discovery was purely his own.

Not even the governor could have forecast this particular oddity. Oddie took a drink and picked up a delectable bit of coal. He chewed it slowly, enjoying its effects and speculated on how much of an edge it would give him.

He thought that maybe this time, the governor had outsmarted himself. Oddie picked up the broom and swept the clean floor vigorously. He hummed a tune and felt optimism surging up like a king tide. Looked to him like Leon Odling had a kind of magic all of his own.

Maybe he could save Eliza after all.

61

Books lay scattered like confetti around the room. Eliza pawed feverishly through the tissue-thin pages of a dusty volume. Her lips spoke silent words as she scanned the print. The grandfather clock chimed as if to keep her grounded to the task at hand. She looked up and lifted her candle. Her heart felt like a lemon in a press. An hour and a half had passed, and she had nothing.

She looked around at the chaos she'd created. Should she carry on for a little longer? Or tidy away the evidence and rethink her strategy? The house lay still and silent around her. Not so much as a mouse stirred. Better carry on. If she quit, she'd be haunted by the books she hadn't opened.

Once more she went to the shelves and peered at the stiff spines of her father's library. Thus far she'd been randomly searching for a clue. Just hoping against hope to find a useful or insightful passage or phrase. But perhaps she should be more specific. What was it that she wanted?

On reflection, she realised the best thing would be an enchantment that lowered her father's guard and made him forgetful of his suspicions. This spell would also need to ensure he drank the draught and woke with no recollection of the events. Trouble was, Eliza had no way of knowing if such a thing existed. And, even if it did, how to go about finding it.

She stamped her foot. "Hell and damnation!" she said furiously. She reached up, grabbed a book at random and wrestled it out of its niche. It was a skinny little volume of faded brown. There was no title, just an imprint of a wand on the smooth surface. When she tried to open it, the pages stayed firmly shut.

A spell she'd come across in her frantic studies surfaced. With a flick of her wand she tapped the book's surface and spoke the words. To her astonishment the book flipped neatly open to a spell that was handwritten in neat copperplate. Her eyes flashed across the verse and she wanted to dance for joy. But she didn't. Instead she slipped the volume into her waistband and madly began tidying up her mess.

It felt like forever before she finally wiggled the last book back into its rightful place. Leastways, she thought they were in the right place, but she couldn't be absolutely sure. Everything was such a jumble and she only had one candle. Then she heard a noise. She froze, ears on stalks. Was her father home?

The thought galvanised her into action. With the one hand clutching the precious book and the candle guttering, she raced back to her room. She'd no sooner snuffed the candle, flung herself into bed and dragged the covers up when she heard someone approaching.

When the door opened she shoved the book under her pillow and played dead.

"Miss? Miss Eliza, are you awake?" a voice whispered.

Eliza nearly expired from happiness. She sat up, throwing back the covers. "Mary, come in!"

Mary crept through the door, fumbling in the darkness. Eliza scrambled out of bed and groped around for matches. After a few aborted attempts, the candlewick caught, and Mary's red hair flamed into life.

"Mary, I'm so pleased to see you! Is all well?"

"I am well, Miss." She hurried over. "Fanny gave me this, Miss."

With trembling hands, Eliza took a small package from Mary. She placed it on her bureau, opening the brown paper carefully. She lifted the light close, the better to see. The aroma of herbs wafted through the room, sweet and heady. Bound in a swaddle of muslin, the spell seemed as innocent as a lavender sachet.

Mary pointed. "Fanny said to tell you that to be most potent it must be steeped in boiling water then cooled enough to drink, but still hot."

It sounded so simple in theory. Still, she was significantly closer to her goal than she had been on waking. With a glance to make sure the door was closed, Eliza led Mary to the fireplace. She stirred the coals and added more fuel. The fire leapt into life and they sank down beside it for comfort.

In the firelight, Eliza could see that her maid was dishevelled. Indeed, her usually braided hair was loose and the hem of her dress muddy. On closer inspection, her sleeve was torn too. "Why, Mary, what has happened? You are in disarray!"

Mary grinned, her small, snub nose wrinkling in amusement. "I met a mob on the Fens but so did the militia! I ran like the wind. The red devils would have had me too, if they hadn't taken a tumble in a bog."

Eliza was intrigued. "A mob? A bog? The militia! What is this?"

"I told you, Miss Eliza. There is a rising against the gentry. Hunger and want make menfolk mad. They'd rather die than go to the workhouse. When no one will listen to words, action is all that is left."

"But the militia is armed."

Mary roared with laughter. "Maybe so, Miss. But they have little use for rifles when they are chin-deep in mud."

Eliza smiled. It did make for a pretty picture. If only Pelham would fall in a bog! She sobered up and inspected her muslin bag.

"Mary, I have so little time. I must put this enchantment to use without delay." She looked up at the clock. Another hour the sun would rise. If her father wasn't home, then she would go to the mill and find him.

"Mary, I want you to go to Fanny's and wait for me. Tell her… tell her…" But Eliza did not know what to say. She shook her head. "Tell her, thank you."

Mary nodded, her eyes welling with tears. "Be careful, Miss Eliza."

Spontaneously they came together, clinging to the comfort of the other. Finally, Eliza broke free. "I will see you later. Promise. Go quickly, while you can."

Without further ado, Mary left the room. Her footsteps faded. And Eliza was alone. She gazed around her room. So snug and warm. It came to her then that she may never see it again. And so, she pulled out her travel bag and set to packing. It was hard to know what to take, for the bag was small and her wardrobe large. But in the end, she was satisfied that she had made wise choices.

Except for the midnight-blue satin and lace nightie. Utterly impractical. But it was divine! Just the thing for… Eliza felt heat racing up her neck. What was she thinking? She was becoming quite the hussy in her old age. But she left the gown where it was.

Right on the top she placed the slim volume of handwritten spells. The verse in question was imprinted clearly on her mind but knowing it was on hand gave her confidence.

Swiftly she dressed. Without her corset, the process was relatively easy. She couldn't manage all the buttons up the back of her riding habit, but her jacket covered it. It'd do. She laced up her boots and looked at the clock. It was twenty to eight. Outside, daylight spread tentative fingers of lemon light over the landscape. The mill stood silhouetted against the grey sky. The driveway remained stubbornly empty. No sign of her father. Time to go.

With her bag in one hand and her wand in the other, she set

off. As she shut the door softly behind her, Eliza felt a wave of grief. One way or another, she would not be coming back. It hurt, for here she had felt loved. She had been happy. Secure. Spoiled. But that was all gone. Like little Comet. She fought an overwhelming desire to rush back, jump into bed and pull the covers over her head. Fear froze her to the spot.

And then, a small shadow bounced down the hallway towards her. Comet raced to her side, leapt up and licked her hand. Eliza crouched down and hugged her, but she was no more substantial than a will-o'-the-wisp. And yet, her bright and merry little spirit did Eliza's heart good. Resolve trickled down her spine like molten steel.

"Come, Comet," she whispered. "We have work to do."

62

Oddie leaned against the door and eyed the coal pile. Or what was left of it. Its reduction led to many questions. The most obvious was, what would happen when it ran out? Without the water wheel the newly emancipated arable land would quickly revert to type. Fen. The governor wouldn't want that. Therefore, the mill must run and the furnaces must burn. Of course, there was a stockpile. But sooner or later the longboat would arrive with its motherlode. And with the longboat came the hauliers. Coal wouldn't carry itself.

Oddie scooped up a bit of coal and crunched it thoughtfully. God but it was good! Then his teeth stilled as it occurred to him how it must look. A man eating what most people considered dirty lumps. He thought of Eliza, with her fragrant, golden hair and delicate ways. What would she think? Would she be disgusted? He shifted the coal onto his tongue and spat it out.

After a moment's hesitation he picked up another bit. Eliza wasn't here. He'd just keep it to himself, he contemplated. Then no harm done. At this stage, he needed the edge. Maybe he could quit later. When he was free. And he would be free. The door would open, sooner or later. Of that, he was confident.

He heard light, quick footsteps approaching. This time he knew to look down when the slit opened. He smiled. "Hello, Boy."

Boy nodded nervously and lifted a brown bag. Oddie took it gently as he could and wiggled it through the gap. Then he peered back out. "Boy, you must listen to me. You must leave this place. There are evil doings here. The master will work his dark arts upon you. Get away. Run as far as you can from this place. And never return."

Boy stared up at him, blinking rapidly. "Master is makin' us a new arm, Mister."

Oddie closed his eyes in despair. The surety in the lad's voice told him it was too late. The boy was enthralled at the prospect. And who could blame him? Oddie pressed on. "It will be a new arm. But he'll take out your heart and put in a pocket watch. And you'll be his toy. Or his slave. For ever."

The boy laughed. A brittle, broken sound. "Hah! He said you'd say that!" And then he made a singularly rude gesture with his finger and slammed the window shut.

Oddie sighed. He'd tried. What more could he do? The boy seemed doomed. Unless Oddie could free himself. Without a doubt, the conversation would be relayed back. The child was already entirely in the thrall of the wizard. It was a troubling thought, for if Elvidge succeeded with his next 'experiment' what would he create? What kind of creature would Boy become? It did not bode well.

He sat down glumly, inspecting the contents of the paper bag. There was a pasty inside. Cold but fragrant. And an apple. He held the fruit to his nose, savouring its scent. His eyes closed as he recalled the small apple tree that grew at the bottom of his garden. Despite its stunted growth the little tree bowed its head every year with the weight of its small, crisp harvest. Behind the tree lay the brook. A cheerful chap that bubbled and splashed across its stony bed. Beyond lay the Fens proper. Acres upon acres, mile upon mile of marsh and finally the sea. Where his lonely little boat bobbed forlornly waiting to sail.

A wave of loneliness lapped over him. Oddie opened his eyes and stared around his prison. He wondered if anyone had missed him. Only Fan and Eliza knew what was happening. Neither seemed placed to reveal the truth. And – indeed – if they did, would anyone believe them? Probably not. Not so long ago, he wouldn't have believed it himself.

He consumed the pasty. It was good. Full of meat and taters in thick gravy with onion. And the apple was sweet enough. Washed down with a dipper of water and a bit of coal, Oddie felt the better for it. His optimism revived as he returned to his work. But, as he shovelled away, he wondered why he did. Work – that is. Puzzled, he down-tooled, the better to think.

Truth was, it had never occurred to him that there was an alternative. Indeed, he'd been shovelling like a man possessed. Which was crazy. Really, there was no reason for him to do so. It was sheer habit. Or perhaps it was a desire to hold on to some normality. An anchor to reason and reality. Or maybe the governor had cast… some kind of spell to make him work. It was possible. The hairs on his arms stood to attention. He must stop!

Yes. There was no surer way of getting attention than by bringing the mill to a halt. Stoking may be a humble occupation, but it was the life's blood of the operation. No fire. No steam. No power. Simple.

To get out, the door had to open. So, Oddie must make it happen. He must get the governor here. Soon. Before Tuesday. Oddie pushed away the possibility that the day had already slipped by. He just couldn't think of it now. He'd go crackers. The priority was to get out. He'd deal with the rest later.

Oddie went to the three furnaces and flicked open the door of the first. The heat was intense. Flames flickering white-hot. He retreated to the back of the room and sat on the bucket. The temperature in the room shot up as the gauge on the furnace dropped dramatically. But Oddie didn't even raise a sweat. Indeed, he found the heat comforting.

And – he had to admit – he felt his spirits risng like a flag up a pole. It was grand to be finally doing something. He felt, for the first time, in control. This time, he was calling the shots. It seemed that he did have a few aces up his sleeve after all. Of course, they may not prove to be a winning hand, but he'd play the hell out of them. The governor had made him for his own purposes. And – from what Oddie could surmise – that boiled down to a pool of slaves to better serve himself and those of his kind. When Oddie failed to meet that expectation, the governor would want to know why. And Oddie would be ready.

He went to the second furnace and opened the door. He sat. He waited. He opened the third. Tense as a coiled spring he waited once more. He couldn't guess how long it would take for the great engine to falter and fail. It was outside his experience. But he guessed it would not be long. As he waited, listening and fidgeting and watching the ovens burn out, time suspended.

The furnaces still glowed red, the fuel inside turning to smoke and ash. The great metal bellies clicked and sighed as the heat slowly subsided. How long had it taken? An hour? Three? More? Oddie couldn't know. But as a pile of ash subsided, flames flickering feebly, he felt sure that steam production must have all but ceased.

This certainty took a hold. Adrenaline surged through his bloodstream. With nothing else to do, he took a long draught of water and grabbed a handful of coal. He'd just swallowed the final piece when he heard footsteps. Not Boy. Bolder. Louder. Booted.

Oddie flexed his hand, bouncing on the balls of his feet. At his core heat began to build. When the door opened he would have just one chance. The governor knew nothing of his coal addiction and its effects. The window of opportunity was small. Surprise was the key. And the key was the prize.

The footsteps echoed louder and louder. And stopped. Bolts grated. A lock clicked. The door swung open. Oddie charged. His shoulder made contact, shoving the door back. He let out a howl of victory as his tormentor went catapulting backward.

Joyfully, Oddie burst out of his prison. His eyes locked on the governor, who lay half dazed on the ground. For a moment, they stared. Both weighing up the other. The ticking in Oddie's chest resonated in the small space. Then, the governor's eyes broke away, darting to the right.

Hyper-aware, Oddie's sights followed. An arm's length away lay the wizard's wooden wand. Oddie shot forward, skidding across the floor. With a wild leap he threw himself to the ground, hands madly grabbing. But the governor was cat-quick. Simultaneously, they laid hands on the wand. Scared witless, Oddie reared back and then smashed his forehead into the governor's face. With a hideous crunching sound, the governor's nose exploded. He went down in a geyser of blood. Oddie didn't hesitate. He pounced, leaning an arm across the governor's throat, pressing down hard.

The governor, thrashing and jerking, made a noise like a filleted fish. But his hand was still clutching the wand. Oddie watched the governor's face turning red, eyes bulging. "Drop it!" Oddie urged. The governor glared up furiously, nostrils flaring. Oddie, running out of patience, pushed down, feeling the governor's Adam's apple spasming convulsively. The governor made a gurgling protest. And then his fingers spasmed and he let go.

With an awkward scrabble of his fingertips, Oddie rolled the wand closer. He felt faint with relief as his hand closed around the curious weapon. He manoeuvred it onto its tip and pressed. The small stick wobbled. It wavered. It bent. And broke. It was the sweetest sound Oddie had ever heard. Tossing the half in his hand aside, he turned his attention to his master.

Elvidge was turning an interesting shade of plum. Spit dribbled in a thin stream down his chin. The whites of his eyes were spiked with red. But there was no pity in Oddie's heart. How could there be? He didn't have one any more. With calm and calculated effort, he shifted his weight, put his hands around the governor's throat and squeezed. As he throttled the life out of the governor, Oddie was filled with a heady sense of power.

He smiled grimly down at his tormentor. "Goodbye, Governor," he said. "See you on the other side."

63

With her skirts around her knees (in an almost inelegant fashion) Eliza ran. The corridor was illuminated by gas lamps and she could see only too clearly what was happening. She held the stitch in her side and forged on, her breath wheezing.

When she reached them, she came screeching to a halt. "Stop! Oddie, stop!" But the stoker was seemingly insensible to anything but the job in hand. It was also clear that her father was close to extinction. Whilst Eliza empathised with Oddie's murderous rage she could not condone it. And, if he were in his right mind, neither would he. Of this she had no doubt.

She darted forward, grasped Oddie's arm, yanking and pulling with all her might. Her father's eyes were glazing over, filling with blood. If he recognised her, he made no indication. Frantic, Eliza tried to claw Oddie away. But he took no more notice than if she were an ant scuttling across his sleeve.

Finally, Eliza's sense reasserted itself. Words scrolled brightly in her mind. She stood up, pulled out her wand and pointed, casting a spell.

It worked like a charm. Which, of course, it was. Her father rolled away, choking and coughing.

Oddie sat up and stared. "Eliza?"

Eliza smiled. "Mr Odling."

He looked dazed. "Eliza, what are you doing?"

Eliza felt her temper rise. What a stupid question. Wasn't it obvious? "I have come to rescue you," she said.

Oddie stood up, frowning. "No, I'm going to rescue you."

She raised an eyebrow and looked pointedly at her parent. Oddie followed her gaze and frowned.

Eliza glared. "And what were you doing?"

Oddie shuffled his feet. "I was… I was…" Then he shook his head like a wounded beast. "Oh God, Eliza!"

Her heart broke. He sounded wretched. His handsome face twisted with self-loathing. Eliza couldn't bear it. She went to him and took his hands. "It's alright, Leon. It's understandable! You've been pushed beyond all endurance. But I couldn't let you. You do know that?"

He broke his hands away, stepping back from her. His handsome features were stark. "What have I become, Eliza? What have I become!"

"You have become my beloved," she said softly. "You have become my beloved."

His dark eyes filled with tears. "I am a monster, Eliza!"

She stepped forward, smiling up into his stricken eyes. "Then you are my own beloved monster, Leon Odling." A tear fell upon her upturned face and she reached up, her finger tracing the short, dark beard. "I love you," she said.

And her words seemed to melt something within him. "You are my world, Eliza," he said simply. Then, he reached, grasping her waist, pulling her hard against the bare breadth of his chest. He smelled of smoke and apples. Faintly she could discern the rapid tick tock of his clockwork heart. His dark head bent, and he kissed her.

For one delicious, delectable moment, Eliza submitted. Until, some sixth sense alerted her. She drew away, breathless. With her hand clasped hard in Oddie's, she turned to face her father. She waited, watching as he reached up to touch the crown of his head. The hand came away red and sticky with blood. He inspected his stained fingers and his mouth tightened. He turned his gaze on Eliza.

"Well, well, well, Eliza," her father said. "It would seem I have underestimated you."

Eliza didn't reply. She scarcely knew what to say lest she make matters worse. Although it was hard to imagine a more torrid scenario. Her heart quaked. She gripped Oddie's hand tight and lifted her chin. "Papa, I am sorry that this has come to pass. But I cannot condone your work any longer. It is my desire to leave peaceably with Mr Odling. And by doing so, I swear that you will never be troubled by our presence again."

To Eliza's chagrin, her father merely looked amused. "Oh, Eliza dear! I am sorry to disappoint, but this I cannot allow. Tomorrow you will be wed to Lord Pelham and thus our humble beginnings will be elevated to that of the highest in the land. This will be key to our success. Through our new connections our revolutionary work will come to the attention of the great and powerful. There will be no end of opportunity!"

Eliza assumed that his grandiose use of 'our' more accurately referred to himself. A snort of derision from Oddie reinforced her sentiments. It seemed improbable that she would have any part of these grand schemes. Her parent's duplicity was outrageous. "As marvellous as that sounds," she said dryly, "I shall have to decline."

Her father let out a long, low, sibilant hiss of anger. His cool façade cracked, revealing an expression of uncompromising cruelty. Eliza took an involuntary step back. He pressed the advantage.

Close up, he was terrifying. He seemed to grow before her eyes, like a supernatural miasma. Eliza felt her spirit contracting and her confidence fade. He whispered words, weaving spells into the hot, smoky atmosphere. She knew what he was about, but could not retaliate, even though she held her wand in her hand. The spell that she had committed to heart evaded her desperately grasping mind. The words faded before her inner eye as she felt a lethargy creeping over her.

Worse, she sensed that Oddie too was succumbing to her father's necromancy. His hand was limp in hers and she felt his strong body wavering. Grief gripped her. What would become of him? Was he fated to shovel coal in this lonely hole for an eternity? Alone and unloved. The thought reignited her willpower. She felt the fish on her wrist flickering. And it all flooded back. What she was. Who she was. And what she wanted.

Bright as moonlight on a lake, words came shimmering into her mind. Clearly and precisely she spoke, the spell falling like raindrops on parched earth. The effect on her father was instantaneous. He shrank and was silenced.

The room settled in relief like a rheumatic old man. In the background, furnaces clicked, pipes knocked and embers shifted and sighed. The air was thick with smoke and fear. Oddie's timepiece slowed to a steady rhythm and his hold on her hand strengthened.

Eliza looked up at him and he smiled. Emboldened, Eliza took a deep breath and spoke the words that she'd been rehearsing. "Papa, give me the key, please."

Without hesitation, her father put his hands in his pocket and drew out a length of chain. Attached at the end was a little silver key. It was such a tiny thing. Then, Oddie stirred. He leaned forward, taking the key into his possession. Which seemed only right.

Eliza sighed. "Thank you, Papa," she said softly. "We will go now and you will wait here until sundown."

Her father gave her a blank stare but made no move as they trod carefully around him and out into the open. The sun had risen in a clear sky. It was bright and beautiful, frost glittering over the grim walls of the mill. The turf lay gilded with silver. She turned to Oddie, her heart overflowing with thankfulness. But her joy was blighted at the expression upon his face.

She turned to where his gaze was fixated. What she saw filled her with dismay.

Pelham made a rictus grin. He waved the pistol at them both. "I don't think so," he said.

Eliza lifted her wand.

But the evil man cocked the hammer. "Try it, do," he mocked. "I will shoot. Make no mistake. I may miss. I may not." He sneered. "Do you want to play?"

She didn't. Whilst it stuck in her craw, Pelham had the rights to it. "What do you want?"

"I want you," he said. "The tin man can take a walk. But you will accompany me back to my home and ready for marital bliss on the morrow."

Eliza felt Oddie's response and gripped him hard. "I will come with you," she said evenly. "But I cannot promise to be the wife that you wish me to be."

Pelham giggled. "Oh, but you will be the wife that I wish. Because if you fail…"

What would happen was lost as the lord's attention fractured. They all turned at the swelling of sound that approached. It was the intense, excitable hum of angry wasps.

Except, as a mob came surging around the building to meet them, the wasps were wingless.

64

At first Oddie couldn't tell who they were. There were many and clearly this was no social call. As they swarmed across the frosted grass, he saw that there were men, women and children. A ragged, desperate crowd.

As they neared, their voices fell to a muted muttering. They stopped at a distance, as if unsure. Now Oddie could pick out familiar faces, people from the Fens, the city and the villages. They were armed. Not with guns and cannon but with pikes, pitchforks and sturdy sticks. And rage.

Then the crowd parted. Oddie's heart skipped a beat as Fanny Flowers emerged. She walked fearlessly across the empty space and stopped before him. She turned her fair face to Lord Pelham, giving him a saucy smile.

As he watched her profile, Oddie realised that it was this aspect that he loved the most. It was this element of Fan that drove him crazy. And he loved her for it.

"Lord Pelham, I thought to find you here." Fanny glanced back at the crowd. "We paid a courtesy visit to your fine house and found you were not at home. So naturally this was the next place we thought of."

Lord Pelham stared at Fan contemptuously. "Your threats don't scare me, Flowers! I'll have you horsewhipped."

A statement that was blatantly untrue.

Fanny lifted a bird's wing of black eyebrow. "No, you won't. You will walk away. Or perhaps run might be the better option. These fine folk have an axe to grind. And they'll happily use you for a whetstone. So, run along. Or I'll not be answerable for the consequences."

Oddie was heartily uplifted by Pelham's discomfort. The lord appeared to be on the edge of apoplexy.

Purple with rage, a giant blood vessel throbbing on his pallid forehead, pistol twitching and jerking, Pelham snarled at Fanny Flowers. "I'll kill you first, you witch bitch."

Oddie's amusement evaporated. Pelham was a menace. A mean and twisted little man who had no respect for womenfolk. Oddie felt he was long overdue for a lesson in good manners. Frankly, he was delighted to oblige.

Despite Eliza's furious resistance, he slipped her grip and walked towards the lily-livered lord.

Pelham squealed, waving the gun wildly back and forth between Oddie and Fan. "Stop, you scum!"

A sentiment that did not endear him to Oddie. Scum! He'd show him what 'scum' could do. It was time to put an end to it. Time to dispose of this pile of human excrement once and for all. The world would be a better place without him.

Oddie advanced. Vaguely, he was aware of Eliza's voice and the thundering of the crowd. Fan watched on wordlessly.

Pelham, perhaps sensing that Oddie was the greater threat, steadied his aim. Though his hands were palsied. "Stop! Or I'll blow your head off."

Oddie shrugged. "Doubtless, the governor can make me a new one." When he was close enough to see the sweat on Pelham's brow, Oddie couldn't quite decide how to finish him. Dismemberment had a certain appeal. But there were children and women present. It'd have to be a crack on his thick skull. Or a thorough throttling. No blood and guts. Very tidy.

With effortless ease, he plucked the gun out of the lord's sticky hands, tossing it aside.

Pelham screamed and collapsed onto the ground, wiggling like a worm. His hands scrabbled frantically at Oddie's legs. "Don't hurt me! Don't hurt me! I'll give you anything you want," he sobbed. Then he lifted his head and stared wildly at Eliza. "Take her! Take her! I'll give you her and… gold. Lots of gold!"

Oddie stared down at the snivelling shell of a man. His rage drained to be replaced with disgust and contempt. There was no glory in snuffing out such a lowlife. Best leave him for the mob. Let them mete out justice. He stepped back.

With a cry of triumph, Pelham launched himself at the pistol. Too late, Oddie realised his mistake. He braced himself as the crazed man came to his feet, face blazing with triumph.

Pelham danced a little jig like a drunken stork. He lifted the gun. "Must be sad to be naught but brawn and no brain, Mr Odling," he crowed. Then, his head jerked back violently. His eyes bulged and the weapon fell to the ground. He put his hands up to his face as a fountain of water came spewing from his open mouth.

Oddie followed the spellbound gaze of the watching crowd. When he laid eyes on Eliza, he was filled with wonder. Gone was the girl. In her place was a woman. A woman who held the power of life over death in her hands.

She stood tall, wand writing invisible ink into the air. Words fell from her lips like music. There was about her an air of intensity, like a peregrine falcon seeking its prey. Eliza Elvidge was magnificent.

Oddie dragged his eyes away from her, in response to the ghastly noise now emitting from Pelham. Oddie watched a small, red fish slipping out between the lord's lips. A ghastly gurgling, gulping sound accompanied the strange birthing. Strangely, the lord caught the fish in his hands. He gazed at it in apparent astonishment. And collapsed. The crowd fell silent.

Not so Fanny Flowers. She walked calmly forward to stand beside Eliza. She smiled a cold, calculating smile. She lifted her voice and cast her own brand of magic. Oddie gasped as the earth beneath his feet began to tremble.

Lord Pelham made not a sound as the ground opened, soil and sod churning and thundering. And then – Lord Pelham was gone. Stones rolled and quivered to a standstill. Dirt shivered. All that was left was a scarred patch of land. A grave without a headstone.

Oddie turned as the crowd stirred as if from a deep sleep. He raced forward, picking up the discarded pistol and hurried back to join Eliza and Fan. It was impossible to predict how the people would respond. The danger was not yet over.

He slipped between them. Eliza leaned into him and he could feel the fatigue in her petite frame. Fanny stood stock-still, neither accepting or rejecting his support. That was Fan's way. The crowd surged forward, and Oddie braced himself. The mob circled rapidly around the disturbed soil, those at the back craning their heads, the better to see.

And then somebody leaned in and spat. "The devil take him!"

The cry went up. "The devil take him!" It echoed across the water and flew upon the wind.

Slowly, they dispersed. One by one they walked past Eliza and Fan. All gave a respectful nod, the men removing their caps, the women bobbing a curtsey. Some reached out to grasp the women's hands briefly.

"Bless you both," a brave few murmured.

None seemed willing or able to look at Oddie, although a few cast quick, furtive eyes upon his metal foot, protruding beneath his trouser leg. Hard though he tried he could not help but mind. It was a cruel blow to be shunned by those he knew by name. Or better.

At last they left, heads bowed to a bitter wind that blew in from the west. Their tattered, threadbare bodies finally were lost as the sun was swallowed by clouds. Starlings gathered in a great murmuration, surfing the sky with wild abandon. A raven cawed and arose from a skeletal tree and the river ran.

Beside him, the two women stirred. Oddie looked down tenderly at one and then the other. His gaze caressed the head of spun gold and the other of black satin. And all he could think was how strange it was that the two women he loved best in this world were witches.

Who would have thought?

65

Eliza felt Oddie's gaze. She leaned away, the better to see him. Caught unawares, he did not have time to hide the expression on his face. He emitted love like light from a lantern. And all doubt fled from her mind. She had done right to destroy Pelham. He was evil. A fact reinforced by the irreverence afforded his grave by the Fen folk. The world was a better place without him.

Boots scrunched in the gravel path behind them. They turned. It was a boy. A ragamuffin with one arm. His small, dirty face was screwed up with angst. Snot dribbled unheeded down his chin and he rubbed red eyes with one clenched fist.

Oddie stepped forward, face creasing with concern. "Boy! Are you alright?"

The child stopped, eyeing them warily. Then he broke down once more. "I want me arm. I was promised!"

Eliza's heartstrings vibrated. Poor little soul. He must be one of her father's acquisitions. Where, she wondered, had this one come from? Not that it mattered. What mattered was that they must get him away. She hurried forward to offer comfort. But when her hand touched his wrist, he jerked away, hurling abuse at her. This at least stemmed his tears. With a rude gesture of his fingers, he darted off.

Eliza made to go after him, but Oddie put a restraining hand on her shoulder. "Best leave him be, my love. He has chosen his allegiance. Though I fear he may live to regret it."

With a shudder, Eliza nodded. She looked at her two companions. "My father is inside. He is under an enchantment, but I do not know not how long it will hold. Do you think…" But she swallowed her words. To think such a thing is one matter. To say it was another.

Of course, Fanny Flowers sensed which direction her mind was moving. "You would destroy him?" There was no hint of judgment in her tone. Only curiosity.

Eliza shook her head. "In all honesty, I do not know. It is clear that he is the orchestrator of this madness. I fear what will happen if he is left unchecked."

Fanny shook her head. "Eliza, you cannot. Indeed, we cannot, even if we so wished."

"Why?" said Eliza.

"Because it takes the power of three," said Fanny. "Three is the only way. For all time, it has been so. Only three of the four can subdue and destroy another."

Eliza was stricken. "So you are saying there is no way! We are only two."

Fanny nodded. "We are. And even if there was another, they may not suit. For the three must be master of the other elements. Earth. Water. And wind. Then, and only then, can fire be overcome."

Eliza frowned. "So, we must find a witch or wizard whose element is wind?"

"Yes," said Fanny.

It didn't sound so difficult. "Well, that's what we must do."

Fanny sighed. "It is simple in theory. But not in practice. There are few wind elementals left. I have never heard of a single one."

How strange, Eliza mused. "But why is that, Fanny?"

"Those that are ruled by the wind have a reputation for fecklessness. They are rumoured to be pranksters and mischief-makers. Over the ages their numbers have… dwindled."

"Dwindled?" said Eliza, thoughtfully. "But how?"

"I don't know," said Fanny. "All I know is that they are few."

"Few, but not extinct," said Eliza.

Fanny shook her head. "Not extinct."

The way forward became clear. "In that case, we will find one. We shall scour the land from Land's End to…" Eliza stopped. Really, her geography was dreadful. What was at the top of the map? She waved her hand airily. "You get my meaning."

Fanny smiled. "I do."

Eliza tucked her wand into her skirts. "Well, we must prepare."

Fanny turned, looking back at the mill. Then she sighed. A sound full of sadness and regret. "I cannot go, Eliza. The Fen folk need me. Hard times have come and will not get better. I must do all that I can to aid them. 'Hedgewitch', they call me, and they are right to do so. For long have I been wed to this land. I would pine away were I to leave."

Eliza felt the truth in her friend's words, yet she sensed there was more left unsaid. And she was afraid for Fanny. "Fanny, what of my father? Are you not afraid?"

A shadow fell, long and black across the frozen ground.

"Well, Fanny, are you? Are you afraid of the governor?" Her father's voice cut through the crisp air like an axe through an apple tree.

Eliza drew in a gulp of frigid air and slipped her wand free. Her eyes darted from Fanny to her father, like startled starlings. A spell scrolled into her mind and she readied to attack. But a sharp look from Fanny stayed her hand.

Fanny turned to Eliza's father. "I am not scared."

Eliza's father smiled. "You love me still a little then, Fan o' the Fens?"

A wicked smirk lit up Fanny's face. "Mayhap just a little."

Eliza felt as if the sky had fallen. "What are you saying, Fanny?" she cried.

Her father laughed, a deep roll of thunder. "You have not told her, Fan?"

Fan shook her head, glancing sidelong at Eliza.

"Told me what?" Eliza demanded.

Eliza's father tutted and shook his head. "Shame on you, Fanny." Then he turned brooding eyes upon Eliza. "What Fanny has not told you, Eliza, is that she is your mother."

"Mercy!" said Oddie.

Eliza could only concur.

66

Well, that really took the biscuit. Just when Oddie felt he'd caught up with the circus parade that was his life, someone threw in another sideshow. Fanny was Eliza's mother. Or so it would seem.

A million questions and uncomfortable observations jostled for pole position in his brain. But ultimately there did not seem anything he could say that seemed useful. Eliza, on the other hand, seemed to have no such qualms.

"My mother! But Father, that is ludicrous. How could she be my mother? My mother is dead," Eliza cried.

Or locked in an asylum, Oddie thought.

Fanny sighed. "Eliza, your father's wife bore no children. She died many years ago."

Eliza swiped angrily at the tears on her cheeks. "All these years I've been grieving for a mother who never existed."

The governor shrugged. "Well, when the wife conveniently died of consumption, I brought you home. No one could prove your birthright."

Then Eliza turned on Fanny. "And you let him!"

Fanny gave a dismissive flick of her hand. "Don't be a little fool, Eliza. Your father did the best for you. As my child you would have been the bastard born scum of a heathen hedgewitch. Instead, you have been raised an Elvidge. The privileged and pampered daughter of a self-made man."

Eliza's eyes narrowed. "You would have let him marry me to that pernicious, perverted and poisonous Pelham!"

Fanny's expression softened. "No, my love, I would never have let that happen."

The governor observed the patch of disturbed earth. "It would seem that – at this point – Lord Pelham is of little consequence," he said.

Oddie could not discern the emotions that lay beneath these observations. Frankly, he would have preferred an outburst of rage, or anything tangible. This calm, distant façade seemed like the calm before a storm. He was firmly of the opinion that all that mattered was extracting Eliza. And quickly.

"Eliza," said Oddie softly. "We must be on our way."

Eliza stirred and turned to him, her blue eyes filled with confusion and sadness. She made no reply but bowed her head to him.

The governor stepped forward, touching his daughter on her shoulder. It was the gentlest of gestures, yet in Oddie's eyes it was laden with menace. Indeed, Eliza shrunk back as if he were a red-hot branding iron.

Without taking eyes off her father, Eliza backed away. "Come, Leon, we shall go." Her voice was strong and clear. The slender wand in her hand steady. Only a solitary tear meandering down her pale cheek gave away the turmoil in her breast.

"I cannot let you go, Eliza," said the governor.

Oddie felt a flicker of hope: the governor no longer had his wand. Perhaps the spell that Eliza had cast still held sway. If so, it boded well for their future. He dared a glance at Eliza to see her features harden into an uncharacteristically calculating look.

"You cannot stop me, Father," she said coldly. "I am no longer the simpering, spoiled child. I am the servant of the water spirit. I have quenched your fire. Do not force me to inflict upon you more ill."

The governor laughed, but Oddie sensed his unease.

The governor turned to Fanny. "Together we can contain her."

Fanny shrugged. "Perhaps. Perhaps not."

An ugly expression spread across the governor's face. He turned on Fanny, looming over her like a great oak. "If you do not aid me, Fanny Flowers, I will have you incarcerated in the asylum. Where you will wither and die like an orchid in the darkness."

Fanny tutted. "No. You dare not. We are the last of the Fair. We are few. Our power diminishes as our world is devoured by greed and avarice. You have been corrupted and perverted by your own desires. Yet, for all that, without me, you are alone. Is that what you want?"

The word 'desire' hung in the air like perfume. Oddie sucked it in, savouring the scent. It smelled like sweet bread fresh from the oven. Or honeysuckle on a warm summer's night. No, it was more the heady scent of rain on parched earth. Then Oddie relaxed, as the answer came to him. It smelled like Eliza. He turned to her, delighted with this revelation.

But Eliza was staring up at him urgently. "Run!" she said.

Oddie blinked. All thought of bread and rain blew away. In the periphery of his sight, he was aware of the governor staring, as if entranced, at Fanny's ethereal face.

Silently, he blessed Fan o' the Fens. And, gripping Eliza's hand, he turned and ran. Beside him, skirts gathered above her knees, his love raced with him. Up the drive they bolted and to the canal.

There Eliza halted, staring wildly around. "Where shall we go, Oddie? Where shall we go?"

Oddie didn't need to think. "Across the Fen and to the sea. I have a coracle." Eliza reached up, cupping his face in her hands. He bent and his lips briefly grazed hers. Then he grasped her by the waist and swung her upon his back.

She squealed but steadied herself, strong, smooth thighs gripping firmly around his waist and her breath warming his cheek. Oddie took off, sprinting down the towpath, leaping a dyke and heading for the lowlands.

Despite the danger, or maybe because of it, he covered the ground effortlessly in great leaps and bounds, joyous as an otter. He rejoiced at the feel of the sun shining on his face, the ice cracking beneath his feet, the bitter wind chafing his bare chest. Eliza was no burden. Oddie would carry her to the ends of the world to keep her safe.

At the triangle of the stream, water meadow and copse that bound his home, Oddie finally stopped. Home. He needed his nets, and rods and change of clothes. Rope and canvas too. There was drink and some preserves. Who knew where the sea may take them?

He ran up the stream, crossed the stones and gently lowered Eliza to the ground. "We must provision ourselves, Miss Eliza."

She shook her skirts to her ankles daintily. "Of course, Mr Odling," she mocked.

He grinned, making his way to his front door. Once inside, he made short work of his list. The bundle was soon tied and readied. With a last fond look around, he turned to leave. As he did so, a sound filled his ears. What on earth? Then it came again, clear and shrill. It was a horn.

Eliza turned pale. "'Tis my father with the hounds! He has them on our scent!"

Oddie hid the terror her words unfurled within him, for it was clear that Eliza's nerve was severely tested. And for good cause. The dogs would tear them apart. As a pack they would be hard to shake. But not impossible. "Eliza, listen to me. We can lose them if we are cunning. Can we not?" To his relief the words had the desired effect.

Eliza ceased her frenzied pacing and took a deep, ragged breath of air. "Cunning," she said. "Yes, of course. I can be cunning." She closed her eyes, eyebrows drawn together. "We can lose the hounds if there is water to break the scent."

Oddie was quiet, unwilling to break her train of thought.

Then she lifted her head and nodded. "Come."

Oddie picked up his pack and followed.

67

The sky was clear. A skein of lavender silk. Eliza could hear the dogs baying but she shut the noise out. Instead she trained her ear to the brook that splashed and tinkled beneath its frozen surface. She concentrated on the sound until it washed through her mind. As the image rippled into her subconscious she felt her fish swimming energetically. And the words came.

She lifted her wand and water fountained from its tip. It arced into the sunshine, filling the air with a million rainbows. They faded, turning to mist. The mist gathered, forming clouds. The clouds grew heavy and black. Rain began falling, lashing the landscape. Drops bounced and skittered across the ground forming streamlets. Eliza exulted, lifting her face to the sky, welcoming the deluge as a daughter. Then, sensing it was enough, she pocketed her wand and turned to Oddie.

Soaked to the skin, he waited patiently, water streaming off his cap, coat and trousers. He looked grimly amused. "That should do the trick," he said.

Eliza ran to him. "I can only hope so. But we must make haste. My father may have a trick or two up his sleeve yet."

Oddie nodded. "I fear I cannot carry this load and you, Eliza. Shall I leave it behind?"

Eliza looked at the bulky pack and weighed up its value. She concluded that Oddie would not take anything that he did not consider essential for survival. "I can manage." She took his hand and they leapt across the stepping stones safe to the other side.

Oddie paused. "Follow in my footsteps. Exactly in my footsteps. The ground is treacherous if you do not know the way," he said, yelling to be heard.

Eliza nodded and followed. At first the going was not hard. A meandering path just visible in the mossy green swathe. Then a copse of stunted trees offering no resistance other than twisted roots to catch a foot in. But when they came to the other side it was into a vast sea of grass. Reeds tall as her head, rattling and clattering beneath the onslaught of rain.

Oddie plunged in, apparently undeterred. Apprehensively, Eliza followed. Unlike the stoker, who stood shoulder-high to the forest, she felt hemmed in on all sides. A feeling that grew apace as they went deeper. Eliza was terrified that she would make a wrong move or get left behind. Time lost all meaning. As did space. Her world narrowed to Oddie's back and the reed jungle.

And then, just as she felt her reserves of strength were used, they stepped out onto a vast plain of marshy land. The air was laden with salt. The rain slowed to a drizzle. At their feet lay the river. It's icy surface slick with water.

Oddie pointed. "We have a long way to go if we walk. But if we skate, we will get there in the hour." He strode across to the riverbank and peered down. Eliza followed, slipping and sliding on the treacherous ground.

Oddie hunkered on the edge and tapped tentatively on the ice. It made a sound like a hollow drum.

Eliza stared anxiously at him. She did not like the sound, though she could not have said why. "Is it strong enough?"

Oddie bent to his bundle and pulled out two sets of blades. "The freeze has been severe. A little rain should not pose a problem. It will hold for our purpose." He held out a pair of blades. "There is less risk on the ice than from the hounds."

It was true. Eliza joined him, and he knelt, deftly attaching the blades to her boots. Dressed now in his heavy coat and cap, his dark hair curling onto his collar, she could not resist caressing the nape of his neck. She rolled the crisp, smooth curls through her fingers. He froze and then looked up. "We'd best be wed, and soon, Miss Elvidge. For I have a yen for you."

Eliza pretended to be offended. She snatched her hand away. Secretly she was delighted. "Don't be presumptuous!" she said. Oddie chuckled but said no more. She could not subdue the smile that played on her lips. In truth, the flame burning bright inside her would not long be denied.

He turned his attention to his own blades, shouldered his bag and stepped onto the ice. Eliza got an attack of the jitters. What if she had forgotten how? After all, she had skated only once and it felt like an age ago.

As if he read her mind, Oddie held out a hand. "You will be fine."

And then they heard it. A shrill, jarring note. The horn. Horror-struck, Eliza turned to Oddie. "He's here!" The deep baying of hunting hounds boomed. Oddie grabbed her hand, pulled her down the slope and onto the frozen river.

Eliza slid around uncontrollably. But Oddie did not let go. He sped away, pulling Eliza in his wake. Leon's legs powering like pistons, they surged on. Eliza held hard to his hand and tried not to be a burden. Behind them the sound of horns and hounds swelled. Eliza glanced over her shoulder. She could see them now. Mounted men with the pack streaming at their heels. How could they travel so fast? There was a sharp sound like gunshot.

"They are coming!" she cried. The dogs broke away, swarming

across the earth. They did not stop at the river. They launched themselves onto the ice. A slavering, baying pack of hellhounds. Eliza could almost feel their teeth sinking into her flesh.

Oddie turned. He swore. He bent his back and forged on. Behind her, Eliza could hear the high blow of galloping horses. Terror snapped at her heels. Soon her father would be close enough to cast a spell!

And then Eliza found her stride. With a sob of relief, she began to skate. At first in jerky steps but then in easy, flowing strides. It helped. The pace picked up, Oddie powering on like a machine. Down the long stretch of river they raced, boats and bridges and buildings a blur. And, gradually, the ferocious sound of the hunt dwindled. Faded. And ceased.

But Oddie did not slow. On and on he went, skates speeding across the ice. And Eliza grew wearier and wearier. She could scarcely feel her legs. She moved mindlessly. Until, ultimately she was just hanging on, fighting to stay on her feet.

As the miles sped by, the marsh gave way to woodland, birch and aspen standing like silver sentinels. Cranes took to the wing and rooks laughed from their perches. Of the hounds there was not a whisper.

And then they came to a plain. Spiky, salty grass spreading down to a distant sandy shore. At long, long last, Oddie slowed, curving away to the bank to stop beside a solitary white willow. Eliza's legs crumpled. She landed in a heap at Oddie's feet. With a cry he bent and drew her back up.

For a moment, she lay her head against him, safe in his strong embrace. She could hear his mechanical heart ticking in his chest. A sound that no longer disturbed. Indeed, it filled her with a sense of wellbeing. It mattered not a jot.

She looked up and smiled. And the most lusted-after lad in Lincoln smiled back. But then Oddie let out a strange, soft sigh. And his clock stopped ticking. He swayed. Panic-stricken, she clung to him, frantically trying to keep him on his feet. Together they sunk to the ground. Oddie stared up at her helplessly, his face chalk white. Lips blue.

Eliza stared down. Stunned. Then – as he drew a ragged breath – she remembered the key.

68

Oddie blinked in the sunlight. With a hand shading his face he sat up. Instantly he was aware of Eliza bending down anxiously.

"Oddie, are you alright?"

He reflected on this for a moment. "I feel fine. But… I'm starving."

Silently she handed over the key. Neither spoke. Then Eliza turned away and scrabbled through his bundle. She hurried back, holding out an apple and a piece of rock-hard cheese. He swallowed them whole. Revitalised, but unsatisfied, he jumped up, hunting through his belongings. With a soft sigh of satisfaction, he found the bag of coal. With a tug, it came free. He unwrapped it, grabbed a piece of coal and crunched it up.

Swallowing, he became acutely aware of Eliza. He avoided her gaze, brushing a few crumbs from his jacket. "Er… thanks." He turned away. He felt he should say something, but his mortification was expanding by the heartbeat.

When her fingers tentatively touched his sleeve, he stilled. His mechanical heart was working overtime but he still couldn't bear to look at her.

"Oddie, look at me. Please."

Reluctantly he turned. And burst out laughing. Eliza's lips, teeth and tongue were black. A smut smudged her cheek. She swallowed. "It's actually quite nice." She pulled out a ridiculous square of handkerchief and patted her mouth, as if she'd just dined on sirloin steak. "Lovely texture," she enthused.

And suddenly everything was alright. In a rush of gratitude, he swooped on her, lifting her off her dainty feet. He pirouetted on the spot, spinning Eliza like a top. Her skirts billowed to reveal a length of shapely, stockinged legs. Then he tossed her high and caught her. While she was too breathless to object he kissed her. Thoroughly.

When he finally put her down, her cheeks were pink and her hair tumbling wildly about her shoulders. She tossed her head, nimbly screwed up her hair, pinning it neatly in place.

"Mr Odling, how ungentlemanly!" Her tone belied her words however. Eliza looked positively delighted.

With a struggle, he contained his desire. "Eliza, we must be off."

The laughter died in her eyes and she glanced fearfully over her shoulder, as if expecting the hounds of hell to materialise on the horizon. A fear not entirely unfounded. She bit her lip and nodded. Then, remembering they were both still on blades, Oddie helped Eliza take hers off. Then freed himself.

He pointed east of the river. "The boat is moored in an inlet. I dare not skate any further for there is too much seawater in the ice. Too weak, you see."

"I see," she said. Then she frowned, glancing around at the great wetlands. "But how can we get to the shore? Is there a path?"

Oddie shook his head. "No path. But there is a way – although it is… unusual."

Eliza's blue eyes widened. "How so?"

By way of answer, Oddie put his fingers in his mouth and whistled. The sound carried high and sweet in the cold air. He waited, eyes scanning the rippling sway of reeds. *Come on, Teddy!*

If Teddy didn't show, they were in trouble. In more ways than one. He couldn't shake the feeling that the hunt was still on.

He turned to Eliza in trepidation as she gripped his arm. "What is it, Eliza?"

Eliza pointed. "Oh Lord! That poor man! We must help him."

Oddie tensed. Was Teddy in trouble? He stared avidly around. But there was nothing. "Where, I can't see anyone?"

"There! There! At twelve of the clock!"

Oddie scanned the reed bed minutely. "What do you see?"

Eliza swallowed. "'Tis a young man, standing at the edge of the reeds." She bit her lip. "He looks mortally wounded. As if he has been… crushed."

Oddie shivered. Now he understood. "It is not a man, Eliza. It is a ghost. It is Ted's poor brother. Saul."

"What happened?"

"Saul tore down the landlord's dykes. They buried him alive in the restoration. It's a common punishment in these parts." Then he heard a familiar sound and turned to see a long, flat barge breaking through the reed bed.

There was a sole occupant. A man as long and slender as a reed, shaggy grey hair sticking out like thatch beneath a disreputable hat. An iron-grey beard flowed down to a length of twine holding up a pair of ancient breeches. He paused, lifted a hand from the long pole propelling his craft and waved.

Eliza took a step back. "Who is it?"

"Ted," said Oddie. "He farms the eels. Skims a meagre living from it but he won't leave his brother."

"Poor man," Eliza murmured. Then she turned. "Oh, he's gone."

Oddie nodded. "Saul is watching out for Teddy. He must know we pose no threat."

Silently, they waited, watching Teddy skimming across the water. He glided gently to their feet. Oddie put out his hands, drawing the craft to rest on the muddy bank. "How goes it, Teddy?"

"Middlin'," said Teddy, in a voice that cracked with lack of use. He appraised Eliza with a pair of deep-set, pale eyes. Apparently she passed muster, for he lifted his hat. "Ma'am."

Eliza smiled. "Teddy, pleased to make your acquaintance."

Teddy nodded and put his hat firmly back on. "You need to take the walk, do you?"

"We do," said Oddie.

Teddy shifted a plug of tobacco in his cheek and spat a gob of juice into the water. "Two sets then?"

Oddie hesitated. Could Eliza do it? No. It wasn't realistic. Like skating, it was easy when you knew how. He shook his head. "Just one set. We'll double up."

The slodger nodded. "One it is." He lay the pole down in the shallow boat's interior. "Hold hard."

Oddie gripped the prow firmly while Teddy levered two long timber stilts over the side. The old man shifted the tobacco and hawked out another stream of yellow. "That'll be the usual fee."

Oddie peered over his shoulder to Eliza. "Open the pack, please, there's a pouch of tobacco." There was rustling as Eliza searched. Then she came and handed over the package.

Teddy weighed it in his hand and pocketed it. "Leave 'em high and dry."

Oddie let go of the boat and snatched up the stilts. "Godspeed, Teddy," he said.

Teddy nodded, picked up his pole and pushed off. The reeds swayed, parted and he disappeared.

Eliza touched one wooden strut. "What is it?"

"They, not it. They are stilts."

"Oh, of course, now I see it! But what have you got them for?"

"To cross the floodplains of the Fen to my boat. It's the only way from here. And besides, no dog will get our trail."

Eliza was silent for a long time. "But there is only one pair," she finally said.

"Yes. But that's no problem. I will carry you on my back." Seeing the expression on her face he smiled. "I can stilt walk as well as I can skate. Been doing it forever."

Eliza's eyes opened wide. "No, Oddie. It's not possible."

They both twitched as if stung. Oddie looked at Eliza. She stared back, white-faced and scared. And it came again. The distant, haunting sound of a horn.

69

Eliza clung to Oddie's broad back like a limpet. She felt sick. The swaying, jerking movement was unbearable. The swag on Oddie's shoulder dug cruelly into her leg. She looked back, terrified of what she might find. But the reeds blocked her view. A dog bayed and she stiffened. Surely they could not follow? Not here.

She shrieked as Oddie stumbled. Then closed her eyes as he righted himself.

"Sorry," he called.

Eliza trembled. She couldn't help it. If they fell, they'd never get astride the stilts again. It had been almost impossible on firm ground. Out here in the shallow, waterlogged land, they'd founder. Or worse. Fall and sink into the silty soil. Was that how the hunt would find them? Bogged and helpless? It was a sickening prospect. With each giant stride Eliza held her breath, expecting the worst. The marsh seemed to spread before them forever.

And then – they were out. The reeds shivering behind and the sea glinting in front. She could have wept with relief. Where was the boat? A horrid thought slipped into her mind. What if it wasn't there? What if it had sunk? Or been blown out to sea in a storm? She looked nervously over her shoulder. Nothing. Thank the gods!

"There!" said Oddie.

And then she spotted it. A tiny skiff, bobbing cheerfully in a small bay. Oddie surged on, the stilts making great progress on the mud flat. Crabs scuttled frantically, alarmed by the invaders.

"Hang on!"

The words had barely formed when Oddie paused, and then, arms outstretched, arced to the ground. Eliza gasped, anticipating the worst. Miraculously, Oddie landed on his knees, hands flat to the floor, face buried in the dirt. He lay still. The only sign of life, a ripple of sea breeze through his hair.

Alarmed, Eliza rolled away and then scrambled back to his side. Her eyes swept over him, but she could see no blood or injury. But a thousand possibilities streamed through her mind, each worse than the last. She shook his shoulder. "Leon! Leon! Are you alright?"

With a jack knife of his body, Oddie rolled over, stilts arcing dangerously. He sat up, shrugged off the bag and began worrying at the straps that attached the stilts to his legs. "Do you hear them?" he said.

She stood awkwardly, pins and needles shooting through her legs. She held her breath the better to hear. Gulls screaming. Sea sucking. Reeds rustling. And – something else. A soft swishing. And then, she saw it. A disturbance. Reeds swaying and bending. "Oddie," she hissed.

Oddie jumped up, unencumbered by the stilts. "What?"

Eliza pointed.

Oddie's eyes narrowed. "What the…" Then he grabbed his pack. "Run, Eliza! To the boat! It's the hounds. They are swimming through the reeds!" He grabbed her hand. "Hurry!"

Eliza broke into a run but staggered. She was wobbly, her legs stiff and awkward. "I can't," she gasped.

Oddie stopped, scooped her up and flung her over one shoulder. Eliza gripped his coat and lifted her head awkwardly.

They streaked down to the sea, Oddie's legs pumping like pistons. Eliza stared at the receding reeds, heart banging on her ribcage, saltwater spraying her uplifted face. Thank goodness! They were in the surf. The boat was not far.

Then she saw it. A huge dark shadow emerging from the reeds. And another. Two great hounds. They stopped, dropping their heads and sniffing the ground. And, with a blood-curdling howl, they came.

"Oddie! The dogs!" she screamed. "Put me down!"

He came to a ragged halt. Eliza slipped down. The water came to her knees, soaking her skirts. But she had eyes only for the two beasts tearing across the mud towards them. Two masses of mean muscle. Yellow teeth sharp beneath snarling lips. A ridge of fur standing erect upon their backs. Panting softly, drool dripping onto clawed feet. At the edge of the surf they stopped.

"Get in the boat," said Oddie.

Eliza glanced at him. He had a knife in one hand and a steely expression on his face.

"No, Oddie." She pulled out her wand. "One for you. One for me."

There was no time for parley. As one, the hounds plunged into the waves. Bounding and leaping, they advanced, eyes blazing. Eliza locked her sights on the one closest, lifted her wand and spoke the words. It was a simple spell. One which had worked before. She waded clumsily backwards, skirts clinging to her calves. The hound kept coming. Closer and closer. She could smell it. Rank. Foul. It hunkered down, growling. Then it yelped and leapt, shaking its head violently. Clamped to its lip was a crab.

But it kept coming, pitiless eyes locked on Eliza. Her back bumped into the boat. Desperate, she waved her wand, her voice ringing out urgently. The water bubbled. Eliza watched a cast of crabs go scuttling up the hound's legs. They ran across its back and up its neck. The hound whimpered, snapping its jaws at the marauders, teeth clacking on their hard shells. It twirled around, shaking and twitching. But to no avail. With a howl of terror, it turned tail and fled.

There was no time to exult. Eliza screamed as she turned to find Oddie locked in battle with the other beast. The hound was on its hind legs, paws planted on Oddie's chest. They were face to face, Oddie straining to hold it back. He held its huge head between his hands. One locked on to each ear. The animal struggled, frothing and foaming at the mouth, jaws deadlier than a mantrap.

Eliza trembled with rage. How dare her father do this? How dare he hurt Oddie! She felt her free will evaporating. Words poured out of her. She lifted her wand. A jet of water shot out, hitting the hound between his shoulder blades. Eliza slid the jet delicately down. And gathered herself for the kill. The water pressure ratcheted up. With a sickening sound the hound's hide split. Blood bursting. Flesh shredding. The beast howled. But Eliza was not moved. Grimly she played the jet over its thrashing body. Until it hung limp. Just gristle and guts.

With a cry of disgust, Oddie tossed the carcass away. It floated in a pink, frothy foam and surfed out to sea.

Eliza shivered and shook as if in the grip of an ague. She looked around anxiously. Scared there were more. But all seemed still. She looked at Oddie. "Is it over?"

He splashed towards her, eyes scanning the marshland. Then he took her in his arms and hugged her hard. "Yes. It's over."

And to her chagrin, Eliza burst into tears. Oddie held her as she poured out all her grief and rage. Finally, she hiccuped. "I'm sorry," she said.

Oddie jerked back with such violence that Eliza's heart skipped a beat. "What? What is it?"

She looked wildly around. "What is it, Oddie?"

Oddie grabbed her hand. "It's alright! I didn't mean to scare you. It's just that you must never be sorry! You are the bravest and the best woman in the world. And I am the luckiest man alive."

Eliza smiled a watery smile. "Oh, Oddie, I would do anything for you."

Oddie grinned ruefully. "I think you already did." Then he lifted his soggy bag out of the water and tossed it in the bobbing boat. He lifted Eliza next and clambered in beside her. It was a snug fit.

He settled on the seat opposite and picked up the oars. "Where to, Eliza?"

"London," she said.

"Why London?"

"I have read that criminals find sanctuary there. So why not us? And it is the nation's seat of learning." She leaned forward, putting her hands on Oddie's knees. "I want to learn, Oddie. Learn all I can. And one day I will return with a sorcerer whose element is wind. And I will destroy my father."

Oddie leant forward and dropped a kiss on the tip of her nose. "London it is!" He picked up the oars. They skimmed across the bay and to the edges of the ocean. Neither spoke. It was enough to simply be alive. To be together. To be in love.

Full steam ahead!